"Taran'atar to Captain Kira."

"I'm here," Kira said.

"And growing too close to the Ascendants," he told her. *"You must reverse your course."* The Jem'Hadar was no longer on the bridge of *Even Odds,* she saw, at least not that she could tell. His countenance filled almost the entire display, with nothing but a featureless background visible behind him. Because of the perspective and slight movement of the image, Kira suspected that he communicated with her via a personal access display device.

"Why?" Kira asked, though she did not truly expect an answer. On the sensor readouts, she saw the fleeing Ascendant ship emerge from the rear of the fleet. It would shortly pass *Even Odds*, which raced in the opposite direction.

"Because I am Taran'atar," he said, and he drew what looked like an energy weapon from the belt of his black coverall. *"I am dead. I go into battle to reclaim my life."*

STAR TREK
DEEP SPACE NINE®

ASCENDANCE

DAVID R. GEORGE III

Based upon *Star Trek*® and
Star Trek: The Next Generation®
created by Gene Roddenberry
and
Star Trek: Deep Space Nine
created by Rick Berman & Michael Piller

POCKET BOOKS
New York   London   Toronto   Sydney   New Delhi   Ashalla

Pocket Books
An Imprint of Simon & Schuster, Inc.
1230 Avenue of the Americas
New York, NY 10020

This book is a work of fiction. Any references to historical events, real people, or real places are used fictitiously. Other names, characters, places, and events are products of the author's imagination, and any resemblance to actual events or places or persons, living or dead, is entirely coincidental.

First Pocket Books paperback edition January 2016

POCKET and colophon are registered trademarks of Simon & Schuster, Inc.

For information about special discounts for bulk purchases, please contact Simon & Schuster Special Sales at 1-866-506-1949 or business@simonandschuster.com.

The Simon & Schuster Speakers Bureau can bring authors to your live event. For more information or to book an event, contact the Simon & Schuster Speakers Bureau at 1-866-248-3049 or visit our website at www.simonspeakers.com.

Manufactured in the United States of America

10 9 8 7 6 5 4 3 2 1

ISBN 978-1-5011-0370-4
ISBN 978-1-5011-0372-8 (ebook)

To Michael David Sperber—
An automotive genius,
A trophy-winning competitive car racer,
And a man who could sell tribbles to a Klingon,
He is a true character and a great friend.
Here's to Murray!

Historian's Note

The events of this novel occur in two different time periods, in both cases directly following the events of *Star Trek: Deep Space Nine—Sacraments of Fire*. The earlier story line begins in December 2377, and continues into February 2378, while the later story line begins in December 2385, and continues into late January 2386.

The land and the people are one.

—Bajoran proverb

Prologue

Flight

December 2385

The warning lights flared to life an instant before the red-alert klaxon resounded through the security office. A crimson glow washed over the banks of consoles in the compartment as the siren shrieked its call to emergency stations. At the master panel, Selten—Newton Outpost's security chief—consulted the readouts and identified the cause of the alarm at once: "Breach in specimen storage." Around him, his alpha-shift staff mobilized immediately, drawing their weapons and racing to their general-quarters assignments. Selten saw them dash through the doorway and past the compartment's rectangular viewport, which looked out onto the adjacent corridor. Only Ensign Connor Block remained in the security office with him, crewing access control.

"All checkpoints are locked down," the ensign reported. "All security doors are confirmed closed and all force fields have been raised."

"Acknowledged," Selten said as he silenced the alarm in the office and restored normal lighting. He then worked the communications controls on his panel, opening a complex-wide comm link that would carry his voice across the subterranean outpost, both on the upper level, where the twenty-one members of his Starfleet Security team protected the facility, and on the lower level, where forty-five Federation Department of Science researchers and technicians lived and worked. "This is Lieutenant Commander Selten. There has been a breach in Corridor Four, Compartment L," he announced, reading the source of the alarm from his console. "All security personnel, report to alert stations. All others, withdraw to your nearest safety compartment." Throughout the complex, various spaces had been set aside and secured for the protection of the scientific team in case of emergency. "This is not a drill."

"Checkpoint data show that seven scientists, including Doctor Norsa, and two technicians entered Corridor Four thirty-seven minutes ago," Block said. "The Changeling visitor was with them." Norsa, an Argelian biologist, served as Newton Outpost's chief of staff. The Changeling, Odo, had arrived in the Larrisint system a week earlier.

Selten operated his console, checking the outpost's internal sensors. He inspected the readouts for Corridor Four, the section of the facility housing all specimen chambers, where the scientists stored both organic and inanimate objects for study. Scans showed rapid movement across a considerable area within and without Compartment L, but no steady combadge signals and no definite life signs. The readings suggested that the ten individuals who had entered the area had all met a violent end, but Selten's exacting Vulcan mind considered that interpretation of events only a possibility, and he concentrated on gathering more information.

The security chief worked his controls, calling up images from the monitors surrounding the compromised compartment. He watched on the display as what looked like a torrent of liquid metal flowed past in multiple locations. Sensors tracked the motion, but they continued to register only indeterminate life signs.

Selten tapped a control surface that tied him in to his entire staff, but not to any members of the scientific team. "We have activity in Corridor Four," he said, "including the movement of a sizable fluidic mass in the direction of the access door." Only a single checkpoint allowed entry to and egress from the specimen chambers. Since Compartment L sat at the farthest reach of Corridor Four, the only direction to travel from there was toward the door.

"Could that be the shape-shifter?" Block asked once Selten had closed the channel. The security chief understood that the ensign did not refer to Odo. Rather, he spoke of the specimen that the Changeling had come to Newton Outpost to help study, which the scientists had listed for the security contingent as POTENTIAL SHAPE-SHIFTER.

"Possibly," Selten said. Although his sensors still detected no definitive life signs, including none corresponding to any known types of shape-shifters, he could conceive of no other reasonable explanation for what he saw. He called up a secondary configuration on his console and accessed the automatically recorded feeds from in and around Compartment L, surveying the images collected in the moments just before the red alert had begun to blare. The first showed Norsa and five other scientists lined up along the viewing ports, gazing down into the outsize chamber. Measuring ten by twenty by fifty meters, the space had recently been expanded to those dimensions in order to accommodate the specimen, which had been discovered on an asteroid by the crew of *U.S.S. Nova*.

Another feed provided a view directly into the chamber. The great silver mass brought to Newton Outpost for study filled the footprint of the compartment, its inert surface rising and falling in sinuous, static swells, giving it a depth of between one and two meters. Selten watched as Odo emerged from the decontamination chamber that led into the compartment. A technician and another of the scientists remained inside decon, while the second technician waited outside in the corridor and observed through a viewport.

Odo peered back over his shoulder, then proceeded once the inner door had glided closed. He took two paces forward, then dropped onto his knees directly in front of the mass, which looked to Selten like a lake of molten metal, frozen into stillness. Odo leaned forward and laid his hands atop its matte silver surface.

The security chief saw the Changeling's hands begin to shimmer. Odo's flesh softened, as though melting. His fingers liquefied, seeming to disappear into the large shape sprawling away before him.

Selten waited to see what would happen—what *had* happened—but for a moment, nothing did. The security chief had never witnessed two shape-shifters merging—*linking,* they called it—but he understood the concept. The living nature of the specimen remained conjecture, though, and so Selten did not anticipate Odo and the great bulk dissolving into each other. It therefore did not surprise the security chief when, after the Changeling's hands deliquesced, the tableau grew motionless.

"The mass is moving rapidly down Corridor Four," Block said. "It is approaching the entry door."

Selten returned his attention to the status panel, but then motion caught his eye. He looked again at the playback on the display and saw that Odo had pulled back from the silver mass, the specimen's shape changing and rushing upward. Its surface, formerly lusterless, suddenly gleamed. At the top of its reach, its amorphous curves shifted, hardening into straight lines and flat edges, forming into contours resembling those of a hammer's head. It surged down, toward Odo. It struck him with tremendous force and sent him hurtling backward. Odo's body impacted the bulkhead hard, flattened, and ruptured. What had been the simulacrum of a Bajoran man exploded into a gold-orange spatter.

"Ten seconds from the door," Block said.

Selten quickly worked his controls to display a live feed from the monitor surveilling the Corridor Four entry. As with all the security checkpoints within the outpost, a large, thick metal door stood closed when not in use. Additionally, the red alert had initiated the automatic lockdown of the facility, and a force field had been activated at each access point within it.

The great silver mass flowed at high speed through the

corridor. It slammed into the force field erected in front of the door. Electric-blue patches sparked into existence as a result of the contact, and jagged streaks spiked across the surface of the specimen. The undulating mass did not reverse its course, but like a dammed river, it collected where its forward progress had been halted, its level rising toward the overhead. Within just seconds, the image on the screen became completely obscured, preceded an instant before by a vibrant blue flash.

"The force field in Corridor Four is down," Block said.

The security chief glanced back at the recordings of the specimen chamber and saw the shining silver mass swiftly expanding. It quickly grew to cover not just the deck of the compartment, but the volume of space above it. The specimen blotted out the monitors within the chamber, but those outside captured the reactions of the scientists. All but the chief of staff lurched backward, away from the viewing ports, while Doctor Norsa threw herself toward the nearest control panel—doubtless in an attempt to sound the alarm or to take some other action—but too late. The still-growing mass burst through the viewports, shattering them and inundating the corridor like a deluge. It swept the scientists from their feet, and Norsa and her colleagues were abruptly lost from view.

"Commander, the door in Corridor Four is showing signs of stress," Block said. "I don't think it's going to hold."

"How can that be?" Selten demanded. In addition to being fitted with force fields on either side, each of the security checkpoints within the outpost had been constructed of multiple plates and installed to withstand powerful forces on their own, including the yields of energy weapons and high explosives. A simple lateral force, even applied by as massive an object as the Compartment L specimen, should not have been able to compromise any of the doors.

At his station, Block worked his controls. "The door isn't being strained from the outside," he said, "but from within."

That's impossible, Selten thought but did not say, recognizing at once the illogic of such words. It didn't matter that the security door had been designed to be not only impervious to liquids, but airtight as well. Clearly, the great shape-changing mass must have adjusted itself finely enough to penetrate whatever infinitesimal openings existed in the structure of the door. That appeared to imply, at the very least, instinct, and quite possibly intelligence. Regardless, it seemed plain to Selten that the object was alive, despite it not showing up as such on sensors.

The security chief also concluded that if the specimen could breach the door from one side, then it could exit through the other. That meant that the safety compartments to which the scientific team had retreated, protected by the same architecture, could no longer be considered secure. For the first time, Selten considered that he might have to order Newton Outpost evacuated.

He switched his display to show the other side of the Corridor Four checkpoint, which fronted on the entry hall of the complex's lower level. Half a dozen standard, single-paneled doors led from there to the science personnel's cabins, living areas, offices, and laboratories. Another closed checkpoint, set opposite Corridor Four, marked the main access to that portion of the facility. Selten saw two of his staff there: Ensign Elise Ehrenreich and Crewman Dozier held their phasers at the ready.

"Pressure inside the door is increasing," Block said. "The exterior surfaces are exhibiting significant signs of strain. They can't hold much longer."

The security chief didn't hesitate. He activated a comm circuit. "Ehrenreich, Dozier," he said, "exit the entry hall at once to Corridor Seven." The two officers acknowledged the order, and Selten watched as they followed his instructions, darting through the single-paneled door that led into the section of the complex containing the scientists' quarters.

A moment later, a section of the Corridor Four security door blew apart. Chunks of metal flew across the entrance hall like shrapnel. The force field on that side of the check-point flickered multiple times as fragments of metal struck it. Rivulets of the silver mass spilled from the gaping hole left in the door and further sparked the force field, which soon collapsed. The damaged door juddered in its track and slid open a meter or so. The entity coursed through the newly opened gap and began filling the entry hall like water flooding into a tub. The force field protecting the other security door glinted blue again and again where the silver fluid washed up against it, until Block ultimately reported its failure.

Selten once more worked the sensors. Though permanently shielded against beaming into or out of its confines, Newton Outpost possessed an internal transporter, and the security chief considered employing it to relocate the entity away from the facility's personnel. Even if no section of the complex could contain the specimen, the security chief conceived of moving the silver mass from one location to another long enough to allow the entire complement of the outpost to board and launch the escape pods.

But scans failed to read the mass as a living creature, or even as a single object. Selten attempted a geographic transporter lock, directing the dematerialization sequence to target a specific location, beginning with the entry hall on the second level. All of his efforts failed.

On the display, the level of the silver mass rose toward the overhead. Before the security chief could order the use of the escape pods, the outpost's operating procedures required him to take one more action. "Initiating intruder defense system," he intoned. Selten would have preferred not to do it—he did not doubt the living status of the specimen, despite the lack of corroborating evidence from his scans—but he also understood the rationale for making abandonment of Newton Outpost the option of last resort. The secret, secure facility hosted important—and in many cases unique—scientific research, in particular providing a haven for sensitive work.

The security chief disabled the safeties on the intruder defense system, then isolated the entry hall on the lower level and Corridor Four. "Releasing nerve agent." On the display, jets of gas blasted from far up on the bulkhead, near the overhead. If the entity took any notice of the measure, it gave no sign. It continued streaming into the entry hall, its level rising. Sensors revealed no slowing of its movement.

"Releasing secondary nerve agent," Selten said, marrying his actions to his words. He did not appreciate the euphemistic label for the weapon, but he used it according to regulations. The first gas he'd discharged rendered many life-forms unconscious; the second left them dead.

"The entry door is now showing signs of internal strain," Block said.

"What about the other doors?" Selten asked. The single panels that led into the scientists' living and working habitats would pose far less of a hindrance to the entity than the heavy-duty security door it had already compromised.

"They're being strained by the weight of the specimen against them," Block said, "but there seems to be no attempt to breach them."

Why not? Selten wanted to know. It could have been that the creature acted out of reflex, seeking to negotiate the second security door because it had already gotten past the first. It also could have been an indication of the entity making a choice, thereby implying intelligence.

Selten adjusted his screen to display the long, wide corridor that stretched between the entry hall on the lower level and the large turbolift that led down from the security deck above. He saw two more of his staff, Lieutenant Rellor Verat and Ensign Diahann Baker, stationed there, standing just in front of the lift doors. The security chief opened a channel to them.

"Verat, Baker," he said, adding a note of urgency to his normally even voice, "the massive specimen from Compartment L is headed in your direction through the main entrance to the sciences section." He hesitated over his next order, but he knew that once the entity made it through the security door, his officers would not have an opportunity to increase the power of their weapons if their first shots failed to stop it. "Set your phasers to kill, and fire on the specimen as soon as you see it." Selten saw them adjust their weapons as they acknowledged their orders.

The security chief consulted the internal sensors again. To his surprise, he noted seven life signs and ten combadge signals back in Corridor Four, corresponding to the locations of the scientists and technicians at Compartment L, but he had no time to address them. Instead, he concentrated on the two life-forms—one Cygnian and one human—he read in the turbolift corridor. "Open the main security door on the lower level and deactivate the second force field," he told Block.

"Yes, sir," the ensign said.

On the display, Selten saw a flash of blue pinpoints as the force field dropped, and then the security door began to withdraw into the bulkhead. The shape-shifting life-form gushed through the opening and onto the tiled floor beyond. Verat and Baker began firing at once. The yellow-red beams of their phasers seared across the length of the corridor and into the silver mass as it streamed forward. The weapons fire showed no indication of hindering the creature at all, much less of stopping it.

The two officers continued to discharge their weapons even as the entity bore down on them. Their dedication to duty and their composure in extremis gratified Selten. He would be sure to note those qualities on their next performance evaluations.

The security chief operated the transporter controls, being sure to neutralize their phasers as he beamed Verat and Baker to the upper section of the outpost. Specks and then streaks of bright white light engulfed the two officers. They vanished just before the life-form crashed across the place they had been standing, like a wave thundering onto a beach. It continued forward, into the force field protecting the turbolift, which sparked blue with the contact.

"Drop the lift to the bottom of the shaft," Selten said. "Then lower the force field and open the doors."

"Yes, sir," Block said as he sent his fingers skittering across his control panel.

Selten didn't believe he had enough information to draw a firm conclusion about the intelligence of the shape-shifting life-form—he reasoned that it could be acting on innate reflexes—but the security chief perceived a measure of knowledge in the creature, which he could only assume it had gleaned from its brief contact with Odo. Though the specimen had been faced with few choices, the path it had taken from its compartment nevertheless appeared to follow the most direct route to the upper level of Newton Outpost and, presumably, to freedom.

Selten opened a channel once more to his staff. "All security personnel, withdraw to the nearest safety compartment." Then, to Block, he said, "Lower the force field at the top of the turboshaft and open the doors there." As he spoke, the security chief operated the transporter again, using the life signs and combadge signals to beam everybody in and around Compartment L to the outpost's infirmary, a secure area always supervised by one of the numerous medical doctors on the staff. "Pressurize the hangar, then lower all force fields and open all doors between there and the turbolift."

"Yes, sir."

On the display, the lift doors on the lower level opened to reveal an empty shaft. The great silver mass heaved into the vertical conduit and arced upward. Its way no longer impeded, its shape smoothed and narrowed as it sped into the turboshaft, making it look like a mammoth silver snake. "Raise the force fields and close the security doors behind it as it clears them," Selten said. While the creature had demonstrated that such measures would not stop it should it reverse its course, they would at least slow it down, which would provide additional time, if necessary, to evacuate the outpost.

The security chief accessed other monitors, starting with the one observing the turbolift on the upper level. The doors stood open on the vacant shaft. Time elapsed—ten seconds, twenty, thirty, a full minute—and then the creature shot out of the turboshaft and whisked down the adjoining corridor. It sped through two open checkpoints, its path clear, then raced past the security office. Selten and Block both stood up at their stations to peer through the one-way port that looked out into the corridor. The creature's shining silver surface reflected the overhead lighting.

Something like an insistent whisper reached Selten's ears, and he realized that, even through the door to the security office, he could hear the sound of the air as the great mass roared past. The size and the speed of the specimen impressed, but as the security chief looked on, something about its lithe motion implied a mind driving its movement. Selten could not explain it, other than to attribute it to intuition, or to infer that his own telepathic abilities touched however dimly upon the creature's awareness. The security chief concentrated for a moment, and he briefly *felt* something, a sense of yearning, there and then gone.

Before the serpentine entity had fully passed, Selten returned to his console, and Ensign Block followed suit. The security chief accessed the monitors in the hangar. He saw that the door to the airlock had withdrawn into the bulkhead, implying that atmosphere had been introduced into the large area. On the deck, markings designated a landing zone, and the outpost's two runabouts—*Neva* and *Loire*—sat off to the side.

The creature bolted through the open airlock. It sliced past the runabouts, its form stretched into an extended silver cylinder. It curved up and toward the interlocking hatches that formed the flat roof of the hangar.

"As soon as its entire mass has cleared the airlock, seal the doors," Selten told Block.

"Yes, sir."

The creature smashed into the center of the hangar's roof. At the point of impact, its body compressed and spread, but not in a circle. It flowed along the line where the two hatches came together. Selten didn't know with certainty that the entity could compromise the roof the way it had the Corridor Four security door, but he did not intend to find out. He focused on the entrance to the airlock and waited as the trailing body of the creature continued passing through it and into the hangar.

"The outer hatch is showing signs of strain," Block said.

The security chief tried to gauge how long he could safely delay before risking serious damage to the outpost, but then he saw the tail end of the creature enter the hangar. "Now," he said at once. "Close the airlock, then open the hatches."

The ensign operated his controls, and Selten saw the airlock doors glide closed. Immediately afterward, the hatches parted and the roof to the hangar opened. Beyond, against a backdrop of stars, light glinted off numerous small objects teeming in nearby space. Located inside a shepherd moon tucked into the rings circling the gas giant of Larrisint IV, Newton Outpost provided nothing but spectacular views.

As the hatch continued to open, the walls of the crater situated directly above the outpost came into view. The creature rocketed out of the hangar, whether of its own efforts or as the result of the atmosphere blasting out into space, Selten couldn't tell. He waited until the entire mass of the specimen had left the outpost, then ordered Block to secure the hatches. The ensign complied at once. The security chief raised the outpost's shields, although he had little confidence that they could long withstand an assault by the creature, which had already proven its ability against force fields.

As the roof of the hangar closed, Selten accessed the external sensors. The specimen still did not read as a living organism, but the security chief tracked its movement. It continued in its tubular shape, twisting among the dust and rocks of Larrisint IV's rings. For three full minutes, it moved away, but then it abruptly changed its path and plunged back toward the shepherd moon at tremendous speed.

Selten quickly worked the outpost's weapons controls. The shepherd moon had been fitted with two phaser banks and a quantum torpedo launcher. The security staff maintained the systems, regularly testing them to ensure their performance, but in the three years Selten had served at Newton Outpost, they had never been fired in defense of the facility.

The security chief targeted both the phasers and the quantum torpedoes. He tracked the path of the creature, but as it neared the shepherd moon, it altered its trajectory. Selten waited to fire, and the deviation increased. The creature had initially been headed for the center of the crater that masked the entrance to the outpost, and then for a spot on the surface, and finally for a point in nearby space.

Mindful of a feint, Selten kept the weapons locked on the silver mass. As it swooped in, it suddenly altered its form. It changed from its long, cylindrical configuration into a complex structure, with what looked like fins and sails, antennae and tails, demonstrating that it possessed far more than the rudimentary shape-shifting abilities it had to that point shown. It remained entirely silver, but nevertheless appeared organic, like some great spaceborne entity. Selten had never seen anything even remotely resembling it. Its appendages rippled, almost as though the creature swam through the void.

The shape-shifter soared past Newton Outpost. Its course changed slightly, and the security chief quickly calculated that the creature had used the mass of the shepherd moon to make the adjustment. Its path bent past the outpost and headed on a course that would take it on a close approach to Larrisint IV.

It's using gravity either for propulsion or for navigation, or perhaps for both, Selten thought. The action could have been the byproduct of mere instinct, but it also could have been the design of an intelligent mind. Selten calculated its flight path and saw that it would bend around the gas giant and slingshot outward, taking the creature out of the Larrisint system.

As the security chief tracked the shape-shifter, wanting to ensure that it did not return to the shepherd moon, he opened an outpost-wide comm link. "This is Lieutenant Commander Selten," he said. "Secure from general quarters. The specimen held in Compartment L has escaped confinement and fled the outpost."

He then checked in with the infirmary. Doctor Leslie Braeden reported two dead and six injured among the scientists and technicians present when the creature broke from captivity. She could not determine the condition of Odo, whose physical essence remained in an unformed gelatinous state. Since being transported to the infirmary after being attacked, the Changeling had shown no signs of life.

Once his staff had reassembled, Selten briefed them on everything that had transpired. The security team followed the progress of the creature, first as it fell toward Larrisint IV, and then as its redirected course took it into interstellar space. Selten prepared a report, then contacted Starfleet Operations.

"Would you classify the creature as a belligerent?" asked Admiral Elizabeth Kadin over a secure subspace channel.

"I cannot make such a determination with any certainty," said the Newton Outpost security chief, "but it clearly could pose a hazard to Federation vessels."

"Understood," Kadin said. *"Is there anything more?"*

"Just one thing," Selten said. "When the creature passed close to me, I sensed what I can only describe at its driving force." The security chief paused, allowing the fleeting impressions he'd received to coalesce into a coherent thought. "Whatever that thing is, it wants something," he finally said. "It wants something, and it wants it *badly*."

I

Descent

December 2377

Captain Kira Nerys stood in Ops and gazed up at the main viewscreen, which hung down from the overhead. She had served for nearly a decade aboard Deep Space 9—for seven years as exec and Bajoran liaison, and then two more as its commanding officer—but she had never grown completely accustomed to its Cardassian architecture. Her discomfort on the erstwhile Terok Nor did not stem from any residual anger or ill will she held for the once and long-time oppressors of her people, for she had fought hard to leave behind the bitterness and hatred so readily fostered within her during the Occupation, and which had then been vigorously renewed during the Dominion War. Far more basic than that, she simply judged the design sense of the Cardassians as awkward and inconvenient. *Who installs a viewscreen in a control center so that everybody has to look up to see it?* Even after her extended tenure aboard DS9, Kira still occasionally stumbled over one of the raised thresholds in the station's doorways. The fact that she sometimes tripped when entering or exiting her own quarters bespoke a style of construction far short of ergonomic.

On the main screen, the resplendent blue-and-white whirlpool of the Celestial Temple spun into view. Just moments before, Kira's first officer, Commander Elias Vaughn, had reported the loss of contact with Starfleet's comm relay in the Gamma Quadrant. The automated, self-contained device kept station in space just outside the Idran system. The relay facilitated subspace communications through the wormhole, but it had abruptly gone silent, not even responding to a simple ping to confirm its continued existence.

Kira had ordered Vaughn to take DS9's chief of opera-tions, Lieutenant Nog, on a runabout to diagnose and repair the problem. Before the first officer had even made it to the lift, the station's alpha-shift tactical officer, Lieutenant Samaritan Bowers, announced the opening of the wormhole. Knowing that the day's schedule included no ships arriving from the Gamma Quadrant, Kira asked to see the vessel on the viewscreen.

The captain peered up and saw a small form—its bow section dark, its aft light—emerge from the center of the Celestial Temple. She could distinguish no details about the ship apart from its compact size and shading. When the terminus of the wormhole swept back in on itself and vanished, Kira could just make out the white portion of the vessel against the black backdrop of space.

From the other side of Ops, near the turbolift, Vaughn asked, "Can you identify that ship?" To Kira, it appeared to be towing another structure.

"Negative," replied Bowers. "There's nothing in the ship registry that matches the configuration. It's relatively small, though. It probably has enough room for only a limited number of passengers."

"Assuming that they're the size of typical humanoids," Vaughn said, glancing over at Bowers.

"Yes, sir," Bowers agreed. He appeared abashed at having to be corrected.

Kira looked to the communications station. "Open a channel," she said.

"Channel open," said Lieutenant Ezri Dax. Only recently returned from Tellar, where she'd undergone Starfleet's Advanced Tactical Training, Dax currently split her on-duty time between alpha shift, when she crewed communications, and beta shift, when she took over for Bowers.

"This is Captain Kira Nerys of Deep Space Nine, to unknown vessel." The station's commanding officer delivered the words in a formal tone. "Please identify yourself."

Kira waited, but she received no immediate reply to her hail. Vaughn walked back around the raised perimeter of Ops to stand next to her. As one silent moment drew into the next, Kira exchanged a look with her exec, and she could see reflected in his expression her own concern: that the unexpected appearance from the Gamma Quadrant of an unrecognized ship bore directly on the failure of the communications relay.

"No response, Captain," Dax said.

"What's their course?" Vaughn asked.

"Not for the station," Bowers said, examining the data on his console. "It looks as though they're heading for Bajor."

Kira's concern grew. Standard operating procedure required all vessels arriving through the wormhole to stop at Deep Space 9. The deviation could have been an oversight, or perhaps even just ignorance, but in either case, Kira should have received an answer to her message.

"This is Captain Kira," she said again. "Identify yourself and state your business in this system or face the consequences." The bellicosity of Kira's language made her uncomfortable. She had uttered such phrases uncounted times before, but doing so had grown more and more difficult of late.

"Captain, the wormhole is opening up again," Bowers said, surprise evident in his voice. Kira watched the viewscreen as the Celestial Temple swirled back into existence. Another shape, resembling the first but wholly dark, flew from within the vortex of blue and white light. "The second ship has a configuration similar to the first," Bowers said, checking his readouts. "It is following the same course." The wormhole once again withdrew into itself and disappeared.

"Is it in pursuit of the first ship?" Vaughn asked.

"Possibly," Bowers said. "I'll scan for weapons—" The lieutenant clipped his sentence short as the Celestial Temple rotated open a third time. The level of Kira's concern increased even before she saw two more ships exit the wormhole, and then five more after that. When scores of ships—a veritable squadron—then materialized, she reached out to Vaughn's arm and urged him forward, a physical manifestation of the order that rose in her mind.

"Get to the *Defiant*," she told him. As he raced toward the lift, she looked over at Bowers. "Red alert," she said. "We're under attack." She didn't know if by *we* she meant the crew and residents of Deep Space 9 or the people of Bajor, but she could not mistake the threat that had so quickly arisen.

The call to battle stations blared through Ops as alert lighting bathed the crew in red tones. "Bowers, go with Commander Vaughn," Kira ordered, assigning the tactical officer *Defiant* would need. Dax had just completed advanced training, but Bowers had both seniority and more experience in the position.

Kira quickly descended the steps to the situation table that sat in the middle of the control center. As Bowers followed Vaughn to the lift, Dax shifted over to tactical, and Lieutenant John Candlewood, the station's newly promoted chief science officer, took over at communications. "Dax, raise the shields," Kira said. "Candlewood, continue our hails."

"Aye, Captain," Candlewood said.

"Energizing phaser arrays and loading quantum torpedoes," Kira said, working controls on the sit table. Starfleet had first made significant upgrades to DS9's weapons and defenses six years prior, in anticipation of hostilities with the Dominion. Since then, the improved systems had performed well, successfully protecting the station from major damage, and possibly even from destruction, on several occasions. They had also been upgraded a second time, not even two years earlier.

As gauges on the sit table showed power coursing into the phaser arrays, and quantum torpedoes loading into launch tubes, Kira glanced back up at the main viewscreen. A second flood of ships had appeared in the center of the wormhole. "Course?" she asked.

"Unchanged," Dax said. "I'm reading two hundred thirty vessels in total, and they're all following the path of the first, which remains headed to Bajor. They have defensive shields that are inhibiting our sensors. Visual scans reveal what appear to be emitters on their hulls, which could be weapons, and the structure that the first ship is towing looks like a torpedo of some kind. Several other ships are also hauling various pieces of equipment."

"Anything, Lieutenant?" the captain asked, peering up at Candlewood.

"Negative," the science officer said. "Still no response, although it appears that our hails are being received."

"Understood," Kira said, and she thought that she understood too well. *Is it going to be this again?* she asked herself. *Another battle? More injuries, more deaths?* Such incidents had always been a part of her adult life—and even before that, as regular occurrences in her childhood. Only the scale had changed. Where as a girl she had first taken up arms against individual Cardassians, and then larger and larger groups of them, she had graduated to firing on well-crewed ships and populated cities. Her justification for doing so did not mitigate the tremendous fatigue she had begun to feel.

"Captain, the first ship is almost beyond our weapons range," Dax reported. Kira glanced back up at the viewscreen, but she hesitated. "Captain," Dax said again, her tone urgent.

"Target the first vessel," Kira said. "Fire phasers."

"Firing phasers," Dax said. The captain peered over at the

lieutenant as she worked the tactical console. Kira waited, and then Dax delivered a verdict. "Direct hit," she said. "Virtually no effect. The vessel is continuing on its course."

"Fire quantum torpedoes," Kira ordered. "Full spread."

Tense seconds passed, and then Dax reported four hits. "The ship's shields are down only eight percent."

"*Eight* percent?" Kira asked, thunderstruck. Four direct, consecutive quantum torpedo detonations would have severely impacted the shields of even the most powerfully equipped Starfleet vessel. How much weapons fire would the crew of Deep Space 9 have to spend to destroy even one of the intruding ships? If Kira loosed Deep Space 9's weaponry on a fleet of conventionally fortified vessels, and even with *Defiant* contributing its own armaments to the effort, she knew that it would be difficult, if not impossible, to prevent all of those ships from reaching Bajor. Within the prior two weeks, a pair of Starfleet vessels—the *Galaxy*-class *Magellan* and the *Norway*-class *Mjolnir*—had docked at the station for maintenance and repairs, while a third—the *Sovereign*-class *Chancellor*—had stopped at Bajor for shore leave for its crew, but all three had since departed the system. Kira could only hope that none of them had traveled too far.

"Open an emergency channel," she said. "Contact any Starfleet vessels within two days of Bajor. Request their immediate assistance, then inform Starfleet Command of the situation."

"Aye, Captain," Candlewood said. "Right away."

Kira reached to the sit table and brought up her own communications display. She would contact Bajor's first minister, Asarem Wadeen, and warn her of the squadron crewed by an unidentified force headed for the planet, with unknown intent. After all that her people had been through, even the possibility of an attack on their homeworld horrified the captain.

As Kira tapped a control to open a comm channel, she saw yet another wave of ships emerge from the wormhole.

Iliana Ghemor listened to the words of her nemesis: *"This is Captain Kira Nerys of Deep Space Nine, to unknown vessel. Please identify yourself."*

In the cockpit of her small ship—of what had been Grand Archquester Votiq's personal vessel before Ghemor had decisively removed him from where he'd stood in her path—she felt rage surge within her. The red-hot nucleus of anger and resentment that she always carried at the heart of her being, that had for so long defined the trajectory of her life, exploded, a star turned supernova in the black pit of space. In her mind's eye, Ghemor envisioned herself taking control of the navigational actuator and swinging the bow of her crimson, bladelike ship around until it pointed toward the old Cardassian ore-processing station that had been usurped by the Bajorans and the Federation. She imagined priming the isolytic subspace torpedo she towed behind her vessel, then launching it and bearing witness as the devastating weapon tore Deep Space 9 apart, and Kira Nerys along with it.

Ghemor's hands hovered over the helm controls. All the pain of her adult life had led her to that moment. It felt like it had been another existence entirely when she'd received word that Ataan Rhukal, her childhood friend who'd eventually become her betrothed, had been killed by the Shakaar terrorist cell on Bajor. The personal tragedy drove her to join the Obsidian Order, the secretive Cardassian intelligence service, which trained her and then transformed her, making her into a replica of Kira Nerys. The Order intended Ghemor to replace Kira in her radical group, and thereby infiltrate the Bajoran dissidents. Before Ghemor could deploy to her assignment, though, one of the Cardassians' own, a depraved *gul* named Skrain Dukat, imprisoned her and kept her as his personal plaything for thousands of days. Her interminable detention robbed her of her freedom, and the unrelenting abuse she suffered took away her will to live, replacing it with a thirst for vengeance.

The great mass of Deep Space 9 showed on Ghemor's sensors like a glowing target. She ached to mete out reprisal to the fountainhead of all her ills, but a just retribution demanded more than the mere death of Kira Nerys—it required agony. For all the misery Ghemor had endured, she needed to repay it, if not in kind, then with some reciprocal version. Her anguish necessitated Kira's own.

"This is Captain Kira. Identify yourself and state your business in this system or face the consequences."

Ghemor laughed. She understood the need for consequences far better than Kira. She did not alter her ship's course, but continued toward Bajor. Her scans showed that a single Ascendant vessel pursued her at close range. She assumed that it must belong to Raiq, who had attempted to contact the Grand Archquester when Ghemor had taken control of his ship in the Gamma Quadrant and headed it for the Bajoran wormhole. The rest of the Ascendant armada followed, the knights clearly driven by the belief that they needed the isolytic subspace weapon to help them achieve the Final Ascension—the generations-long quest of their people to find and become one with their gods.

Her sensors also showed a Starfleet vessel powering up at Deep Space 9. It didn't matter. None of it mattered. She would reach Bajor ahead of them all, and once she had, she would unleash the might of her weapon on its people—on Kira's people. Ghemor would bring her enemy to her knees by destroying that which she held most dear.

An alert sounded in the cockpit, and Ghemor consulted

her control panel to see that Deep Space 9 had fired its weapons in her direction. The phaser blasts slammed into the shields of her vessel, but she barely felt their effects. Starfleet could not match the technology of warfare employed by the Ascendants.

Another warning pulsed, and then four quantum torpedoes exploded against the shields. Ghemor identified a dip in the protective envelope encompassing her vessel, but nothing that would distract her from her goal. Kira wanted her to identify herself and state her business. Ghemor would make her purpose known soon enough. Kira would look upon the destruction of her people and her world, and then find the responsibility for the act laid at the captain's own feet.

And then Ghemor would finally end Kira's miserable, treacherous life.

A circle of darkness appeared ahead of the ship, quickly growing to reveal a field of stars within it—or perhaps beyond it. Raiq quickly surveyed her instruments, trying to make sense of what she saw. *Except I already know, don't I?*

Not that long ago, the Archquesters—the leaders of the Ascendants' Orders—had come together for the first time in millennia, seeking clarity on what many knights viewed as portents of the End Time. At the gathering, an alien woman appeared in their midst and declared herself the Fire, a figure prophesied by scripture. As presaged by the holy texts, the Fire claimed that she would lead the Ascendants to the Fortress of the True, where they would finally be judged by their gods and burn beneath their gaze, with the worthy among their ranks uniting with them.

In pursuit of that goal, a young Quester named Aniq had previously managed to acquire a metaweapon, which she had subsequently enhanced by arming it with transformative fuel. It had been Raiq's understanding that the powerful explosive device would be utilized within the Fortress, facilitating the burning of the Ascendants and their joining with the Unnameable. After uncounted generations, the Final Ascension at last seemed within reach.

But then, on the cusp of the Fortress, the Ascendant armada had come upon the long-concealed homeworld of the Eav'oq. In the distant past, the last of those heretics had escaped extermination by going into hiding. The Fire ordered a squadron of ten ships to destroy the lone remaining city on the planet.

To Raiq, the proposed action had seemed more than simply apt. It promised closure, and carried with it a sense of symbolism that bordered on the poetic. There, in the star system where the Ascendants would finally locate the portal leading to the Fortress of the True, they would execute one last tribute to their gods by eradicating the blasphemers who had escaped their wrath.

Raiq had watched as Aniq had delivered the metaweapon to the Grand Archquester's vessel, to be safeguarded during the attack. A squadron of ten Ascendant ships then headed for the Eav'oq world. Excitement churned within Raiq.

But then she had seen the Grand Archquester's vessel break away from its position at the front of the armada. The distinctively colored ship darted forward, and for a moment, Raiq assumed that Votiq, or perhaps the Fire, had chosen to participate in the obliteration of the Eav'oq. But sensors did not show the vessel turning in the direction of the planet. Rather, it continued along the course the Fire had set for the armada—which meant toward the Fortress of the True.

The Grand Archquester's ship towed the metaweapon behind it.

Raiq's excitement that her people would soon enter the Fortress and stand before the True had transformed into fear that she and the others would be left behind. She immediately opened a channel and hailed Votiq. When she received no response, she did not try a second time. Instead, she contacted the armada and sounded the alarm.

There had been no time for consensus, and Raiq hadn't waited for it. Instead, she started in pursuit of the Grand Archquester's vessel and the valuable cargo it towed. She tried to imagine Votiq absconding with the metaweapon and seeking to utilize it for his own purposes, but she couldn't. He had lived longer and spent more time on the Quest, in the service of his people, than any other existing Ascendant. Raiq could not conceive of him wanting to abandon the Orders so that he could stand alone before the Unnameable.

It's the Fire, Raiq had thought as she'd pushed her own ship to its limits. *If she truly is the Fire.* It sickened Raiq to harbor suspicions of a figure foretold by prophecy, but she could not deny the distrust building within her. *Would the Unnameable really have sent an alien to guide us?*

Raiq had followed the Grand Archquester's vessel on sensors. It pleased her that scans showed the rest of the Ascendant armada falling into formation behind her. She peered out through the transparent canopy of her own ship and searched for any visual sign of Votiq's vessel.

That had been when space had blossomed before Raiq. A great frenzy of light and movement wheeled around in brilliant shades of blue and white. Even before she entertained a conscious thought about what she saw, a thrill like an electric charge coursed through Raiq's body. There could be no doubt about the wonder before her: the gates that would lead her and the rest of the Ascendants into the Fortress of the True.

Raiq had felt elation and fear in equal measure. She saw the Grand Archquester's vessel ahead of her, a dark knife-edge towing the subspace weapon, advancing directly toward the center of the kinetic radiance. Raiq glanced at her display to see a series of readings that made little sense. Votiq's ship still appeared on her scans—

And then it had vanished. Raiq looked up to confirm the disappearance, and saw that she had a choice to make. Suddenly at the boundary of the spectacle, she could either continue forward or turn away.

Exhilarated beyond measure, and yet also terrified, Raiq had taken the only action she reasonably could. After an existence lived exclusively on the Quest, seeking out and eliminating sacrilege while searching for the Fortress, she could not turn away from the realization of all her striving. She pulled her hands away from the control console before her, then watched as her ship drew ever closer to the coruscating field of light.

Raiq's vessel had shuddered as it had crossed through the gates of the Fortress. A rich blue light enveloped the cockpit. Great luminescent streamers twined past, and beyond them, sequences of white rings appeared to define a vast cylinder. On the periphery of the region through which the ship moved, concentric loops formed, expanded, and faded away.

As Raiq had gazed out at a sight as beautiful and wondrous as she'd expected, her vessel had continued to buck and heave. She examined her console and saw that powerful stresses threatened the integrity of her ship's hull. Sensors showed wave intensities increasing asymmetrically, escalating externally but not internally—an occurrence she previously would have thought impossible. In the region surrounding her vessel, a centripetal force of unknown origin somehow acted on the imaginary mass of neutrinos. Proton counts climbed sharply, and spatial discontinuities propagated, seemingly at random.

Raiq had looked back up through the canopy of her ship, not only eager at long last to lay her eyes upon the form of the Unnameable, but deeply curious as well. As she searched the writhing panorama ahead, her vessel quaked again, hard, and nearly threw her from her seat. She knew that she needed to compensate for the fractured space around the ship and the strains on the hull. She worked to reconfigure the navigational deflector, then tied her scans into the helm to accommodate the discontinuities.

When Raiq had raised her head again, she'd seen the black disc expanding in the distance, like a hole opening in the fabric of reality. She consulted the sensors to identify what she saw. She wanted an explanation other than what it looked like to her, but then the kaleidoscope of shifting colors and forms fell away, and the ship shot back out into normal space.

Anticipation and hope drained out of Raiq, replaced by dread and disappointment. Stars shined in the firmament, none of them in patterns she recognized. Off to one side, a structure composed of arcs and circles and angles hung in space like some great skeletal sentinel. Directly ahead of her, sunlight from the nearest star glinted off the deep, purplish red of the Grand Archquester's vessel as it continued speeding away.

Confusion colored Raiq's thoughts. Her zealous faith told her to trust in the prophecy that heralded the coming of the Fire, and in the Fire herself, but her lack of understanding about what had just happened provoked doubt. Had Raiq just entered the Fortress of the True, and if so, then why had she not encountered the Unnameable? Had she been deemed unworthy? Or had the Fire led her not into the Fortress, but into—and through—some other construct?

Raiq turned and peered behind her ship through its transparent canopy. At first, she saw no indication of the Fortress or the gates through which she had passed. But then a dizzying gyre of blue and white light appeared like a dawn in the eternal night of deep space. From within the dazzling display emerged ranks of Ascendant ships.

What is happening? Raiq asked herself. She had no answers, but she vowed to herself that she would get some. She turned back to her control console and sent her ship in pursuit of the Grand Archquester's vessel.

Suddenly, red-yellow beams cut through space from the structure—probably a space station—and into the Grand Archquester's vessel. Raiq checked her sensors to see that the weapons had not resulted in any damage to Votiq's ship. She considered returning fire, but she did not want to overstep her authority. She waited a moment, and then a quartet of bluish white bolts flashed out of the space station and into the Grand Archquester's ship.

Raiq primed her vessel's own weapons. For the moment, she did nothing, following Votiq's lead, but she would not stand idly by for long. She continued on in pursuit of the Grand Archquester's ship, ready for any battle that might come.

"We will prepare our planetary defenses, Captain, but . . ." On the main viewscreen in Ops, Asarem did not complete her sentence, but Kira understood the first minister's meaning just the same. A number of weapons platforms orbited Bajor, supplemented by several ground-based installations, while Ashalla and the other large cities possessed deflector grids. Those measures, commensurate with similar fortifications on other Federation worlds, could protect against the weaponry of a single starship, or even that of several vessels, but they had not been designed to withstand an attack by an entire fleet.

"We don't know their intentions," Kira reminded the first minister, though the words sounded unconvincing even to the captain. Overlooking the possibility—and perhaps the likelihood—that the invaders had destroyed the communications relay in the Gamma Quadrant, their large fleet, their refusal to respond to repeated hails, and their direct course for Bajor did not suggest benign objectives.

"We'll reach out in peace to welcome them," Asarem said, *"but considering that they've declined to reply, I doubt that our efforts will meet with success."*

"No," Kira agreed. "Probably not."

"Keep me informed," the first minister said. *"Asarem out."* The viewscreen went dark, and Kira saw Candlewood work a control on his panel to close the channel. An image of the wormhole reappeared, another phalanx of ships streaming from it.

"How many ships in total?" Kira asked.

"Nearly seven hundred," Dax said.

"Captain," Candlewood said, "the *Defiant* has just left the station."

"Acknowledged," Kira said, pleased that Vaughn would be on the scene to deal with the situation, but unsure exactly how she should have him proceed. Hundreds of alien ships had unexpectedly entered the Bajoran system through the wormhole, running with shields energized and with apparent armaments, but they had yet to make an offensive move. Kira had fired the first shots, to little effect, but she did not want to wait to respond further until an attack had been loosed against Bajor. If she chose—

"Captain, two ships that have just come through the wormhole are a close match to a known configuration," Dax said.

"Show me," Kira said.

The image on the main viewscreen shifted, magnifying a single vessel so that it filled the display. To the captain, the streamlined, almost tubular design resembled a Starfleet warp nacelle. It did not appear to possess any running lights, and Kira doubted that its black hull would have been visible had the vibrant form of the Celestial Temple not been open behind it.

"The match comes from an historical database," Dax said. "More than a hundred years ago, a squadron of six such vessels attacked a Federation starship and its landing party in the R-Eight-Three-Six star system. The Starfleet crew were there to investigate a city that had been destroyed on the second planet. They repelled the assault, but two months later, they were on hand when five more of those vessels showed up and attacked—" Dax abruptly stopped speaking and looked over at Kira. "They attacked Pillagra."

The name struck Kira like a slap across the face. "The Bajoran colony." She had learned as a girl about the settlement, which had been founded more than a hundred years earlier. Though Pillagra had ultimately thrived, Kira knew that the original colonists had faced tremendous adversity, though she didn't recall the incident Dax had referenced.

"Yes," the lieutenant said, referring to a readout on the tactical display. "All of the attacking vessels were ultimately destroyed . . . actually, the master of the last vessel self-destructed. Captain Kirk of the *Enterprise* reported that they identified themselves as the Ascendants."

The Ascendants. The name sounded familiar to Kira, but only vaguely, like a detail she might have read out of a history text long ago. "Who are they?" she asked. "Where are they from?"

"Unknown," Dax said. "There have been no other recorded encounters with them, but—" The lieutenant peered up from her console and over at Kira. "—Kirk described them as religious zealots who specifically targeted the Bajorans."

That did more than merely suggest a motivation for the

sudden appearance of the fleet entering the system and heading for Bajor. "What were the offensive capabilities of those ships?" Kira asked.

"Checking," Dax said as she worked the tactical console. "The *Constitution*-class *Enterprise* and the *Miranda*-class *Courageous* faced five of those vessels at Pillagra. The Ascendant ships were highly maneuverable, but they were equipped with standard shielding and only low-yield laser cannon."

"That doesn't sound too formidable," Kira said.

"It might not sound that way," Dax said, "but the *Enterprise* suffered considerable damage and the *Courageous* was destroyed. The physical Bajoran colony was also wiped out, although the two Starfleet crews were able to save the colonists."

"Can you evaluate those ships out there now?" Kira asked, gesturing toward the viewscreen. "Is there any way to compare them to the ones that attacked Pillagra?"

"At the very least, the ships coming through the wormhole have more powerful shielding," Dax said. "Because our scans are being deflected, we can't accurately assess their offensive capabilities, but it would be reasonable to assume considerable advancement over the course of a century."

Kira nodded. She'd reluctantly reached the same conclusion. Something else Dax had said troubled the captain even more. "Starfleet described the Ascendants as religious zealots," Kira said. "Was there a reason that they attacked a Bajoran colony?"

Dax studied her console. "According to Captain Kirk, the Ascendants sought to annihilate the Bajorans because they falsely worshipped the 'True.'"

"The *True*?" Kira echoed. "Were they referring to the Prophets?" The captain puzzled over the information and wondered about the meaning of *falsely* worshipping. Whatever the intentions of the Ascendants, it suddenly became clear that it likely had something to do with the Bajoran religion.

Kira first thought to contact Pralon Onala, but the kai had left Bajor several days earlier and had yet to return. She had traveled into the Gamma Quadrant, to the fourth planet of the system that a little more than a year before had shifted three light-years, to a volume of space that encompassed the other terminus of the wormhole. Pralon had gone to Idran IV as part of a cultural exchange with the Eav'oq, a species whose surviving members had reappeared after fifty thousand years secreting themselves away in folded space, in something like a meditational trance.

They claimed that they were hiding from a race of fanatical beings bent on wiping them out, Kira recalled hearing. Opaka Sulan, Odo, and Jake Sisko had all been present when the Eav'oq had returned to normal space. The captain wondered if those fanatics could have been the same zealots who had attacked Pillagra a century prior, and who at that moment were sending hundreds of ships toward Bajor. Kira didn't know, but she believed that the events unfolding before her probably had something to do with her people's faith. She considered contacting Opaka or the Vedek Assembly, but instead chose to seek guidance from another source.

The captain looked to Candlewood at the communications station. "Open a channel to Bajor," she said. The lieutenant operated his panel, then nodded to her. The captain peered back at the viewscreen. "Kira Nerys to Benjamin Sisko."

By the time Asarem Wadeen returned to the reception room, she had spoken with Kira Nerys twice. The first time, Kira informed her of a fleet of alien vessels pouring out of the Celestial Temple, and the second, the captain identified the apparent invaders as historical aggressors against the century-old world of Pillagra. Asarem immediately contacted Minister of Defense Fandor Jelt so that he could prepare Bajor's fortifications, and then she charged Second Minister Ledahn Muri with apprising the rest of the government about the situation. Once the first minister had dealt personally with her diplomatic visitors, she intended to speak directly with the Bajoran people in a planetwide address.

Asarem reentered the reception room, shadowed by Jasmine Tey, one of the security staff assigned to protect her. The first minister looked around the large, high-ceilinged chamber, where she had earlier been meeting with the Eav'oq delegation prior to embarking on a day of events scheduled across Bajor. Paintings adorned the walls, interspersed with decorative plants, and tall tables stood scattered about the empty room. Asarem did not immediately see Itu and his two peers, but then she spied them through an open doorway off to her left. She headed in that direction.

The three Eav'oq looked to the first minister more like works of abstract art than actual living beings. They had slender, tubular bodies that rose three-quarters of a meter taller than Asarem. A row of eight long, lissome pink arms circled their upper frames, and they walked on eight shorter but no less nimble legs, which seemed to intertwine when they moved.

As Asarem approached the doorway, the Eav'oq in the center of the group turned toward her, spinning in place as crisply as a child's top. The first minister recognized Itu from the gray color of his single eye, which spanned his narrow face. The other two members of the Eav'oq party, Evo and Onan, each had a soft-yellow eye, distinguishing them as female members of their species.

Asarem stepped out onto the balcony to join her visitors. To either side of the wide platform, at an attentive but respectful distance, a pair of Militia officers, a woman and a man, accompanied the Eav'oq. Beyond the railing at the edge of the balcony, the verdant springtime panorama stretched away toward the wilderness that bordered that side of the capital city. As the summer months rapidly approached in Ashalla, the landscape had grown colorful, with clutches of wildflowers abounding like vibrant splashes of paint on a green, monochromatic canvas. The twitter of birds filled the air, as did the redolent scents of fresh growth, including the heady fragrances of *nerak* and *kidu* blossoms.

"I am sorry for the delay," Asarem told her guests.

As Evo and Onan whirled where they stood to face the first minister, Itu's eye curled up at the ends, in much the same way that a humanoid mouth formed a smile. When he spoke, he did so with a melodic voice that had a singsong quality to it. Asarem's universal translator converted the continuous tones into more ordinary speech. "We understand that you must attend to affairs of state." Although he eschewed any sort of a title that branded him as the leader of the Eav'oq, Itu functioned in his people's dealing with Bajor as, at the very least, their de facto spokesman.

"I'm afraid that a troubling, possibly dangerous situation has arisen," Asarem said. "A large number of alien ships have unexpectedly entered our solar system. They refuse to respond to our attempts to speak with them, and they are heading directly toward our planet."

The ends of Itu's eyes slipped down. "And you are concerned for the welfare of your people."

"I am," the first minister said. "But I'm also mindful of protecting the three of you while you are visiting our world." She signaled with a gesture to the two nearby Militia officers, who immediately strode over to her. "Major Carlien and Lieutenant Onial will escort you to a secure shelter in the foundation of this building." Asarem looked to the red-haired Carlien Anra, who nodded her acknowledgment of the order.

"Is there a reason you see the influx of the beings in these vessels as a potential threat," Evo asked, "other than their unforeseen arrival and their inability or unwillingness to communicate with you?"

"There is," Asarem said. "We have found a report in our records that once, long ago, a squadron of such ships attacked a Bajoran colony and obliterated a city. We also believe that, prior to that incident, they destroyed two other Bajoran colonies, along with their entire populations."

"That is most unfortunate," Itu said. Despite his words, he spoke in his usual unhurried, easy manner. In the three days since he and his fellow Eav'oq had first arrived on Bajor, Asarem had grown accustomed to the tranquility with which they comported themselves. "Perhaps it would be wise for us to contact our own people to apprise them of the situation."

Although the first minister showed no outward sign of it, the suggestion frustrated her. She had intentionally avoided revealing that the fleet on its way to Bajor had emerged from the wormhole, which likely meant that it had passed through the Idran system. Asarem had not wanted to alarm her guests when they could do nothing to alter events, but while she felt justified enough to omit such a fact, she would not lie or even dissemble when engaged directly about it.

"I'm afraid that won't be possible at the moment," she said. "The communications relay in the Gamma Quadrant is not currently functioning. It might have been disrupted by the arriving fleet."

"Are you saying that the alien ships have come through the Anomaly?" Onan asked, employing the Gamma Quadrant nomenclature for the wormhole. Despite the implications of the question, Onan offered her words as calmly as her comrades had.

"Unfortunately, yes," Asarem said. "I must stress that there is no indication that Idran Four has been attacked. In fact, the fleet began coming through the wormhole not long after the Starfleet crew on Deep Space Nine lost contact with the communications relay. If an offensive was launched against your people before that, then we would have expected to receive some sort of distress signal from them."

"But they could be under attack right now," Evo noted. Amazingly, her comportment remained serene.

"I'm afraid that's so," Asarem admitted. "Ships are continuing to enter our system through the wormhole, but as soon as it is safe to do so, Captain Kira intends to send some of her crew to your world. In the meantime, since we can do nothing about Idran Four, I must insist that my security team takes you to safety."

"Yes, of course," Itu said.

Asarem walked back into the reception room from the balcony and started toward the tall doors that led to the atrium of the building. Tey fell in beside her. The Eav'oq followed, the skitter of their many-legged steps punctuated by the booted footfalls of the Militia officers accompanying them. By the time the first minister reached the doors, though, Itu had stopped. Asarem turned back toward him, as did the rest of the group.

"Is something wrong, Itu?" she asked.

"You told us that the ships entering your system belong to 'historical aggressors,'" Itu said. "Does that mean you know who they are?"

"We know almost nothing about them beyond their past acts, and even much of that is speculation," Asarem said. "But they appear to be a race of religious extremists."

Itu's eye narrowed, almost to the point of disappearing

from his face. He looked to Evo and Onan, and then back to Asarem. "Who are the aliens?"

"They call themselves the Ascendants."

The air of calm about the three Eav'oq vanished. Evo spoke to Itu so rapidly, and perhaps using so many colloquialisms, that Asarem's translator failed to interpret most of her words. She also gesticulated wildly, her eight arms a tangle of confused movement. Onan looked on, shifting her weight not just from side to side, but onto each of her many legs, lending her body a circular motion. Itu's eye remained squinting and straight.

Asarem waited only a moment before she attempted to settle the Eav'oq. She called out their names, until they at last gave her their attention again. "Forgive us," Itu said. "We are understandably agitated. You are aware that our culture was once almost completely destroyed."

"Yes." Asarem did not know the details of the account, only that the Eav'oq had been driven nearly to extinction, which had caused the survivors of their race to shift the location of their solar system and to go into hiding for millennia. She inferred from the context what Itu would next tell her.

"The Ascendants were responsible," he said.

Even expecting to hear that, Asarem felt sick to her stomach. It suggested that Idran IV and the Eav'oq might already be under siege. It also made it more difficult to imagine that the fleet on its way to Bajor had peaceful intentions.

"I will make sure that Captain Kira sends assistance to Idran Four as soon as it's possible to do so," promised the first minister. "In the meantime, it is all the more imperative that we get the three of you to a secure location."

"No," Itu said. "It is not."

The sudden declaration surprised Asarem, and it also vexed her. Because of the potential danger ahead, she felt it necessary for her to deal directly with the Eav'oq visitors, but she didn't have time to do so for more than a few minutes; far more important responsibilities awaited. "I'm sorry," she told Itu, "but I'm going to have to insist."

"First Minister," Itu said, and finally his eye opened again. "The Eav'oq were brutalized by the Ascendants. We have seen firsthand the ferocity and single-mindedness of their religious belief. With their return, I fear for the survival not just of my people, but also for the inhabitants of Bajor. I want to help."

"I appreciate that," Asarem said, and she meant it, but she also perceived time slipping away as the Ascendant fleet drew ever closer. "If there was some way in which I thought you could help, I would avail myself of it."

"You must instruct your people to disavow their religion," Itu said. "They needn't do it in their hearts, but outwardly, they must assert their atheism. In that way, they can rob the Ascendants of their motivation."

The first minister shook her head. "If only it were that simple," she said. "Even if we could speak to every person on Bajor before the Ascendants reach us, there would be no way to hide the evidence of our true beliefs: our books, our artwork, our temples, all of the institutions dedicated to the Prophets . . . the Orbs. There isn't sufficient time to mask it all, but I don't think it would matter if we could; there will always be Bajorans who will refuse under any circumstances to deny their faith." Asarem remembered too well courageous men and women standing up to Cardassian oppression during the Occupation, proclaiming their trust in the Prophets even as they were tortured to death. "Our beliefs are too much a part of who we are as individuals and as a society for us to be able to conceal them."

"Of course," Itu said. "I understand. The Eav'oq almost perished because we mantled our civilization with a deep awareness and appreciation of the Siblings. When the Ascendants came, we did not think to veil our knowledge, but if we had attempted it, I can see now that we would not have succeeded."

"Then, please, accompany my officers to safety." Though they said nothing, both Evo and Onan gave the impression of agreeing with the first minister. They looked to Itu as though waiting for his approval. He did not give it.

"First Minister, there may yet be something that I can do," he said.

"Itu—" Asarem started, but the Eav'oq spoke over her.

"When the Ascendants reach Bajor," Itu said, "let me meet with them."

Kira's desperate attempts at contact and her empty threats had ceased, but transmissions from Archquesters in the Ascendant armada besieged Iliana Ghemor. Initially, she ignored them, making note only of the particular ship from which each message originated, but not listening to any of them. Ghemor pushed the Grand Archquester's vessel to its top sublight speed, confident that no other ship—whether Ascendant or Starfleet—could overtake her. Her long-range scans of Bajor revealed freighters and transports in orbit, and coming and going, but no starships of any consequence with which she would have to contend.

When aft sensors showed that the entire armada had made it through the wormhole—thousands of vessels trailed after Ghemor—she at last surveyed some of the incoming messages. In the musical speech of the Ascendants, Ghemor heard many emotions: anger, confusion, fear, disappointment. Regardless of what they felt, most of the Archquesters seemed to believe that the armada had followed the Fire into the Fortress of the True, and then out of it. They posed questions about what had happened, and why, and they sought clarification and direction. Many wanted to speak to Grand Archquester Votiq.

Ghemor had anticipated such reactions, and she had planned for them. She opened a channel to the armada—not just to the Archquesters, but to all of the knights. "To my Ascendant followers," she said, imbuing her voice with the gravitas that had become a part of her since her encounter with the Prophets—or the Unnameable, or whatever the entities in the wormhole called themselves—for hadn't those mysterious, powerful beings set her on the path that would ultimately lead to her vengeance? They had, and she would complete her journey, wielding her form of justice as though it had been divinely sanctioned.

"This is the Fire," she intoned. "We have just passed through the Fortress of the True. All of you—even those doubters among you—know this. You observed it for yourselves, you sensed its majesty and power, felt the great presence that looked down upon us."

As Ghemor delivered her address to the faithful, indicators on the communications console winked off, signaling a decrease in the number of incoming transmissions. "We were cast out by the Unnameable," she continued in a solemn tone. "The True looked down upon us from on high, but they did not find us worthy to burn beneath their gaze and join with them. They did not find us deserving." She paused in order to emphasize her next words: "Not *yet.*"

The messages from the Archquesters had almost completely stopped. Tension and anticipation filled the cockpit around Ghemor, almost as though the Ascendants in the vessels spread out in space behind her had propelled a wave of desperation ahead of them. She understood that many of them believed her, but even if some didn't, she knew that they all *wanted* to believe. That was why they had accepted her leadership without question. It would allow her to provide them with the impetus to at last deliver to her what *she* wanted.

"In the Fortress, the True spoke to me," Ghemor went on. "They commanded the Ascendants to their destiny. We have but one final act to perform, one last deed to commend ourselves to our ultimate fate. We must annihilate the blasphemous population of Bajor, the planet that lies ahead of us."

The communications panel grew wholly dark. Ghemor knew that the army she had assembled and led exulted in her words. They understood heresy, and they recognized it. They not only had long experience in eliminating those aliens who dared to worship the Ascendant gods, but they reveled in that great cause.

"We will return to the Fortress of the True and face the Unnameable," Ghemor said, her voice ringing out with purpose, "once we have laid waste to Bajor."

Raiq peered through the transparent canopy of her vessel into the depths of space. She could not discern the Grand Archquester's vessel in the blackness, but the light of the system's star occasionally glinted off the surface of the metaweapon. Raiq felt no nearer to Votiq and the Fire, and no farther from them, than when she had first begun her pursuit. Her sensors confirmed the fact: her ship paced theirs.

Raiq had listened to the Fire's address to the Ascendants. The words and the sentiments behind them roused her. Like all her fellow knights, she had spent her entire existence on the Quest, searching for the Fortress of the True. To know that they had almost reached their goal, that they would soon achieve their greatest aspiration and that of generations past, threatened to overwhelm her. It almost seemed enough to discover that she had actually entered the Fortress, no matter for how brief a time.

If the Fire is telling the truth. The suspicion troubled Raiq—especially if she would soon burn beneath the gaze of the Unnameable. But she felt skeptical. It occurred to her that the Ascendants had done more than accept the Fire at her word: they had placed many millennia worth of hopes and struggles in her hands. They had traveled so long and so far, only to surrender their self-determination in the final moments, across the final distance, to an alien stranger among them.

But all of this was foretold by scripture. How often had Raiq read the sacred texts? How many times had she digested the holy words, internalized them, converted them into motivation and optimism and bearing. Like all her fellow knights, she had used scripture as a guiding light, a means of illuminating the path of her life. But while that light glowed brightly, it did not reveal every detail ahead.

Is that why there is nothing in the hallowed writing about the Ascendants entering and then leaving the Fortress of the True before the Final Ascension? Raiq wanted to know. *Or is it because that's not a part of the Unnameable's plan for us?*

Each question begat doubt, and each doubt, another question. *Am I not worthy?* Raiq asked herself. *Or is this when and where and how I fully prove myself to the True?*

Despite her uncertainty, Raiq chose to follow her intuition, which had, after all, been shaped by her experiences on the Quest and her understanding of the Ascendants' purpose. She found that she honestly believed that she and the rest of the armada had followed the Fire into and then out of the Fortress of the True. Even with her misgivings about the actions of the Fire, Raiq felt that, from the fragments visible to her, she could almost make out the completed mosaic. She believed that the End Time had come, and that the reckoning of the Final Ascension would soon be at hand.

And how will that happen? Raiq wondered. For her, all of the pieces fit together: the gathering of the Arch-questers, the appearance there of the Fire, the discovery of the metaweapon and the harvesting of its fuel by Aniq, the return of the Eav'oq on the threshold of the Fortress, and the presence nearby of a new breed of heretics. It made sense to her that the Ascendants, right there and right then, should demonstrate their reverence for the Unnameable by committing one final, glorious act on their generations-long crusade to rid the universe of those who dared to worship the True.

And then we will burn. The thought coursed through Raiq like an electric charge. She envisioned returning to the Fortress, where the Ascendants would face the judgment of the Unnameable, with the worthy among the knights enveloped in a sea of flame to join with their gods.

To Raiq, that meant detonating the metaweapon—not on the world of blasphemers ahead, but in the Fortress, as a means of uniting the Ascendants with the True. But it remained unclear whether the Fire meant to use the device on the population of heretics on the planet they approached, or if an attack by the armada would suffice. She had to find out.

Either way, regardless of what the Fire intended, Raiq vowed to make sure that her people would have what they needed when they faced the Final Ascension.

At last, the wormhole closed. Ezri Dax reported the event from her position at the tactical station, and she saw the captain immediately look up from the situation table at the main viewscreen. If Kira felt relieved, she gave no indication. Instead, she gazed over at Dax.

"How many ships?" the captain asked.

Dax had been tracking the number, reporting it whenever it reached a milestone: *One hundred. Five hundred. A thousand.* The size of the Ascendant fleet had grown beyond any expectations she'd had when the first waves of ships had appeared, and well past the ability of Deep Space 9 to mount a defense of Bajor. *Which is why we should have acted sooner and more decisively,* she thought, not for the first time.

"Thirteen thousand one hundred seventy-one," Dax said. Kira had fired on the first ship, and when that had failed to produce a positive result, she had sheathed DS9's weapons. Attacking the trailing end of such a sizable fleet, even if completely successful, would have little impact on the many ships ahead of them, already well on their way to Bajor. Dax had waited for the captain to give further orders to discharge the station's phasers and quantum torpedoes on the invaders, but that moment had never come. The lack of action confused the lieutenant, but more than that, it frustrated her. Had Kira chosen even to attempt to make good on the warning she had issued to the Ascendants, the DS9 crew might have been able to prevent them from bringing their entire fleet through the wormhole.

I would have made that call. Ever since she had first taken the center seat aboard *Defiant* more than a year and a half earlier, during an attack by rogue Jem'Hadar that had resulted in the death of the ship's commanding officer, Tiris Jast, Dax had discovered a vein of leadership within her. Both Kira and Vaughn had supported her request to shift her career path from the sciences to command. Since then, Dax exchanged her position as a counselor for that of second officer on DS9, and exec aboard *Defiant.* More than that, she consistently demonstrated her abilities, and she added significantly to her education, both on the job and in the classroom—including her most recent participation in Advanced Tactical Training.

My decision would have been to launch an all-out assault

on an invading alien force, she thought. The experience and instruction Dax had gained over the prior twenty-one months had contributed to her confidence to such an extent that she recognized when her superiors erred in their command decisions—particularly when, in their places, she would have issued different orders. She had a great deal of respect for both Captain Kira and Commander Vaughn, but she had of late grown restive serving under them.

Maybe it's this place, Dax thought. She had made her way through Starfleet Academy with the objective of serving aboard a starship, with its continually changing locales, rather than on a space station, with its fundamentally static environment. She did get to function as *Defiant*'s first officer, and even occasionally as its commander, but—

But Sam's out on the Defiant, *and I'm stuck here.*

Except that there was more to the way Dax felt than just any one specific assignment. She had never really chosen to come to Deep Space 9; needing a steadying influence after Ezri Tigan had joined with the Dax symbiont, she had accompanied Curzon and Jadzia's old friend Benjamin there. Initially, she thought she would leave the station and return to her posting on *U.S.S. Destiny,* and later, she considered resigning from Starfleet, but then she connected with the people on DS9—or *reconnected*—and decided to stay.

And then Julian and I developed feelings for each other, Dax thought. *Or maybe we just danced around his residual feelings for Jadzia, and hers for him.* It had taken Ezri and Julian a long time to get together, and less time to discover that, despite their genuine affection for each other, they did not belong in a romantic relationship.

The tactical console emitted an alert, and a secondary display came to life. "Captain," Dax said at once, "the wormhole is opening again." Dax redirected the view on the main screen away from the rear of the alien fleet even before Kira asked her to do so. Once more, radiant eddies of light curled open in shades of blue and white. Dax expected yet another rush of Ascendant ships to appear, but instead, she saw only a single vessel. A moment later, the wormhole receded into nothingness, withdrawing back into its subspace lair.

"Magnify," Kira said, even as Dax worked her controls.

"It's much larger than any of the other vessels we've seen," Dax said. She read off its dimensions, then glanced at the viewer. The ship appeared somewhat boxy, with a hull that looked like a mélange of contrasting engineering designs. Dax consulted the sensors again. "The ship is heavily shielded," she said.

"Is it an Ascendant vessel?" Kira asked.

"It is following the same path, but it doesn't resemble any of the other ships," Dax said. "Its shields are also configured differently, but my attempts to scan the interior of the vessel are still being blocked."

"Open a channel," Kira said.

"Hailing frequencies," Candlewood said.

"This is Captain Kira Nerys of Deep Space Nine, to unknown vessel. Please identify yourself."

Dax assumed that they would receive no response, but then Candlewood said, "Captain, we're being hailed."

"Put it on-screen."

Dax peered over at the main viewer, unsure of what she would see. The image of the ship disappeared, and then Dax felt her mouth drop open in surprise as she saw a Jem'Hadar standing alone on what looked like the vessel's bridge. She recognized him at once: Taran'atar.

When he heard her voice, Taran'atar at first thought that the message had come from *Even Odds'* dropship. Sensors had shown Kira pursuing him in the auxiliary craft, from the surface of Idran IV and toward the Anomaly, but she shouldn't have been able to close the gap so quickly. When the captain then asked him to identify himself, he checked the communications console and saw that the transmission came not from behind the ship, but from ahead and off to starboard—from Deep Space 9.

Taran'atar immediately suspected the treachery of Iliana Ghemor. Back on Idran IV, Kira had contacted him aboard *Even Odds* to tell him that the mad Cardassian woman had taken control of the Ascendant fleet, and that they had in their possession a subspace weapon of some kind. He didn't know how the captain had learned that information, but he trusted her.

On Idran IV, the Jem'Hadar had also heard the urgency in Kira's voice. He trusted that, too, because he felt his own sense of resolve with respect to Ghemor. She had been thought lost inside the Anomaly, but if she had returned, she posed too much of a threat for Taran'atar to allow her continued existence.

The Jem'Hadar opened a channel to Deep Space 9. On the main viewscreen on the *Even Odds* bridge, the tiered spread of Ops appeared. Taran'atar recognized members of the DS9 crew—Lieutenant Ezri Dax, Lieutenant John Candlewood, Ensign Aleco Vel, and others—but he focused on the woman standing at the situation table in the middle of the scene: Captain Kira Nerys.

"Taran'atar," she said.

"Captain Kira." He wondered which of the two was the imposter—the woman who had been recovered by the crew of *Even Odds* from an Orb floating in the Gamma Quadrant, or the woman who regarded him from the center of DS9's operations center. Before Taran'atar had chosen to leave the space station and return to the Dominion—a journey he had never completed—he had encountered multiple "versions" of

Kira Nerys, including the surgically altered Iliana Ghemor, as well as Kira's doppelgänger in an alternate universe, who functioned under the title of Intendant. It seemed reasonable to assume that either the woman he had left behind on Idran IV or the one facing him on the viewscreen, or possibly even both, were not the genuine Kira.

"What are you doing here?" she asked. *"Are you a part of the fleet that has entered the Bajoran system? Is this a Dominion operation?"*

"I am part of neither the fleet nor the Dominion," Taran'atar said. He noted that the woman he spoke with wore a Starfleet uniform, rather than the civilian clothes attiring the woman he had left behind on Idran IV. She also had shorter hair. More than those surface differences, Taran'atar saw in the few words she had just uttered a demeanor at variance with that of the woman with whom he had spent so much time on *Even Odds*. The Kira on the viewer conducted herself with a stiffer back, a sharper tongue, a more authoritative bearing.

But she is *Kira,* Taran'atar thought. He had grown to know her well enough to feel confident in that determination. *But then who has been aboard* Even Odds?

Taran'atar considered his time spent with *that* Kira. When she had first been brought aboard, he had noticed the superficial changes in her, but he had also been certain of her identity. She had shown a greater calm than he had previously seen in her, as well as a watchfulness that contrasted with the headlong manner he had come to know.

They are both *Kira,* Taran'atar concluded, trusting his instincts. *They're both Kira, but at different points in her life.* Time travel seemed the likely explanation. He considered the various permutations—him moving into the past or into the future, or the captain doing so—and deduced that the Kira recovered in the Gamma Quadrant must have arrived in the present from a time yet to come. Among other things, that would explain how she could have known that the Bajoran kai had been visiting Idran IV, and that Iliana Ghemor had taken command of Ascendant forces.

"If you are not with the Ascendant fleet," Kira asked, *"then why are you here?"*

Taran'atar contemplated how to respond to the captain's question. He could lie, or prevaricate, or simply elect not to reply at all. But it occurred to the Jem'Hadar that the Kira aboard *Even Odds* had been determined to return to the Alpha Quadrant and Deep Space 9, and to save the kai and to stop Ghemor. He would honor her wishes.

"I am in pursuit of the Ascendant fleet," Taran'atar said. He glanced at the sensor readouts and saw the thousands of vessels heading for Bajor. He also noted that the dropship had not followed him out of the Anomaly. If the Kira he'd left behind in the Gamma Quadrant had indeed come from the future, then perhaps she had chosen not to reenter the Bajoran system for fear of disrupting the timeline. The Jem'Hadar did not necessarily agree with Starfleet's Temporal Prime Directive, but Kira did serve as one of the space service's officers, and so she might have wanted to abide by their strictures.

"Why are you pursuing the Ascendants?" Kira asked. *"What do you know about them?"*

Again, Taran'atar deliberated about how he should answer the captain's question. In the end, he decided to tell her what the other version of Kira Nerys had told him. "I want to stop them from attacking Bajor," he said. "They are being led by Iliana Ghemor."

The name cut through Kira like a knife. For a moment, she could say nothing. The last time she had seen Ghemor had been when the two of them, along with Ghemor's counterpart in a parallel reality, had fallen into the Celestial Temple. There, the three women encountered the Prophets, who communicated with them via the images of people in their lives. They declared the mirror Ghemor the Voice, and then reinserted her into her life so that she could function as Their Emissary in the alternate universe. They likewise returned Kira to her own existence to act as Their Hand—whatever that meant. They also dubbed Iliana Ghemor the Fire, and then They extinguished her.

Or at least that's how I interpreted events, Kira thought. Ghemor had posed a grave threat, not just to Kira, but to the people of Bajor in two different realities. The captain naturally construed the insane Cardassian's disappearance from the Celestial Temple as evidence that the Prophets had dealt with her, consigning her to some well-deserved and distant fate.

Or maybe that was just wishful thinking. In either event, Kira had never expected to see Ghemor again—and she had certainly never *wanted* to see her again. It pained her to think of the madwoman leading a fleet of religious extremists against Bajor.

I let it happen, Kira thought. She had warned the crew of the first alien ship that, if they did not identify themselves and their reasons for entering the system, she would fire on them, but she had barely carried out that warning. Her attack on that vessel had proven ineffective, and when groups of ships soon swarmed out of the wormhole, continuing the battle quickly became a losing proposition. With no conclusive evidence that the fleet threatened Bajor, Kira did not want to risk the lives of more than seven hundred fifty crew members on DS9, and more than five thousand civilians.

Finally, she addressed Taran'atar. "Have you been searching for Ghemor since you left the station?" Kira had given the Jem'Hadar the choice of remaining on DS9 or taking a decommissioned Bajoran scoutship wherever he chose, to do whatever he chose. For his own sake, she had wanted him to stay, but he hadn't; he had boarded the old space vessel and immediately taken it through the wormhole into the Gamma Quadrant. She assumed he intended to return to the Dominion, likely to face the punishment he believed he deserved for failing in the assignment Odo had set him.

"*No, I have not pursued Ghemor until now,*" Taran'atar said.

"How did you find her?"

"*I didn't,*" Taran'atar said, as though speaking in riddles, but then he offered an explanation. "*I was just informed by a reliable source that she is leading the Ascendants. I was also told that the fleet possesses a subspace weapon.*"

"What?!" Kira said, alarmed. "What kind of subspace weapon?"

"*I do not know,*" Taran'atar said. "*I only know that Ghemor and the Ascendants are taking it to Bajor, presumably to launch it against the population there.*"

No, Kira thought, and on the heels of that, *Why?* But she knew why: Ghemor held Kira responsible for all the miseries in her life, and she sought to avenge herself upon the captain. Clearly, the deranged woman counted a devastating assault on the people of Bajor as the beginning of her retribution.

And something else occurred to Kira. The Prophets had called Ghemor the Fire. That name took on a new meaning when juxtaposed with the possibility that she would detonate a subspace weapon on the surface of Bajor.

"Will more Ascendant ships be arriving through the wormhole?" Kira asked.

"*No,*" Taran'atar said with welcome certainty. "*Long-range sensors revealed no other ships anywhere near the Idran system.*"

Kira nodded, then posed a critical question: "Can you stop Ghemor?"

"I do not know," Taran'atar told her, *"but I will not rest until I have done so or died in the attempt."*

Kira's path seemed obvious. "Take me with you," she said.

"Captain—!" Dax started, but Kira raised a hand to stop the tactical officer before she could say more.

"Whatever Ghemor is doing, she's doing it to punish me," Kira said. "If I can get close enough and get her attention, maybe I can redirect her anger away from Bajor and toward me."

Kira waited as Taran'atar regarded her stoically. She didn't know what to expect from the Jem'Hadar. He'd been gone from Deep Space 9 for almost a year—for longer, in fact, than the amount of time he'd spent on the station. She thought that she had come to understand him, at least to some degree, and she had even come to like him, but she had no illusions about being able to accurately predict what he would do.

At last, he said, *"Ghemor is my responsibility."* Then he reached to a control panel on the bridge of his ship. The screen blinked, reverting to an image of the boxy vessel, on its way past the station and toward Bajor.

"Dax," Kira said, "what's his course?"

"The ship is following the path of the Ascendant fleet," the lieutenant said.

"Get me the *Defiant*," Kira said.

"Channel open, Captain," Candlewood said.

"Deep Space Nine to Commander Vaughn." In the moment before her first officer responded, Kira felt torn. With the Ascendant fleet having bypassed DS9, and the station not under attack, she wanted to recall *Defiant* so that she could board it, take command, and defend Bajor—but she also did not want to waste any time by diverting the ship away from the invaders.

Defiant's bridge appeared on the main viewscreen. *"Vaughn here,"* said Kira's first officer. He sat in the command chair. His daughter, Ensign Prynn Tenmei, crewed the combined conn and ops console just ahead of him. Kira also saw Nog at an engineering station, and Bowers at tactical. *"Go ahead, Captain."*

"Commander, we've just learned that Iliana Ghemor is leading the Ascendant fleet," she told him, "and that they have a subspace weapon at their disposal."

Vaughn thought for a moment, and then asked, *"Is that the torpedo being towed by the first ship?"*

"Unknown, but you should assume that it is," Kira said. "Can you overtake that ship before it reaches Bajor?"

"Not if they maintain their present speed," Vaughn said. *"We're pacing the ship, but not gaining on it."*

"We've heard back from the nearest Starfleet vessels. The *Mjolnir* and the *Bellerophon* are on their way, but they're both a day out," Kira said. "What if you left the system and went to warp?"

Vaughn looked to his daughter. *"Ensign Tenmei?"*

The flight controller worked her console, obviously calculating the projected course. Without looking up from her station, she said, *"It'll take some time to climb out from the plane of the ecliptic to be able to go safely to warp, and then to descend back into the system to Bajor. It will necessarily lengthen the distance of our journey, but we should be able to arrive much closer to when the first Ascendant ship reaches the planet."*

"Do it," Kira ordered.

"Go," Vaughn told Prynn, and the ensign set to operating her controls with a fluid ease.

"Commander, it is imperative that you locate and neutralize the subspace weapon before it can be detonated," Kira said. "Push the *Defiant* if necessary, but you have to stop Ghemor."

"Understood."

Kira then informed her first officer about the arrival of Taran'atar. Though usually unflappable, the redoubtable Vaughn looked surprised. He wondered aloud about the timing of the Jem'Hadar's reappearance, and its possible significance, but Kira had no answers for him.

When the captain finished speaking with Vaughn, the image of *Defiant*'s bridge disappeared from the viewscreen, replaced by that of Taran'atar's ship, receding into the distance. As the Jem'Hadar and Vaughn raced toward Bajor, chasing the Ascendant fleet and the specter of Iliana Ghemor, Kira felt helpless. She knew that she had a responsibility to remain on the station to help ensure its defense, but the captain genuinely believed that she alone might hold the key to stopping the former Obsidian Order operative. In addition to the Cardassian seeking vengeance against her, the Prophets had on two separate occasions referred to Kira as Their Hand; that made her think that They meant her to act on Their behalf in the current crisis. Specifically, she thought that she might be able to offer up her own life in order to prevent a devastating attack on Bajor.

Kira left the situation table and mounted the steps to the raised outer level of Ops. She stopped beside Dax at the tactical console. "Have Lieutenant Chao and a security team take a runabout into the Gamma Quadrant. Verify that there are no more Ascendant vessels approaching the wormhole. If they detect additional ships, they are to return at once. Otherwise, the lieutenant is to assess the communications relay, and if possible, repair it. Once that's done, I want them to check on the status of the Eav'oq, as well as the kai's delegation on Idran."

"Yes, sir," Dax said.

"You're in command."

Dax peered at her with a look of confusion. "Captain?"

"I'm taking a runabout to Bajor," Kira said. "Putting myself in Ghemor's path may be the only way to stop her. Contact First Minister Asarem, apprise her of Taran'atar's information, and tell her I will shortly be contacting the Emissary."

Dax looked as though she wanted to say more—no doubt to protest the captain's decision to leave the station. Kira didn't give her the chance. Instead, the captain turned on her heel and strode toward the lift.

As she neared Bajor in the Grand Archquester's ship, Iliana Ghemor examined the sensor readouts. Scans showed several weapons platforms in orbit, along with a collection of Bajoran assault ships distributed above the planet—but no obstacles of any real consequence to her. She did see a Federation starship rapidly approaching, but it would arrive too late to interfere with her plans.

As she expected, the communications panel indicated an incoming transmission from Bajor. Ghemor accepted the audio portion of the message, and a man's voice delivered a warning. *"To the Ascendant vessels approaching our planet, this is Overgeneral Manos Treo of the Bajoran Militia. Do not enter orbit. You are not authorized to remain in this system. Withdraw at once or we will fire upon you."*

It surprised Ghemor to learn that the Ascendants had been identified. As far as she'd known, the Bajorans had never had any contact with the zealous aliens—as evidenced by the continued existence of a civilization on the planet. Ghemor could not imagine the Grand Archquester and his people allowing the devout Prophet-worshippers to survive.

Obviously, the Bajorans had somehow learned about the Ascendants, but she deemed the fact irrelevant.

Ghemor navigated toward the planet, two of its five moons visible beside it. She settled Votiq's ship into a high orbit, then ran a status check on all systems. As Overgeneral Manos reiterated the Bajorans' threat, the Cardassian confirmed the optimal operating condition of her vessel. She paid particular attention to the powerful shields she'd erected around both her ship and the metaweapon she towed behind it.

A chime sounded on the main console, signifying incoming fire. Ghemor ignored it. Instead, she accessed a control panel for the metaweapon.

The ship suddenly quaked beneath phaser fire. The shields readily dispersed the main force of the blast, and the inertial dampers quickly stabilized the hull. Ghemor noted that the phaser had been fired from the closest of the orbital weapons platforms. Sensors also showed a squadron of the nearest eight Bajoran assault vessels bearing down on her position.

Unconcerned by the capabilities of the Bajoran Militia, Ghemor operated the control panel she had just configured. She initiated the arming sequence for the metaweapon before she scanned the surface of Bajor. She searched for the largest city she could find. She knew that the yield of the isolytic subspace weapon would be considerable, and liable to obliterate a significant portion of the planet's surface, but because of the unpredictability of such devices, she wanted to target the most populous area in order to ensure the greatest possible loss of life.

A second phaser blast rocked the ship. Ghemor again checked her shields, which remained essentially unaffected by the attack from the weapons platform. A moment later, the Bajoran assault vessels closed to within firing range and initiated a fusillade. Phaser beams pounded into Ghemor's ship. Confident in Ascendant technology, she ignored them.

Ghemor completed her scans of the planet's surface and selected the capital city as her target. She quickly programmed it into the guidance system of the metaweapon. She also set the course of her own ship to take her away from the planet and back to Deep Space 9, where she would bask in Kira's anguish before finally ending the Bajoran's miserable life.

As Ghemor's hand hovered over the launch control, she once more examined the sensors. The eight Bajoran vessels continued to fire, but she knew that even a coordinated assault on the metaweapon would not be sufficient to penetrate the torpedo's shields before it reached the surface. Nor would phasers—whether ship-, platform-, or planet-based—trigger the device on its descent through the atmosphere, though even if they managed to do so, Bajor would still suffer tremendous destruction.

On the verge of exacting her vengeance, Ghemor felt more than satisfied. By virtue of all that she had suffered, all that she had endured, she had finally become the answer to her own piteous prayers, the fulfillment of her own dark desires. Unexpectedly, she had truly transformed herself into the Fire.

Ghemor launched the metaweapon.

Raiq tracked the Grand Archquester's vessel on sensors as it maneuvered toward orbit. Scans showed weapons platforms and ships protecting the planet below. None of the defenses appeared particularly formidable.

As Raiq continued on her intercept course, at last making up distance as the Grand Archquester's ship decelerated, she detected a transmission from the planet's surface. She activated a display on her control console, and the image of a pale, dark-haired humanoid appeared. *"To the Ascendant vessels approaching our planet,"* he said, *"this is Overgeneral Manos Treo of the Bajoran Militia. Do not enter orbit. You are not authorized to remain in this system. Withdraw at once or we will fire upon you."*

The words meant nothing to Raiq. Her sensors revealed torpedoes and emitters for energy weapons on the platforms and Bajoran ships, and similar emplacements on the planet's surface, none of which posed much of a threat to her vessel. Instead, she focused on her communications display, and the face of Overgeneral Manos Treo. He looked like any number of other fleshy humanoids whom Raiq had encountered on the Quest. He had small eyes, blood-veined whites around brown irises, and ebon pupils. His mouth cut across his countenance like a jab from a knife: short, straight, and sharp. Black hair crowned his head.

Raiq ignored all of that, and more. She stared exclusively at his nose—more specifically, at the bridge of his nose, which showed a series of horizontal ridges. Raiq had seen such a physical feature before, on an alien woman, on a world where the Ascendant had once crash-landed.

Opaka Sulan.

The woman and her wards had seen to Raiq's medical needs, ultimately restoring her to full health. As a consequence, the Ascendant had generously declined to eradicate them, despite that Opaka Sulan spoke of worshipping an order of false gods she called the Prophets. Looking back, Raiq had come to believe that the woman had lied to her, that she had willfully hidden that her people actually dared devote themselves to the True—and further, that Opaka Sulan belonged to a strain of heretics newly discovered by the Ascendants.

And here is more evidence, Raiq thought. The Fire had

spoken of the Unnameable demanding that the Ascendants vanquish a last race of violators. At first, the thousand or so remaining Eav'oq seemed a natural target, but Raiq's sensors showed billions of the wrinkle-nosed unclean on the world below—a far more impressive tally to deliver as a final offering to the True.

Up ahead, the Grand Archquester's vessel slowed further as it achieved orbit. The Bajorans plainly took note. They repeated their warning, then punctuated it by firing an energy weapon from a defense platform. The shields protecting the Grand Archquester's ship—and the torpedo hauled along behind it—endured the blast with ease.

As Raiq studied her scans, she saw a power increase on the metaweapon, indicating that its arming process had begun. A feeling of dread gripped her. She wanted to believe that the powerful device should be utilized against the planet of heretics ahead, that the immolation of its blasphemous population would serve the Ascendants well as the ultimate sacrament before they submitted themselves to their gods for judgment.

But why use the metaweapon? Raiq asked herself. Why not just send the Ascendant armada down to attack the planet's surface? The thousands of ships could readily leave the Bajoran civilization in ruins.

Aniq had modified the metaweapon so that it would not only destroy, but transform. Raiq had heard her describe it as a means of initiating the Final Conflagration. Surely the destruction of yet another heretical species did not count as important as the facilitation of worthy Ascendants joining with the True.

Another red-yellow streak flashed through space, followed by a prolonged salvo from an approaching squadron. The energy beams slammed into the Grand Archquester's vessel and the precious cargo it towed. Raiq again checked her sensors to verify the ineffectiveness of the attack. When she did, she saw the guidance system in the metaweapon had been activated—probably to accept a programmed target.

Panic threatened Raiq. Her people had at long last arrived at the End Time, and they stood on the brink of the Final Conflagration, and beyond it, the Final Ascension. She could not risk losing the tool that would bring them there.

Raiq quickly worked her console. She remained just out of range for what she intended, and although she could never have imagined taking action against the Grand Archquester—much less against the Fire—she would do what she had to do for her people. She only hoped she would not be too late.

Time seemed to pass with interminable slowness. Raiq could do nothing but wait as she approached the Grand Archquester's ship. She could see the shape of it against the blue-green world below. She anticipated seeing the torpedo dropping away and soaring toward the planet's surface.

And then her ship had drawn close enough to that of the Grand Archquester. Raiq operated her console, then examined the sensors. At that moment, the engines of the torpedo carrying the metaweapon engaged.

The subspace device didn't move.

The tractor beam Raiq had deployed held the torpedo fast. She continued scanning the metaweapon, and saw the power to its drive system increase. She adjusted the strength of her tractor beam accordingly.

A hum rose in her ship's cockpit. The countervailing force of the metaweapon's engine taxed her tractor emitter. Sensors showed the torpedo's drive straining as it fought to free itself and begin its destructive run toward the planet. If the engine failed catastrophically, the explosion would not trigger the subspace weapon; it would only destroy it.

An indicator suddenly glowed on Raiq's panel. She tapped

the control beside it, accepting the incoming transmission. It originated on the Grand Archquester's ship.

"Release the metaweapon!" The voice, filled with fury, did not belong to Votiq, but to the Fire.

Raiq opened her mouth to speak, but words failed her. *How can I defy the Fire?* It suddenly occurred to her that in her attempt to ensure that her people would burn beneath the gaze of the Unnameable and join with them, she might instead affirm her own lack of worthiness, and in so doing, forever bar herself entrance into the Fortress of the True.

"Deactivate your tractor beam now!" the Fire demanded.

Raiq reached to the control that would free the metaweapon. She hesitated, her hand hovering over the console. She felt the significance not just of her own lifetime spent on the Quest, but that of uncounted generations past.

"You will do as I order. I am the Fire."

"No," Raiq said, the word barely more than a whisper. She expected an eruption of anger, but heard only the whine of the tractor beam.

And then the cabin quieted. Raiq checked her scans and saw that the metaweapon had been shut down. The torpedo remained motionless, fixed between her tractor beam and that of the Grand Archquester's vessel.

For a moment, only the faint hiss of background radiation on the open channel intruded into the silence. Then the Fire said, *"Raiq, you must release the metaweapon."* She spoke slowly, but with unmistakable authority.

"With respect, Fire, I am reluctant to do as you request," Raiq said. "Our people require the subspace weapon so that we can burn before the Unnameable, and in that way, merge with them."

"The Unnameable do not need assistance to burn their faithful, nor to join with them," the Fire said. *"What they require of us is that we perform one last sacrament, that we*

make one last offering to them, before they allow us to make the Final Ascension."

That makes sense, Raiq thought. *It sounds right.* But so did her own perspective.

Unsure why she had become so convinced of her position, Raiq decided to seek clarity. "May I speak with Grand Archquester Votiq?"

"No, you—" the Fire began, but then she hesitated for the first time that Raiq had ever heard. *"That is no longer possible."*

Alone in the cockpit of her vessel, Raiq flinched. She had not necessarily expected the Fire to permit her to speak with Votiq, but the finality of the words troubled her. She wanted to ask questions, but felt that she didn't dare. A stillness settled around her, but she found no calm in it.

Eventually, the Fire said, *"The Grand Archquester perished inside the Fortress of the True."*

Votiq, dead? The idea rattled her to the core. For more than half a century, for a large portion of Raiq's life, Votiq had led the Ascendants in the Quest. He provided strength, leadership, and direction, but perhaps more than that, he offered the remaining population of knights a touchstone— to each other, to the interpretation of the sacred texts, and to generations past. He bridged the gulf between what had been and what could be. He helped illuminate the darkness and drive Questers and Archquesters ever onward.

"We should not mourn the Grand Archquester," said the Fire, as though grieving came naturally to the Ascendants. *"He died where he always hoped he would. Now we must do what is necessary to ensure a similar fate for all of us."*

Had the Fire just implied that the Unnameable had taken Votiq during their journey through the Fortress? She thought that she had, and she wanted to believe her, but she had to admit the truth of her uncertainty. The notion that the Fire had killed the Grand Archquester in order to abscond with the metaweapon seemed shocking, even melodramatic—but not necessarily untrue.

"As required by holy writ," Raiq said carefully, "I will notify all of the knights about the loss of Votiq." Her own audacity terrified her; the sacred texts contained no such fiat, though such an action plainly made sense. Once Seltiq, the eldest Ascendant after Votiq, learned of the Grand Arch-quester's death, she would by law take over that position.

Raiq expected the Fire to challenge her on her claim of scriptural imperative, but she didn't. *"Very well."* Raiq didn't know if she felt more surprised by the Fire's words or the note of resignation in her voice, but both called her identity into question.

"I will speak with the new Grand Archquester," Raiq said, "and I will seek her guidance."

Once more, she expected the Fire to fly into a rage, to rebuke her for brazenly disobeying her wishes. Instead, she only said, *"Be quick about it."*

"Yes, Fire," Raiq said, and she ended the transmission. She then opened a channel to the entire Ascendant fleet, which she saw on sensors had just begun to arrive at Bajor. She would do as she'd told the Fire she would, informing her people of the loss of Votiq, and then speaking with his successor.

Never had Raiq's doubts been stronger.

Benjamin Sisko stood inside a dimly lighted observation lounge, looking out through one-way glass. The primary operations chamber of the Musilla Consolidated Space Center sprawled away from him on the other side of the port. Scores of Bajoran Militia officers staffed the extensive complex, most of them seated at banks of consoles arranged before walls of viewscreens.

Sisko knew that the Musilla CSC oversaw the spaceborne traffic around Bajor. Personnel there coordinated launches and orbital insertions, departures and arrivals. They also served to monitor external threats to the planet, with control over weapons platforms and ground-based defenses, and links to Militia spacecraft.

Interspersed with numerous smaller displays, a triad of large screens dominated the convex, three-sided front wall. Sisko saw views of defensive emplacements from around the globe, facilities that housed powerful phaser emitters designed to reach belligerents in orbit. He also spotted installations that supported, launched, and landed Militia vessels. Mostly, though, he studied scenes from space, images captured by monitors on weapons platforms and Bajoran ships. One of the larger viewscreens showed a terribly disconcerting sight: a massive array of vessels on approach to Bajor. The display conjured up Sisko's time in the Dominion War battling fleets comprising Jem'Hadar, Cardassian, and Breen forces. He shuddered at the thought of the Federation facing another conflict like that, particularly one that imperiled Bajor.

Sisko had come to Musilla from his home in Kendra Province after Kira Nerys had contacted him, not as her friend, nor even as her former commanding officer aboard Deep Space 9, but as the Emissary of the Prophets. During the time they'd served together on the station, Kira had recognized the importance of the role Sisko played in her religion, but she had also done well to respect his privacy. Rarely did she call upon him as the Emissary, and so he took her doing so that day very seriously—despite that, in the fifteen months since his return from the Celestial Temple, he'd felt disconnected from the Prophets.

Sisko's erstwhile first officer had wanted to inform him about the large fleet of vessels coming through the wormhole and heading for Bajor. Under normal circumstances, he likely would have taken no action. Kira knew her job as a Starfleet captain and how to run the station, and she had a good crew. Sisko also did not want to intrude on the responsibilities of First Minister Asarem and Kai Pralon. But Kira had chosen to get in touch with him because of the nature of the approaching force: a race of violent religious extremists.

At Kira's request, Sisko had spoken with the first minister, offering his assistance if needed. Asarem asked him to transport out to Musilla Province, to the city of Ilveth, home to the planet's Consolidated Space Center. One of the first minister's aides, Enkar Sirsy, escorted him to a conference room, where he met with Asarem and a delegation of Eav'oq from Idran IV. The first minister detailed for Sisko what little information the Bajorans and Starfleet possessed about the Ascendants. An Eav'oq named Itu then described what his people knew of them, corroborating the description of them as zealots bent on exterminating those who dared either to worship the Ascendant gods, or to venerate other deities.

Afterward, Asarem had gone to the Space Center's operations chamber. Sisko, wanting to avoid overstepping his bounds by accompanying the first minister there, followed Enkar to an observation lounge. The Eav'oq, declaring their aversion to violence, remained in the conference room, declining to witness whatever defensive measures the Bajorans might take.

Sisko watched as Militia personnel in the operations chamber monitored and responded to the encroachment of the Ascendant ships. On one of the large main displays, he saw a Bajoran weapons platform fire its phaser bank at a purplish red, knifelike vessel that trailed a torpedo behind it. The ship looked as though it had established itself in orbit. The phaser beam appeared to have no effect on the ship, which did not retreat from the attack, or respond in any observable way. Sisko waited for what would happen next, dreading an all-out assault on Bajor when the entire Ascendant fleet arrived.

On another of the large displays, Sisko saw several Bajoran assault vessels headed toward the Ascendant ship in orbit. At the same time, on a smaller screen, the image of Ezri Dax appeared. The lieutenant conversed briefly with Asarem, who then quickly stalked in Sisko's direction. The door to the observation lounge glided open, and the first minister strode inside.

"Mister Sisko," she said, forsaking both of his titles— Captain and Emissary—as he'd requested of her months prior, not long after he'd returned from the Celestial Temple. "We've just heard from Lieutenant Dax on Deep Space Nine with updated information. She says that Captain Kira will be contacting you shortly. She also tells us that the Jem'Hadar observer has come back to the Alpha Quadrant. He claims that the Ascendants are being led by Iliana Ghemor, and that their fleet is carrying a subspace weapon."

The news could not have been worse. When last heard from, perhaps a year earlier, Ghemor had been pursuing a personal vendetta against Kira, showing no compunction against harming or even killing anybody who stood in her way. If she deployed a subspace weapon on or near Bajor, it could do considerable damage to the planet, and the resultant deaths could number in the millions, or even in the tens of millions.

Or even worse than that, Sisko thought. He remembered a gruesome tale that he'd first heard at Starfleet Academy, and which he'd later confirmed when he'd served as a junior officer at the Federation embassy on Romulus. Nearly a century prior, a species adversarial to the Empire had detonated an isolytic subspace weapon in proximity to the Romulan world of Algeron III. The explosion caused the underlying structure of space to tear, and when power sources on the planet attracted one end of the growing fissure, catastrophe followed. Algeron III had been shredded, costing the lives of its more than seven hundred million inhabitants.

"Obviously, they have to be stopped," Sisko said. "They can't be allowed to employ such a weapon."

Asarem nodded, but she wore a grave expression. "The problem is that Deep Space Nine reports the Ascendant ships have powerful shields, and it's unclear if Militia weapons can stop them," she said. "The two closest Starfleet vessels are on their way to Bajor, but they won't arrive for at least a day."

Before Sisko could ask about *Defiant*, a tone sounded, followed by the soft voice of a computer interface. *"Incoming transmission for Asarem Wadeen."*

The first minister crossed the lounge to a companel in the far wall. She activated the device with a touch, and Kira's face appeared on the display. Sisko noted at once that she was no longer on DS9, but aboard a runabout. *"First Minister, this is Captain Kira."*

"I'm here, Captain," Asarem said. "And I'm with Mister Sisko."

"Then Lieutenant Dax has updated you about the situation?"

"She has," Asarem said. "What is your status?"

"Since we've confirmed that there are no more Ascendant vessels approaching the wormhole in the Gamma Quadrant, I'm on my way to Bajor aboard the Yolja," Kira said. *"Taran'atar is ahead of me in a civilian vessel. He is also in pursuit of Iliana Ghemor. Meanwhile, Commander Vaughn has taken the* Defiant *to the edge of the system so the ship can go to warp and reach the leading edge of the Ascendant fleet as quickly as possible. He should arrive before long."*

"And you've had no contact with any of the Ascendants?" Asarem asked.

"No," Kira confirmed. *"They have refused to reply to any of our hails."*

"They are not responding to messages from Bajor either," Asarem said. "At this juncture, Overgeneral Manos believes we have no choice but to defend ourselves." Manos Treo, Sisko knew, served as the commandant of the Bajoran Militia, reporting directly to the Minister of Defense, Aland Novor. "We have opened fire on the lead ship from a weapons platform, and a squadron of our assault vessels is closing."

"I'm not sure how effective your weapons will be," Kira said.

"Have you any other recommendations, Captain?" the first minister asked, her voice tightly controlled.

"I might," Kira said. *"That's why I wanted to speak with the Emissary."*

"I'm here, Captain," Sisko said. Again, he noted Kira's use of his religious title. Since departing the Celestial Temple and returning to Bajor, Sisko's relationship with DS9's commanding officer had been conducted almost completely on a personal level. They usually addressed each other by their given names.

"Emissary, I've been weighing our options, trying to determine the best course of action to face down the Ascendants and Iliana Ghemor," Kira said. *"I feel . . ."* She looked away for a moment and off to the side, as though attempting to gather her thoughts. *"I feel that some great plan of the Prophets is unfolding."*

"A plan?" Sisko believed that, during his sojourn in the Celestial Temple, he had come to comprehend, at least to some degree, the minds of the Prophets. He even thought that he might have contributed to their understanding of humanoid existence. But his memories of those experiences had faded with time, and although he had been left with the feeling that the Prophets watched over Bajor, and even set certain events in motion, he had also come to recognize that their guardianship took place at an extremely high and distant level. Where once he'd trusted that he might one day fully fathom the intricate tapestry they had woven for the Bajorans, he had subsequently abandoned any such hope.

"*If not a plan, then something that They have . . . something that They have foreseen.*" Kira said, clearly trying to find the right words to voice her thoughts. "*I feel like something important is going to happen, and They've set the proper participants in place: you are Their Emissary, They called me Their Hand and Ghemor the Fire. In whatever is about to happen, it seems like there's a role to be played by the Ascendants, who are vicious religious fanatics. Even Taran'atar's reappearance feels . . . portentous.*"

Sisko empathized with Kira's presentiment. He knew well what that felt like: to have a strong sense of foreboding, mixed with the instinct that a full understanding of events lingered just beyond the ability to clarify. His exposure to the Prophets had brought him many such moments— though none in recent times.

And yet Sisko didn't hesitate to respond to Kira. He had his own intuition about the situation, about the actions required to provide Bajor the best chance for survival. His ideas derived not from some mystical connection with the Prophets, though, but from his long experience as a Starfleet officer and leader. "Captain, you need to speak directly with Iliana Ghemor," he said. "You need to get and keep her attention, to distract her. Itu, one of the Eav'oq, has volunteered his help, and so I think he should communicate with the Ascendant fleet for the same reason. We need to delay the use of their subspace ordnance, in order to allow the *Defiant* time to sweep around to the forward edge of the Ascendant ships so that Commander Vaughn and his crew can locate and destroy—or at least secure—the subspace weapon."

Sisko looked to the first minister. She offered no objections, and Kira acknowledged the new tactic before signing off. Past Asarem, through the port, rapid movement caught Sisko's attention. He looked to one of the large viewscreens, which showed Bajoran vessels opening fire on the lead Ascendant ship.

The first minister must have read the expression on Sisko's face, because she spun toward the glass wall that looked out on the operations chamber. She observed for only a few seconds before she turned back around. "Accompany me, Mister Sisko," she said, the tone of command in her voice unambiguous. Although he in no way served under her authority, he did not object. Instead, as Asarem strode quickly from the room, Sisko fell in behind her.

Kira informed Vaughn of the plan—at least to the extent that it could even be called a plan. The captain believed Taran'atar's report of Iliana Ghemor's return, and of the existence in the Ascendant fleet of a subspace weapon, but Starfleet and Bajoran forces knew nothing definitively about the location of either. It seemed reasonable to think that the Cardassian could be traveling in the lead ship, and that the torpedo it hauled could be carrying the metaweapon, but such suppositions could also turn out to be incorrect.

After speaking with Vaughn, Kira worked *Yolja*'s main console to broadcast on all hailing frequencies. Only minutes separated *Defiant* from a rendezvous above Bajor with the forward edge of the Ascendant fleet, so she needed to delay Iliana Ghemor for only a short period. The captain did not necessarily expect the gambit to work, but considering the circumstances, she could think of no better strategy than to heed the advice of the Emissary.

"Kira Nerys to Iliana Ghemor." She waited, unsurprised

as the seconds stretched out and her hail went unanswered. She tried a second time and met with the same result. "Come on," she said under her breath, and then offered up a couple of choice Bajoran epithets. Kira rarely swore, but when she did at that moment, she visualized bellowing the words directly at Ghemor.

Which would be like screaming into my own face, she realized. Still, the notion of confronting the Cardassian madwoman appealed to her. Previously, Kira thought that the Prophets had contended with Ghemor either by imprisoning her or by sending her away somewhere—or possibly even by ending her miserably unhappy life, an act that could have been considered a kindness. But if the former Obsidian Order operative had found her way back to Bajor, then it likely meant that she had come seeking her revenge.

Maybe I can use that against her, Kira thought. She worked her controls and leaned toward the runabout's main console. "Kira Nerys to Iliana Ghemor," she said again. "The Prophets might have released you, but they clearly didn't give you back your life, otherwise you wouldn't be back here so desperately looking to fulfill your vendetta against me."

Kira waited, hoping for a response, but none came. "Of course, I didn't really expect a coward like you to show your face," she said, continuing her transmission. She paused for effect. "That is, I didn't expect you to show *my* face, since you no longer have one of your own." The barb felt juvenile to Kira, a taunt intended to dig at Ghemor's ego and sense of self.

The captain inspected *Yolja*'s sensors. She saw a group of Bajoran assault vessels swarming around the two Ascendant ships closest to Bajor, while a broad span of the Militia awaited the rest of the invading fleet, the thousands of alien ships swiftly nearing. Meanwhile, *Defiant* raced toward the planet from outside the system, and Taran'atar's ship gained on the Ascendants as they slowed on their approach to the planet.

As Kira tried to figure out another means of provoking a reply from Ghemor, a familiar but somehow foreign-sounding voice rustled up out of the comm. *"You've discovered that I am here,"* said Iliana Ghemor. *"No doubt you are congratulating yourself for doing so, as if your possessing such knowledge would make a difference."* Kira heard her own tones and inflections, but they also sounded off to her, as though Ghemor for some reason chose to overpronounce her words. The captain tracked the signal, not surprised to find that it sourced from the lead ship of the Ascendant fleet.

Kira wanted to have a conversation with the woman who had once intended to take her place. She preferred a calm dialogue with Ghemor, in an attempt to reach her through sympathy and compassion, or short of that, by way of logic and reason. But Kira had not only followed the destructive trail of the Cardassian's chosen path—a path strewn with rubble and bodies—she had also dealt with her directly, had looked into her eyes and seen her instability. More even than that, Kira also witnessed the long, tragic tale of Ghemor's life, laid bare by the Prophets for Their own examination. The captain beheld the events that had taken the young Cardassian woman from a privileged existence and a promising future down into the depths of madness. Kira could imagine no reprieve from that abyss, no means of her reaching down into that pit and making any sort of meaningful connection.

Because of that, she tried instead to figure out how to incite Ghemor's anger, and in that way keep her talking and preoccupied. "I'm not congratulating myself any more than if I'd run across a dead gutfish," Kira said, referring to a Cardassian animal notorious for the foul odor it discharged when it died. "It doesn't require much effort to locate the source of such a stench." The words tasted mealy in Kira's mouth.

To the captain's surprise, Ghemor laughed—not a great chortle or cackle or bray, but a soft, measured chuckle that sounded perfectly sane. *"You're trying to bait me,"* the Cardassian said. *"For what possible purpose? To keep me busy while you attempt to mount some sort of grand defense for your people?"* Again, Ghemor chuckled, but with an added tinge of derision. *"I see the one starship headed for Bajor from outside the system, and the other two smaller vessels chasing the armada—one of them carrying you—but those won't be enough to eliminate the Ascendants, or even to turn them away. And neither will the assault vessels headed up from the planet, or the weapons platforms in orbit. All that is left is the rending of Bajoran flesh and the gnashing of teeth."*

"I am here," Kira said. "I am the cause of your misery. You do not need to punish innocent people for my crimes."

An indicator amid *Yolja*'s communications controls flashed on, signifying the initiation of a visual component in Ghemor's transmission. Kira activated the display mounted in the bulkhead to her left. Ghemor apparently wanted her to see something, but the captain didn't know what to expect. What she saw surprised her.

Iliana Ghemor stared back at Kira, but not with the face the captain had expected. Rather than a duplicate of her own Bajoran features, she saw the ridges and scales, the ash-colored complexion and slick, dark hair that defined a Cardassian countenance. The overall effect resembled Kira, and she recognized that *other* version of herself. More even than observing Ghemor looking like her mirror image, it jolted the captain to essentially see herself in the guise of Bajor's historical oppressors. Nearly seven years earlier, Kira had awoken to such a view, abducted by the Obsidian Order and surgically altered to resemble Iliana Ghemor in an attempt to unmask Ghemor's father as a dissident within Central Command. Seeing herself as a Cardassian back then had been disturbing, but it troubled her nearly as much to discover that Iliana had reverted to her Cardassian self.

"Do I look like somebody who subscribes to the fable of Bajoran innocence?" Ghemor asked. *"But of course I knew that you would be here, Captain. I counted upon it."*

"Then deal with me directly."

"Oh, I will," Ghemor said. *"And you know that I will. I've already told you what I intend to do."*

"To become the Emissary?" Kira said. "To get your life back?" She recalled Ghemor's plan to fulfill Trakor's first prophecy in an alternate universe so that she could become a religious icon there. She believed that when she did, the Prophets would restore her existence, allow her to eliminate every other Kira in all the different realities, and make her whole.

"Don't you see, Captain?" Ghemor asked, gesturing to her own face. *"The Prophets have already given me my life back. I am no longer some bastardized iteration of Kira Nerys. I am Iliana Ghemor, proud and devoted daughter of Cardassia."*

"Then why are you here?" Kira asked. She knew the answer, but she wanted to keep Ghemor talking. "If your life has been made whole, you should go live it."

"Oh, I am doing that, Captain," Ghemor said. *"And right now, I'm about to satisfy myself by making you a witness to what is about to unfold."*

"Come face me if you must," Kira said, softening her voice to issue her plea, "but there's no reason to do anything more than that."

"But there is reason," Ghemor said. *"There is the suffering I endured for five thousand days. Five thousand. I am here to repay your actions."*

"Then do what you have to do *with me*," Kira said.

"I am dealing with you," Ghemor insisted. *"I told you that when I finally met the Prophets, that They would see inside me,*

just as They did with your Emissary, and that They would then
understand what I needed to do to get my life back. That is
exactly what happened."

The claim did not just sound patently absurd to the
captain; it also angered her. Kira had encountered people
who'd found tortuous ways of justifying their actions—
including Bajorans who twisted the canonical writings in
order to rationalize their own bad behavior. The Cardassians had taken such a position with respect to the Occupation, which they called the *Years of Deliverance*, asserting
that they had come to Bajor not as oppressors, but essentially as social workers wanting to elevate the lives of the
backward natives.

"The Prophets did not tell you to attack Bajor in order
to make yourself whole," Kira said, absolutely certain of her
declaration.

"You are so misguided," Ghemor said, almost as though
she felt sorry for Kira. *"Why else would the Prophets have given*
me an army to lead?"

An army, Kira echoed in her head, and then expanded
on the thought. *An army of religious zealots, with a history of*
attacking Bajorans. Kira didn't believe that the Prophets had
handed over the control of such an adversarial and seemingly formidable force to a vengeful madwoman, but why
had They *allowed* it? The Ascendant fleet had come through
the wormhole. In the past, the Prophets had closed the passage linking the Alpha and Gamma Quadrants to prevent
the Jem'Hadar fleet from passing through it, and Kira felt
sure that, through the power of the Orbs, They had fostered
the destruction of the parasite queen, ending the infestation
of Bajor. Why wouldn't They have taken some sort of action
to stop Ghemor and the Ascendants?

"You suddenly seem less talkative when your gods act dif-
ferently from your expectations of Them," Ghemor said. *"But*

They are evidently just gods, and They are seeing fit to punish your people for their terrorist activities against Cardassia, and you for your transgressions against me."

"That can't be what's happening," Kira blurted, confident in the virtue of the Prophets. Except she could hear that the determination in her voice sounded more like desperation—or maybe even like denial. *Am I trying to convince Ghemor of my trust in the Prophets, or am I trying to convince myself?* So rarely had Kira faced personal doubts in her faith that the very concept felt foreign to her.

"You can protest that it can't be happening," Ghemor said, *"but it already is: the Ascendants are here, I am leading them, and you will watch your world perish in flames—the result of a long series of events that started with you and your Shakaar resistance cell."*

"Iliana," Kira began, her tone beseeching, "if I could change what happened to you, I would."

"I don't want your help or your pity, Captain," Ghemor said. *"All I want right now is for you to watch."* Ghemor, who looked so much like Kira despite her Cardassian features, leaned forward until her face filled the display. *"I want you to watch—and suffer."*

The screen went dark, leaving Kira alone with her doubts as she sped toward Bajor, the Ascendant fleet, and Iliana Ghemor.

Seltiq sat alone in the cockpit of her blade-shaped vessel—a vessel that, in less exigent circumstances, she would have had to coat with a crimson finish to identify her new position. She would also need to take custody of the Eye of Fire at some point. Instead of planning such actions, though, she slowly leaned away from the communications panel and closed her large golden eyes. For just a moment, she allowed her mind to drift from the litany of Ascendant voices trilling forth from all across the armada.

So much had happened of late. The sheer quantity of dramatic incidents loomed over Seltiq like some terrible menace, the collective weight of recent events almost too much for her to bear. In addition to all of that, she had just learned that Votiq had perished. The news shocked her, despite the Grand Archquester's advanced age of nearly four centuries. For more than five decades, ever since the death of his predecessor, Votiq had led the Ascendants on the Quest. His absence would leave a hole in the fabric of their existence.

But it won't, Seltiq admitted to herself. By virtue of her status as the eldest knight among the surviving Archquesters, she immediately advanced to Votiq's leadership position. She would miss him, owing to their long comradeship, but with his succession prescribed by the holy texts, the Ascendants would endure, and the Quest would continue without interruption.

It was not the fact of the Grand Archquester's death that surprised Seltiq—not much younger than he, she understood well the rigors and pitfalls of advanced age—but the particular timing of his demise. It seemed cruel to think of Votiq spending so long pursuing his dream—pursuing the dream of *every* Ascendant—only for him to die on the verge of attaining that dream. According to Raiq, the Fire had implied that the Grand Archquester had burned beneath the gaze of the Unnameable when the armada had passed through the Fortress, meaning that, if the True had deemed him worthy, then he had actually achieved his lifelong goal. To herself, Seltiq questioned such a turn of events. Nothing in scripture even hinted at a separate Final Ascension for individual Archquesters, not even for the highest ranking among them.

I don't have time to think about that right now, Seltiq told herself, her eyelids fluttering back open. The need for her to take action as the new leader of the Ascendants preempted her consideration of Votiq's fate, but she also recognized the personal expedience in finding a reason to avoid doubting the veracity of the Fire. In Seltiq's lifetime, she had never once deviated from orthodoxy, and on the threshold of the Fortress of the True, she did not intend to begin doing so.

Over the communications system, via audio only, the new Grand Archquester listened to one Ascendant after another as they expressed their evaluations of the current situation, as well as their concerns and their recommendations on how to proceed. Many believed as Raiq did, that the knights should attack the planet of heretics ahead using only their ships and the conventional weaponry they carried, preserving the subspace device for use in facilitating the Final Ascension. Others felt that the metaweapon should be unleashed on the newly found blasphemers, if only to expedite the battle and bring about the reentry of the Ascendants into the Fortress of the True as soon as possible.

Seltiq considered the divergence of opinions expressed to her—opinions she had sought after informing the armada about Votiq's death, her assumption of his post, and the Fire's identification of the false worshippers who called themselves Bajorans. The new Grand Archquester would have to choose one path or the other, or find an alternative. She would—

A light on the communications panel flashed on, indicating an incoming transmission from beyond the armada. Seltiq saw that it originated on the surface of the planet ahead. She had earlier listened to several such messages, though she hadn't responded to them. Once Seltiq's automatic interpreter had translated the content of those previous transmissions, she'd heard the apparent leader of the heretical population—who identified herself as Asarem Wadeen, First Minister of Bajor—initially attempt to commence a dialogue with the Ascendants, and later to blindly appeal for peace. The new Grand Archquester had been witness to many such pleas during her time on the Quest. As always, she found that the sad, desperate beseeching of the unholy sickened her.

Seltiq tapped a control, curious what new entreaty the heretic leader would make on behalf of her people. The new Grand Archquester expected once more to hear the imploring words of Asarem Wadeen, but instead, a masculine voice emerged from the communications panel, its tone pitched in a low register. The native language of the speaker, different from that of the Bajoran, flowed calmly, not in discrete words, but in a continuous hum, more like meditation than conversation. The message also possessed a strange, distinctly alien quality to it, quite different from either the musical speech of the Ascendants or the more prosaic tongue of most humanoid species Seltiq had encountered, including that of the Bajorans.

Despite the exotic flavor of the transmission, the automatic interpreter deciphered it at once, with no lag whatsoever. Seltiq grasped at once the reason for the immediacy of the translation: the linguistic computer didn't have to decode the language because it already knew it. The new Grand Archquester checked the communications panel for the identity of the speaker's species. What she saw jolted her: the message came from an Eav'oq.

Seltiq sat motionless, stunned by the revelation. She listened to the Eav'oq, who called himself Itu, as he sought to converse with the leader of the Ascendants. Finally, Seltiq worked a control to access the visual component of the message. She had never seen an image of an Eav'oq, but she had read accounts of them. Despite those literary descriptions, she did not feel prepared for the full extent of their alien nature. Itu had a long, tubular body, with a tangle of gangly pink limbs encircling his upper torso. One wide, gray eye covered his slender face.

For a few moments, Seltiq did nothing but stare at Itu on the display. When the Eav'oq did not receive a response from her or anybody in the armada, he tried to unilaterally negotiate for the lives of the Bajoran people. Itu spoke of eons past, referencing a tale out of antiquity that all knights knew well: the failed attempt of the Ascendants to exterminate the Eav'oq, an event that had led to a schism among the Orders, leading to the Great Civil War.

The words of the heretic enflamed Seltiq. Itu's life and the very existence of his people seemed to mock the Ascendants, pointing up their failures even as the knights prepared to meet their gods. But something else troubled Seltiq even more: the armada had entered the Fortress of the True on one side of the galaxy and had exited on the other, far from where they had begun. How had Itu navigated the distance between his homeworld and Bajor? The Ascendants had seen nothing of the Eav'oq for millennia, allowing the unholy aliens ample opportunity to travel great distances. Still, the proximity of both Itu's planet and Bajor to the Fortress suggested another possibility—namely, that Itu himself had journeyed through the realm of the Unnameable.

The idea of a heretic traversing such holy territory repulsed Seltiq. It also raised uncomfortable questions in her mind: *How could the Eav'oq even have discovered the Fortress? If they had, and if they'd entered it, then why had the True not immediately smote the profane aliens? Why had the Eav'oq been permitted to leave the Fortress?*

The answers all at once seemed clear to Seltiq. The True had allowed Itu, and perhaps other Eav'oq, through the Fortress in order to point the way for the Ascendants. There could be no clearer sign that the Unnameable demanded one final sacrament—the destruction of Bajor—before the advent of the Final Ascension.

Seltiq jabbed at her control panel, ending the transmission. The image of the Eav'oq disappeared at once from her display. Then she worked communications and opened a channel.

The time had come for the new Grand Archquester to lead the Ascendants into battle.

Iliana Ghemor waited, but she would not wait long.

As she listened to the debate progressing among the Ascendants, she looked out into space through the dome atop Votiq's vessel, which she had rendered transparent. The blue-and-white globe of Bajor dominated the view, with two of its moons hanging in space above it, one nearby, and one farther away, just above the planet's horizon. Sunlight glinted off an orbital weapons platform, and pinpoints of movement marked the rise of assault vessels from the surface.

Ghemor wanted nothing more at that moment than to successfully launch the devastating power of Raiq's subspace missile against Kira's people. The Cardassian visualized the weapon soaring out of sight on its way toward the planet. She imagined the device detonating and tearing through subspace, undermining the fundamental structure of the space-time continuum. The resulting cataclysm would rip Bajor to tatters. The planet might survive the onslaught, individuals and even groups might find their ways to safety, but the civilization that had given rise to so many problems for the Cardassian Union, that had hosted the murder of her betrothed, that had birthed the bane of Iliana Ghemor's existence—that civilization would never be the same.

And Kira Nerys will witness it all.

While the Ascendants continued to deliberate about

how they should vanquish the population of Bajor, Ghemor checked her sensors. As the last of the armada assembled in orbit, she saw that *Defiant*, the Federation starship assigned to Deep Space 9, would arrive shortly. A second vessel—which read not as Starfleet, but as a civilian ship, with strong shields and virtually no weaponry—would also reach Bajor soon. Kira Nerys followed in a runabout, too far away to make a difference, but close enough to monitor the Ascendant attack.

Of greater import, Ghemor detected no Starfleet vessels on long-range sensors. She felt certain that Kira had sent out an alarm, but apparently the Federation had no reinforcements stationed near Bajor. The Ascendants would have to contend with *Defiant*, but a lone starship would not be enough to stand in Ghemor's way. Before long, she would either fire the subspace weapon, or the Ascendant armada would descend on Bajor. The latter course would require more time to complete, and it would progress less spectacularly, but it would still prove effective. The Ascendant ships would leave Bajoran cities in ruins and set fire to what remained. Poisons would choke the air. Arable lands would blacken. Waters would vaporize. Blood would spill.

Ghemor considered firing on Raiq's ship so that she could use the subspace weapon against Bajor, but she felt that doing so would cross a line. She did not want to lose control of the Ascendants, or worse, to make an enemy of them. She needed their armada to ensure her vengeance on Kira's people, and once that had been accomplished, to finally put an end to Kira. Ghemor had endured too much to allow herself a misstep.

For the moment, she awaited word from the new Grand Archquester. As she did so, an alert sounded in the cockpit just before another phaser beam carved through space from the closest Bajoran weapons platform. It slammed into

Votiq's ship, but once more, the defensive shields barely registered a dip in power levels or effectiveness.

Ghemor heard another chime. Scans showed the eight Bajoran assault vessels that had earlier fired on her coming around for another attack run. She quickly energized her own ship's weapons. She targeted the two lead vessels and tapped a trigger on her console. From emitters on either side of the ship's bow, brilliant white circles of energy darted out into the void, expanding in diameter the farther they traveled. Ghemor watched as the baryon pulses found their marks. Jagged bands of blue light erupted around the two lead Bajoran vessels like a violent but localized electrical storm. The faux lightning faded and then vanished as the weapon drained the shields of energy.

The eight assault vessels leveled a phaser salvo at Ghemor's ship. The red-yellow beams buffeted her shields, which remained largely unaffected. Ghemor locked on to the two lead vessels again and fired a pair of tetryon bolts. Fiery green spheres streaked from the bow of her ship and caught their targets as they tried to veer off. A jet of gas burst from the flank of one vessel as it vented atmosphere through a breach in its hull, and then it broke into pieces. The second ship exploded in a blaze, reduced in an instant to fragments that intermittently reflected the Bajoran sun as they tumbled through space. The other assault vessels sped away.

Suddenly, a flash of light blossomed in the distance, off to starboard. Ghemor looked in that direction and saw a great deal of movement: clusters of Bajoran assault vessels leaving the atmosphere and reaching space, waves of Ascendant ships arriving in orbit, weapons platforms discharging their phasers. When she spotted a series of bright bursts at the far edge of the armada, she examined her sensors to find that *Defiant* had arrived from Deep Space 9, and that the Starfleet vessel had already engaged the Ascendants.

Seltiq is taking too long, she thought. Ghemor couldn't wait any longer for the new Grand Archquester to make a decision about whether or not to utilize the subspace weapon against the Bajorans. Ultimately, it didn't matter whether the Ascendants obliterated Kira's people in the span of a heartbeat or in a full rotation of their world, just as long as Ghemor's nemesis suffered through it.

The Cardassian reached for the communications panel, intending to contact Seltiq, when a tone signified an incoming transmission—from the new Grand Archquester. Ghemor opened the channel. The image of the nascent leader of the Ascendants appeared on a screen, and Seltiq identified herself.

"Fire, I have listened to the voices of many knights," the Grand Archquester then said. Ghemor thought that she spoke with the poise earned from a long life. *"I want to satisfy your request to use Aniq's subspace missile against the heretics on the planet ahead. Many Ascendants support such an action, but far more seek to employ the metaweapon as a means to help us burn before the Unnameable and join with them. All agree, though, that we must first annihilate the heretics as one last sacrament before we reenter the Fortress of the True. I submit to you that we can accomplish that goal without resorting to the use of the subspace weapon."* If Seltiq felt any anxiety about contravening the wishes of such an important figure in her religion, Ghemor couldn't tell.

"I retract my intention to use the subspace weapon against the Bajorans," the Cardassian said. She could not risk losing the loyalty of the new Grand Archquester, much less that of the majority of Ascendants who opposed her plan. She quickly worked to deactivate the metaweapon. "I have disarmed the missile. I am content to allow the armada to strike the planet and level its population of blasphemers."

For the first time, Seltiq hesitated. She blinked her big

golden eyes. She obviously hadn't expected her conversation with the Fire to proceed so smoothly. *"I am pleased, Fire,"* the new Grand Archquester said.

"Our goals are the same: to burn before the Unnameable in the Fortress of the True," Ghemor lied. "To make that happen, let us embark on the final sacrament. I will keep the subspace missile with me and protect it from harm while the Ascendants eradicate the heretics."

Ghemor waited to see if the new Grand Archquester would resist her intention to retain custody of the meta-weapon. She didn't—but then how could she? Seltiq could not question the integrity of the Fire.

Instead, Ghemor listened as the new Grand Archquester quickly contacted Raiq and ordered her to deactivate her ship's tractor beam, releasing the subspace missile into Ghemor's care. Once the younger Archquester had complied and withdrawn from her position, Seltiq then opened a channel to the entire armada. She informed the Ascendants of her joint decision with the Fire to preserve the metaweapon for their use inside the Fortress of the True, and also of their shared determination to eliminate one more heretical culture from the cosmos. "Assume planetary-advance formation," she said, ordering the Ascendant legion into an offensive configuration. *"And then,"* she said, finishing by issuing a one-word command: *"Attack!"*

Iliana Ghemor observed through the transparent dome of Votiq's ship as the Ascendant armada started toward Bajor. For the moment, she would relish her role as a spectator, fully aware that Kira would be watching too—watching, and powerless to prevent the coming massacre. If for some reason it became necessary, though—if the Ascendants faltered, or if the Bajorans somehow manufactured a miraculous defense—Ghemor would not hesitate to use the subspace weapon against all of them, or against Kira herself.

* * *

Raiq did as the new Grand Archquester ordered, pressing a control to deactivate her ship's tractor beam. Some part of her expected that as soon as she released the subspace missile, the Fire would launch it at the planet ahead, regardless of her word that she would not. The thought caused Raiq tremendous anxiety, which did not abate when her fear did not materialize. Any treachery perpetrated by the Fire—or by the woman who at least purported to be the Fire—did not trouble her as much as her own skepticism did.

How can this be happening? Raiq asked herself. After a lifetime of more than a century spent in service to the Quest, with a mind-set absolutely dedicated to orthodoxy, how could she suddenly question the foundation of her entire existence? *And not just of my existence,* she realized, *but that of all Ascendants.* Scripture foretold the coming of the Fire, whose arrival in turn augured the End Time, when the surviving knights would embark on the Path to the Final Ascension. For Raiq to doubt the word of the Fire, or worse, for her to distrust the truth of the Fire's identity, placed her squarely on the brink of heresy.

"What is wrong with me?" she asked herself. She spoke softly, her musical voice shaky and sounding thin even in the compact space of her ship's cockpit. Raiq felt distraught, her thoughts awash in doubt and shame. How would her profane turn of mind affect her when she burned beneath the gaze of the Unnameable? Would it still be possible for her gods to find her worthy of joining with them? Could her fall from grace impact the Final Ascension for the rest of her people?

Raiq didn't have the answers to any of her questions, but she needed to find them. She did not want to wait to discover whether or not she had offended the True beyond the possibility of her redemption. She also discovered that she could not live with the idea that she had doomed all the Ascendants to burn before the Unnameable without then being elevated into their pantheon.

But what can I do?

Raiq considered taking an action that previously would have required no deliberation from her whatsoever: helping to exterminate the heretics on the planet below. But if her lifetime of unwavering devotion to the Unnameable, if all the cycles she had spent on the Quest, if the thousands of blasphemous cultures she had helped to extinguish, if the billions—perhaps even trillions—of heretics she had helped to destroy—if all of that failed to warrant her burning before the True and then joining with them, would attacking the Bajorans alongside the rest of her people actually make a difference?

No, it wouldn't, she decided. *But something else might.*

After disengaging her vessel's tractor beam from the subspace weapon, Raiq had retreated from the Fire's ship—which until a short time ago had been Votiq's ship. As the new Grand Archquester ordered the Ascendants to strike at the planet of heretics, Raiq for the first time in her existence disobeyed a direct order from the leader of her people: she turned her vessel away from Bajor. She would not take part in an action that could have no possible effect on her Path to the Final Ascension. But she reasoned that, if Votiq could, on his own, burn beneath the gaze of the Unnameable and join with them, then she could at least try to do the same thing.

Raiq set course for the Fortress of the True.

Defiant hurtled toward Bajor. In the center of the bridge, beneath the red glow of alert lighting, Commander Elias Vaughn listened to the strained whine of the impulse en-

gines, alert for any indication that he pushed the bantam
ship too hard. In the nearly two years he had served as the
first officer of Deep Space 9, he had come to know *Defiant*
well, owing particularly to his captaining the vessel during its three-month exploratory mission into the Gamma
Quadrant. Equally as important—or perhaps more so—he
knew the crew. He had met few engineers as naturally
adept as Lieutenant Nog, who at that moment had the
sublight drive functioning at 117 percent capacity.

Vaughn leaned forward in the command chair, his gaze
fixed on the main viewscreen. On the journey from the
station, he had spoken multiple times with both Captain
Kira and Bajoran Minister of Defense Aland. There had
been some positive news: Lieutenant Commander Ro and
Lieutenant Chao had taken a runabout into the Gamma
Quadrant, and while they'd discovered that Starfleet's communications relay had been destroyed, they'd found that no
more enemy ships were headed for the wormhole. They also
confirmed that, while the Ascendants had attacked Idran
IV, the Eav'oq had suffered no casualties. Kai Pralon and
her cultural delegation had also survived, and Ro and Chao
had accompanied the Bajoran spiritual leader and her party
back through the wormhole to DS9. Vaughn did not know
what to make of the return of Taran'atar, but the rest of
the information that Kira and Aland had imparted—about
Iliana Ghemor, about the Ascendants, and about their subspace weapon, not to mention that the nearest Starfleet vessels would take a full day to reach Bajor—could not have
been more dire.

On the main viewer, the Ascendant fleet, thousands of
ships strong, sprawled in a massive formation above Bajor.
Aland had relayed his intention of mobilizing the assault
vessels of the Bajoran Militia, in addition to utilizing the
weapons platforms in orbit, but Kira's initial attack on the

Ascendants, as well as the brief historical record on the zealous aliens, suggested that far more than that would be needed to stop them. And if they did possess a subspace weapon, then the Bajorans faced a truly grave threat.

"Are you confident about the location of Ghemor's ship?" Vaughn asked. Scans had so far not detected any subspace weaponry within the ranks of the Ascendant ships. Vaughn hoped that meant that the invading fleet did not actually have such a weapon, but he also knew that it might simply mean that they had shielded it from sensors. Whatever the case, finding the mad Cardassian woman and dealing with her directly seemed the most likely means of forestalling an attack on Bajor and its people.

"I've identified Ghemor's ship based on the comm data Captain Kira provided after their contact," said Bowers, who worked at the tactical console on the port side of the bridge. He raised his voice to be heard over the high drone of the overworked impulse drive. "It was the first Ascendant vessel through the wormhole, and the first to reach orbit. It's still towing what looks like a missile behind it."

"Set a direct course," Vaughn ordered.

"Aye, sir," said Prynn from the conn and operations station. "She's positioned at the very heart of the Ascendant force. We'll have to pass through a sizable portion of their fleet to get there."

"Do it," Vaughn said. "Avoid their ships as best you can. Lieutenant Bowers, report tactical status."

"Shields at maximum. Phasers energized, quantum torpedoes primed and loaded."

"Very good," Vaughn said. "Lieutenant Nog, what are—"

"Captain," Bowers interrupted. "I'm reading more weapons fire at Ghemor's location." The tactical officer worked his console, clearly seeking more detailed information. "One of the orbital platforms has discharged its phasers again . . . and the squadron of eight Bajoran assault vessels that fired earlier have resumed an attack vector."

On the viewer, in the distance, isolated yellow-red flares colored the sky above the planet. They did not last long, nor did they repeat immediately. Vaughn hoped that meant the Ascendants had not come to Bajor to do battle, although their refusal to answer hails and the historical record strongly suggested otherwise—as did the presence of Iliana Ghemor among them.

"I'm now reading return fire," Bowers reported. During Deep Space 9's assault on the lead ship, and again when the Bajoran Militia had initially taken aim at it, the Ascendant ship had not engaged its attackers. "Sensors are showing an oscillating, high-energy baryon beam directed onto the two lead Bajoran vessels." Vaughn noted that, with the exception of Prynn, who did not take her gaze from her console, every officer on the bridge had turned their attention toward Bowers. "The Bajorans are responding with a coordinated phaser barrage . . . the Ascendant ship is firing again . . . what read as tetryon torpedoes—" Bowers looked up from his panel and over at Vaughn. "The two lead Bajoran vessels have been destroyed."

Vaughn snapped his head toward the main viewer, as though he could see across the kilometers of space to the confrontation that had just occurred. *Two volleys, and two lost ships,* he thought, more than a little concerned about what that implied about the offensive capabilities of the Ascendants. The Bajoran assault vessels might have been older ships, with aging systems, but it still should have taken longer than it had to destroy them.

"Coming up on the edge of the Ascendant fleet," Bowers announced. A moment later, a knife-edged ship appeared on the viewscreen. Vaughn watched the perspective shift as Tenmei adjusted *Defiant*'s course, yawing it to port. The Ascendant ship slipped away in the opposite direction.

"Captain!" Bowers called out just before *Defiant* shook violently. The sudden movement threw Vaughn against the side of the command chair, but he managed to hold himself in his seat. The alert lighting blinked off, leaving the bridge illuminated only by the glow of control consoles, but then it resumed. "We've taken a baryon beam to our aft starboard flank."

"Shields are down to seventy-nine percent," Nog said. The number shocked Vaughn. With just one shot, the Ascendant ship had reduced the effectiveness of *Defiant*'s shields by almost a quarter. Such a powerful weapon did not bode well for Vaughn and his crew.

"Return fire," Vaughn ordered. "Phasers and quantum torpedoes, full spread."

"Aye," Bowers said. Characteristic feedback tones rang out across the bridge, signifying the firing of the ship's phasers and the launching of quantum torpedoes. Vaughn noted that the ambient noise in the compartment had quieted just as Nog explained why.

"Velocity is down to ninety percent of full sublight speed," said the operations chief. "One of the impulse reactors was knocked offline. I'm cycling it back up."

"Direct hit on the Ascendant ship with phasers and one quantum torpedo," Bowers reported. "Sensors are showing minimal damage. They're swinging back around."

"Quantum torpedoes," Vaughn said at once. "Three shots, staggered attack. Target their weapon emitters."

Vaughn didn't hear Bowers respond, but the sound of torpedoes being dispatched again resounded across the bridge, once, twice, a third time. On the main screen, the view had been locked—doubtless by Ensign Cathy Ling, who worked the communications console—onto the attacking Ascendant vessel. Vaughn saw it nimbly elude the first two quantum torpedoes. The blue-white fireballs soared past it and detonated in the distance with dazzling intensity. The third caught the ship on the port side of its blade-shaped bow, but not before the Ascendant fired again, sending out what looked like expanding white circles of energy in *Defiant*'s direction.

"Evasive," Vaughn said, but he could already perceive a change in the ship's momentum as the inertial dampers compensated for alterations to *Defiant*'s course. Prynn had clearly anticipated his order—she might even have acted before he'd spoken. Vaughn waited for the Ascendant weapon to land, but no impact came.

"We scored a direct hit," Bowers said, "but their shields registered only an eight percent drop."

Not enough, Vaughn thought. If it took ten or twelve quantum torpedoes to bring down the shields of just one Ascendant ship, and with thousands of their vessels hanging over Bajor, it didn't require higher mathematics to know that *Defiant* didn't carry anywhere near enough ordnance to make much of a dent in the invading fleet.

We'll do the best we can, Vaughn thought, *but first we need to find and disable the subspace weapon.*

"They're firing again," Bowers said.

"Continue evasive action," Vaughn ordered, leaping from the command chair and over to lean in beside Prynn. "Can you get us through to Ghemor's ship?"

Prynn continued to operate the flight controls without looking up. "I can snake our way past their ships, but we need all the impulse reactors online," she said. "And if they're firing on us . . ." She did not have to finish her statement for Vaughn to take her meaning.

As if to validate Prynn's concerns, another ship appeared in the center of the viewscreen. Shaped essentially the same as the first, it also looked different, with several cylindrical projections topside and keel. It quickly swam out of sight as Prynn pitched *Defiant*'s bow down.

"Torpedoes, full spread," Vaughn barked.

"Torpedoes, aye," Bowers called back, but then a thunderous roar filled the bridge. Inertial dampers failed for an instant as the deck lurched laterally. Vaughn flew sideways and landed hard on his left shoulder.

"We've taken another hit with a baryon beam," Nog yelled out above the din as Vaughn climbed back onto his feet. "Shields down to fifty-six percent."

"Two quantum torpedo strikes on the second ship, but their shields are still up hard," Bowers announced. "Both ships are in pursuit."

"Captain, we've got company up ahead," Prynn said. Vaughn looked at the main screen just in time to see three more Ascendant ships approaching in a triangular formation before the starscape canted and they disappeared from view. "Other ships are positioning themselves to block our way."

"How many ships?" Vaughn wanted to know.

"Incoming!" Bowers cried out. Vaughn rushed to the command chair and grabbed for its arm. He steadied himself as another Ascendant weapon pounded into *Defiant*'s hull.

"Shields at twenty-nine percent," Nog said.

We can't take much more of this, Vaughn thought. *How many more hits before our shields are down? Two? One?*

"Scores of ships are moving into our path," Prynn said. "Others are moving to intercept."

Vaughn strode back over to Prynn. "Get us out of here," he told her. The crew would be unable to help the people of Bajor in any way if *Defiant* went up in a fireball. Once more, the stars on the viewscreen skewed as Prynn set the ship onto a serpentine path.

"Several ships up ahead," she said.

"Avoid them if you can," Vaughn said. "Bowers, fire at

will. Rig quantum torpedoes for mine function and seed them behind us."

"Aye," Bowers said. "Firing phasers and quantum torpedoes. Initiating mine-deposit program."

"Viewer astern," Vaughn said.

"Viewer astern," echoed Ling. The image on the main screen changed to show the area behind *Defiant*. Bajor slid into and out of sight as Prynn continued to weave a path out of the Ascendant fleet. Vaughn saw two of the alien ships doggedly chasing *Defiant*. Both of them fired their weapons, but Prynn's deft piloting succeeded in eluding them.

An intense blaze of light brightened the viewscreen. "One of the ships trailing us struck one of the quantum mines," Nog reported. Vaughn saw an Ascendant vessel deviate from its course, then straighten in its flight. That's when a second brilliant glow erupted onscreen. "The same ship hit another mine," Nog said. "They're slowing . . . and turning back toward the main body of the fleet. The other ship is following."

"Ensign Tenmei?" Vaughn asked.

"Space ahead isn't clear, but there are only a few Ascendant ships," she said. "I can get us through."

Vaughn nodded, then stepped back and sat down in the command chair. He'd known that it would be problematic for one starship to challenge a fleet thousands of ships strong, but he'd hoped that Prynn might be able to thread the needle and get them to Ghemor and the subspace weapon. He had also believed it possible that *Defiant* might prove a paladin against the smaller vessels, even despite the large number of them.

When Vaughn looked again at the main screen, he noticed that Ling had switched to a forward view. For the moment, he saw no Ascendant ships in their path. *But that's not the direction we need to go.*

"Open a channel to Bajor," Vaughn said. "I need to talk to the first minister."

On the bridge of *Even Odds*, Taran'atar sat at the sensor station and studied its readouts. Just ahead of his purloined craft, the thousands of Ascendant ships had arrived at Bajor, and the Jem'Hadar watched as they established in orbit what he recognized as a military formation. It struck him that they intended to attack the surface of the planet. Unlike their assault on Idran IV, when the Ascendants had sent ten ships to strike the lone Eav'oq city, they would deploy their entire fleet against Bajor. Taran'atar could read it in the movements of their vessels. And while he had managed for a short time to stave off the Ascendant's attempt to destroy the Eav'oq city, that had required the use of *Even Odds'* superior shields. He could not hope to fend off thousands of Ascendant vessels, nor did he believe that Bajor's own defenses would stand against them for very long.

What can I do? he asked himself. In the Gamma Quadrant, Kira Nerys had sent him after the Ascendants—had wanted to accompany him in pursuit of their fleet—but why? He understood that the captain would willfully face insurmountable odds to protect her people, even if doing so assured her death. For most of his life, Taran'atar had felt the same way with respect to the Founders: nothing had meant more to him than risking his own existence in their defense.

But the Captain Kira who had demanded that the Jem'Hadar transport her aboard *Even Odds* so that they could both protect Bajor was not the same Captain Kira he'd encountered on the Alpha Quadrant side of the Anomaly. The former revealed information—the presence of Iliana

Ghemor among the Ascendants, their possession of a subspace weapon—that she could not realistically know. At least, she couldn't know in any straightforward manner, and Taran'atar once more suspected that the Captain Kira with whom he had spent more than a hundred days aboard *Even Odds* had come from the future.

The Jem'Hadar again asked himself why, but the answer seemed obvious: Kira wanted to enlist his aid in stopping the Ascendants from destroying her people. Perhaps they had already done so in her lifetime, and she had then traveled into the past in search of a means of preventing the catastrophe. But that also implied that Kira believed Taran'atar, or perhaps the two of them, could somehow stop the Ascendants.

That makes no sense, the Jem'Hadar thought. While a sophisticated vessel equipped with some impressive technologies, *Even Odds* could not possibly provide an adequate defense against thousands of Ascendant ships. Sensors had just shown *Defiant*, a powerful starship, retreating beneath an onslaught of the bladelike vessels. Additionally, if Iliana Ghemor and the Ascendants actually did have a subspace weapon at their disposal, then he had even less chance of protecting Bajor.

And then he saw it. A potential solution did rest with him, and not with *Defiant* or Deep Space 9, not with a planetful of Bajorans or either version of Kira Nerys. He could not be sure that the action he proposed to take would succeed, but he could conceive of no other course that would allow for even the smallest possibility of victory.

Taran'atar rose and hurried over to the communications console. He knew that Kira had left the Federation space station aboard a runabout, in pursuit of either Taran'atar or the Ascendants, or perhaps both, because she had continually tried to contact him from her vessel. He quickly recorded a brief message to her and transmitted it to the runabout.

Then Taran'atar grabbed a tablet from atop a neighboring console and charged out of the *Even Odds'* bridge.

Sisko stood in the operations chamber of the Musilla Consolidated Space Center, beside Bajor's first minister and its minister of defense. After his conversation with Kira, Asarem had invited him to join her. Sisko did not feel particularly comfortable doing so, either in his role as the former commanding officer of Deep Space 9 or as the Emissary. He had not served in Starfleet for two years, and although he had not shared the fact with anybody—not even with Kasidy—he had not experienced even the slightest connection with the Prophets since his return from the Celestial Temple fifteen months earlier.

The three large display screens on the front wall of the chamber showed views from orbit, where thousands of Ascendant ships assembled in a manner that indicated they intended to launch an offensive against the planet. Bajoran weapons platforms and assault vessels had already proven ineffective in combatting the invaders, and a message from Commander Vaughn told a similar story about *Defiant*. If the Ascendants attacked, then even discounting Taran'atar's report that Iliana Ghemor and the aliens carried a subspace weapon as part of their arsenal, Bajor teetered on the precipice of annihilation.

As Sisko observed the movements of the invading fleet, a Militia officer approached Asarem. A tall woman with a rigid posture, she wore the insignia of a colonel. Sisko did not recognize her, but given her position within the Space Center, he assumed that she functioned as a right hand to the head of the Militia, Overgeneral Manos.

"First Minister," said the colonel, "Captain Kira is asking to speak with you."

"Route it over here," Asarem said, gesturing toward an uncrewed console.

"Right away," the colonel said, and she hurried back to her own station.

Asarem motioned to Sisko and Aland that they should follow, then she headed over to the empty console. She did not sit, but leaned in over the chair and activated the panel with a touch. The seal of Bajor appeared briefly on-screen, replaced a second later by the face of Kira Nerys. Alone in a runabout, she wore a determined expression. She looked in turn at Sisko and Aland, but she addressed her comments to Asarem.

"First Minister, Taran'atar just sent me a message," she said. *"He told me that he thinks he might be able to prevent the impending attack."*

"How?" Asarem asked.

"He gave no details," Kira said. *"I can play his message for you."*

"Please."

Kira reached forward and tapped a control surface. Her image vanished in favor of the Jem'Hadar's. Sisko studied what little he could see of the control stations in the background, but he did not recognize the configuration. *"Captain Kira, this is Taran'atar,"* he said in a rich, resounding voice. *"I believe I can stop Iliana Ghemor and the Ascendants. You should not approach them, nor should the crew of the* Defiant. *All Bajoran vessels should withdraw at once."* He offered no sign-off, but the message abruptly ended, and Kira reappeared on the display.

"After receiving the transmission, I tried to contact him," she said, *"but he's not responding."*

"What do you think he intends to do?" asked Asarem.

"I don't know," Kira said. Sisko thought she tried to conceal the frustration she felt, but he had worked side by side with her for seven years, and he knew that the lack of detail Taran'atar had provided vexed her.

Minister of Defense Aland shifted from one foot to the other, then spoke up. "Captain, is it possible that the Jem'Hadar soldier is in league with these Ascendants?" he asked. "Iliana Ghemor at one point did hold him in her thrall, did she not?"

"She did," Kira allowed. *"My instincts tell me that Taran'atar is acting on his own, and that he genuinely wants to prevent Bajor from being attacked. It's possible that Ghemor is controlling him again, but why would she or the Ascendants want me and our assault vessels and the* Defiant *to pull back? We've already seen that Bajoran ships are no match for theirs, and even Commander Vaughn couldn't find a way to stand against such a large and powerful fleet."*

"Then you recommend doing as the Jem'Hadar says?" Asarem asked.

Kira looked away from the screen for a moment, as though reviewing the present situation one final time. At last, she peered back at the screen and said, *"Yes, I do."*

The first minister looked to Aland, and the two officials seemed to share an unspoken communication. "Very well," Asarem said. "We'll take it under advisement. In the meantime, please continue trying to reach the Jem'Hadar. Keep us informed if you learn anything more."

"Yes, Minister," Kira said.

"Asarem out." The Bajoran leader reached to the console a second time and ended the transmission. She then turned to Sisko. "Do you have any thoughts, Mister Sisko?"

Numerous ideas passed through his mind, mostly in the form of questions. How could one person, aboard one ship, hope to combat a fleet of thousands? Why did Taran'atar want Kira, *Defiant*, and the Bajoran assault vessels to withdraw? Did he carry some sort of unthinkably potent weapon aboard the ship he piloted?

Without warning, the answer drifted up in Sisko's mind.

It didn't arrive in a mystical flash, like an Orb experience or a *pagh'tem' far*—a sacred vision. He wished it had. Contact with the Prophets, no matter how vague or indefinite, no matter how oblique or mystifying, at least would have carried with it the imprimatur of the powerful, noncorporeal beings who watched over the people of Bajor. Such experiences had initially confused and frustrated Sisko, but he had learned not only to live with those numinous moments, but to mine valuable insights from them.

And, he had to admit to himself, *I just want contact with the Prophets again.* When he had originally arrived at Bajor, when he and Jadzia had discovered the wormhole and its inhabitants had first communed with him, he had resisted his sudden elevation to the status of religious icon. Over time, though, his life changed dramatically. He successfully dealt with the emotions of losing his first wife, in no small part because of his experiences in the Celestial Temple. He also became interested in, and even enamored of, the culture and people of Bajor, to the point where he considered himself one of them. He came to accept his place in Bajoran society, and then to use his position to help safeguard its citizens, often aided by what he learned from his strange and intermittent interactions with the Prophets.

At that moment, with a fleet of religious zealots in orbit, poised to strike at Bajor, Sisko would have welcomed such assistance. Instead, he had to settle for his own intuition. It came born not of deities or alien entities, but from his training, his long tenure in Starfleet, and his many experiences. One word—*Algeron*—emblazoned itself in his mind, and although he knew that it came from his own memory, it nevertheless carried the force of revelation.

He looked to the first minister. "Shut it down," he told her.

Asarem's brow creased in obvious confusion. "Shut what down?"

"Bajor."

Asarem Wadeen felt her eyes widen as she stared at the Emissary. "What do you mean?" she asked him. Although she had worked only occasionally with Benjamin Sisko during his command of Deep Space 9—she had served at the time as Shakaar Edon's second minister—she knew all the good he had done for the Bajoran people, all the personal risks he had taken on their behalf. Most believers readily accepted him as the Emissary of the Prophets, but even those few who didn't could not deny everything that he had accomplished for Bajor.

"Shut down every power source on the planet," Sisko said.

"Captain," Aland said, either forgetting Sisko's preference for the simple honorific of *mister*, or intentionally addressing him as one military officer to another. "All of our orbital weapons platforms draw secondary power from the surface. Our largest cities have shield generators to protect them in case of attack. Our ability to monitor what's happening in space, to direct our assault vessels, this very facility . . ." He spread his arms wide, clearly taking in the whole of the Musilla Consolidated Space Center. "It all requires power."

"Of course it does," Sisko said. "But I know what Taran'atar is going to do, and we have to shut down as much as possible before he does."

"If you know something—" Asarem started, but Sisko cut her off.

"I do, and I'll explain it all, but if we don't start shutting down the power right now, Bajor might not survive," he said. To Asarem's surprise, he reached up and took hold of her by her shoulders. "Not just the Bajoran people, but the planet itself."

"What?!" Aland said. "Do you think—"

"Yes," Sisko said, not waiting for the minister of defense to finish his question, but the two men seemed to understand each other.

"There are hospitals," Asarem said. "People on public transport—"

"We can drop medical facilities from the main power grids, and switch them over to emergency generators," Aland said. "People will be trapped in lifts and public transportation, transporters will be inoperative . . ."

"Recall your ships from orbit," Sisko said, "but leave the weapons platforms active."

"Of course," Aland said, and then he peered over at Asarem. "An emergency shutdown will cause havoc everywhere. Do I have your authority, First Minister?"

Asarem looked from Aland to Sisko. The former commanding officer of Deep Space 9 held her gaze. "Are you sure?" she asked him.

"I am," he said. He hesitated for perhaps the space of a heartbeat before uttering the words she needed to hear. "I am the Emissary."

Kira paced the main cabin of *Yolja* liked a caged *pugabeast*. She had pressed the runabout to its maximum impulse speed, but it felt to her as though the vessel sat in its hangar aboard Deep Space 9, drawing no closer to Bajor and the alien fleet that threatened it. Forward and back she paced, around the freestanding console that stood just ahead of the transporter platform at the aft end of the compartment. Every few circuits, she leaned in over the main console and checked the sensors.

I really thought I'd grown more patient with age, Kira thought. *With age, and with greater responsibilities.* Waiting had never been her forte, all the way back to the days of her youth, when she could do nothing quickly enough to rid her world of Cardassian occupying forces. But she truly believed that her time serving under Captain Sisko in a more structured environment, and then her two years in command of DS9, had taught her the value of facing down adversity with forbearance. At that moment, though, she thought she would get out and push *Yolja* if it would get her to Bajor even a second sooner.

The captain had not yet decided whether to comply with Taran'atar's instructions. As she stopped at the runabout's main console, she saw that many of Bajor's assault vessels had begun to withdraw from orbit, and *Defiant* remained just beyond the spread of the Ascendant fleet. She could also see from the way the alien ships gathered that they would shortly commence an attack on Bajor. The realization made her blood run cold. She felt helpless, still too far away to do anything to aid her people, although she saw that Taran'atar's vessel had almost reached the rear edge of the Ascendant formation.

Kira started away from the forward console when contrapuntal movement on the sensor display drew her eye. She leaned over the panel and watched for a moment as a ship at the leading edge of the invading fleet soared in the opposite direction. Kira sat down at the console and studied the readings. She expected to find the pilot of a Bajoran assault vessel attempting to penetrate the enemy ranks, but scans showed the ship as one of the Ascendants' own.

The captain followed the progress of the blade-shaped vessel as it sped along a straight path away from Bajor. Kira projected its linear course ahead. It did not surprise her to discover it on a direct path to Deep Space 9, and beyond it, to the Celestial Temple.

Kira decided she would attempt to contact the ship's pilot. She reached toward the communications panel, but just then, a series of tones indicated an incoming transmission. Kira tapped a control surface, half expecting to come face-to-face for the first time with an Ascendant, with the pilot to whom she had been about to send a message, but instead, the image of Taran'atar appeared on the monitor.

"Taran'atar to Captain Kira," he said.

"I'm here," Kira said.

"And growing too close to the Ascendants," he told her. *"You must reverse your course."* The Jem'Hadar was no longer on the bridge of his ship, she saw, at least not that she could tell. His countenance filled almost the entire display, with nothing but a featureless background visible behind him. Because of the perspective and slight movement of the image, Kira suspected that he communicated with her via a personal access display device.

"Why?" Kira asked, though she did not truly expect an answer. On the sensor readouts, she saw the fleeing Ascendant ship emerge from the rear of the fleet. It would shortly pass Taran'atar's vessel, which raced in the opposite direction.

"Because I am Taran'atar," he said, his voice rising and his eyes widening. He drew what looked like an energy weapon from the belt of his black coverall. *"I am dead. I go into battle to reclaim my life."*

Kira heard the fiery words, and she suddenly understood what Taran'atar intended to do. Part of her wanted to stop him, to tell him that he did not need to sacrifice his own life for the sake of the Bajoran people. But she couldn't. She couldn't, even though she realized that, despite his words, he would not actually reclaim his life.

The captain operated her controls and brought *Yolja* to a stop. On the sensor panel, Taran'atar's ship soared past the retreating Ascendant vessel. Kira made no mention of it, nor did Taran'atar. Instead, he continued his recitation.

"This, I do gladly, for I am Jem'Hadar," he said. *"This, I do gladly . . . for my friend Kira Nerys."* The words startled the captain. It shocked her simply to hear Taran'atar alter the oath he had sworn all his life, more so because he invoked her name and called her his friend.

"Victory is life," Kira said. "I will remember you."

Taran'atar said nothing more, but he leveled his weapon at a target offscreen and squeezed the triggering pad. A beam of coherent blue light streaked from the weapon's emitter. At once, a sickly shrieking noise blared out. It did not sound like a voice, or even like something natural, and yet it evoked the impression of pain.

Not just pain, Kira thought. *Agony.* "What—" she started to ask, but Taran'atar began to scream. His image wavered, as though from a display or transmission malfunction. He dropped the padd he carried, and it landed screen side up. Kira watched from that perspective as he continued to fire his weapon. The air around him seemed to grow thin, not like colors dulling in bright sunshine, but as though the reality of the scene had somehow weakened.

Taran'atar raised his empty hand in a defensive posture, in a way that made Kira think that some sort of creature would soon be upon him. He continued to fire his weapon, and to cry out, but the piercing screech grew in volume and nearly drowned out all other sounds. Taran'atar suddenly appeared to fade, and then the air thickened around him and brightened, until nothing more showed but a glowing field of white light.

Kira lifted her hand in front of her face and tried to endure the brilliant glare by observing it through her fingers, the display unable to compensate for the intensity of what it showed. Ultimately, the captain had to look away. When she did, she saw the interior of the runabout's main cabin thrown into bleak relief.

And then the compartment quieted and the lighting returned to normal levels. Kira turned back to the main console to see that her transmission with Taran'atar had ended. She quickly consulted the sensor readouts.

Taran'atar and his ship were gone.

With Seltiq's order for the armada to attack Bajor ringing in her ears, Iliana Ghemor gazed out through the transparent canopy of her ship. In all directions, Ascendant vessels moved into position and assumed an attack posture. A glance at her sensors showed every ship's shields at maximum power, and all their weapons energized. At long last, her revenge was at hand.

Ghemor checked her scans once more and saw that the vessel Kira piloted no longer flew toward Bajor. Rather, it had stopped in space. *Still close enough for her scans to show the Ascendants reducing the surface of her homeworld to ashes.*

Ghemor's sensors also showed the other ship approaching the rear of the armada. It did not read as a Starfleet vessel, nor like any other she had ever seen. Ghemor worked her controls to scan it in greater detail, wanting to know about its offensive and defensive capabilities, but before she could, its signature blinked. The ship vanished for a moment before reappearing and seeming to rapidly expand in size, like concentric ripples in a body of water, but in three dimensions. An alert on her display identified the growing spheres as subspace waves.

Alarmed about the deployment of some formidable weapon that could incapacitate or even destroy the armada, Ghemor set a course to flee, but too late. The waves propagated faster than they could have in normal space and swept through the Ascendant ships. None of the vessels showed any ill effects as the subspace oscillations passed, but that was not what Ghemor feared.

As rapidly as she could, she rearmed the subspace weapon, then launched it toward the surface of Bajor. She watched the missile streak away. Suddenly, the view before her quivered. Color drained from everything she saw—no, not the color, but the essence of everything. Reality all at once felt weak and insubstantial.

Ghemor held her hand up before her face. She flexed her fingers, testing her own physicality. As she did so, the light in the cockpit increased in intensity, and the air appeared to gain some measure of . . . heft.

Through the rising glow, a point of light flared into existence. Ghemor looked out through the transparent canopy of her ship once more and saw that the subspace waves had reached the missile even before it had entered the atmosphere. The metaweapon detonated, and Ghemor had just enough time to hope that the explosion would still destroy every living thing on Bajor.

Then space tore asunder.

"Captain," said Bowers at the tactical station, "sensors are detecting a . . . an eruption of subspace."

Vaughn stood up from the command chair, uncertain just what the lieutenant had reported. "An eruption?" he asked, making no effort to hide his confusion.

"Aye, sir," Bowers said. "I've never seen anything like it. It's as though a region of subspace has come unmoored, penetrated into normal space-time, and is now gushing through the aperture."

"Where?"

"I've isolated the area on scans," Nog said. "It's near the trailing edge of the Ascendant fleet, away from Bajor."

"Put it on-screen," Vaughn ordered. "Maximum magnification."

"Yes, sir," said Ling. She worked her console, and the Ascendant ships displayed on the main viewer winked off, replaced by a region of seemingly empty space. Vaughn saw nothing.

"Lieutenant Bowers?" he asked.

"Charting a representation of the eruption," Bowers said. The viewer changed again. In the center of the screen, bright blue spheres began emerging from a single point, expanding as they moved outward. "The lines denote subspace waves."

"Is it an Ascendant weapon?" Vaughn asked.

"I don't think so," Bowers said. "There was a ship at that location, but it wasn't an Ascendant vessel. It was Taran'atar's ship."

"It *was* his ship?"

"The eruption appears to have destroyed it," Bowers said.

Despite the news of Taran'atar's sudden demise, Vaughn thought he saw a ray of hope. "Did Taran'atar launch a weapon?" he asked. "Are the subspace waves destroying the Ascendant ships?"

"Negative," Bowers said. "It appears to have been the violence of the eruption that blew apart Taran'atar's vessel. The subspace waves are passing over the Ascendant ships without effect."

"Captain," Nog called out, "Ghemor has launched the missile towed behind her ship. It's headed for Bajor."

Vaughn supposed that many people—perhaps *most* people—would have felt a sense of dread at that moment. Taran'atar had reported that the Ascendants possessed a subspace weapon—a devastating destructive device—and the *Defiant* crew suspected the missile Ghemor towed behind her ship to be that weapon. They would apparently find out shortly, but the people of Bajor could pay a significant price for that knowledge.

The possibility that the weapon could cause mass casualties saddened Vaughn, especially since the circumstances denied him and the *Defiant* crew the capacity to prevent such a calamity. Rather than dread, though, he felt a sense of futility. During his long tenure in Starfleet, most of which he had spent in Intelligence, Vaughn had helped avert numerous tragedies—events that, had they been allowed to reach fruition, would have resulted in untold death and destruction. But he had not always succeeded in his missions, which often left him with the enervating feeling that he could have—*should* have—done something differently. More even than his failures, though, the simple need for somebody like him—somebody to stand against tyranny and terrorism, against avarice and powermongering, against benighted self-interest and crippling ignorance—had spawned an abiding cynicism within him. Vaughn found it difficult to reconcile the evils of the universe with his natural desire merely to live a happy life.

Except on our mission to the Gamma Quadrant. Vaughn's command of *Defiant* on a three-month journey into unexplored space had proven the most fulfilling assignment of his career. But that had been more than a year prior, and while he'd enjoyed his posting to DS9, he had more often been charged with stopping various factions from achieving nefarious goals than he had been with discovering the marvels of the universe. *And here I am again, facing down a madwoman attacking a planetary population with a terrible weapon.*

"Put it on-screen," he said.

"Yes, sir," said Ling, and the scene on the main viewer shifted once more. The bright blue-green orb of Bajor appeared. A horde of Ascendant ships hung in space above it. One graphic identified Ghemor's stationary vessel, while another tracked a shape moving toward the planet.

A possibility suddenly rose in Vaughn's mind. "Superimpose the subspace waves," he ordered. Bowers complied at once, and the expanding concentric spheres appeared at the edge of the screen, moving toward Bajor. They traveled faster than the missile Ghemor had launched, and the outermost subspace wave quickly overtook it. When it did, the point of intersection exploded in a brilliant flash of white light.

"What happened?" Vaughn asked, though he already knew: Taran'atar had done something in an attempt to save the people of Bajor.

"The subspace waves have triggered the missile," Bowers said. "Scans show that it was a subspace weapon, with a yield—" The tactical officer abruptly stopped talking, then looked up from his console with a grave expression on his face. "It was an *isolytic* subspace weapon."

Vaughn knew the destructive power of subspace weapons in general, but an isolytic version could literally tear apart huge tracts of the space-time continuum. As if to confirm his understanding, a great, dark gash appeared on the main viewscreen, a fissure somehow blacker than space itself. It tore like a streak of lightning above Bajor, originating at the point of the missile's detonation and jagging back toward the nearest vessel: Ghemor's ship. The hull cleaved in two before disintegrating in a coruscation of rusty gold, as though reduced to its component atoms. Vaughn thought— he *hoped*—that the destruction might seal the fracture that had opened in space.

It didn't.

The rent in space-time multiplied, ripping the structure of reality apart in different directions. The ruptures zigzagged from one Ascendant ship to another, ripping them to pieces before causing them to crumble into nothingness. One of Bajor's weapons platforms, and then another, split apart before degenerating into nothingness. Several assault vessels that had not cleared the area in time were minced to pieces. Some of the Ascendant ships began to move away from the advancing destruction, but Vaughn knew that power—and in particular warp power—attracted the subspace tears. The reason for the message that Kira had passed on from Taran'atar—that *Yolja* and *Defiant* should stay away from the Ascendant fleet, and that the Bajoran assault vessels should retreat—became abundantly clear.

"Shut down the warp drive," Vaughn said.

"Sir?" Nog said, peering over at him from his engineering station.

"We can't outrun the fissures at sublight speed, and if we go to warp, we'll only drag them along behind us until we slow. Shut down all noncritical systems, and prepare to eject *and* detonate the warp core." If they timed it correctly, they could use the exploding core to seal the subspace breaches.

"Yes, sir," Nog said, and he set to work at his console.

On the viewscreen, space continued to splinter, destroying one Ascendant ship after another as it did so. Vaughn feared that at any moment, one of the clefts in space-time would head toward Bajor. If any of the world's power supplies drew the subspace splits, the entire population—and even Bajor itself—would be at risk of destruction. As Vaughn and his crew looked on, though, the framework of broken space spread, but not in the direction of the planet.

"Captain," Bowers said, "several of the fissures are growing close to Endalla."

Endalla! Bajor's largest natural satellite, the moon possessed a basic ecology, with a thin but breathable atmosphere, and liquid water on the surface. No advanced fauna had evolved there, but simple flora had. Over the previous few years, several thousand scientists had taken up periods of residence on the planetoid to perform local research.

"Ensign Tenmei, set course for the nearest fissure, maximum impulse," Vaughn said. "Lieutenant Nog, are we prepared to jettison the warp core?"

"We will be shortly, Captain," Nog said. "Shutdown protocols are proceeding."

"Ensign Tenmei, take us in close enough for us to fire the warp core directly into the breach, but no closer," Vaughn said. He thought to tell Prynn that if any new fissures formed in the direction of *Defiant*, she should immediately withdraw, but such a strategy held no chance for success, since the subspace ruptures generated at faster-than-light speeds.

"Yes, sir," Prynn said.

As *Defiant* once more came to life around the crew, Vaughn moved back to the command chair and sat down. "Show me Endalla," he said.

"Yes, sir," said Ling.

The chain-reaction destruction of the Ascendant fleet disappeared from the main viewer, and Endalla took its place. Occasional streaks of white showed above the mostly brown-and-green globe. "How long before the subspace fissures overtake the moon?" Vaughn asked.

"It's impossible to predict with accuracy," Bowers said, "but probably between thirty and ninety seconds."

"And how long before we're close enough to fire the warp core into a breach?" Vaughn asked.

"At least five minutes, Captain," Prynn said. Vaughn wondered if any of the crew could hear the dismay she tried to keep out of her voice.

"Raise Endalla," Vaughn said.

"Channel open," Ling said.

"*Defiant* to Endalla research facilities," Vaughn said. "This is Commander Elias Vaughn."

Long seconds passed without a response. Vaughn was about to speak up again when an image appeared on the main viewscreen. Perhaps in his forties, a Bajoran man did not look to the companel at which he stood, but back over his shoulder. Behind him, several other people scurried about, and Vaughn could hear the white noise of commingled voices and what he thought might be an alarm.

When the man turned around to face the companel, Vaughn identified himself again. The man said, "I'm Goros Kly. I'm a botanist."

"Mister Goros, a series of subspace fissures has opened up in orbit of Bajor," Vaughn said. "You need to shut down all of the power supplies on Endalla."

"Minister Aland just contacted us," Goros said. "We're trying to shut everything down right now, but there are eleven different facilities on Endalla, each with their own power sources. We don't have a centralized shutoff."

"Do you have vessels on which to leave Endalla?" Such an evacuation likely wouldn't provide a solution, Vaughn knew, since the ships would have active power sources.

"We have a few small vessels for emergencies," Goros said, "but not enough to fit more than a small number of people."

"Then do your best to shut down the power," Vaughn said. "The *Defiant* is going to attempt to seal the subspace fissures."

The man nodded, then looked back over his shoulder again. He called out to somebody who hurried past, but Vaughn could not make out his words. When he finally turned to the companel once more, Goros said, "I have to go." He stabbed at the companel with one hand, but apparently missed the deactivation control. The channel between *Defiant* and Endalla remained open as the man hurried away.

Vaughn looked over at Ling and made a slashing motion with his hand across his throat. The ensign nodded and tapped at her controls, severing the communications connection with the Bajoran moon. The view of Endalla returned to the screen.

"Captain, we're ready to eject the warp core," Nog reported.

"Very good," Vaughn said, rising once more from the command chair. He paced forward to stand beside Prynn. "Ensign, bring us parallel with the fissure, keel facing it," he said. "Coordinate with Lieutenant Nog as to distance. I want the core to enter the fissure and detonate at the same time, ten seconds after we eject it. Be prepared to maneuver the ship appropriately if a new fissure opens in our direction."

Both officers acknowledged their orders, then worked with each other to determine how best to execute them. Vaughn returned to the command chair. Until *Defiant* reached a fissure and jettisoned their rigged warp core into it, he could do nothing but hope that the scientists on Endalla would survive long enough for that to make a difference. But Vaughn had to agree with what the Ferengi Rules of Acquisition had to say about hope: it didn't keep the lights on.

Time seemed to elongate as *Defiant* rushed forward. The ninety seconds Bowers had estimated before a fissure reached Endalla came and went, but the moon remained untouched by the unfolding disaster. *But is it disaster,* Vaughn asked himself, *or salvation?* Bowers reported that almost all of the Ascendant fleet had already been destroyed, and that it appeared only one ship would escape the expanding subspace fractures, the one that had started away from Bajor before Ghemor had launched the missile.

Though not a religious man, Vaughn had personally felt the influence of the Prophets, and the commander had to ask himself if he thought they had a hand in what was transpiring over Bajor. Only minutes earlier, the planetary population faced an invading fleet of zealots led by a mentally and emotionally unstable Cardassian bent on exacting her revenge on them. Whatever Taran'atar had done aboard his ship had turned the tables. If such a dramatic reversal did not suggest divine intervention, then Vaughn didn't know what did.

As they drew to within two minutes of reaching a fissure, Prynn began counting down in increments of ten seconds. After fifty seconds, Bowers spoke up.

"Captain, a fissure is about to reach Endalla."

By the time he'd finished speaking, Bowers' words had come to pass. On the viewscreen, a dark, angled shadow sliced into Bajor's largest moon. Vaughn almost could not credit what he witnessed. The red glow of flames spread across the face of Endalla as though the entire orb had been set alight all at once. The effect lasted only a moment, and then the fires died, as though extinguished by a great wind. Later, an analysis of *Defiant*'s sensor readings would show that the moon's thin atmosphere had been ripped away, some of it pulled down into subspace, and the rest blasted out into the void.

What remained of the moon barely resembled Endalla. Where soil and plant life had once painted the surface in browns and greens, only the dull gray of a dead world remained. Bowers quietly announced that scans showed no indications of the scientific installations that had been established there, and no signs of life.

"Coming up on a fissure," Prynn said. Without needing an order, Ling adjusted the main screen to display the path ahead of *Defiant*. Vaughn felt a sense of oppression leave him as the image of the lifeless moon winked off, though he knew his relief was chimerical; he no longer had to endure looking at the place where so many had perished. If the Prophets could be considered deities, and if they actually had protected the Bajoran people from the Ascendants, then it could only be said that they were cruel gods.

On the viewer, a ragged stretch of space showed not the black of infinite distance, but the nullity of nonexistence. It looked like a vast chasm in the sky. Its tenebrous opening gave Vaughn the impression of the gaping maw of some impossible spaceborne creature.

"Bringing us in over the fissure," Prynn said.

"Preparing to eject the warp core," Nog said. As *Defiant*'s bow pitched upward, Ling kept the viewscreen focused on the fissure.

"Five seconds," Prynn said, and then she counted down to one.

A feedback tone sounded in the bridge, not too dissimilar from the one that accompanied the launch of a quantum torpedo. "Warp core away," Nog said. On the viewer, the long, cylindrical core shot out into space from the ship's keel.

"Ensign Tenmei, get us out of here," Vaughn said, but Prynn had already engaged the ship's impulse drive. "Viewer astern." He resisted the temptation to count down from ten in his head.

As the ebon tendril of subspace faded into the distance, an atmosphere of anxious expectation settled over the bridge crew. They all waited to see if their efforts would halt the fracturing of space above Bajor, or if more would need to be done. Vaughn also assumed that they all also wondered if some new fault in the continuum would reach out and smite their ship.

When ten seconds had passed, *Defiant*'s warp core exploded.

Through the forward viewport of *Yolja*, Kira saw a blue-white flash of light above Bajor. Her sensors told her that the *Defiant* crew had jettisoned their warp core into one of the subspace fractures, and she presumed Commander Vaughn had ordered its destruction in an attempt to combat the shredding of space brought about by Ghemor's weapon. She could only hope that it would work.

Even if it does, it's too late for the people on Endalla, Kira thought bitterly. She had lived so much of her life—first under the yoke of Cardassian oppression, and then later, during the Dominion War—with not just the threat of death hanging over her, but with its reality a consistent presence. She had somehow survived one battle after another, unexpectedly making it into her middle thirties, but so many of the people around her had perished along the way—family, friends, comrades-in-arms. In some ways, she had become inured to such deaths; they did not incapacitate her emotionally, and she functioned in their wake. At the same time, the pain had never gotten easier to bear. Even the deaths of innocent strangers, such as the scientists on Endalla, gnawed at her spirit.

Of course, more than the lives of people she did not know had just been lost. She wished she could thank Taran'atar for his sacrifice, though he doubtless would have eschewed her gratitude. If his final, seemingly desperate act worked—and it seemed at that moment as though it would—he might have saved the entire population of Bajor.

After the destruction of Taran'atar's ship, Kira had done essentially as the Jem'Hadar had suggested. She did not turn *Yolja* and speed away from Bajor, but she did bring the runabout to station-keeping. She followed what took place next, both on sensors and via a magnified view of Bajor on a screen. By the time the subspace waves that Taran'atar had set in motion reached *Yolja*, they barely registered as a spatial disturbance.

Kira had observed, though, as those same ripples in the foundation of space-time sparked Ghemor's subspace weapon. She watched cracks form in reality itself, which then began swallowing up the ships of the Ascendant fleet. It did not take long for her to realize that Ghemor's missile had not simply been a subspace weapon, but an *isolytic* subspace weapon. Nearby power sources drew the fractures and then bred new ones.

Staring through the forward port, Kira saw the blue-white light of *Defiant*'s exploding warp core spread. It moved along sharp-edged paths, forming a misshapen latticework that could only be the network of spatial fractures the isolytic weapon had caused. Then, just as quickly, the light started to fade.

Kira examined her sensors. She noticed first that *Defiant* and its crew had escaped the ejection and destruction of their warp core. But where Endalla only moments earlier had scanned as a living, inhabited world, its current readings depicted it as little more than a sterile rock in space. Likewise, the skies above Bajor, so recently filled with thousands of ships massing for an attack, sat empty, every Ascendant vessel annihilated by the shattering of space-time.

Every vessel but one, Kira realized.

The captain refocused her sensors in search of the Ascendant ship that had fled from Bajor prior to Taran'atar taking action. She had notified Dax about the rogue vessel, and she knew that the lieutenant would handle the situation as best she could. Although Vaughn had reported the considerable strength of both the Ascendant ships' shields and weapons, Kira had confidence that Deep Space 9 could stand against a lone aggressor. The course of the vessel, though, concerned her; it continued on a direct heading for the wormhole. The captain didn't know if the remaining Ascendants intended either to flee, to bring back reinforcements, or to damage the Celestial Temple, but an entire fleet of their people had just attempted to destroy Bajor. Kira wanted answers.

Closer to the Ascendant ship than anybody else, she turned *Yolja* and set out in pursuit.

Raiq piloted her ship at top speed through the solar system, her course taking her precisely toward the entrance to the Fortress of the True. She did not know what else she could do, and yet she feared that the gates would not open for her. She had sinned grievously—she had not only distrusted the Fire, but had acted against her—and she'd been rebuked for it by the new Grand Archquester.

The new Grand Archquester. Raiq still found the account of Votiq's individual Final Ascension suspicious, but as she rushed away from the location of the greatest catastrophe in the Ascendants' history, she hoped to the core of her being that the Fire had been speaking the truth. If so, then the goal Raiq had pursued every moment of her life, the goal her people had relentlessly sought throughout the millennia, remained ahead of her, a tantalizing possibility that meant everything to her, that gave shape and meaning to her existence. If not—

If not, then I have nothing, she thought, not without bitterness. Her past—more than that, the entire history of the Ascendants—would prove worthless and empty. Her future would no longer exist in any form that she recognized. And in between the cycles gone and the cycles yet to come, in her present, she would for the first time in her life be utterly directionless.

What have I done? Raiq asked herself. *What have my doubts wrought?* She had questioned both the honesty and the judgment of the Fire. Believing that the Ascendants needed Aniq's subspace weapon to help bring about the Final Ascension, Raiq had prevented the long-awaited prophet from employing the device against a planet of heretics. The new Grand Archquester ordered the release of the missile, but Seltiq also agreed with Raiq about how it should be used. *Were we both wrong? Should we simply have acquiesced to the Fire's plan? Would that have made a difference?*

Raiq had so many questions, a jarring reality when juxtaposed with the virtual certainty in which she had lived her life. She was accustomed to having answers provided to her, and not having to search them out herself. To her horror, she discovered that questions carried far more implications.

But Raiq could not stop herself from asking: *Did I bring this cataclysm down upon us?* She could only answer: *Maybe.* Maybe if she had not intervened when the Fire had initially launched the missile, it would have reached the surface of the planet and wiped out the billions of heretics there. Maybe, having performed one last sacrament for the Unnameable, the Ascendants would at that moment be headed for the Fortress of the True, on their way to the Final Ascension.

Except we did not act as Ascendants, Raiq realized. They had taken the Fire at her word that a race of heretics inhabited the planet, but doing so ignored the rites and procedures established eons prior. The Ascendants visited the cultures they happened upon, observed them, judged them. Only after they had taken that time and made those efforts, and only if circumstances warranted, did they then perform a cleansing.

Was that it? Raiq wondered. Had the Fire been sent not just to guide them to the Fortress of the True, but to gauge their suitability for the Final Ascension? Had the Ascendants failed the last task they had been given, and thus denied the opportunity to reenter the Fortress?

Does it even matter? As far as Raiq knew, all of her people had perished, their ships wiped out by their own subspace weapon. As she'd fled the armada, her sensors had offered up confused readings, and so she supposed that one or two vessels, perhaps even more than that, might have somehow escaped. The notion seemed born out of desperation, but she clung to it.

But if any other Ascendants had survived, wouldn't they also be headed for the Fortress of the True? Raiq examined her sensor console. An unfamiliar ship followed closely behind her, and farther ahead, two similar vessels moved toward her from the direction of the space station located near the Fortress. Raiq also saw an attempt to communicate with her from the trailing ship. Though she doubted it, she supposed that another Ascendant could have captured the vessel and used it to escape the yield of the subspace weapon. She tapped at a control, and a voice filled the cockpit of her ship.

"This is Captain Kira Nerys of the Federation station Deep Space Nine, to the Ascendant ship." The automatic interpreter immediately translated the words from the language of Opaka Sulan's people to that of the Ascendants. *"Stop your vessel at once, deactivate your weapons, and lower your shields. You have invaded this system and attacked us, but we do not seek confrontation with you. We want only to talk."*

Raiq stabbed at her controls, ending the transmission. After a lifetime spent on the Quest, she would not yield so near to its end. She told herself that it did not matter that she would face the Final Ascension alone. She would burn beneath the gaze of the Unnameable, and even if they found her unworthy, at least the end would be at hand.

Raiq accessed the controls for her ship's baryon pulses and tetryon bolts.

Aboard Deep Space 9, in Ops, Dax studied the tactical console. She wished she could use *Defiant* to intercept the fleeing Ascendant vessel, but the starship remained at Bajor, its crew consulting with the first minister and other officials, and studying the aftermath of all that had taken place. Dax had dispatched two runabouts, *Platte* and *Volga*, but after speaking with Commander Vaughn, she wanted to send out two more. According to the first officer, the bladelike ships possessed both formidable armaments and durable shields.

Captain Kira, in pursuit of the Ascendant vessel herself, had just contacted the station, though, and she had opted for different tactics. Because DS9 currently hosted only civilian vessels, the captain wanted the balance of the runabout fleet to remain in their hangars, out of sight, but ready to launch in defense of the station. Dax tried to persuade her, without success.

She saw on the tactical console that the Ascendant vessel rapidly neared the two runabouts, with Kira following close behind aboard *Yolja*. Lieutenant Commander Ro Laren and Ensign Jang Si Naran crewed *Platte*, while Lieutenant Rey Alfonzo and Ensign José Chavez had taken out *Volga*. The captain's orders had been, foremost, to keep the station safe, and second, to capture the Ascendants alive.

Sensors showed that the paths of *Platte* and *Volga* would soon intersect that of the Ascendant vessel. The two runabouts flew on staggered courses rather than in formation so that they would provide more than a single target. Dax aimed one of the station's outer sensors and set it for maximum magnification. The two runabouts appeared on the main viewscreen in Ops, *Platte* ahead and off to starboard, *Volga* behind and off to port. In the distance, the Ascendant vessel became visible, though it appeared as little more than a black surface barely reflecting the light of the Bajoran sun.

Dax ordered Lieutenant Candlewood to tap into *Platte*'s communications. She immediately heard Ro attempting to contact the approaching vessel. *"This is Lieutenant Commander Ro Laren to the Ascendant ship,"* the security chief said. *"You have entered this system without authorization. You are instructed to power down your weapons and bring your ship to a halt. We do not want to fire on you, but we will do so if necessary."* Not surprisingly, Dax heard no response. The captain had similarly failed to provoke a reply.

On the viewscreen, the Ascendant vessel grew in size, though Dax could still make out scant detail, the ship's knife-shaped hull offering little to see when viewed from in front of it. Suddenly, two dazzlingly white beams surged from the ship, independently targeting the two runabouts. The bright, expanding circles of energy slammed into *Platte* and *Volga*. Dax eyed the status readouts for both and saw that their shield power had been reduced by a third.

The two runabouts immediately returned fire with their phasers. The Ascendant weapons quieted as the vessel dived away, neatly evading the red-yellow beams. *Platte* reacted quickly, maneuvering to cut the attacker off, while *Volga* swung around and raced back along its original path, ensuring that the runabout remained between the Ascendant vessel and DS9.

From a point offscreen, the white beams—a pulsating baryon charge, according to Dax's sensors—resumed firing. Both struck *Platte* amidships. Dax saw a flurry of blue pinpoints flickering along one side of the runabout, a telltale sign of a failing shield. Before she could even check *Platte*'s status, the runabout deftly whirled on its vertical axis, protecting its collapsing shield as three bright green bursts landed on the hull.

As Dax studied *Platte*'s condition on the tactical readouts—one shield gone, two others on the verge of breaking down—she also spied the strength and composition of the Ascendant vessel's second weapon: powerful tetryon torpedoes. The lieutenant didn't know how much more fire *Platte* could take, but she made a command decision to take no chances. She dropped the station's shields, then worked the transporter.

As a familiar whine rose in Ops, Dax saw the Ascendant vessel reappear on the viewscreen, headed toward *Platte*. The enemy ship fired on the runabout at point-blank range, sending a combined barrage of baryon beams and tetryon torpedoes crashing into it. As the Ascendant vessel veered off and resumed its course toward the wormhole, a fiery explosion consumed *Platte*.

Dax snapped her head up to look at the small transporter stage on the periphery of Ops. It hummed in operation, but remained empty. She opened her mouth to call out for assistance—*I'm not a transporter expert, I need help*—but her hands moved across her console as though driven by a mind of their own.

Or maybe driven by Tobin's mind, she thought. A former host of the Dax symbiont, Tobin had been a skilled engineer by trade; he'd even taken part in the initial testing of a transporter prototype. Although Ezri had learned to cope with the numerous memories of Dax's previous hosts, and even to take strength from those lifetimes of experiences and abilities, she wondered if she was earning her own way.

But I did earn this, she told herself. *Starfleet just prepared me for this.*

Dax took in the readings on the transporter console and understood instantly that either the radiation from the Ascendant vessel's weapons or the shock wave from *Platte*'s destruction had affected the rematerialization sequence. She had pulled Ro and Si Naran's patterns from the runabout, but they had been distorted in transit. Dax needed to determine the source of the corruption and compensate for it.

She called up a visual model of the patterns and immediately recognized interference from radiation. Without even thinking about it, she engaged an appropriate filter, crosscircuited the transporter from *A* to *B*, and reenergized the materialization sequence. When she looked back up at the transporter stage, Ro and Si Naran stood there. Dax immediately raised the station's shields.

"Did the *Platte* make it?" asked Ro as she and Si Naran started down the stairs from the transporter stage.

"No," Dax said, and she peered over at the main viewer. *Volga* raced across the screen, firing phasers and microtorpedoes. Several connected with the Ascendant vessel, but it immediately struck back with its baryon weapon. *Volga*'s shields flared and held, but Dax saw that another hit would take them down.

"Open a channel to the *Volga*," Dax said.

At the communications station, Candlewood worked his controls. "Channel open." Ro and Si Naran crossed Ops to stand by the tactical station.

"Dax to Alfonzo. Pull back."

"Sir, we've compromised their shields," Alfonzo said. *"A few more microtorpedoes should bring them down."*

"Your shields won't last that long," Dax said. "Pull back *now* and return to the station."

"Aye, sir." On the viewscreen, *Volga* swerved from its course, peeling away from the Ascendant vessel. Dax worried that the enemy ship might pursue the runabout, but instead, it resumed its heading for the wormhole.

"Lieutenant," said Candlewood, "we're receiving a message from the captain."

"Put her on speaker." Dax assumed that Kira had followed the clash with the Ascendant vessel on the sensors of her own runabout.

"Yolja to Deep Space Nine."

"This is Dax. Go ahead, Captain."

"Lieutenant, do not send any more runabouts after the Ascendant ship."

"Agreed, Captain," Dax said. She did not say that she'd had no intention of risking additional lives. She knew that Kira wanted to question the surviving Ascendants, but Dax did not judge that opportunity worth losing anyone.

"Did you successfully beam out the Platte *crew?"*

"Yes, sir, we did."

"Good work, Lieutenant," Kira said. *"Keep the station locked down. I'm going after the Ascendants."*

The idea seemed like a bad one to Dax. "Captain, they already destroyed one runabout, and very nearly a second one."

"Their shields are down to sixty percent," Kira said. *"That should give me a fighting chance."*

"Captain, this is Ro," said the security chief from beside the tactical console. "You shouldn't go alone. You can beam me aboard as you pass the station." Dax's jaw tightened at the interruption.

"Negative," Kira said. *"I'll do this myself. Dax, I need you to keep the station secure. Report everything that's happened to Starfleet Command, and request that the* Mjolnir *and the* Bellerophon *stay at Deep Space Nine once they arrive, at least until we can obtain a new warp core for the* Defiant.*"*

"Yes, sir." Ops suddenly brightened, and Dax looked to the viewscreen to see that the wormhole had opened, bathing the control center in its brilliant illumination. She watched as the Ascendant vessel flew into it, and then as the swirling currents of blue and white light folded in on themselves until no hint remained of their existence. "Captain—"

"I saw it," Kira said. *"I'm not far behind. If you don't hear from me in one hour, assume that I've been lost, and call Commander Vaughn back to the station aboard one of the* Defiant's *shuttlecraft."*

"Yes, sir." Dax knew the wealth of Vaughn's Starfleet experience, and she consequently understood the logic of recalling him to command the station in the captain's absence. Still, it bothered the lieutenant; it almost felt as though Kira did not trust Dax in command.

That's foolish, Dax chastised herself. After all, Kira actually *had* left her in command of the station. Moreover, Dax had not been promoted to the position of Deep Space 9's second officer all that long ago.

"Kira out."

Dax heard the tones that signaled the closing of the comm channel. She looked across her console at Ro, whose expression left little doubt that she thought the captain was making a mistake by chasing the Ascendant vessel by herself. But then Ops brightened again, and Dax gazed up at the viewer to see the wormhole opening once more.

A moment later, *Yolja* soared into the maelstrom.

The second ship limped away. Raiq briefly considered altering course to go after it, but decided against it. Her own vessel had taken some damage from the aliens, and so close to her goal, she did not want to jeopardize her chances of reaching it.

Raiq saw on her navigational instrumentation that she approached the spatial coordinates at which she had exited the Fortress of the True. Excitement brimmed within her, mixed with the nauseating certainty that she would be unable to find the gates. After all, the Ascendants had set out to prove their worthiness by performing a final sacrament for the Unnameable, and their armada had been wiped out, unable to vanquish a population of alleged heretics. It stood to reason that their failure demonstrated they were unfit to burn beneath the gaze of the True.

But then the emptiness of space bloomed before Raiq. A great, spinning formation of blue and white light rushed out of nowhere and twisted open. Emotion like none Raiq had ever experienced—not even when she had first passed through the gates—filled her so completely that she felt as though she might physically burst. She navigated her ship into the brilliant light, and then—

And then Raiq returned to the Fortress of the True. She beheld it as she had the first time: in awe. Opulent blue light swaddled her through the transparent canopy of her vessel. She saw enormous, glowing white rings as she soared past them, as though she traveled through a great tunnel, one that would carry her from the ordinary universe of Questers and heretics and heathens, into the sublime realm of the Unnameable. Circles formed, grew, and vanished on the periphery of the space, imbuing the journey with an even greater sense of motion.

The same forces that Raiq had encountered on her initial trek through the Fortress pummeled her ship once more. She modified the settings of the navigational deflector, using sensors to compensate for the spatial discontinuities. The turbulence eased, and the ship grew more stable.

In the cockpit of her vessel, Raiq waited, her emotions equally split between anticipation and apprehension. Would she burn before the True and be found worthy, or would her gods find her wanting? Would she join with the Unnameable, or be reduced to nothing more than a pile of cinders?

At that point, it didn't matter. She either would achieve the goal of every Ascendant who had ever lived, or she would relieve herself of the burden of false hope. At a minimum, the Quest would finally be at an end, and she felt thankful for that.

Except that it does matter. Raiq heard her own voice as a whisper, far back in her consciousness. *It does matter whether I join with the Unnameable.* She tried to convince herself that attaining the goal for which she and all her people had forever striven would lend value and meaning to the terrible loss they had just suffered. She tried to convince herself, but she couldn't. *I want this for myself,* she confessed. *I want—*

Up ahead, a circle of darkness appeared in the center of the flowing colors and shapes of the Fortress. Expectation thrilled through Raiq. She watched with wide eyes, eager to behold the True, and yet also uneasy.

The moment did not last. The round, black region expanded as she neared it, and with horror, Raiq recognized it from her first voyage through the Fortress of the True. The urge to slam her eyes shut nearly overwhelmed her, but she could not look away, even as she saw the gleam of starlight ahead.

Raiq's ship plunged through the opening and back into normal space. She identified arrangements of stars. *I'm back where I started,* she thought.

Without much thought, Raiq reached to the navigational controls and slowed her ship to a complete stop. Then she turned the craft so that she could look back at the path she had just traversed. The gates to the Fortress of the True had already folded back in on themselves and disappeared from view.

It's not the Fortress, she thought. *It's a subspace bridge . . . or a wormhole . . . or an interdimensional passage.*

Raiq closed her eyes and screamed.

As soon as *Yolja* emerged from the wormhole into the Gamma Quadrant, Kira saw the Ascendant vessel, even before she registered the chime of the proximity alert. She also realized that the ship had halted in space and turned in her direction. She quickly examined the main console to confirm the runabout's shields, then she reached for the phaser and microtorpedo controls.

To the captain's surprise, the Ascendant vessel did not fire on her, nor did it move. Kira brought *Yolja* to a halt, wondering if something had happened. Could the Prophets have intervened?

Of course, They could have, Kira thought. She also knew that her gods did not generally act so directly. For years, They had worked through the Emissary, though even he did not always comprehend Their will.

And what about me? Kira asked. *The Prophets called me Their Hand.* But she did not know what that meant, any more than she understood what They intended her to do.

Kira knew that the Prophets did not exist or act in a linear fashion, but she felt that she might already have failed in her role as the Hand. What more obvious situation could have a need for Their instrument than the arrival of a fleet of religious extremists? Kira had done little to combat the danger the people of Bajor had faced. And although the Ascendants had ultimately been stopped, thousands of scientists on Endalla had lost their lives.

Up ahead, clearly visible through the forward viewport of the runabout, the Ascendant vessel remained motionless. Kira opened a channel and tried once again to hail the invader. She received no response.

An alarm signaled in the main cabin of *Yolja* as the Ascendant ship fired its pulsing white beam. Kira moved her hands to the weapons panel, but before she activated the phaser or microtorpedo controls, she hesitated. The Ascendant's weapon had missed the runabout.

Confused, Kira scanned the enemy vessel. To her surprise, the sensors encountered none of the interference that had previously prevented the collection of detailed readings from any of the Ascendant ships. More than that, Kira saw that its shields had come down.

What's going on? During their attack on Bajor, and in

the brief historical account of their destruction of the Pilla-gra colony, the Ascendants had been nothing but relentless. Kira knew that the vessel just ahead had taken phaser and microtorpedo hits, and that its shields had been weakened, but they had not failed completely.

Kira used the sensors to scan the ship again. She read one life-form aboard. She located the Ascendant vessel's shield generators and found them intact. As she reviewed the readings, she saw the enemy's power levels drop further—not just on its shields, but on every ship's system: weapons, engines, life support. It was as though the Ascendant was surrendering.

No, not surrendering, Kira realized. *Committing suicide.* She thought about the fact that the Ascendant on that ship had been part of a fleet comprising thousands of her people, and that they had all perished. The captain tried to under-stand what the loss of so many must mean, and she readily found a frame of reference: the Occupation. In her own life, Kira had watched so many friends and comrades die. It had never grown easier, and many times, it had seemed almost too much to bear.

Kira reopened a channel and attempted once more to contact the Ascendant. Again, she received no response, but the sensor displays changed, showing that the engines of the enemy ship had begun a buildup to overload. In just seconds, she saw, the vessel would be reduced to dust.

Without hesitation, Kira erected a containment field around the compact transporter platform at the rear of *Yolja*'s main cabin. She then locked on to the cockpit of the Ascendant vessel and beamed out its lone occupant. The materialization sequence had just completed when the enemy ship exploded.

Kira stood up from her position at the runabout's main console and walked to the back of the cabin. The Ascendant stood on the transporter platform. At first glance, the captain thought it might actually be an artificial life-form. Tall and perfectly proportioned, it had an outer surface that gleamed silver. It had large, golden eyes, with radial lines around the outer edges. When it blinked, though, it lost any impression it gave that it might be an android.

The captain opened her mouth to say something, but the Ascendant dropped to its knees, then fell back against the rear of the transporter compartment. Its body began to tremble, and Kira wondered if it had been hurt during its altercation with *Platte* and *Volga*. She moved to the freestanding console in front of the transporter platform, intending to configure a sensor panel so that she could scan the alien for injuries, but then she stopped, realizing what she saw.

The Ascendant wept.

Interlude

Aftermath

February 2378

For what felt like the tenth time that shift, Ezri Dax sat at the situation table in Ops and reviewed Deep Space 9's external sensor logs. The same four ships remained docked at the station as yesterday: a Frunalian science vessel, a Rigelian transport, and a pair of freighters, one Alonis and the other Gallamite. As well, no ships had entered the orbit of Bajor, and the wormhole hadn't opened for any vessel other than one of DS9's own runabouts. Only the position of *Defiant* on its patrol of the system changed, and that hardly qualified as new, different, or interesting.

Six weeks had passed since the Ascendants had invaded the system and marched toward Bajor. The incident marked the latest in a series of demanding events that included the parasite crisis, Dax's trip to Trill with Julian and everything—both personal and professional—that happened there, and the entire convoluted situation involving Taran'atar and Iliana Ghemor. Dax faced all of those challenges, meeting her career responsibilities with considerable success. In many ways, though, Dax felt that her forward progress in Starfleet had stalled.

She thought back to before all of that, to *Defiant*'s three-month exploratory mission into the Gamma Quadrant. Much had taken place during the expedition, not all of it easy or positive, but despite the difficulties she'd endured, she could not deny that those had been the three best months of her career. Afterward, back on DS9, the captain assigned her to crew the communications console so that she would have a dedicated position in Ops. That allowed Kira and Vaughn to guide her as she settled into her posting as the station's second officer.

But then nothing happened, Dax thought. At least, it had seemed that way to her. She wanted to grow in her new position, wanted something different from what she had. Change did not happen quickly enough for her, or profoundly enough.

After serving for a year as second officer, she had applied for Advanced Tactical Training. Although DS9 already had an alpha-shift tac officer in Sam Bowers, Dax still believed that expanding the scope of her abilities would only make her a more valuable officer and help advance her career. After completing her training on Tellar and returning to the station, she chose to work alpha shift at communications and beta shift at tactical as she made the transition from one to the other.

Since the incident with the Ascendants, DS9 and the entire Bajoran system had been on high alert. *Mjolnir* stayed a week on patrol, and *Bellerophon* two, until a new comm relay could be put in place in the Gamma Quadrant, and a new warp core could be installed on *Defiant*. The station typically stocked a spare core, but the DS9 engineering staff had recently used it on *U.S.S. Erdős*, after the *Archimedes*-class starship had suffered a warp-system failure in an encounter with a cosmic string. After that, Commander Vaughn spent his shifts aboard ship, ensuring the safety of the Bajoran system, and he took Bowers with him. That left Dax as the de facto first officer aboard the station, working in Ops at tactical during alpha shift.

For the last week, Kira had been away on leave, and Dax had taken on the mantle of command. She'd looked forward to it, recalling the times during *Defiant*'s mission to the Gamma Quadrant when she'd captained the ship. To that point, though, the command experience aboard the station hadn't measured up to her expectations—not by a considerable measure.

And neither has my time at tactical, she thought. Dax hadn't expected her new skills to change her career overnight, but after two months—including the last week in command—she had started thinking about what else she could do. *Maybe I'm just not cut out for Starfleet. Maybe—*

Across the sit table and up the stairs, in Dax's line of sight, the lift ascended into Ops. It carried a single passenger: Quark. The Ferengi barkeep technically didn't have clearance to enter Ops—the lift shouldn't even have conveyed him there—but during her time on DS9, Dax had never known any rules or security measures to limit Quark.

"Lieutenant," the Ferengi said, even before the open lift had fully reached the deck. "I have a complaint." He held a cylindrical container upright between his two hands. He wore one of his tailored, varicolored jackets, the one that always put Dax in mind of a flyover view of farmland.

"Quark, when don't you have a complaint?" She looked up to the communications console and exchanged a look with Lieutenant Candlewood, who rolled his eyes.

"I appreciate the delicate nature of your ears," Quark said as he exited the lift and headed down the steps toward the lower, center level of Ops. "Imagine what I have to endure hearing with ears this big."

"It's always about size with you men, isn't it?" Dax retorted.

Quark reached the lower deck, paced up to the sit table, and deposited his container atop it. "I guess you would know, Lieutenant, since you've been a man . . . what, three times?"

Dax shook her head. She should have known better than to trade rejoinders with the barkeep. Jadzia had been able to keep up with him, but he always seemed to have a riposte for Ezri. "So what's your complaint?"

"May we talk privately?" Quark asked, gesturing toward the tallest set of stairs that led out of the center deck and up to Kira's office.

Dax offered a heavy sigh, which did not reflect any

annoyance with Quark—Ezri liked the barkeep, as had Jadzia before her—as much as it did her general sense of dissatisfaction. She immediately regretted her reaction. *That's not a sign of leadership,* she berated herself. "Of course," she said. "We can talk in the captain's office." She did not want any of the crew thinking that she had any delusions about replacing Kira Nerys.

Dax deactivated the padd she'd been reading and set it down on the sit table. Quark followed her up the steps and through the tall, patterned doors that led into the captain's office. Inside, Dax looked to the seating area off to the right, but then she circled the wide desk and sat down behind it. That left Quark to stand facing her. She saw that he had carried the cylindrical container with him, and he set it down on the desk.

"So what can I do for you, Quark?"

"You can help me with this," he said, uncapping the cylinder, reaching in, and pulling out an elegant cut-glass bottle filled with a pale-blue liquid.

"You want me to have a drink with you?"

"No," Quark said, but then he seemed to think better of his response. "I mean, yes, of course, that would be lovely, but that's not why I'm here. I need you to speak with Ensign Hava and get him to release my shipment."

"And why is Ensign Hava unwilling to release your shipment?" Dax already assumed that she would have to speak with the security officer to learn whatever details Quark either omitted or altered.

"I don't know," the barkeep said. He set the bottle down on the desk with a thump. "Maybe he's receiving a payoff from one of my competitors."

"Of course," Dax said. "It couldn't be that Romulan ale is illegal." She had recognized the notorious alcoholic beverage on sight.

Quark grunted. "The Federation has too many rules and regulations for its own good," he said with patent disgust. "But it also needs to make up its mind. I had Starfleet officers in my bar toasting the end of the war with Romulan ale. *You* were one of them."

"I remember," Dax said, though she actually didn't. There had been at least a couple of nights after the end of the Dominion War when she'd overindulged. "But that was then, this is now. You know that our relations with the Romulan Empire haven't been exactly smooth lately."

"Of course I know that," Quark said. "It's increased my Beta Quadrant shipping costs."

"Okay, so then you know about the new embargo, and you can understand why Ensign Hava impounded your shipment of Romulan ale," Dax said. "Forgetting for a moment that this is a security matter and you should be seeing Commander Ro about it, what do you expect me to do?" Dax felt the beginnings of a headache. She knew that the Ferengi had an on-again, off-again . . . what? Romance? Flirtation? Affair? Whatever the descriptor, he had some sort of personal relationship with Ro, which likely meant that he didn't want to jeopardize that by going to her with his problem.

"I want you to order the ensign to release my shipment," Quark said, "because this—" He swept up the heavy bottle and brandished it in the air. "—isn't Romulan ale."

"It's not?" Ezri had enjoyed the sometimes-licit, sometimes-not beverage on two or three occasions, but several other of Dax's previous hosts—particularly Curzon and Jadzia—had boasted an intimate knowledge of it. "Shall we do a taste test?"

Quark put the bottle back down, then laid both of his palms on the desktop and leaned toward Dax. "I didn't say that it didn't *taste* like Romulan ale."

Dax rubbed a finger in a tight circle on her temple. "All

right," she said, "so your shipment looks like it and tastes like it, but it's not Romulan ale." She stood up. "What do you take me for, Quark? Stop wasting my time." She made her way out from behind the desk and headed for the door.

"Lieutenant," Quark said, "I'm telling you the truth."

Dax stopped and faced Quark. "Why should I believe that?"

Quark shrugged. "Because of the One Hundredth Rule of Acquisition: 'When it's good for business, tell the truth.'" Dax scoffed, but the barkeep persisted. "I have ears, so I know that it's illegal to import Romulan ale. But it's not illegal to *make* it."

"What?"

"I have a supplier out by the Typhon Expanse," Quark said. "Most of the ingredients used to make Romulan ale are generic, like water and yeast. The key elements are the grains for brewing, and the berries for taste and the unique coloring. My supplier imports *kheh* and *dorish* from Terix Two, and *alota* fruit from ch'Havran. Grains and berries aren't on the embargo list."

"Clever," Dax said, genuinely appreciating Quark's well-deserved reputation as a sly operator. "Except that makes it sound like what you have there really is Romulan ale."

"If it's not produced within the Empire, then it's technically not Romulan ale."

"And I'm sure you share that technicality with your customers."

"I abide by the Thirty-ninth Rule of Acquisition: 'Don't tell customers more than they need to know.' Plus, just because the Romulans wouldn't want me calling it Romulan ale doesn't mean I can't."

"Uh-huh," Dax said, skeptical of the entire scheme. "Do you have proof of your claims?"

Quark whisked a Ferengi padd from the inside of his jacket. "I have all the details right here," he said.

Dax resisted the urge to sigh again. "All right," she said, plucking the device from Quark's hand. "I'll look into it."

"Thank you, Lieutenant."

"Is there anything else?"

"Just a reminder that, after the war, when Romulan ale was still legal in the Federation, one of my customers who especially enjoyed it was Commander Vaughn," Quark said. "So I'm sure he'd like having it available in the bar again."

"I'll keep that in mind," Dax said drily. She turned toward the doors, which parted before her, and started back down into Ops. As Quark followed after her and headed for the lift, Dax returned to the lower deck. She waited until the barkeep had disappeared from view before tossing his padd onto the situation table, where it clattered to a stop beside her own padd.

As Dax sat back down, Candlewood asked, "What was that all about?"

"It was just Quark in his eternal pursuit of profit," Dax said, shaking her head. She knew that part of the job description for officers aboard a space station, and specifically command officers, included dealing with the civilians aboard. On Deep Space 9, that necessarily meant dealing with the merchants on the Promenade, but that did not strike Dax as a good use of her time or abilities. She didn't really understood how Captain Kira and Commander Vaughn managed it.

Dax thought about reviewing the information on Quark's padd, but she decided she would do it later. Instead, she picked up her own padd so that she could finish reviewing the external sensor logs, but her gaze moved over the data without reading it. She had been in a foul mood before, and Quark's visit to Ops hadn't improved it.

What's wrong with me? she wondered. She hadn't always

been so cynical. For the second time, she considered whether or not she really belonged in Starfleet.

But it wasn't always like this, Dax reminded herself. She had been enthusiastic when she'd been posted to *Destiny,* and her time on the ship had been satisfying. Similarly, her three-month stint as *Defiant's* first officer had fulfilled her.

Maybe it's not Starfleet, she realized. *Maybe it's the posting.* Dax certainly got along with her crewmates, and some of them had become good friends. Despite sporadic flare-ups with Julian since they'd parted ways, they both managed to keep their on-duty interactions professional.

But the station . . . As Dax thought about it, she saw that she had come to view Deep Space 9 as an insular environment. That seemed impossible on the face of it, given the amount of interstellar traffic that passed through the place. Still, circumstances didn't change all that much for her from day to day, week to week.

Is that it? Dax thought, feeling as though she might have uncovered the source of her discontent. *Do I need a different setting? Not on a space station rooted in one location, but aboard a starship that's exploring the galaxy?*

The notion of leaving DS9 for good divided Dax's emotions. She had grown close to a number of her crewmates— Elias Vaughn, Sam Bowers, Mikaela Leishman, Simon Tarses—and it would be hard to leave them. And yet the possibility of serving once more aboard a starship definitely appealed to her.

It's not just the station, though, is it? Dax asked herself. *It's also about me—about my identity.* Ezri Tigan had never intended to be joined, had never trained for it, had never even fantasized about it. Despite the supposed joys and benefits of merging with a symbiont, she had never considered pursuing such a path. Circumstance had left her without much of a choice.

Joining had been an intense experience—an experience that, early on, had come close to overwhelming her. She quickly came to understand the inexpressible harmony Ezri and the Dax symbiont shared, but she also had trouble coherently navigating through a flood of memories and emotions not her own—at least, not her own in a way that she recognized. Eventually, the voices in her head blended into one coherent perspective: Ezri Dax, and the echoes of all the previous hosts of the symbiont became a single entity.

But I am the sum of my parts, she thought. *I am Ezri and I am Dax, but I am also Lela Yurani, Tobin Fendus, Emony Odaren, and all the rest of the hosts.* Maybe, in truth, she was more than that, a collection of lives and experiences that exceeded their mere combination.

But I want to be more even than that, Dax admitted to herself. *More—and* different. She didn't want to be a member of the Trill ruling council, as Lela had been. She didn't want to be an engineer like Tobin, or a gymnast like Emony. She wanted to forge her own unique self, rather than define herself too closely to how any of Dax's prior hosts had: as a Trill Symbiosis Commission member, as a pilot, as a musician, as a diplomat.

Or as a Starfleet officer on a space station.

Ezri Dax had done more than make peace with being joined; she had come to relish the knowledge and wisdom that came with having effectively lived for a quarter of a millennium. Still, she sometimes found her recollection muddled, and her sense of self tenuous. Sometimes, she found herself relating closely to Jadzia—uncomfortably so. The two had both served under the command of Curzon's friend. The two had both been attracted to Julian, and though they had taken different courses, they had both declined a long-term relationship with him.

And we both made our home on Deep Space Nine. Ezri

had tried to convince herself that was a small detail, a simple echo that did not wholly define either her or Jadzia, but she had never entirely convinced herself of that argument. How could she, when such significant aspects of her own existence—her career in Starfleet, her posting to DS9, her life on the station—mirrored those of Jadzia.

I have to do something, she thought.

Dax didn't know what she would do. She only knew that she would have to make some major changes in her life.

Kira looked up as the bend in the gently flowing river carried her canoe along a steep stone wall. The rock face rose impressively high above her, and it actually angled out slightly over the water, but she judged that, with the numerous cracks she saw, it would not be too difficult to scale. She had no intention of doing any climbing during her trip, but she could never stop herself from examining her surroundings, either for a means of escape, or for an avenue of attack.

I was taught well, Kira thought. She'd spent most of her life struggling to free her people, and almost a decade since then as a soldier on Deep Space 9. *But not just as a soldier,* she corrected herself. She also functioned as an aide, as a liaison, as a diplomat, as a leader. Still, she could not deny that she considered herself a woman of action.

As the easy current of the upper Elestan River pulled Kira into the shade thrown by the escarpment, the air temperature dipped noticeably. She appreciated the break from the hot summer sun. It took a moment for her eyes to adjust to the shadows, but when they did, she saw a thick wood marching up to the other side of the river. She had reached the edge of the Graldom Forest, where she intended to set up camp for the night. She would continue on in her canoe for

perhaps another hour, which would leave her with enough time before sunset to find a suitable place to camp.

Kira had rarely taken extended leave during her service aboard Deep Space 9. Throughout her years in the Resistance, there had been no such thing as a holiday. Consequently, on the station, she most often sought rest and renewal in ways long familiar to her: by meditating at the small shrine she kept in her quarters, by immersing herself in the sacred texts, and by visiting the Bajoran temple on the Promenade.

After everything that had happened since she'd taken command of DS9, though, she'd found herself almost swept away by a growing sense of fatigue. From the N-vector viroid that infected the station two years earlier, through to the days of the Ascendant invasion, a series of threatening events demanded her continual attention and labors. Additionally, so many of those incidents impacted her directly, including her attainder by the Vedek Assembly; a mind-controlled Taran'atar attacking and almost killing her; the replacement of her damaged heart with an artificial organ; her encounters with the two versions of Iliana Ghemor; and her contacts with the Prophets, within and without the Celestial Temple.

In the days immediately after the Ascendant invasion, Kira had worked hard to ensure the safety of both DS9 and the entire Bajoran system. She coordinated with Captains Kalena Hoku and Nthanda Naidoo of *Mjolnir* and *Bellerophon*, respectively, to patrol on both sides of the wormhole while *Defiant* underwent repairs and the installation of a new warp core. Kira also dispatched her own crew in runabouts to replace the comm relay in the Gamma Quadrant. She held services on the station for the scientific teams lost on Endalla, and she attended a memorial on Bajor.

Kira had also reviewed *Yolja*'s sensors logs, as well as those of *Defiant*, in an attempt to determine precisely what had

happened to result in the destruction of the Ascendant fleet. She assigned DS9's primary science officer, Lieutenant John Candlewood, to oversee a detailed analysis of those readings. Neither he nor anybody else could reach a definitive conclusion about what had taken place in what people had begun calling the *Even Odds* disaster—although nobody seemed to want to talk about the fact that without the destruction of the peculiar vessel, the Bajoran people might have faced a loss of life that would have dwarfed what they had endured under Cardassian oppression.

Even Odds had been identified by, of all people, Jake Sisko. While visiting his grandfather on Earth, he saw images of the ship on the comnet, and he immediately transmitted a message to Benjamin on Bajor. More than a year and a half prior, Jake had been rescued in the Gamma Quadrant by the crew of *Even Odds*. Nobody could explain how Taran'atar had come to be aboard the ship, or whether or not its crew had perished with him. Lieutenant Candlewood believed that the boundaries between the normal space-time continuum and its underlying, foundational dimensions had somehow been broken down aboard *Even Odds*, resulting in subspace waves emanating from the newly opened aperture.

Sensor sweeps around Bajor by the crew of *Bellerophon* had confirmed that the explosion of *Defiant*'s warp core had sealed the fractures in space. Endalla read as geologically stable, but it had been transformed from a living, breathing world into a dead, airless rock. Not a single individual who'd been on the moon survived, nor were any of their bodies recovered.

A thorough search of the historical record provided little additional information about the Ascendants. The only recorded encounter with them had been by the crew of *Enterprise* a century earlier, at Pillagra, although they had been believed responsible at that time for the destruction of

two other Bajoran colonies, Gelladorn and Velat Nol. Itu gave an account of his people's historic experiences with the Ascendants, which had driven the Eav'oq into hiding for millennia. After the attack on Bajor, Itu and his diplomatic team returned to their own world, and later sent a message requesting that they be left alone while they processed the meaning and implications of what had taken place.

Kira shook her head, as though physically trying to clear her thoughts, and her canoe rocked from side to side. Back on Deep Space 9, the measures she usually employed to find peace of mind hadn't worked. The captain considered paying a visit to Phillipa Matthias or one of the station's other counselors, or even simply talking with some of her friends, but she didn't quite know what to say about how she felt—not that she was particularly inclined to have those sorts of conversations anyway. She also thought about speaking with one of the vedeks on DS9, but she feared they would pronounce her assertions of contact with the Prophets as orb shadows or even delusions; Bajorans believed fully in their gods, and that They communicated with Their people by way of various types of visions, but not that They spoke directly with anyone other than the Emissary.

Five weeks after the invasion, when *Mjolnir* and *Bellerophon* had departed, and life aboard the station had returned to normal, Kira put in for a two-week leave on Bajor. She decided to hike alone along the foothills of the Glyrshar Mountains, to Densori's Landing, where she would take to the water, traversing the Elestan down to the Graldom Forest. She hoped that the solitude and the physical activity would allow her to take her mind off her troubles and find a way to renew herself.

After a while, the escarpment fell away and Kira paddled back out into the sunlight. The swollen orange orb of B'hava'el had descended low in the sky, and so the captain scouted for a good location to go ashore. When she spotted a small riverside clearing, she headed for it. She pulled her canoe up onto the bank and secured it, then collected her rucksack and carryall, and she traipsed inland.

Inside the wood, Kira's feet pushed into a soft bed of fallen needles. She smelled the strong scent of pine. The muffled twitter of birds reached her from above, accompanied by the sawlike hum of *lopa* bugs. At one point, she startled a *hyurin*, the fist-size rodent scampering away from her.

When Kira judged that she had walked far enough from the river that its burble would not keep her awake through the night, she found a patch of level ground and dropped her gear. She slipped off her flotation vest—thin and comfortable when dry, it expanded to a buoyant form when immersed in water. As she unpacked and pitched her tent, she could not help thinking of her days on the run in the Resistance. *Except that tents and sleeping rolls would have been considered luxuries.* She'd had similar thoughts often on her trip, and not for the first time, she wondered why she had chosen to take her leave in a way that approximated her life during the Occupation.

Don't be so melodramatic, Kira chastised herself. Nobody chased her through the forest, nobody pointed a weapon in her direction. She would not drift off to sleep that night alert for the sound of approaching footsteps, fearful that she would wake to find herself in Cardassian custody—if she even woke up at all. Her life had changed significantly since those days, and in all ways for the better.

Then why do I feel so unsettled? Kira had taken leave because she'd felt troubled, and she'd thought that time away from the burdens of command would necessarily fix that. *But it's not being the captain of Deep Space Nine that's upsetting me.* Each day that had passed with no real change in her mind-set had brought her closer to that admission.

The night before, as she strived to relax enough to sleep, she replayed the decisions she'd made and the actions she'd taken once it had become clear that the Bajoran system faced an alien invasion. Starfleet Command had not found fault with her leadership, but she searched for the mistakes she was sure she'd made. Fortunately, the physical demands of her dawn-to-dusk hike that day caused her to drift off despite her agitation.

Kira finished setting up her tent, then laid out her bedroll inside it. Although she didn't really need a fire—she'd brought a portable cooking pad with her—she made several trips back to the river to find stones. She formed them into a circle by her tent. She hunted down some dead wood and kindling, then used a flint to ignite a flame.

By the time Kira had prepared and eaten her evening meal, night had fallen on Graldom Forest. The daytime heat gave way to crisp air, but she warmed herself by the fire. The capering flames dredged up more memories. She pictured her mother and father, her two brothers, Reon and Pohl, bathed in the flickering light of a small stove in the Singha refugee camp. She recalled Furel and Lupaza, Reyla and Mobara, comrades in the Resistance, sitting around a campfire in one of the many caves in which they'd hidden.

They're all gone now, Kira thought. *All of my family, and almost all of my friends from that time.* Her recollections didn't sadden her any more than they ever did; she had long ago accepted such losses, for to do otherwise would have been to dishonor their memories and to relegate herself to a sort of walking death.

The darkness deepened around Kira, out beyond the meager glow of the fire. Dull aches suffused her legs from all of the hiking she'd done that week, while she felt deeper pain in her shoulders after her first day on the river. She realized that she wanted nothing more at that moment than to sleep—preferably without dreaming—but as she moved to extinguish the fire, she realized that she hadn't checked the padd she'd brought with her.

Kira reluctantly pulled her carryall from inside the tent, not really wanting to find if she'd been sent a message, but knowing that she should. She shuffled through the contents of the tube-shaped bag until she found her padd. She activated it and saw at once that she'd received a message from Vedek Yevir Linjarin.

There had been a time when an attempt by Yevir to contact her would have elicited a strong reaction from Kira— somewhere on the spectrum between frustration and anger. The vedek had not that long ago served as a lieutenant in the Bajoran Militia. Posted to DS9, he had a chance encounter with the Emissary, which altered the trajectory of his life. Walking among the people on the Promenade, Benjamin Sisko approached Yevir, touched his shoulder, and counseled him that he didn't belong there, that he should go home. In that moment, Yevir understood that he had to that point wasted his dull, inconsequential life, and he felt called to religious service. Within hours, he resigned from the Militia and returned to Bajor. The next day, he became a novice and began his religious studies.

Kira had heard the story several times. Yevir apparently reveled in telling it, and though it easily could have been a tale told—even though true—as a political calculation, the captain believed the profundity of the incident's impact on him. It actually inspired Kira, and reminded her of her good fortune that she knew the Emissary not just on a professional basis, but as a friend.

Yevir's personal story resonated with many others, among the laity and beyond, which helped explain his meteoric rise through the ranks of the Bajoran clergy. He advanced from novice to prylar to ranjen to vedek in just two years, an astonishingly rapid progression. Many believed that he would someday become kai, though he had not submitted his name for consideration by the Vedek Assembly when they had chosen a new spiritual leader the previous year.

Yevir characterized his beliefs as conservative, which differed from how Kira felt about her own faith. Never had the vedek's traditionalism been more on display than after the discovery of the Ohalu texts, which proclaimed the Prophets not as gods, but as powerful and benevolent aliens. Opinion divided sharply among the vedeks about how to handle the controversial material, with Yevir strongly advocating for keeping what he considered heretical documents from ever being made public. When Kira uploaded translations of the texts in their entirety to the Bajoran comnet, Yevir spearheaded efforts to have Kira attainted—efforts that succeeded, at least for a time, in excommunicating her from the Bajoran faith.

But while the vedek identified as conservative, Kira had discovered that she could not always use that as a predictor of either his interpretation of religious tenets or on what side of an issue he would fall. To his credit, he did not appear to react to issues based upon the accepted views of orthodoxy; rather, he seemed to study matters on a case-by-case basis, and with an open mind. His overtures to the Oralian Way, an ancient Cardassian religious group, marked one example of Yevir acting contrary to popular traditional thought.

Kira played the message. *"Captain Kira, I hope you are well, and that you are finding peace on your travels."* Yevir spoke calmly, almost languidly, but his sharp-eyed visage betrayed the exactitude with which he chose his words. He and Kira had spoken several times over the last month, including just before the captain had taken her leave. Always perceptive, he plainly had discerned the disquiet within her. *"I am loath to contact you during this time away from your duty,"* Yevir continued, *"but I am concerned that Raiq has reached a critical juncture."* The Ascendant, after much public debate on Bajor and even in the wider Federation, currently resided at the Shikina Monastery in the Bajoran capital of Ashalla, though her legal status remained unresolved. *"She still has many questions, but she is also distrustful of virtually everybody."* Yevir paused, signaling his intention to emphasize what he would say next. *"Everybody, that is, except you."*

Kira could not be entirely sure why Raiq had come to trust her. It might simply have been because the captain had been the first person the Ascendant had encountered after the isolytic subspace weapon had wiped out the rest of her people. Or perhaps Raiq had been influenced by Kira's unwillingness to fire on her unprotected vessel. But the captain also wondered if it had anything to do with what she had said to the Ascendant aboard *Yolja*, or in the hours and days afterward, aboard DS9.

Six weeks earlier, in the Gamma Quadrant, Kira had beamed the Ascendant onto her runabout, into a containment field erected around the transporter platform. The gleaming alien crumpled to her knees and fell back against the rear bulkhead, her body quaking. "I am Kira Nerys," the captain told the gleaming alien. "I am the commanding officer of the space station on the other side of the wormhole."

At that, the Ascendant raised her head. " 'Wormhole'?" she said. Kira's universal translator rendered the word in Federation Standard, but the captain heard the unexpectedly musical quality of the uninterpreted speech.

The Ascendant's paroxysms of grief abated as she stared at Kira. The captain saw no tears on her face, nor anything that approximated them, but she remained convinced that the alien had been crying—or whatever the equivalent might be for her species. "Yes, a wormhole," Kira said, thinking that perhaps the word failed to translate in whatever device the Ascendant used for communication. "A subspace bridge physically linking two points distant from each other in normal space."

"Then it is not the Fortress of the True," the Ascendant said, looking away from Kira. "Or maybe . . . maybe it is. There's nothing in the scriptures that would contradict that." She seemed to be speaking more to herself than to the captain, apparently debating some sort of religious idea. "Or maybe," she went on, peering back up at Kira, "the Fortress is a myth. Maybe *all* of it is a myth." Despite that she had uttered it, the suggestion clearly angered her.

"I don't know," Kira said. "I don't know what it is you're talking about, and I don't know why your people came here to destroy my people." In truth, the historical record spoke of the Ascendants who attacked Pillagra a century prior objecting to the Bajorans falsely worshipping the True, but she wanted to hear about the reason behind the invasion directly from the alien.

"We were told that you are heretics," the Ascendant said.

"But our religion is not your religion. We do not worship your gods."

"There is but one set of real gods. Either you worship them or you do not."

Kira didn't know whether or not to reveal details about the Bajoran culture, but since the Ascendants already felt justified in attacking Bajor, she did not see how the truth could make things worse. "We worship the Prophets, not the True."

"On the Quest, we have learned that just because a race of aliens calls the gods something different from what we do does not mean that they are not our gods."

"And that was reason enough to want to destroy us?"

"Blasphemers must be vanquished, either because they worship false gods, or because they dare to worship the

True," the Ascendant said. "So it is written, so it must be done."

"Unless it's all a myth," Kira ventured, echoing the doubts already expressed by the Ascendant, who seemed to deflate at the words. The captain thought of the Ohalavaru and their belief that the Prophets were not divine. "You did not personally participate in the attack. You stopped the launch of the subspace weapon, and then just before the attack began, you fled."

The Ascendant dropped her head. "I believed that we needed the weapon to help us join with the True in the Fortress." The vision of somebody detonating an explosive device of any kind, let alone an isolytic subspace weapon, within the Celestial Temple chilled Kira. "It might be that my acting against the Fire doomed my people."

The words resonated in Kira's mind: *the Fire*. She recalled the Prophets dubbing Iliana Ghemor with that title before sending her away. At the time, Kira had believed that They had removed Ghemor as a threat to Bajor, but that had obviously not been the case. The captain's mind reeled as she wrestled with the meaning of it all. She knew better than to think that she could know the minds of the Prophets, but for just a moment, the answers seemed almost in her reach.

"Why did you flee?" Kira asked.

The Ascendant shook her head, a gesture that appeared to carry the same meaning as it did for many other humanoid species. "I ran from the situation because . . . I think because I was trying to outrun my own heterodoxy."

"Your faith did not align with that of the other Ascendants?"

"For all of my life, it did . . . until now." The expression of sadness on her face transcended species.

"Is that why you lowered your shields?" Kira asked. "So that I would fire on you . . . so that you would die?"

"My doubts do not deserve to live."

The articulation of the Ascendant's guilt struck a chord in Kira. It seemed a terrible—and unnecessary—burden. "We all have doubts," she said. "That does not make us unworthy of our faith." She hesitated, searching for the right words. "Sometimes, answering our doubts can strengthen our beliefs."

"You have doubted?"

"I am an imperfect adherent," Kira said, admitting something difficult even to think about. The Prophets had called her Their Hand, and yet confronted with an existential threat to all of Bajor, she had accomplished almost nothing. She had been little more than a bystander as the Emissary, First Minister Asarem, Minister of Defense Aland, Captain Vaughn, and even the Eav'oq diplomat, Itu, had handled the situation. "I am imperfect, but I strive for better understanding."

Again, the Ascendant shook her head. "I no longer know what to believe."

Kira felt the Ascendant's pain. The loss of friends and family brought terrible anguish, but life could eventually go on. *If you lose the core of who you are, though, you could lose all hope.*

The captain had stepped up to the containment field surrounding the transporter pad and lowered herself to her knees. She faced the Ascendant at eye level. "Maybe if we talk . . . if we work together . . . maybe I can help you figure it out."

In front of her campfire, Kira blinked. She realized that, lost in recollection, she hadn't heard anything of Yevir's message after his mention of Raiq. She operated the padd to replay it.

"Captain Kira, I hope you are well, and that you are finding peace on your travels. I am loath to contact you during this

time away from your duty, but I am concerned that Raiq has reached a critical juncture. She still has many questions, but she is also distrustful of virtually everybody . . . everybody, that is, except you.

"*In recent days, Raiq stopped speaking,*" Yevir went on. "*A doctor confirmed that there was nothing physically wrong with her. She continued to read the Bajoran canon, and also to record, from memory, Ascendant scripture. We cannot tell with certainty, but she might be attempting, or planning to attempt, a comparative analysis.*"

Kira understood why such an appraisal threatened Yevir: while he kept an open mind about most issues, he did not appreciate what he considered attacks on Bajoran religious doctrine. The captain did not worry about people who did not believe as she did, or even about those who judged her faith as misguided. After the invasion of the Bajoran system, though, it made sense to fear that more Ascendants might one day arrive and feel justified in launching another attack—although Kira believed Raiq's claim that the fleet had comprised every living member of her people.

"*Today, Raiq finally responded to my efforts to communicate with her,*" Yevir said. "*As I mentioned, she has many questions. I endeavored to answer them for her, but she quickly became frustrated, and it was clear that we had difficulty making ourselves understood by one another. Vedek Kyli volunteered to speak with Raiq, but their conversation did not last long and produced the same results. Afterward, Raiq suggested that, if she was going to talk with anybody, it should be with you. I know that you are away, but if you can find any time at all to contact her, I think that it would help her. I also think it might aid all of us here at the monastery in establishing a level of trust with our guest.*" The message ended and the screen went dark.

Kira took note of Yevir's use of the word *guest* in referring to Raiq. Just a month and a half earlier, it would have been unthinkable. Invaders bent on destruction are rarely invited to stay.

Kira had brought Raiq back to Deep Space 9 and imprisoned her in the most secure cell on the station. Starfleet promptly preferred a number of charges against her, mostly minor offenses such as criminal trespass and failure to respond to officials, simply so that they could continue to detain her legally. First Minister Asarem directed the Bajoran Militia to conduct an investigation into Raiq's actions during the invasion, with the aim of charging her with whatever crimes she had committed. Starfleet Command ordered a full and detailed report from Kira.

Raiq initially spoke with several of the people who visited her. Members of the Ministry of Law traveled from Bajor, both to take her statement and to provide her legal counsel. An officer from Starfleet's judge advocate general's office on Empyrion VI also arrived with an offer of representation. Unfamiliar with such procedures, Raiq declined to have anybody speak on her behalf. She understood that she would face judgment and punishment, but such prospects did not appear to concern her. Kira got the distinct impression that Raiq believed she could battle her way out of custody if she chose to do so. The captain worked with Ro Laren to make sure that couldn't happen.

As time wore on, Raiq became more reticent in communicating with visitors, other than with Kira, and also with members of the Bajoran clergy, about whom she seemed very curious. She answered the captain's questions, which primarily focused on the series of events that began with the Ascendant fleet entering the Idran system in the Gamma Quadrant. As far as Kira could tell, Raiq had actually broken few laws. She had not been part of the ten-ship squadron that had fired on the Eav'oq city of Terev'oqu. Similarly, she had not attacked any of the Bajoran vessels that had been sent to meet the Ascendant threat, or even any of the automated weapons platforms. Raiq even prevented Iliana Ghemor from launching the isolytic subspace weapon when first the Cardassian had tried to do so. By the time the Ascendants moved into attack formation and started toward Bajor, Raiq had already decamped the fleet and set course back toward the wormhole. She did fire on a pair of runabouts, *Platte* and *Volga*, destroying the former, but with no loss of life.

The question of what the authorities in the Bajoran and Federation governments should do with Raiq, apparently the last surviving member of her species, became a thorny question. Some believed her actions merited serious punishment. Others pointed to her preventing Ghemor's initial attempt to launch the metaweapon as a mitigating circumstance, and they suggested that she deserved probation, if not an outright pardon. Some called her a zealot, others a religious exile. Public rage at the Ascendants for their attempted genocide transmuted in some quarters into sympathy for Raiq, who many believed had exhibited great courage in acting against her own people. The fact that she had stopped Ghemor from using the isolytic subspace weapon because she'd hoped to use it for another purpose, and that she'd still wanted to destroy the Bajorans with conventional weapons, got lost during the discourse.

After Raiq spent two weeks imprisoned on Deep Space 9, the Federation and Starfleet agreed to allow Bajoran officials to take full charge of the matter. Extradition took place at once. Raiq was remanded into Bajoran custody and taken to a maximum-security facility outside Ashalla to await trial. Several high-profile vedeks, including Yevir, visited with her. Some—again, including Yevir—concluded that Raiq was the victim of religious indoctrination, oppressed by a society that did not permit dissenting opinion or even freedom of expression.

Just before Kira had begun her leave, Asarem Wadeen had accepted the recommendation of the Ministry of Law, reached in concordance with Raiq and Yevir, that the Ascendant be granted probation for her crimes and released into the custody of the Shikina Monastery. The captain agreed that justice would not have been served by incarceration. Kira hoped that Raiq would be able to find peace after an entire life essentially devoted to destruction.

The captain held up her padd and activated its communications interface, then contacted Yevir. She expected to transmit a message, but then the channel opened and his face appeared on the display. "Vedek Yevir, I didn't expect to find you available," Kira said. "I just reviewed your message."

"I made myself available tonight, Captain, just in case you chose to contact me," Yevir said. *"I'm glad that you did."*

"I'll be happy to talk with Raiq," Kira said, "although I'm not really sure what either she or you think I can tell her."

"It is also unclear to me just what Raiq is looking for," Yevir said, *"and I suspect that it may be just as unclear to her. Regardless, it does seem that you and she have developed a rapport."*

"I'm not entirely certain why that's the case," Kira admitted, "but as I said, I'll be happy to speak with her. I'm heading back to Deep Space Nine in six days, so I'll visit the monastery before I do."

Yevir looked down, and Kira could see that he had more he wanted to say. She waited to see whether or not he would. When he peered back up, he said, *"I'm aware that you are on leave, Captain, one that I have no doubt is well earned."* Kira heard no sarcasm or dismissal in the vedek's tone. Though she and Yevir had opposed each other in the matter of the Ohalavaru texts, they had also had contact with each other since, and in every instance, they had both conducted themselves on a professional level. *"I am therefore asking you this knowing that it is an imposition, but would it be possible for you to speak to Raiq tonight?"*

Kira looked away from her padd and over at the fire. She wondered if the dancing flames showed on her face. She did not actually want to talk with Raiq just then—not because she didn't want to interrupt her time away from DS9, but because the Ascendant's circumstances and her questions somehow touched too closely on some of the uncertainty that she had been feeling. The captain decided, though, that she did not want her own struggles to interfere with Raiq's attempts to make sense of recent events and beyond.

"Very well," Kira said. "When you and I finish speaking, I will contact her."

"I wonder," Yevir said, *"would you mind if we transported you from your location to the Shikina Monastery? I believe that your communication will be more effective if it takes place in person."*

Before she could stop herself, Kira sighed. She did not really mind the idea, but she felt too tired to have to deal with Yevir or anybody else at the monastery. Still, she agreed with the vedek about the superiority of a face-to-face conversation, rather than one conducted over a padd. "Why don't you beam Raiq to my location?"

"I . . . don't know, Captain," Yevir said. "While we are not legally responsible for Raiq, it is our tacit understanding with the first minister and the minister of law that we are to supervise her for as long as she remains on Bajor."

"The Shikina Monastery is hardly a stronghold," Kira said. "Do you honestly believe that you could keep Raiq there if she chose to leave?"

"No, of course not," Yevir said.

"Then if she wants to talk to me tonight, transport her here."

The vedek took a moment to respond, but he eventually

acquiesced. Several minutes later, he contacted Kira again to say that Raiq did indeed want to visit her. Shortly after that, the Ascendant materialized in a hail of shimmering white light.

Raiq greeted the captain cautiously. The two hadn't seen each other in some time, and the Ascendant appeared to need to ease into renewing their acquaintance. Kira stood up and offered Raiq the pad on which she'd been sitting, then she retrieved her carryall and emptied it inside her tent. She laid out the bag on the ground for herself.

"Vedek Yevir tells me that you've been studying the Bajoran holy texts," the captain said as she sat down, bringing her knees up and wrapping her arms around them. Raiq followed suit, lowering herself onto her haunches. Her exoskeleton mirrored the red of the campfire, making her look as though flames engulfed her.

"Yes." Kira waited, but Raiq seemed disinclined to say more.

"What have you read?"

"*The Prophecies of Trakor*, *When the Prophets Cried*, and *Shines the Celestial Temple*," Raiq said.

"Those are some hefty tomes," Kira said. "Have you formed any opinions?"

"It is . . . difficult." Kira nodded, realizing how uncomfortable it must have been for an individual of such obviously strong beliefs—*ingrained* beliefs—to expose herself to the teachings of another religion. "There are many . . ." Raiq began, but her musical voice quieted before she finished her thought.

"Many differences?" Kira prompted.

Raiq did not respond, and the captain worried that she might have somehow offended her. Kira waited a moment, then opened her mouth to apologize. Before she could, Raiq said, "No. No, not differences. There are many . . . similarities."

The declaration surprised Kira, just as it had apparently surprised Raiq. The captain didn't know much about Raiq's religion beyond the imperative to eradicate both those who venerated false gods, and those who dared to worship the Ascendants' gods, whom they called either the True or the Unnameable. That alone made it hard to imagine that Raiq's faith could have much in common with Kira's. "How are they similar?" she asked.

"In myriad small ways, but most disturbingly in some areas of major significance," Raiq said. "What you call the Celestial Temple undoubtedly equates to the Fortress of the True. Your nine Tears of the Prophets parallel the nine Eyes of Fire. And the descriptions of your gods, the nature of them, their mysterious ways . . . it is plain to me that the Prophets are in reality the Unnameable."

The conclusion dismayed Kira. "Then you believe what Iliana Ghemor . . . what the Fire . . . told you," she said. "That my people are heretics, that we falsely worship your gods." *Does that mean she believes it is her duty to wipe out the Bajoran people?*

Raiq bolted to her feet, and for just an instant, Kira thought the Ascendant might attack her. But then she turned and strode away, past the campfire and to the edge of the circle it illuminated. "It is that simple no longer," she said. "For my entire life, and for millennia before, it was an uncomplicated equation: Continue the Quest. Search for the Fortress. Along the way, rid the universe of heretics. Come the End Time, follow the Fire on the Path to the Final Ascension. Enter the Fortress, burn beneath the gaze of the True, and for the worthy among the Knights, join with our gods."

Kira didn't know what in particular troubled Raiq, and she didn't know what to say or what to ask. Instead, she waited, and at last, Raiq walked back and faced her across the campfire. "But the Final Ascension never took place," she said, spitting the words as though they were poison in her mouth. "If the Celestial Temple *is* the Fortress, then when we first entered it, why didn't we burn beneath the gaze of the True? Why were we not judged? And if the Celestial Temple is *not* the Fortress, if the Prophets are not the True, then your people are not the heretics the Fire claimed them to be. You worship false gods, but you do not falsely worship the Unnameable. Your destruction would not have been worthy of a final sacrament. The Fire . . ." Raiq raised both hands to the sides of her head, as though trying to keep it from exploding.

"The Fire lied to you," Kira said as gently as she could. Even though all of the Ascendants but Raiq had perished, the captain still wanted to disabuse her of the notion that the Bajoran people deserved to die.

Raiq dropped her hands to her sides. "It seems obvious to me now that the one who led us to the Fortress . . . or to the Celestial Temple . . . was not actually the Fire."

But she was, Kira thought. *Iliana Ghemor was the Fire. The Prophets declared her so.* But she did not say that to Raiq. *Because if Ghemor was the Fire, and she was meant to lead the Ascendants here . . . what did that mean?*

Raiq looked up, as if to see the stars, but when Kira lifted her gaze as well, she could see no patch of sky through the forest canopy. "We followed an imposter," Raiq said. "We allowed ourselves to be pulled from the Quest . . . and now I am the only one left."

"What do you intend to do?"

Raiq peered over at Kira with a puzzled look. "I am doing it," she said. "I am searching for the meaning in what has happened. I must discover how I have erred so that I can move forward, so that I can reinitiate the Quest."

The level of Raiq's commitment to her faith impressed Kira. Despite the vast differences between Bajoran and

Ascendant, and what they each believed—no matter whatever correspondence there might be between the two creeds—the captain related to the strength of Raiq's piety. In following their faith, all but one of the Ascendants had perished, and yet the sole survivor sought to understand where she and her people had gone wrong so that she could recommit herself to her beliefs. Kira wanted to help her, wanted to guide her along her spiritual path, but—

But how can I? she wondered. *I need guidance in my own life.* Kira felt exhausted from years and years of battle, but she actually thought that the bulk of her fatigue stemmed from her inadequacy in playing the role the Prophets had intended for her. She did not believe herself worthy of the designation "the hand of the Prophets."

I have to do something, she thought. *I must earn the place the Prophets have set for me.*

Kira realized that she would need to recommit herself to her faith. It would require effort—not just praying, not just reading the canon, not just attending temple services. It would necessarily entail study and exploration, of both her religion and her own inner life. It would take time. Maybe that meant that she would have to step away from command, or perhaps from military service entirely. At that moment, Kira didn't know just how she would change her circumstances, only that she had to do so.

She gazed at Raiq, into her large golden eyes, which seemed even in stillness to be constantly, desperately searching for something. Kira could imagine the same look in her own eyes. "Maybe," she told Raiq, "we can look for what we each need, together."

II

Transit

December 2385

In the simulated morning aboard Deep Space 9, Captain Ro Laren tapped the chime control next to the door, then stepped back to stand beside Pralon Onala. A pair of Bajoran Militia officers attended them. The two, a woman and a man, functioned as security for the spiritual leader.

The kai had arrived on DS9 the previous night, in response to an invitation from Ro to tour the new starbase, which had begun full operation only a few months earlier. Pralon had not announced her visit ahead of time, even to the captain. In part, that had been because Ro's offer to show the kai around Deep Space 9 had been a pretext, and the kai understood that. In reality, the captain wanted to speak to Pralon about Altek Dans, the man who had emerged from the wormhole on an Orb, apparently carried out of Bajoran history. Because of recent events—the assassination of the UFP president, the initial arrest of the first minister's chief of staff for the crime, and then the revelation that Ishan Anjar, Bajor's representative on the Federation Council, had conspired to kill Nan Bacco and succeed her—Asarem Wadeen and her government had been reluctant to deal with Altek's situation.

The door panel glided open. Altek stood just inside, tall and dressed in fashionable togs—black slacks and a sleek, two-toned crimson shirt—looking more like he had just stepped out of a modern clothier's than out of the past. His short, dark hair complemented his handsome, sculpted, clean-shaven face. Since his arrival, his tanned complexion had faded a shade or two.

"Captain Ro," he said with a wide, winning smile. When Altek had decided that he wanted to go home to Bajor, his request had essentially met with silence from the Bajoran government. It had been Ro's idea to enlist the aid of the clergy, and Vedek Brandis Tarn had in turn suggested inviting the kai to the starbase. When Pralon had arrived under the guise of visiting DS9 for the first time, the captain had informed Altek that the kai would indeed meet with him.

"Doctor Altek," Ro said, and she made formal introductions.

"Won't you please come in?" Altek asked, stepping aside and motioning into the living area of the guest quarters he had been assigned.

"Thank you," Pralon said, entering the tasteful but generically decorated cabin. Ro followed her inside, while the Militia officers took up positions in the corridor, on either side of the door.

"May I offer you some refreshments?" Altek asked. He moved past Ro and the kai to a seating area, where a small sofa and two overstuffed chairs surrounded a low, circular glass table.

"A cup of *deka* tea, thank you," Pralon said.

Altek chuckled as he headed toward the replicator on the far side of the compartment. "I've never heard of that," he said, "but I'm sure that this machine has."

"Why don't you sit down with the kai and I'll get the tea," Ro suggested. "What would you like?"

"I suppose I'll try some of the tea," Altek said. "After all, if I want to return to Bajor, I should get accustomed to what we're eating and drinking these days." The effort to casually bring up his desire to go back to Bajor, and to count himself as one of its people, struck the captain as clumsy. It also seemed out of character for the socially adept doctor. Ro guessed that he must be nervous.

Ro walked over to the replicator and ordered three cups of deka tea, while Pralon sat down on the sofa, and Altek took a chair across from her. "Where did you grow up on Bajor?" the kai asked, deftly mixing pleasantries with the purpose of her visit.

"I was born in Revek, but when I was very young, my family moved to Davenesh," Altek said. "I attended medical school in Joradell and then stayed there when I became a doctor."

As the replicator hummed and delivered Ro's order in a haze of white light, Pralon said, "I'm sure it won't surprise you that I've never heard of any of those places."

"No, not at all," Altek said. "Just as I'm sure it won't surprise you to discover that, before I came to Deep Space Nine, I'd never heard of the title *kai*."

Ro walked over with a cup of tea in each hand. She set one down before Pralon, who looked elegant in her traditional robe and matching headpiece. The lavender vestments set off her silvering blond hair and brought out the blue in her blue-green eyes. The captain put the other cup down in front of Altek. They both thanked Ro before Pralon responded to the doctor.

"Actually, it does surprise me some," she said. "The title of kai goes considerably far back in history. It was given to spiritual leaders even before all the people of Bajor united as one world."

"Though I never met her, and though nobody ever called her kai, I was aware of the woman whom people looked to as the Bajoran spiritual leader," Altek said. "Her name was Denoray Lunas."

"I don't recognize either the surname or the given name," Pralon said, "much less the entire name."

Ro carried her own cup of tea over from the replicator. She set it down on the table and sat in the unoccupied chair. "There are several officers in my crew who studied Bajoran history at university," the captain said. "I assigned one, Aleco Vel, to lead a team in researching from what period Doctor Altek might have come. Lieutenant Aleco and the others conducted several interviews with the doctor and then used the information they collected to search the archives. So far, they haven't found anything to help identify his origin."

Pralon shook her head slowly. "Although much is known about the First Bajoran Republic, and the Second, there are still lengthy periods in our history that are undocumented and unremembered." The kai paused, then asked Altek, "Do you have any intuition about what's happened to you? Any sense, no matter how fleeting, about your situation?"

"No—" Altek began, but then he stopped abruptly. "Actually, I've come to believe what Captain Ro and her crew believe: that I somehow traveled through the Celestial Temple, and in doing so, also journeyed forward in time."

"Does that not seem like a fantastical idea to you?" the kai asked.

"To me, it does, of course," Altek agreed. "But as I understand it, it's something that's commonplace now."

"Not 'commonplace,'" Ro interjected, "but yes, there have been more than a few recorded instances of travel backward and forward in time."

"I didn't believe it at first," Altek said. "I thought that perhaps I'd been drugged, or that I was the victim of an elaborate hoax. But I've been here for more than three months, and there just doesn't seem to be any other reasonable explanation—unless maybe I'm really in a coma and this—" He waved his hand in an arc above his head, a gesture manifestly meant to include the entirety of Deep Space 9. "—is all a figment of my unconscious mind."

Pralon raised her eyebrows. "I've been called far worse things than that," she said, and both Ro and Altek laughed. The kai smiled, and it felt to Ro as though some of the natural tension in the meeting had eased.

Pralon leaned forward and picked up her cup from its saucer. She sipped at her tea, then put it back down. "Doctor," she said, "I'm going to assume that the conclusion Captain Ro and her crew have come to is correct, that you have come forward from Bajor's past. Such an occurrence involving the Celestial Temple, as I'm sure you've been informed, is not without precedent. I also have confidence in the analytical abilities of the captain and the people in her charge." The offhand compliment surprised Ro; in her experience, the kai did not engage in either flattery or hyperbole, and so she appreciated the gracious words. "That being the case, what is it that you expect? What do you want from Bajor and its people?"

The questions, phrased so bluntly, sounded to Ro almost like accusations. She felt the urge to say something to the kai, to defend Altek. The captain had spent many hours with him during his time on the starbase, and she had become utterly convinced of his authenticity. She didn't think he deserved to be treated like a suspected criminal.

Before she could say anything, though, the doctor responded. "I want nothing," he said, his voice even, "other than to go home." He did not act as though Pralon's questions had offended him.

"But where, exactly, is home?" the kai asked. "There is no such place as Revek or Davenesh or Joradell. None of the people in your life are still alive, nor is there even any record of their existence. How do you propose to return home when home as you knew it no longer exists?"

Again, the captain found Pralon's words combative, although the kai kept her tone free of suspicion. In her younger days, Ro probably would have spoken out, and harshly. *And that wouldn't have helped matters,* she thought, *other than to make me feel self-righteous for a few moments.* She recognized that the kai might be testing Altek's reactions, intentionally trying to bait him, for he certainly would face considerable scrutiny if he did go back to Bajor. For his part, he reacted to the pointed questions with equanimity.

"I only want to return to the world on which I was born, and on which I lived all of my life until I somehow ended up here," Altek said. "I seek no special place, no special recognition—or *any* recognition."

The kai nodded slowly, then leaned forward on the sofa. "Let me ask you, Doctor Altek, if you believe that the Prophets have special plans for you."

For the first time since meeting Pralon, Altek appeared flustered. His face flushed and he moved back in his chair. "I don't . . . I don't know how to answer that," he said. "It seems clear to me that, if I'm to be permitted to go back to Bajor, your hope is that I do so quietly. As I've told you, that's what I want, too. But the truth is that, if the Prophets *have* sent me here, They must have done so for a reason."

"What reason?" the kai asked.

Altek blinked before answering, and the captain thought she saw in that minutest of hesitations something in his eyes. *Does he know why he's been sent here?* Ro asked herself. In all the time she'd spent with him, she'd seen no indication that he did. The kai didn't seem to notice the pause, and Ro wondered if she'd imagined it.

"I don't know," Altek said. "I would not presume to know the minds of the Prophets."

Pralon leaned back on the sofa. Her gaze seemed appraising to Ro. "That is a wise answer," the kai said. "And it's almost a direct quote out of *Shines the Celestial Temple*."

"I have been reading some of the canon," Altek said, with no hint of guilt or embarrassment. "I guess it's made an impression."

"That is good to hear," Pralon said. Her voice carried no implication, but Ro appreciated the kai's intellect enough to know that she must already have formed some opinion about Altek. The captain expected Pralon to say more, but instead, she seemed content to let the doctor speak.

Altek sat forward, moving to the edge of his seat. It almost seemed to Ro as though he and the kai were involved in some sort of elaborate dance, the two of them shifting positions as they evaluated each other. "I don't know if the Prophets have sent me here for some particular purpose," Altek said. "Whether or not They have, I do not intend to search for that purpose. I have to believe that, if I am here for a reason, it will come to pass on its own."

"You sound almost fatalistic in your outlook," Pralon said.

"No, I wouldn't call myself a fatalist," Altek said. "But if some things are predetermined, then there's no point in me or anybody else trying to stop them or help them along." For the first time, he took hold of his teacup and raised it to his lips.

As Altek set his tea back down, the kai asked, "Do you like it?"

"Not particularly," the doctor said without hesitation. Then he smiled. "But like most things, I can probably get used to it."

Pralon smiled with just one side of her mouth, an expression Ro took to mean that the kai understood the subtext in Altek's words. "It's often important to be adaptable," Pralon said. "I wonder if you would consent to me exploring your *pagh*."

Altek looked to Ro questioningly, then back at the kai. "I've encountered the term," he said. "I gather that it refers to a person's essence."

"To their life-force, yes," Pralon said. She stood up from the sofa and circled the low glass table. "If you would permit me to touch your ear . . ."

Again, Altek looked to Ro. She nodded, and he tilted his head to one side. The kai reached forward and slowly traced her forefinger along the pinna of his left ear, and then pressed her thumb to his lobe. Altek shuddered once, but he did not pull away.

The kai closed her eyes, her chin lifting slightly. "Your pagh is stalwart. It is . . . it was lost," she said. "But no more. You are . . . you are . . ." Pralon opened her eyes. "You are here to stay."

Altek looked up at the kai. "That's good," he said, his voice quiet. "I would not be quick to leave home in the same way again."

"You won't." Pralon turned her eyes to the captain, and Ro suddenly felt naked, as though the kai could see her life-force without having to make physical contact. Ro had never liked the sensation of somebody feeling not just at her ear, but down into the core of her being. Contrary to the Bajoran tradition of wearing an earring on the right ear, she used to wear one on her left, not just to assert her disbelief in the divinity of the Prophets, but also to deter members of the clergy from attempting to read her pagh. Once she'd been promoted to the position of first officer aboard the original DS9, though, she'd made the decision—after an enlightening conversation with Commander Vaughn and some serious self-examination—to wear no earring at all.

The kai dropped her hand from Altek's ear. Still gazing at Ro, she said, "It is not my place to offer apologies for the Bajoran government. Nevertheless, I am personally sorry about the lack of responsiveness you've received in this matter."

"We appreciate that you're here now," Ro said.

Pralon stepped back over to the sofa, but she did not sit down. "It is also not my wont to make excuses for other people, but I do hope you can appreciate the political climate that has prevented a swift and definitive decision regarding Doctor Altek's return to Bajor."

Ro nodded. She understood that the kai referred not only

to the assassination of President Bacco and everything that followed, but also to the recent actions by the Ohalavaru. The sect had attacked the Bajoran moon of Endalla and unearthed what they declared to be proof that the Prophets were not gods, but merely members of a powerful alien species. Those events had yet to be made public, but Ro assumed that they soon would be—if for no other reason than that it would be virtually impossible to keep such a momentous claim a secret.

"I do believe what you and Captain Ro have told me," the kai told Altek. "I have concerns about allowing you to come back to Bajor right now. Even if you do not seek attention, you will likely receive it anyway. Your story is not yet known, but it is only a matter of time before it becomes a matter of public record."

"I truly wish only to blend in to Bajoran society," Altek said. "I just want to try to live a normal life."

"I know," Pralon said. "And it is the *right* thing to provide you that opportunity. But it is complicated. I need to meditate on the issue before I can decide what will be best for all concerned—including you, Doctor."

Altek stood up, as did Ro. The meeting clearly seemed at an end. "Thank you for seeing me, Kai Pralon."

"It was a pleasure to meet you, Doctor, and thank you for the tea, Captain." Ro realized that she hadn't even taken a sip from her own cup.

The kai walked around the sofa and toward the door, which slid open at her approach. Before she left, she turned back to the sitting area. "I will be leaving for Bajor tomorrow," she said. "I invite you to join me in the temple later for evening services, Doctor."

"Thank you," Altek said. "I'd like that."

"I would welcome your presence as well, Captain."

Ro nodded and offered a smile, but said nothing. The

kai did not wait for any more of an answer than that. She continued through the door, which closed behind her.

Altek looked at Ro. "What do you think?"

"I think that if there's any chance at all that you can go back to Bajor sometime soon," Ro said, "it lies with the kai."

"Where have you been?!"

Nog peered over to the freestanding companel from where he stood in the doorway to his uncle's office. Quark had called out even before the panel had completely opened. *Of course,* Nog thought. *He heard my footsteps approaching and recognized them.*

"I've been away," Nog replied, realizing at once that such a response would hardly satisfy his uncle.

"I know you've been away," Quark said with obvious annoyance. "What I want to know is where."

Nog debated whether to flee the familial interrogation—*Haven't I answered enough questions lately?*—and come back later in the day. In other circumstances, he probably would have. He didn't have to report for duty until the next day, though, and so he had a free afternoon, which he hoped to put to good use. "Uncle, please," he said, stepping fully inside the office. The door panel slipped closed behind him, dampening the olio of voices and the clink of glassware outside in the bar. "I'm a Starfleet officer. You know we can't always talk about our assignments."

"Then it's true," Quark said, slapping the Ferengi padd in his hand down on the surface of the companel. "You hunted down President Bacco's assassins."

Nog felt his mouth drop open, and he forced himself to close it. It shouldn't have surprised him that his uncle had obtained classified information. Quark had contacts all over the Alpha Quadrant—not to mention in the Beta and Gamma Quadrants as well. *But Uncle also knows how to bluff,* Nog reminded himself. Quark might merely have deduced the nature of Nog's assignment based on the timing of events on the starbase, Nog's departure, and the public reporting about the capture of the president's assassins. *Or he might just have wildly guessed.*

"Uncle, I'm an engineer," Nog said. "Why would Starfleet send me on a military mission?" He had asked himself the same question when he'd first learned the purpose of the Active Four unit to which he had been assigned, even though Lieutenant Commander Kincade had already made mention of Nog's extensive battlefield experience—a fact Nog typically preferred not to think about.

"Why would Starfleet send you on a military mission?" Quark blustered. "Because you're in Starfleet, which is a military organization."

"We consider ourselves explorers and diplomats first."

"Really?" Quark said, sounding not at all convinced. "Do you engage in a lot of exploration and diplomacy on this starbase?"

Nog rolled his eyes at the snide question, but it actually pleased him that his uncle cared enough about his welfare to be upset. *And if he knew the truth, or even suspected it, he'd have good reason to be upset.* Nog had indeed been recruited as part of a covert team charged with capturing Nan Bacco's killers—although, as it turned out, not to bring them to justice, but to allow Baras Rodirya and his coconspirators to eliminate them. Since leaving Deep Space 9, Nog had been shot at more times than he cared to recall. He felt fortunate to have survived the ordeal.

Of course, he couldn't tell his uncle any of that. Beyond the classified status of the mission and its details, Nog wouldn't want Quark to worry about him the next time he received orders that took him away from the starbase. Still, between tracking down Onar Throk and his collaborators, dealing with Galif jav Velk and Baras Rodirya's other accomplices, and then getting debriefed by what seemed like every officer in Starfleet Intelligence, Nog had been gone for more than three months, so he had to tell his uncle something.

"There are a lot of jobs in the galaxy that require the expertise of an engineer," he said vaguely. "And Starfleet doesn't necessarily want to share every detail with everybody."

Quark waved a hand dismissively through the air, as though even the concept of somebody keeping information from him offended his sensibilities. Nog expected his uncle to quote one Rule of Acquisition or another—perhaps the 135th: *Listen to secrets, but never repeat them*—but instead, he came out from behind the companel console he used as a desk, crossed the room, and took hold of his nephew by his upper arms. "Are you all right?" he asked, and the honest concern in his eyes moved Nog.

"I'm fine, Uncle." Nog slapped his hands against his own chest. "Everything intact. No new parts." It amazed Nog that he could make such a joke, that he had come so far emotionally after losing his leg a decade prior, during a battle with the Jem'Hadar. At the time, even after being fitted with a fully functioning prosthetic replacement, he'd still had trouble thinking of himself as a whole person.

Vic helped me with that, he remembered warmly. Nog missed his friend—which, after letting his uncle know that he had returned safely to DS9, formed the second reason he had come to Quark's that afternoon. Because of a series of technical incompatibilities and other issues, Vic Fontaine's program had been confined to running in a holographic testing unit ever since the destruction of the original space station more than two years earlier. Just before Nog had left for his covert assignment, he had finally made progress in uploading Vic's complex matrix from the tester and getting it to run, at least partially, in one of his uncle's new holosuites, but there still remained a great deal of work to be done.

As Quark let go of Nog's arms and moved back around the companel console, he said, "Have you spoken with your father? He's got some addlepated idea about normalizing the currency exchange . . . something about eliminating the intrinsic unfairness of high-speed transactions . . ." He finished his comment with a disapproving grunt, but Quark clearly just wanted to make sure that Nog had let Rom know that he was safe.

"I talked to Father just before I came here," Nog said.

"It's amazing he hasn't been overthrown yet," Quark grumbled, referring to the nearly ten years Rom had spent as the Grand Nagus of the Ferengi Alliance. Already, though, his attention had returned to his padd, which he retrieved from atop the companel.

"Uncle, I was hoping you'd let me into a holosuite this afternoon," Nog said. "I'm not on shift until tomorrow morning, so I thought I'd continue my work on Vic's program."

"The holosuites are for paying customers," Quark said without looking up. It seemed as though he spoke out of reflex.

"Uncle, I know you want to be able to run Vic's program again," Nog said. "He brought in a lot of business." Quark continued working on his padd. "Uncle, I need a holosuite."

"What?" Quark said, at last glancing over at Nog.

"I want to work on Vic's program."

"Vic? Oh, a friend of yours stopped in while you were away," Quark said. "He worked on the software and interface."

Nog felt a tingle shoot through his lobes—and not the good, *oo-mox* kind of tingle. "What?!" he said, crossing the office to stand directly across the companel from Quark. "Uncle, how could you let somebody else work on Vic's program? I told you how delicate the matrix is. Somebody unfamiliar with it could easily cause permanent damage. We could lose Vic."

Quark shrugged. "You could just reboot him."

"Uncle!" Nog said, his voice rising in alarm. "Then Vic would lose all of his memories, all of his experiences . . . he wouldn't be the same Vic Fontaine anymore."

"He hasn't been in one of my holosuites in two years, and I seem to be surviving," Quark said. "Besides, it wasn't my fault. Broik let them into a holosuite."

"'Them'? I thought you said *one* person worked on Vic's program."

"I said one of your friends came by. He had somebody with him."

Nog looked down and shook his head, his concern for Vic growing. It would have been so easy for somebody unacquainted with Vic's matrix to—

"He left you a message," Quark said.

"What? Who?"

"Your friend who worked on the program." Quark looked around his office, then reached to a shelf behind him. He pulled out another padd and examined it. "Here it is," he said, handing it over across the companel.

Nog grabbed for the device and quickly scanned its contents. He found a file marked FOR NOG and activated it. When a face appeared on the display, he felt a surge of relief: it was Geordi La Forge.

Nog knew few better engineers than La Forge. The two had worked together for a short time when both had served aboard *U.S.S. Challenger*. Nog would have preferred to be the only one permitted to work on Vic's program, but if he had to choose another engineer to do so, it would have been La Forge.

"Hello, Nog," the recording began. *"I'm sorry that I missed you on my visit to the new Deep Space Nine. You've got quite a facility here, and you and Chief O'Brien did a fine job helping design it."* The encomium from an engineer as fine as La Forge gratified Nog.

"I came to the starbase because it was very important for a friend of mine to speak with Vic Fontaine," La Forge continued. *"We weren't aware that Mister Fontaine was a hologram, or that there were problems with his matrix. I looked at the program and saw the work that had been done on it—I'm guessing those were your efforts. It looked like you were close to solving all the incompatibilities and other issues. I made a few modifications myself, just in how the emitter array handles the power."*

"Yes, the power distribution," Nog exclaimed. "I knew I was on the right track."

"I managed to bring the program online, but not in the entire holosuite." Nog had encountered a similar difficulty the last time he'd worked on the program. *"My friend did get a chance to speak with Vic Fontaine. I wanted to let you know that I think the issues with power are being exacerbated by the high resolution of the new holosuites. I think you might need to reroute the main buses. I've appended a file detailing all the work I did, and some suggestions for what you might try next."*

"Yes," Nog said, thrilled by the news.

"Be well, Nog." The display on the padd blinked, and a link to a data file appeared.

"Uncle," Nog said at once. "I need a holosuite *right now*."

Nog worked through the afternoon and into the evening. Well past dinnertime, he contacted Broik and ordered a grub steak and an *eelwasser*, and it delighted him when Ulu Lani delivered it to the holosuite. The last time Nog had been in the bar, before he'd departed on his classified mission, the beautiful Bajoran woman had actually flirted with him. She did so again that night, making him promise that he would take her to Vic's casino and nightclub once he succeeded in restoring the program.

Now I have two good reasons to make the program work, Nog thought. *Vic . . . and Lani.*

The evening hours wore on, and the night grew long. Nog made sure he fully understood both the work La Forge had done, and the recommendations he'd left. He attempted to power up the holosuite and upload Vic's matrix twice, and both times, only a strip of it showed in the center of the compartment. Undeterred, he soldiered on, until just after midnight, when he thought he had finally solved all of the issues.

Nog kneeled down before the simulation tester. The gray metal cube balanced on one vertex atop a black base. An isolinear optical rod—a piece of old Cardassian technology that held Vic's program—filled one of the four input slots, and a series of indicator lights burned in different colors. An optical data network cable ran from an open access panel in the bulkhead, across the deck, and over to the tester.

If I can just get the program to load fully once, Nog thought, *I can transfer it to the starbase's storage drives.* That would provide added stability to Vic's matrix, which had continued to run for the two years it had been inside the testing unit. Nog felt thankful that La Forge had been able to upload the program to a holosuite and run it, and that he and his friend had gotten to speak with Vic, however briefly, because that confirmed that the matrix hadn't degraded.

Nog reached to the tester and activated the upload. Immediately, the deck, bulkheads, and overhead vanished, replaced by photons and force fields organized by Vic's program. It filled the entire holosuite. Nog felt elated—but only for a moment.

As he looked around, he saw a setting unfamiliar to him. He saw no tables and chairs, no stage, no bar. He did not hear the chirrups of slot machines or the roar of voices around gaming tables. He saw none of the furniture in Vic's apartment.

Instead, Nog stood in a dingy, poorly lighted hallway. Scuffed, uneven planks formed the floor, and several grimy doors lined the space. A dirty window at the end of the hall looked out onto a brick wall. He neither saw nor heard anybody.

By degrees, the painfully obvious truth sank in: Nog had failed. Sorrow overwhelmed him. He didn't know if his tampering that day had altered Vic's program, or if it had been something that La Forge had done. It didn't matter. Vic had been lost.

As Nog put out a hand toward the wall to steady himself, he heard a muffled thud behind him. He spun around quickly, but the hallway remained empty, stretching away to a set of stairs that led down to the left. The noise must have come from behind one of the closed doors.

"Vic?" Nog said, his voice tentative. He no longer believed that he would ever see his friend again—at least not the same friend he had once known—but he didn't want to give up hope. He took a step down the hall and stopped at the nearest door, upon which hung a pair of numbers, both 2s, with the second hanging askew. Nog listened. He heard nothing more.

Nog moved to the next door, on the other side of the hall, marked with the number 23. "Vic?" he called out again, a little louder and steadier. His hope seemed desperate, but—

A footstep reached Nog's ear, and the door in front of him suddenly swung open on a creaky hinge. He instinctively stepped backward, but then somebody lunged forward, seized his arm, and pulled him through the doorway.

Nog tried to keep his balance as he staggered forward and past whoever had grabbed him. The door slammed behind him, and when he turned—

When he turned, he fixed his gaze on Vic Fontaine. Nog had not seen or spoken with his friend since the destruction of the original Deep Space 9. Thrilled, Nog took a step forward, but then he stopped.

Vic did not look the same. Nog worried again that the program had been changed or damaged, and that the man standing in front of him was not the friend he had known. Instead of the formal attire Vic donned when he entertained, or the natty outfits he favored when not onstage, he wore a pair of shapeless brown pants and a checked, long-sleeve shirt. Worse, Vic appeared as crumpled as his clothes, as though he had slept in them, but only fitfully.

But then Nog saw recognition in Vic's eyes. "Kid!" he said excitedly, though the word came out of his mouth as a loud whisper.

Relief flooded through Nog. "Vic," he said, "it's so good to see you."

"Shhh," Vic urged him. "Keep your voice down. The walls have ears."

Nog thought he must have heard Vic wrong because he could make no sense of the last thing he'd said. *The walls have ears?* Nog peered around, imagining huge lobes hanging around the room, but he saw only fading, cracked plaster. A rusting, iron-framed bed pushed up against one side wall, its mattress sagging and its sheets in tangles. A bare bulb hung by a wire from the ceiling, throwing a dim, yellow cast over everything. A gauzy piece of fabric covered a single, small window, a sickly red pall glowing on it from somewhere out in the night. The threadbare curtain ruffled inward, pushed by stale currents of air. The room in no way resembled the hotel attached to Vic's casino.

When Nog looked back at his friend, he saw a concerned expression on his face. *It's more than concern—it's anxiety . . . maybe even fear.* "What is it?" Nog asked, careful not to raise his voice. "What's wrong?"

In response, Vic pushed back one sleeve of his shirt and checked his wristwatch. "I can't talk right now, Kid," he said, still speaking in hushed tones. "There's somewhere I gotta be." He rushed to the bed, got down on his knees, and reached beneath the mattress. He pulled out a small, shop-worn satchel, rose, and headed for the door.

"Wait," Nog said, louder than he'd intended. He reminded himself to keep his voice low before he continued. "Where are you going? Why can't you talk?" He gazed around at their shabby surroundings, then asked, "What is this place?"

"It's the Fremont-Sunrise Hotel," Vic said, one hand grasping the doorknob. "Meet me back here tomorrow evening."

Before Nog could say anything more, Vic pulled the door partially open. He stuck his head out into the hall and peered in both directions. An instant later, he threw the door wide and bolted out of the room.

Nog stood there, dumbfounded. For a long time, he had worried about his friend, concerned that his program would fail while hosted in the simulation tester. It had never occurred to him that something might have happened to Vic in his own world. *But what* has *happened?*

Nog rushed out into the hall. It was empty, but he heard Vic's footsteps thundering down the staircase. Nog thought about trying to follow him, but that didn't seem like a good idea.

Not knowing what else to do, he stepped back inside the dismal room. He looked around, searching for any clue that might help make sense of what he'd just experienced. When his gaze alit on the window, he raced over to it, swept the flimsy curtain aside, and leaned over the sill.

A dark thoroughfare passed in front of the hotel. A flickering streetlamp proved inadequate to penetrate the shadowy fronts of the dilapidated buildings that crawled away in both directions. Nothing moved on the street until Vic ran outside. Nog wanted to call out, wanted to try to stop his friend, or help him in whatever way he could—for he surely seemed to be in some sort of trouble—but he remembered Vic's admonition not to speak too loudly. Instead, Nog watched as his friend sprinted down the street, his footfalls clicking along the surface of the road. Half a block down, Vic turned sharply and disappeared into a gloomy alley.

For several minutes, Nog didn't move, hoping that his friend would reappear. He didn't. Nog finally stepped back from the window, wondering what had just happened. He had found Vic, and then just as quickly, lost him again. He once more considered making his way out into the night to try and find his friend, but he knew virtually nothing about the layout of 1960s Las Vegas.

"Computer," Nog said, but then he hesitated. He had been about to order Vic's program saved, which would protect it from any possible problems with the simulation tester, as well as from the risks associated with future uploads. But he also recognized that once he secured the matrix in DS9's memory banks, he would also be storing the incident that had just occurred.

I don't have a choice, he thought. *And it doesn't matter, anyway: it's not as though it's possible to move backward or forward in time in Vic's program.* Doctor Bashir's friend Felix had created a very special bit of code, one that unspooled in real time, and with as much fragility as real life.

"Computer," Nog said, "save and end program." Around him, the run-down hotel room evaporated like a mirage disappearing in the desert. Nog disconnected the simulation tester and the ODN cable, then reset the access panel in place. He took one last look before exiting the holosuite and heading for his quarters, where he would try to get at least a few hours of sleep before his duty shift started.

He could only hope that, when he returned to the Fremont-Sunrise Hotel the next night, he would find Vic there.

Lieutenant Commander Selten strode into Newton Outpost's infirmary. He crossed the empty antechamber to the main ward. He had never seen it so busy. Patients filled six of the eight bio-beds. In another compartment nearby, he knew, the bodies of T'Pret, a technician, and Bruce Prestridge, a scientist, had been placed in stasis; both had been killed during the creature's escape from captivity.

As Selten observed for a few moments, he saw that two of the medical doctors on staff tended to the injured, aided by a third doctor functioning in a nurse's role. Across the ward, propped up on a bio-bed, the outpost's chief of staff, Doctor Norsa, looked over and saw the security chief. She motioned to him, but before he walked over to her, he waited until one of the attending physicians had a moment to speak with him. "How is Doctor Norsa?" Selten asked Gellish, a Denobulan neurosurgeon.

"She's suffered a concussion," he said. "She lost consciousness, but we've confirmed that she has no bleeding in the brain. We've given her an analgesic for her headache and an antiemetic for her nausea. Doctor Norsa should make a complete recovery, but she may experience other symptoms in the coming days or even weeks. The prescription is rest."

"She'd like to speak with me."

Gellish glanced over his shoulder at Norsa. "If there's

something she needs to tell you or that you need to find out, fine," he said. "She's foggy at the moment, so please don't take any longer than is necessary, and certainly no more than five minutes."

"Understood," Selten said. "Thank you, Doctor." The security chief crossed the room to Norsa's bio-bed. The chief of staff looked up at him.

"Commander," she said, and though Selten understood her perfectly, she sounded as though she spoke with a swollen tongue in her mouth. "I understand the creature is off the outpost."

"It is," Selten confirmed. "It has departed the shepherd moon, altered its course utilizing the gravitational field of Larrisint Four, and is headed out into space."

"You're implying the creature is intelligent."

"Yes," Selten said. "It is possible that it is acting out of instinct, but when it came very close to me, I sensed emotion, a yearning—"

"I did too," Norsa said, sitting up quickly. She listed to one side, and Selten reached over to take firm hold of her. As he helped her back against the pillows, Gellish came over.

"Please," the doctor said. "She needs to rest."

Selten nodded, then leaned in and told Norsa, "I'll speak with you later." As he stood back up, she reached for his arm.

"Wait," she said. "Has the outpost been damaged?"

Selten looked to Gellish, who gave a tight nod. "The ports around Compartment L have all been shattered, and the security door leading to Corridor Four has been compromised, but the outpost has suffered no structural damage and no breaches."

"Good," Norsa said. "That's good." She closed her eyes, but as Selten took her hand from his arm, she looked up at him again. "One more thing: How is Odo?"

Selten looked to Gellish once more, who said, "We're

still treating him." Without giving Norsa the opportunity to ask another question, he said, "Now, I must insist that you get some rest."

Norsa nodded slowly. "Yes, Doctor."

Selten and Gellish walked away from the bio-bed together. Once they had crossed the ward, the security chief quietly asked, "What injuries has the shape-shifter endured?"

"Come with me," Gellish said.

Selten followed the doctor out of the main section of the infirmary, down a short corridor, past the operating theater, and into the isolation ward. A half-dozen sealed chambers lined the circular compartment. Gellish motioned toward an observation port, the only one through which light shined. The two men walked over together.

The security chief saw another bio-bed inside the isolation chamber, as well as a small table and chair, and a computer interface set into a bulkhead. The diagnostic panel above the bio-bed appeared operational, but it showed almost no activity. No body lay on the pallet—at least no humanoid body. Rather, a transparent container sat there, perhaps a meter tall and the same in diameter. A grayish sludge filled it three-quarters of the way to the top. Selten did not detect even the slightest motion in the container; he would have expected some movement in a liquid, simply from air currents passing across its exposed surface.

"That's the shape-shifter?" the security chief asked.

"That's Odo, yes," Gellish said.

"I saw a recording of the creature attacking him," Selten said. "It looked as though his body . . . his *form* . . . spattered against a bulkhead."

"I watched the recording, too," Gellish said. "Very disturbing."

"Is he dead?"

"Possibly," the doctor said, and then he shook his head.

"Probably, I think, but there's just no way to tell at the moment. Odo's body *did* spatter, and the morphogenic particles it's composed of became noncontiguous, striking the bulkhead and the deck at different points. But as the particles on the bulkhead slid down, they pooled together with those on the deck, which could suggest some sort of autonomic reflex. We collected all of it and brought it here, but since then, it's lost its lustrous color, which could be a marker of injury, sickness, or death." Gellish shook his head again. "I'm afraid we just don't know enough about the physiology of shape-shifters to reach a definite conclusion."

"All right, Doctor," Selten said. "Keep me informed."

"Of course."

The security chief made his way back through the infirmary and headed for the turbolift. He would return to the upper level of the installation so that he could check the external sensors. He wanted to know where in the Larrisint system the creature had gone, and whether or not it still posed a danger to Newton Outpost.

Ro sat down on the small sofa in Altek's quarters while he went to the replicator. "What can I get you, Captain?" he asked.

Ro thought about having a glass of springwine, or perhaps even something harder, but she still had work to do that night. She had spent the latter part of the morning and most of the afternoon taking Kai Pralon on a tour of the starbase. After she and her officers hosted the kai and her party to a dinner—an affair ably catered by Quark—she decided to accept Pralon's offer to attend evening services at the Bajoran temple. She did so mostly to curry goodwill with the kai regarding Altek's situation, but she had other reasons as well. Ro had not been to services in some time, and she discovered that she had a desire to go. She also thought that it would please Altek.

"Nothing for me, thank you," Ro said. "I have to head to my office soon. I still have a report to prepare tonight and two late meetings." The tasks all involved the Ohalavaru extremists who had attacked Endalla with explosives in order to expose a large subterranean structure. They claimed the complex construction to be a falsework the Prophets utilized to initially anchor the wormhole in the Alpha Quadrant, and around which they built the moon in order to conceal it. Ro would meet with her security chief, Lieutenant Commander Jefferson Blackmer, so that he could update her on any additional information he and his staff had uncovered on their Ohalavaru prisoners, who would shortly be extradited to Bajor. She would then consult with First Minister Asarem Wadeen regarding the official actions her government would take on the matter, and the timing of them. After that, she had to ready a status report for Starfleet Command.

And I should check on Desca, the captain thought. The previous night, Ro's first officer, Colonel Cenn Desca, had publicly—and drunkenly—assailed Kai Pralon, calling her a liar and the Bajoran religion a hoax. The kai had taken the incident in stride, and despite the awkwardness of having one of the starbase's senior officers involved in such an embarrassing episode, Ro thought that any negative effects would prove short-lived. She had a much greater concern for Cenn on a personal level. His faith, which played a significant role in his life, had been shaken by the Ohalavaru contentions. For that reason, she had relieved him of duty for a few days, so that he could concentrate on coping with his emotions.

From over by the replicator, Altek said, "You are tireless, Captain."

Ro laughed. "Hardly," she said. "I'm actually exhausted, but we all have our duties to perform."

"Your crew is fortunate to have such a dedicated leader." Altek ordered an Altair water from the replicator, which appeared in a tall glass.

As he walked over toward the sitting area in his guest quarters, Ro said, "For somebody born before Bajor ever made contact with aliens, you've developed cosmopolitan tastes pretty quickly."

Altek held up his glass as though in a toast. "It's a whole new universe for me," he said. "I might as well experience it."

"I also notice that you've taken well to the replicator."

Altek set his glass down on the low circular table, then sat down, not across from Ro, but beside her on the small sofa. "It's a remarkable device," he said, pointing over at the replicator. "Astonishing, really. It seems like such an incredibly useful tool, not just technologically, but socially. When you can take any raw material—and the universe certainly contains a lot of otherwise-useless matter—and you can fashion it into the necessities of life, what need is there for want? And once you can provide everybody with food and clothing and a place to live, it frees society to pursue loftier goals: art, science, exploration. It should obviate the justifications for war."

"You'd be surprised," Ro said, unable to prevent herself from thinking about what had happened to President Bacco and what that had nearly wrought: another war with the Tzenkethi, and maybe even with the whole of the Typhon Pact. "But you're right. The advent of the replicator helped the Federation eliminate poverty and homelessness, and to advance medicine considerably." She thought back to the UFP survey courses she'd taken at the Academy, one of which had focused on the impact of technology on modern life. "In many ways, the development of the replicator gave societies the chance for their cultural morality to progress."

Altek smiled at her. "Thank you, *Professor* Ro."

The captain laughed again. "I had a hard enough time making it to class as a student," she said. "If I was the teacher, I'd probably never go."

"Oh, I don't know," Altek said. "You strike me as somebody who'd make a fine educator."

"I think you need to get to know me better before saying something like that."

Altek's lips curled up slightly on one side, a small, lopsided smile that had the effect of stripping away ten or more of his forty-plus years. "I hope to."

The romantic implication startled Ro. She had spent a great deal of time with Altek during his months on the starbase—more and more as time had worn on—but she'd attributed that to her responsibility to help him acclimate to his new surroundings, meaning not just to DS9, but to the twenty-fourth-century Milky Way. They were contemporaries in terms of age, and she could not deny that she found him attractive, but she spent most of her days, and even many of her nights, working to fulfill her responsibilities as the commanding officer of an enormous starbase. What little time she put aside for romance, she shared with Quark.

Except he and I have hardly seen each other since the new Deep Space Nine became fully operational, she realized.

When Ro didn't say anything, the moment threatened to become awkward, but Altek quickly moved past his comment. "Listen," he said, "I want to thank you for all you've done for me."

"It's my duty," Ro said, but she heard the curtness in her voice, which ignored the very real affection she had come to feel for Altek. "It's also been my pleasure," she added. "I know what it's like to feel like an outsider, so I'm happy that I could help."

"I'm also grateful for your advice to enlist the aid of the clergy," Altek said. "I really believe that Kai Pralon will help me get back to Bajor, whether it's tomorrow or sometime further in the future."

"I think so, too," Ro said. "I've always found her to be an honest person, dedicated to doing the right thing, no matter how difficult it might be. I'm confident that she'll make sure you're permitted to return to Bajor."

"Apart from all of that, I also enjoyed meeting her."

"She's very charismatic, and a strong leader for the faithful, I think." Ro had not cared much for her predecessor, Winn Adami, nor for the previous kai, Opaka Sulan. Winn had always seemed too political and too self-interested, and Opaka too ungainly as a public figure. Pralon Onala carried herself with assurance but not ego, a shrewd leader aware of all the machinations of those around her, who always acted for the benefit of those she served.

"I also want to thank you for attending services this evening," Altek said. "I know you don't believe, so I'm assuming you did it to avoid offending the kai while she was here to consider my request."

"You're welcome," Ro said, "but the truth is that I didn't do it for you. Not entirely for you, anyway. I didn't decline the kai's invitation in the first place because I didn't want to insult her, but when I thought about it, I realized that I did want to go—not just for the kai or for you, but for myself."

"I'm glad, but why?" Altek asked. "If you're a nonbeliever, why would you want to go to the temple?"

"I've never been comfortable with labeling myself," Ro said. "I used to call myself a nonbeliever, and I wore an earring on my left ear to let every Bajoran I met know that. I stopped doing that a few years ago when I realized that it didn't matter what words I used to describe myself, or that others used to describe me."

"It only matters what's in here," Altek said, pressing the flat of his hand to his chest.

"Exactly," Ro said, gratified that Altek understood her. "My views are also in flux. Some things have happened lately that have caused me to question my disbelief." Where Cenn Desca had taken to heart the declarations of the Ohalavaru that the Endalla falsework demonstrated the mortal nature of the Prophets, Ro's opinions had moved in the opposite direction. Nothing about the discovery of the falsework or the claims of the Ohalu extremists had come out yet, though, and so the captain could not discuss it with Altek.

"I have to say, it pleases me to hear that," Altek said. "I felt comforted this evening in the temple. I'd like to think that you could feel that, too."

"It's not as though I haven't attended religious services in my life," Ro said. "My father was devout, and he taught me. Later, my uncle sent me to assist the local vedek at the temple, but . . . I became very rebellious around that time, so it didn't last long." Ro thought back to her childhood and her teen years, to a mother too depressed by the death of her husband to raise their only daughter. The captain recalled her uncle Vanka with more fondness than she'd felt for him when he'd selflessly taken her in. She always believed that she'd been forced to grow up too quickly—as so many children of the Occupation had.

"Anyway," Ro went on, "I remembered the sense of community I often experienced when I went to the temple. I just decided that I wanted to feel that again."

"I'd think you'd get that from being the leader of such a large crew," Altek said.

"Oh, I do," Ro quickly agreed. "But there's so much diversity in Starfleet—in all the Federation—not to mention in the itinerant guest population we have on the starbase. All of which is a good thing, but sometimes it's nice to be among people who share your heritage."

"I can understand that," Altek said. "Especially now that there's nobody I have a common history with."

"I'm sorry."

"No, it's all right," Altek told her. "I wasn't complaining . . . well, not much, anyway. But I am becoming accustomed to life in the future." As though to prove his assertion, he reached for his glass of Altair water and took a long pull.

"I think I might finally be getting used to it, too," Ro said. She chuckled, and Altek joined her.

"You know, believe it or not, if the kai is able to clear a path for me to Bajor, it's going to be hard for me to leave the station. I've really grown to like it here." He reached over to the table to set down his glass, and when he reset himself on the sofa, he had gotten much closer to Ro. Before she knew it, he leaned in and pressed his lips to hers.

Ro pulled back, surprised. She gazed into Altek's eyes, unsure how to react. She felt his desire—passionate, sexual, but more than that . . . romantic. And had similar feelings been sparking in her? She thought that—

Altek leaned in and kissed her again. That time, she kissed him back.

Benjamin Sisko walked through the corridor, sensing the vitality of his ship around him. He had woken early that morning after a night of interrupted sleep, his excitement making it impossible for him to doze for very long. Despite that, he did not feel at all tired, although he suspected that the adrenaline pumping within him would leave him exhausted that night.

Ro Laren walked beside Sisko. When he had contacted her aboard Deep Space 9 to inform her that his crew had completed their preparations, she had routinely notified the on-duty dockmaster, Ensign deGrom, to release the clamps binding *Robinson* to the starbase's *x*-ring, and to confirm a clear path to the wormhole. Ro had then asked to come aboard to meet with him. Despite Sisko's eagerness to finally begin the mission his crew had for so long been denied by circumstance, he did not want to refuse the captain the tradition—practiced unevenly throughout Starfleet—of personally seeing a commanding officer off at the start of a long journey. It also helped that the *Robinson* crew, as enthusiastic as its captain for the voyage to come, had their schedule running thirty minutes ahead.

Ro had transported over from DS9 and met Sisko in his ready room. Their meeting had been professional and cordial. Although the two officers had not grown close, they had worked together a great deal over the previous two years, with *Robinson* assigned to patrol the Bajoran system for most of that time. Ro had wanted to offer Sisko her best wishes for a safe and successful mission.

As he escorted her through the ship, back to the transporter room, they ended up talking mostly about Elias Vaughn. His name arose when Ro revealed that it had been Vaughn, when he'd been about to take command of *James T. Kirk*, who had shared the ritual of one officer seeing off another in such circumstances. Sisko then spoke of how the late captain's love of exploration had helped nurture a similar passion in him.

They reached the ship's active transporter room on Deck 6 and walked inside. Crewwoman Jentzen Spingeld, a petite human, stood at the compartment's freestanding console. "Captain Ro will be beaming back to Deep Space Nine," Sisko told the transporter operator. "Contact the Hub to let them know."

"Aye, sir," Spingeld said, and she immediately worked her controls.

Sisko walked with Ro over to the transporter platform,

but she turned to face him before mounting the step up. "Captain Vaughn also told me about another custom," she said. "When one officer bids farewell to another who is about to take his crew out on what is expected to be a particularly long expedition, the officer remaining behind bestows a small token on the one departing." If Ro carried anything with her, Sisko had not seen it during the time she'd been aboard *Robinson*. "In my case, when I saw Captain Vaughn off, he realized that I had probably never heard of such a ritual, and so he actually presented me with a gift. He and I were close . . . in many ways, he was like a father to me."

Ro glanced down for a moment and took a breath before continuing. Sisko could see her holding back her emotions. "I know that you and I have only a professional relationship, Captain, but I have a great deal of respect for you. In the spirit of Elias Vaughn, I wanted to give you something . . . something that would have some meaning. I thought about trying to find an old map from Earth, or a book about the first interstellar flight by humans, but I decided that I wanted something more personal, at least on my part, as a way to express my appreciation for you as a fellow officer, and also to commemorate all you've done for Bajor."

"I'm touched, Captain," Sisko said.

Ro said nothing more, and for a moment, Sisko wondered if he'd missed something. But then she held one hand out between them and uncurled her fingers. In her palm lay a Bajoran earring. "It's not fancy or made from valuable materials," Ro said, "but my father gave it to me. After he died, I didn't wear it for a long time, but I kept it. When I finally did put it on again, I wore it on the left side as a symbol of protest."

Sisko felt his eyebrows lift, surprised by the personal nature of what Ro revealed.

"I stopped wearing any earring when I became exec on

Deep Space Nine," she went on. "I'm no longer sure how I feel about the Prophets or my people's religion, but I'm more open to it today than I have been since I was a girl."

"The Bajorans have a lot to offer," Sisko said. "I don't know if I'll ever live among them again, but I still count myself as one of them."

"I understand," Ro said. Sisko worried that she would bring up his role as the Emissary of the Prophets—a role he didn't believe he'd occupied since his return from the Celestial Temple—but she didn't. "I wanted you to have this. I thought you might someday want to give it to that beautiful little girl of yours." Ro held her palm out to Sisko, and he allowed her to pour the earring from her hand to his.

"Thank you, Captain," he said. "This means a great deal to me. I'm moved by your generosity and your thoughtfulness."

"It's my privilege, Captain." Ro climbed up on the transporter platform, and Sisko glanced over at Spingeld.

"Deep Space Nine reports ready to receive Captain Ro," the crewwoman said.

"Good sailing to you, Captain," Ro said. "I'll see you in two years."

"Thank you," Sisko said again, and then he ordered Spingeld to energize the transporter. Amid the familiar whine and the white brume of dematerialization, Ro departed *Robinson*.

Sisko left the transporter room, headed for the bridge. Around him, the ship felt like a living being, its muscles tensed and ready to spring. The deck hummed with the operation of the warp drive, on standby but coursing with power.

As the captain passed members of his crew, he saw expressions of anticipation everywhere, and a few smiles impossible to suppress. He almost could not believe that the time had finally come. His crew's extended mission of exploration had been tabled for so long that he half expected a last-minute communication from Admiral Akaar, informing him that *Robinson* would be required elsewhere.

No, not this time, he thought as he entered a turbolift. Sisko had spoken just the night before with Admiral Herthum. Starfleet's new chief of Starfleet Operations had assured him that he saw no impediments to *Robinson*'s mission. Herthum also added that he would look to Sisko's voyage, which represented a return for the Federation to the Gamma Quadrant, as a significant milestone in a new era of exploration.

"Computer," Sisko said as the turbolift rose toward the bridge, "what is the ship's time?"

"The time is zero-eight-fifty-one hours," came the reply in the standard female voice with which Starfleet had imbued its computers for decades.

"Reroute turbolift," Sisko said. "Deck Nine."

The turbolift slowed to a halt, then reversed direction. It traveled only a short distance downward before it stopped and the doors opened. Sisko walked out and quickly strode into the corridor. He would have just enough time before he needed to be on the bridge.

Sisko entered the quarters he shared with his family almost at a gallop. Kasidy and Rebecca sat at the dining table to his left, eating breakfast. They both looked up at him.

"Daddy!" Rebecca said, and she jumped from her chair and ran over to him.

"What are you doing here?" Kasidy asked, also standing up. "I thought you had a ship to run."

"I do," Sisko said, squatting down to let Rebecca throw herself into his arms. He squeezed her tightly to him. "But I wanted to come see my girls before the big moment."

Rebecca pulled back to look at him. "You mean the launch?" she said.

"That's right," Sisko told her. "In just a few minutes, the *Robinson* will be leaving Deep Space Nine and traveling through the wormhole into the Gamma Quadrant. And then . . ." He left his sentence hanging, trying to coax his daughter into finishing it. She did.

"And then we go exploring," Rebecca said. "Where no one has gone before."

"Perfect," Sisko said, and he hugged his daughter to him once more. Then he stood up and held his arms open to Kasidy, who walked over into his embrace. "This is what we've all been looking forward to," he said. "It's going to be a great big adventure."

"Then, Daddy," Rebecca said, "shouldn't you be going to the bridge?"

Sisko laughed. "Yes, I should." He kissed his wife, then bent and kissed the top of his daughter's head. "I'll see you two later." As he headed out into the corridor, he heard Kasidy asking if Rebecca wanted to watch through the ports as *Robinson* traveled through the wormhole. The closing doors cut off his daughter's response, but he didn't doubt that she would want to see the spectacle.

At precisely zero-eight-fifty-nine hours, Captain Benjamin Lafayette Sisko took the command chair in the center of *Robinson*'s bridge. A view of Deep Space 9 showed on the main viewscreen. The ship's first officer, Commander Anxo Rogeiro, sat to his right, and the ship's counselor, Lieutenant Commander Diana Althouse, to his left. The captain took a moment to gaze around at his command crew, then opened a comm channel that would carry his voice to the rest of the ship.

"Attention, all hands," he said. "This is your captain. We are about to embark on a journey into unexplored space. A few years back, the *Robinson* completed a six-month voyage into the Gamma Quadrant. Those of you who served aboard the ship then know how satisfying such a mission can be. Those of you who have joined the crew since then will now find that out for yourselves."

Sisko saw that the officers on the bridge had turned in their chairs to watch him as he spoke. "We set out now in the name of the United Federation of Planets, in the hopes of exploring strange new worlds, of seeking out new life and new civilizations, of boldly going where no one has gone before." Until the words had left his mouth, he had not known that he would quote from the Starfleet charter when addressing his crew. "Sisko out."

Just ahead of the captain, Commander Gwendolyn Plante and Lieutenant Commander Sivadeki turned back to the operations and conn stations, respectively. "Commander Plante," Sisko said, "ship's status."

"All department heads report ready for launch," Plante said, and the captain could hear the smile through which she spoke. "All systems show green."

"Viewer ahead," Sisko ordered.

"Viewer ahead," Plante confirmed, and with the tap of a control surface, a field of stars appeared on the main screen.

"Commander Sivadeki," Sisko said, "set course for the wormhole."

"Course laid in, Captain," the flight controller said at once.

"Ahead one-half impulse power."

"One-half impulse, aye."

The thrum of the sublight drive rumbled through the deck as *Robinson* started forward. On the viewscreen, the Bajoran wormhole appeared as though out of nothingness, a bustle of circular motion. Its blue branches unfurled around its white center like a great celestial hand opening, as though the Prophets themselves reached out for the starship.

Seconds later, *Robinson* surged directly into the spectacle, on its way to territories unknown.

Lieutenant Commander Selten sat at a table in a conference room located on the lower level of Newton Outpost. He typically attended meetings there only when new and potentially dangerous objects or specimens had been scheduled for delivery, but he had been invited by Doctor Gellish, who presently stood in as chief of staff while Doctor Norsa recovered from her concussion. A day after her injury, Norsa's existing symptoms had intensified, and she displayed new ones: dizziness, ringing in her ears, and a general fogginess of thought.

According to Gellish, he anticipated that the discussion he intended to oversee could have security implications for the outpost. Along with Selten and the acting chief of staff, five others had assembled around the large, rectangular table, all of them scientists who had been studying the specimen in Compartment L. Norsa usually led the team, but she remained in the infirmary, and the seventh member, geneticist Bruce Prestridge, had been killed during the creature's escape, his neck broken when he'd been thrown awkwardly against a bulkhead. Gellish had brought the others together to discuss possible treatments for Odo.

Two days after the creature's flight from the outpost, the Changeling had shown no improvement in his condition. Uncertain about the possible effects on Odo of his brief link with the specimen, the medical staff continued to keep the shape-shifter in an isolation chamber. His semiliquid form, ash-colored and unmoving, had not changed since the incident. Perhaps not coincidentally, one of the issues that had caused the scientists to seek Odo's assistance—namely, their inability to determine whether or not the specimen was alive—had come to apply to the Changeling. It also remained unclear whether his biomimetic cells had somehow been forced into replicating the specimen's physical appearance, or if they had done so either through his conscious effort or reflexively.

The dialogue in the conference room had to that point lasted nearly an hour. The scientists detailed what they had done to revive and restore Odo—including placing him in a nutrient bath and surrounding him with different types and wavelengths of energy—but they reported no improvement. Beyond what they had already tried, they could not reach anything approaching a viable methodology on how to treat Odo. From what Selten heard, he gathered that the difficulty underscored the fact that Federation science possessed limited knowledge about the physiology of shapeshifters.

When the conversation flagged, Selten asked, "Who has the most medical experience with Changelings?"

Across from the security chief, sitting in the center of one long side of the table, Doctor Mennil Farran spoke up. A Lendrin, he stood more than two meters tall, had a long, white mane, silver eyes, and a bony protrusion that curved downward from his brow. Light dots of natural pigment speckled his nose and cheeks. "Doctor Norsa," he said, and then he looked to his colleagues for confirmation. They all offered words and nods of approval.

"I understand that Doctor Norsa has the most experience among the staff of the outpost," Selten said, "but is that true with respect to the entire Federation?"

The scientists glanced around at one another, offering general murmurs of disagreement. "No, certainly not," Farran finally said. "No Changelings were captured, either alive or dead, during the war, limiting the amount of research about them. Their leader surrendered herself into the custody of the Federation as part of the armistice, but she has declined to allow us to conduct even noninvasive medical tests."

To Farran's right, Doctor Vika Leth said, "The majority of what little we know about Changelings comes from the medical record of Odo." A Mizarian, she specialized in the study of biological regeneration. "The two primary physicians who served aboard Deep Space Nine during Odo's time there had more experience than anybody else."

"Were they asked to join the study of the specimen?" Selten wanted to know.

"We invited both Julian Bashir and Girani Semna," Farran said, "but both declined."

Selten had heard of Bashir, a Starfleet officer. After the doctor's recent actions at Andor, most of the Federation had. Bashir had been taken into custody by Starfleet so that he could stand court-martial for his actions. Selten didn't know whether or not the trial had yet taken place.

"I can make a request to Starfleet Command for assistance from Doctor Bashir," Selten said, "but I think it is unlikely that they would permit outside contact with him. What about Doctor Semna?"

"Doctor Girani, actually," Farran said. "She's Bajoran, and I believe that's she's practicing medicine on her homeworld."

"That's right," Leth agreed. "She was posted to Deep Space Nine as part of her planet's Militia, but she chose not to transfer to Starfleet when Bajor joined the Federation."

"Does it make sense to attempt to enlist her aid?" the security chief asked.

"Yes, I think so," Leth said, and Selten saw nods all around the table. "Since we're not talking about the study of a specimen, but an attempt to save a life, I'm sure she would do whatever she can to help."

Selten looked to Gellish. "Doctor, as the acting chief of

staff, would you make that request? Go through Starfleet Medical if you need to, but in this situation, I think direct contact is advised."

"Of course," Gellish said. "In the meantime, barring any negative change in Odo's condition, we'll continue to do what we've been doing, with the hope that we can prevent any deterioration."

Selten waited a beat to see if anyone would say anything more, but the meeting had clearly come to an end. As the scientists rose and prepared to leave, the security chief collected the padd he had brought with him and quickly exited the conference room. He made his way out to the entry hall, where technicians worked to repair the door that the creature had breached and forced open as it had fled. Two of his security staff stood guard there, and they or others would guard the access point until the door had been mended.

Selten headed for the turbolift and took it up to the first level of the outpost. He entered the security office, where several of his staff monitored the installation and the planetary system. He intended to check on the status of the creature, but before he could, a member of his staff looked up from his console and spoke to him.

"Sir," said Ensign Connor Block, "we've been tracking the creature on long-range sensors. It has exited the system and gone to warp."

The news surprised Selten. Spaceborne organisms did exist that had the capability of traveling faster than light, but they possessed complex and very specialized structures to allow them that capability. The scientists had found nothing like that with respect to the creature. *Of course, as a shapeshifter, it can presumably take many forms.*

"So far, it is maintaining a linear trajectory," Block continued.

"What is its bearing?" Selten asked.

"Sir," Block said, "it's on a direct course for the Bajoran system."

Ro tapped at the door chime and waited, unsure whether she should have come down to the residential deck. She had accepted an invitation a few days earlier from Quark to have dinner in his quarters, something they hadn't done in quite a while. She'd contacted him from her office just half an hour before the time she'd been supposed to meet him, apologizing and saying that she had too much to do, and that she wouldn't be able to get together after all. Quark made it easy for her, telling her that he understood, and also that it worked out well for him because he had a lot of things to take care of at his Public House, Café, Gaming Emporium, Holosuite Arcade, and Ferengi Embassy. They agreed to reschedule sometime soon, but the captain could see the disappointment on Quark's face.

I need to be honest with him, Ro told herself. To do that, though, she would first have to be honest with herself. *Whatever that means.*

In front of Ro, the door glided open. Until that moment, she didn't know what she'd expected to see—anger, grief, distress . . . some sort of strong negative emotion. Two nights previously, Cenn Desca had railed at the kai, drunkenly—and publicly—lambasting her for foisting the lie of the Prophets' divinity upon the Bajoran people. Although those who witnessed the tirade could not possibly understand its source—the Ohalavaru discovery and their associated claims had yet to be announced to the general population—Ro certainly did.

A week earlier, as he'd reported on the events on Endalla, Cenn had appeared on the brink of an emotional breakdown. When Cenn returned to the starbase after dealing with the Ohalavaru, the captain suggested that he pay a visit to Lieutenant Commander Matthias so that she could assign him to one of the counseling staff. *When he didn't do that, I should have made it an order,* Ro thought. Instead, she encouraged him to take some leave, and to use that time off to settle his mind. Cenn demurred, telling her that he preferred to keep himself occupied, and that discharging his normal duties would allow him to do that. Ro empathized with his attitude, as she'd often felt the same way.

But then he exploded at the kai, Ro thought. She blamed herself for allowing the situation with Cenn to get that far. At that point, she ordered him to see Matthias, and also to take five days of leave.

That had been just two nights prior. Since then, Matthias reported that she had taken on Cenn's case herself, and that he had already been to see her for a pair of counseling sessions. Despite that, Ro did not expect her first officer to recover emotionally—at least not fully—for quite some time.

But standing before her and gazing out from just inside the doorway of his quarters, Cenn Desca looked fine. He wore civilian clothes of a modern Bajoran style—casual dark-blue slacks and a layered, aqua-colored sweater. Ro realized she'd thought that when she made her unannounced visit, she might find him drinking, but he had clear eyes and an attentive expression.

"Captain," he said. "I wasn't expecting you. Please come in."

"Thank you," Ro said. Cenn stepped aside and she walked past him. Once more, what she saw surprised her. Nothing had been thrown around the cabin, no dirty dishes had been left on the dining table, nothing seemed out of place.

"Please have a seat, Captain," Cenn said, moving toward the sitting area. "Can I get you something to drink?"

"No, nothing, Desca, thanks." She sat down in a comfortable chair, and Cenn did so as well.

"I guess I don't have to ask what brings you here, Captain."

"No, I'm sure it's obvious," Ro said. "But I'm not here as your commanding officer, Desca. I'm here as your friend."

"I appreciate that," Cenn said. "I know I worried my friends and crewmates with my behavior the other night—and I certainly didn't make a favorable showing before the kai."

"She told me that, given the circumstances, she understood," Ro said. "The kai had nothing negative to say about you, and only offered her concern."

"Yes, well, she's not the spiritual leader of billions for no reason."

Ro nodded in agreement. She had always found Kai Pralon reasonable and forgiving. The conversation lagged for a moment, and the captain rushed to fill the silence before it extended. "I'm glad that you've been talking with Commander Matthias."

"She's really helped me in the last two days," Cenn said. "It's been good just to talk to somebody about everything that's happened. Since the whole story hasn't come out yet, I can't mention it to any other of my Bajoran crewmates or friends. Commander Matthias isn't Bajoran, but her husband is, so she has a better perspective than most on what all of this means."

"I'm glad she's helping," Ro said. "I also want you to know that you can come to me, Desca." The captain immediately realized why Cenn hadn't chosen to speak with her, and he immediately confirmed her suspicion.

"You're not a believer," he told her. "I don't mean that in a pejorative way—" Cenn stopped and chuckled. "How could I mean it that way, when it turns out that you were right all along? It's just that, if I talked with a friend, I would want it to be with somebody who would understand in an organic way what it would be like to lose your faith—no, not to lose it . . . to have it ripped away from you." Cenn's jaw clenched, and Ro saw him make a conscious effort to calm himself. She sensed the deft hand of Phillipa Matthias at work.

"Does what happened really have to rob you of your faith?" Ro asked. "You've believed in the Prophets for virtually all your life, haven't you? And those convictions have served you well." The captain glanced over to the corner of the compartment, to where Cenn kept a small shrine.

The shrine was no longer there.

Ro then peered over at a set of shelves where Cenn had displayed handsome hardbound editions of the complete Bajoran canon. Even as a nonbeliever, Ro could easily appreciate the artistry and craftsmanship required in the creation of the beautiful illuminated manuscripts. Like the shrine, they too were gone. She looked back at Cenn, and he started answering her questions even before she asked them.

"It's not a matter of conviction," he said. "It's about faith. And faith is something that you either have or you don't. You can't manufacture it. Either it's there inside you, a piece of who you are, or it's not. I had faith. Now I don't. I can't pretend to believe in something that I know to be a lie any more than you can."

"But that means that you're taking the Ohalavaru at their word," Ro said. "Just because they interpreted their discovery on Endalla as a falsework used in creating the Celestial Temple doesn't mean that they're right. And even if they are, their conclusion that it proves the Prophets aren't gods doesn't necessarily follow."

"It does, though," Cenn said. He sounded sad, even disconsolate, but also accepting. "With respect, Captain, you weren't there. You didn't see what I saw . . . the vastness of it . . . the incredible complexity . . . the advancement it represented, not just in technology, but in conception. I'm not an engineer, so I can't tell you about how the construct I saw could be used to anchor a wormhole, or how a moon could be built around it and made to look naturally occurring . . . but I could *feel* all of that. I got so angry at the Ohalavaru . . . slammed one of them into a wall . . . because I knew the claim they were going to make about the false-work even before they made it . . . because I could see it for myself."

"Maybe you're wrong," Ro ventured.

"No," Cenn said. "I'm not. I wish I were, but I'm not." He spoke not with self-pity, but with resignation.

Ro stood up from her chair. She wanted to go over to Cenn, take him by the arms, and shake him. Instead, she extracted herself from the sitting area and crossed the room, over to where her first officer's shrine used to stand. When she looked back over at Cenn, she said, "I have to tell you, Desca, that the Ohalavaru discovery has me rethinking my own beliefs."

"What?" Cenn asked. "What do you mean?"

"I mean that this entire situation has had the opposite effect on me than it's had on you," Ro said. "The report you submitted on what you saw on Endalla . . . it's actually moved me *toward* recognizing the Prophets as gods."

Cenn didn't say anything for a few seconds, as though he had difficulty processing what Ro had just told him. Finally, he said, "I can't say that doesn't surprise me, because it does. But I'm also happy for you. I truly hope that, if you reach a place of belief, of faith, that it gives you great comfort."

"Maybe you can help me," Ro said, though she recognized her attempt to re-engage Cenn with the Bajoran religion could not have been more transparent.

"I'm sorry, but I don't think I could do that," Cenn said. "Even if I was staying."

"What?"

"I didn't intend to tell you like this, but I've tendered my resignation from the Bajoran Militia," Cenn said. "I was going to visit your office first thing in the morning to tell you."

Ro paced quickly back over to the sitting area and stared down at her first officer from behind the chair she'd been using. "Desca, you can't just run away from this." She wanted to stop him from doing something rash, just as she had done with her chief of security a week earlier, when Blackmer had attempted to resign. But Colonel Cenn did not serve in Starfleet, and so Ro did not have the same authority. "You've been in the Militia since the end of the Occupation. That's seventeen years. You've built a life for yourself."

"But that life no longer suits me." Cenn sounded certain. "I'll just have to build another one."

"Doing what?" Ro asked. "You've loved your time in the Militia."

"I don't know," Cenn said. "I only know that whatever I choose to do, it will be somewhere beyond the Bajoran system."

"Oh, Desca," Ro said. She circled the chair and sat back down again. "Please don't be rash." She leaned forward, her manner urgent. "You should allow some time to pass before changing your life so dramatically."

"My life has already been changed dramatically, and there was nothing I could do to stop it," Cenn said. "Do you know when word of the Ohalavaru discovery will be made public?"

"I actually expected the kai might make the announcement today," Ro said. Pralon Onala had departed the starbase for Bajor the previous night, after attending evening services. "I'm sure it will come sometime in the next few days."

"I thought it might," Cenn said. "My preference is to be far away from here when it is announced. The reaction is going to be frenzied and loud."

Ro agreed. "I remember what happened when the Ohalu texts were released to the public."

"That's why, ten minutes ago, I booked passage on an Alonis freighter leaving at midday tomorrow."

Ro shook her head. "No, Desca," she said. "You can't go so quickly. You might be able to get away from the furor that's going to erupt, but you can't just run away from what you think and feel."

"I do want to thank you for everything," Cenn told her. "For your leadership and your trust in me, and for your friendship.

"Desca, please," Ro said. "I'm convinced that—"

The electronic chirp of the starbase's comm system sounded. *"Hub to Captain Ro."*

"This is Ro. Go ahead, Vel." Lieutenant Aleco worked as duty officer on beta shift that evening.

"Captain, we've received a message from a Federation research facility," Aleco said. *"Priority one."*

Ro and Cenn looked at each other. "I'm on my way," she said. "Ro out." She stood up and told her first officer, "I urge you to reconsider before leaving Deep Space Nine."

Cenn rose as well. "I'm sorry, Captain."

"So am I, Desca," Ro said. "So am I." Then she strode purposefully toward the door, on her way to the Hub.

For once, his uncle hadn't made him beg to use a holosuite. It might have helped that Nog had yet to tell anybody that he'd fixed Vic's program, meaning that Quark believed it still required repair. *It was more than just that,* Nog thought. It almost worried him, since his uncle had seemed distracted and . . . well, forlorn. Then again, the barkeep could certainly be moody, with the typical cause being an extra slip of latinum in cost here or one fewer strip of latinum in payment there. Nog didn't feel that he really needed to worry about Quark. Besides, the engineer had his own problems.

Nog entered the holosuite, anxious about what he would find. A major reason he hadn't mentioned that he'd fixed Vic's program was because it wasn't entirely clear to him that he actually had. To be sure, it had looked vastly different when it had activated in the holosuite the night before. In the brief time he'd seen Vic, Nog thought that he sounded, looked, and acted like his old self—despite his run-down surroundings, shoddy clothing, and rushed manner—but it could be that the matrix had decayed during the two years it had been running in the simulation tester.

"There's only one way to find out," Nog said, and his voice produced a slight echo in the unadorned space. He set down the hologram simulation tester, which he'd brought with him as cover; he no longer needed it, since he had stored Vic's matrix in the starbase's memory banks. "Computer, run program Bashir Sixty-two."

In the fraction of a second it took for the holosuite to come to life, Nog worried that his success in finally loading Vic's matrix would prove temporary. He needn't have. Just as he had the previous night, he found himself in a dingy corridor, fronted by a number of closed doors. Nog quickly moved to the one marked with the number *23*, where he had found Vic. He rapped lightly on the door, and when he received no response, he tried to turn the knob, without success.

Feeling as though he had loaded one of Doctor Bashir's

old-time spy programs, Nog looked both ways down the empty hall. Satisfied that he was alone, he moved close to the door and whispered his friend's name. He still heard no reply, and when he listened carefully, his sensitive ears told him that Vic's room was empty.

Disappointed, but committed to seeing his friend again, Nog waited. Twenty minutes passed quietly, and he considered leaving the seedy hotel to look for Vic, but he didn't want to risk missing him. After another thirty minutes, Nog finally heard footfalls on the stairs. He waited expectantly, but as the steps shuffled upward, he knew that they did not belong to Vic.

At the end of the hallway, a shadowy human shape appeared, barely visible in the dim lighting. Stooped over, his grubby clothes hanging about him in tatters, the man staggered forward. He carried a brown paper bag in one hand, and as he lifted it to his mouth, he finally took notice of Nog.

"Whaddaya want?" he said, his words coming out in a croak. "I ain got nuthin." He edged to the opposite side of the hallway from Nog, lost his balance, and fell shoulder-first against the wall. Nog automatically took a step forward to help, but the man snarled at him. "Nah, I toll ya, I ain got nuthin!"

"All right, all right," Nog said, backing away, holding his hands up to show that he meant no harm. "I don't want anything."

The man pushed away from the wall and lurched forward. The scent of alcohol and unwashed flesh preceded him. As he got closer, Nog backed away, wanting to avoid appearing as any kind of threat. When the man reached the door marked *22*—or almost marked *22*—he fumbled in the pocket of the loose jacket that hung from his shoulders like a tarp. Two rumpled tissues fell out and onto the floor. Eventually, he extracted a key, and after several abortive tries, he managed to slide it into the lock. He opened the door and nearly toppled into the room beyond, but then found his way back to slam it closed.

Frustrated, Nog walked to the end of the hallway and went down the stairway. He came to a landing halfway down, then turned a corner and descended the rest of the way. A checkered black-and-white floor filled a squarish, poorly lighted lobby. A short hallway connected to another that appeared to run beneath the one on the level above. From behind a metal grate, in what basically looked like a cage, a gruff, unshaved human peered out at him.

"Excuse me," Nog said to the man. "I'm looking for—" He stopped, unsure Vic would want him to use his name— or if Vic himself had used his own name in that place. "I'm looking for the man in room twenty-three."

"Yeah?" the man said. "Whaddaya want me to do about it?"

"I was just wondering if you've seen him?"

"I don't see nuthin."

Nog shook his head. He liked Vic, and he enjoyed visiting him at his casino and in his apartment, but he didn't understand the Earth of that era. He eyed the door to the street, which stood ajar, and he thought again about going out to look for Vic. Maybe if he—

The intercom trilled. *"Commander Nog,"* came the voice of Ensign Zhang Suyin, who crewed the communications console in the Hub during gamma shift. *"Please report to Captain Ro in the conference room in thirty minutes, at twenty-two-hundred."*

The time told Nog that gamma shift had started while he'd been in the holosuite. He wondered why the captain needed to see him—and probably other members of the command crew, since she wanted to meet in the conference room. At least he would have time to go to his quarters and change into his uniform beforehand.

Because he currently wore civilian clothes, he did not have a combadge with him. "Computer, end program," he said, and the run-down hotel lobby disappeared, replaced by the cool, blank bulkheads of the holosuite. Nog walked to the door and tapped at the companel there. "Nog to the Hub," he said. "Message received. I'll be there."

Nog picked up the simulation tester. On his way out of the holosuite, he vowed to come back later that night if possible, and if not, then to return the next night. He wanted to find Vic and make sure he was all right. At that moment, he had a bad feeling about whatever had happened to his friend.

Quark paced back and forth in his office, working on a padd to calculate his expected balance. He factored the latest interest fluctuations coming out of the Ferengi Central Reserve against the micro-compounding policies of the Bank of Luria. He checked the current time and—

And I should be having dinner with Laren right now, Quark thought. He hadn't seen much of her in recent days, and nothing at all of her in private. *It hasn't been just the last few days,* he reminded himself. *It's been ever since the new starbase opened for business.*

Quark didn't resent Laren's position or responsibilities. He knew that she took great satisfaction in her command, probably not least of all because it had come as such an unexpected occurrence in her professional life. She'd encountered trouble in her Starfleet career on more than one occasion, and she'd made her share of enemies—including the present commander in chief of Starfleet Command, Admiral Akaar. Fortunately, Laren had also drawn other officers staunchly to her side, such as Kira Nerys and Elias Vaughn, and that, coupled with an exemplary service record since arriving at the original Deep Space 9 nearly a decade prior, had made it possible for her to move up the ranks.

I can remember when we talked about leaving the old station together, Quark thought. With Bajor joining the Federation and off-world Militia operations being absorbed into Starfleet, Laren had believed her days numbered. At the time, before he had hit on the idea of incorporating the Ferengi Embassy into his establishment, Quark had also viewed UFP encroachment as the likely end to his business prospects on DS9. *Maybe we should have left together.*

"Stop it," Quark told himself. Staying in the star system had actually brought him some of the business success he had sought for so long. His place on Bajor, which he'd established after the destruction of the original station, had been wildly popular when DS9's operations had temporarily moved planetside, and, under the management of Treir, it continued to turn a healthy profit. His new bar, on the new starbase, had hit a few lulls here and there, but for the most part, it had earned him more latinum than even he had forecast.

Too bad I can't seem to hold on to it.

Quark stopped pacing, looked at the padd in his hand, and reprimanded himself for his drifting attention. Laren—and even thoughts of Laren—had the capacity to divert him from business. He might have been able to deal with that, had she been his only distraction, but other subjects consumed his time, his concentration, and worst of all, his profits.

In the bulkhead in front of Quark, rows of muted but active monitors brought news from comnets all over the quadrant, raw material for his powerful data-mining programs. He liked to think that his system rivaled that of Yridian information merchants. The majority of the data displayed there related directly to his business, either to inventory and other items for one of his two bars, or to deals that he hoped to negotiate or had already set in motion. Several other of the displays kept him apprised of local matters—streaming in from Cardassia, Bajor, and Deep Space 9 itself. At that moment, he noticed the new Federation president, Kellessar zh'Tarash, speaking on one monitor, and Kai Pralon Onala on another.

Two of the screens, though, showed images from places in which he had no business interests, either real or prospective: the cloud city of Stratos on the planet Ardana, and the crystal city of Geopolis on Janus VI. For a while, Quark had told himself that he'd pursued the matter as diligently as he had, for as long as he had, because he believed it would restore a long-term asset to his balance sheet. But the hunt had taken up so much of his time, concentration, and profits that he could no longer lie to himself about it.

Quark looked away from the monitors and checked the time. He saw that several minutes had gone by since he'd completed his calculations, and so he had to start all over again. When he once again reached an expected value for the balance on his account at the Bank of Luria, he quickly moved to the freestanding companel console he used as his desk. He initiated a secure data-link to the Lurian Commerce Net, worked through the copious, complex, and critical protections, then at last accessed his account. He quickly compared the tally listed there with his own calculation. As he always did, Quark breathed a sigh of relief when he saw that the figures matched, down to the last strip, slip, and scintilla of latinum.

After that, he took a deep breath. He separated out a fraction of his holdings and marked it for transfer, specifying the various routing and security data. Before he could change his mind, Quark executed the transaction.

Regardless of the reason necessitating the withdrawal of funds from any of his accounts, doing so always caused him anxiety. It also made his lobes grow cold. Allowing the diminution of his profits for any reason ran counter to every Ferengi sensibility. The very first Rule of Acquisition said: *Once you have their money, you never give it back.* Quark had always interpreted that as: *Once you have any money, you never give it* to anybody.

He quickly operated his companel to record a message. "Viray, I've transferred the funds you requested," he said. "You now have enough to hire a ship to take you from Ardana to Janus Six. I've studied the report you sent from Stratos and . . ." Quark stopped and paused the recording, trying to formulate exactly how to phrase his apprehensions to Mayereen Viray, the Petarian private investigator he'd hired to find Morn. The loquacious Lurian had walked out of Quark's establishment on Bajor a year and a half earlier, and he'd never returned—although he had shortly thereafter sent a courier to settle his bar tab in full. Two other detectives had failed to find Morn, but Viray had tracked him to Stratos, and from there to Geopolis.

Quark wanted to voice his concerns—his *legitimate* concerns—to his investigator without offending her. She had made it clear that she liked neither to waste her time, nor to work for people not wholly committed to their own goals. Bearing that in mind, Quark queued his message back and resumed recording. "I've studied the report you sent from Stratos, and the evidence you provided is suggestive, and even in part compelling. I hope when you arrive at Geopolis, though, you are able to find something *concrete*. Keep me informed."

As Quark reviewed his recording, he heard a sudden din out in the bar. When he had closed the door to his office, he had not closed the inner, soundproof panel. He quickly transmitted his message to Viray, then hied across his office. When he opened the door and stuck his head out, he saw down the corridor and out into the large, main room of the bar. Past the half wall that separated his establishment from the main Plaza walkway, a crowd rushed by, their combined speech an intricate amalgam of sound. Quark concentrated in order to extract individual voices from the acoustic mixture. He heard anger, distress, confusion.

". . . to the temple. I want to hear what Vedek Novor has to say . . ."

". . . the first minister shouldn't allow any analysis . . ."

". . . if you ask me, it's just more Ohalavaru terrorism . . ."

". . . the kai can't possibly believe . . ."

The kai, Quark thought. He had just seen her on the comnet. He took a moment to watch those flooding past the bar and saw almost exclusively Bajorans. Quark quickly retreated back into his office and moved to the companel. With dexterity born of experience, he restored the audio to the Bajoran feed and replayed it from the beginning of Kai Pralon's appearance.

Quark listened with interest as the spiritual leader spoke of an attack by Ohalavaru extremists on Endalla. Without equivocation, she denounced the actions, which had put a number of Starfleet officers at risk, although there had fortunately been no loss of life—unlike five-plus years prior, when members of the Ohalu sect had first set their sights on Bajor's largest moon.

Pralon went on to explain that the two actions were apparently related, part of a plan by certain Ohalavaru to prove their beliefs. To that end, they had succeeded in uncovering a previously unknown installation hidden beneath the surface of Endalla. The kai noted that First Minister Asarem would later address the people of Bajor about the matter, but that the government would likely send scientists and engineers, along with a contingent from the Vedek Assembly, to study what the Ohalavaru had found.

The Vedek Assembly? Quark wondered. *If they need to send scientists and engineers, why would they need to send members of the clergy?*

Pralon answered that question by making a statement Quark thought far more inflammatory than when the entirety of the translated Ohalu texts had been posted to the Bajoran comnet. The kai quoted Ohalavaru claims that the installation they had uncovered provided proof that the Prophets were not gods. Pralon went on to say that she did not herself put any credence in those allegations, and that she was sure an examination would demonstrate their falseness conclusively—but Quark doubted that many Bajorans had continued listening after hearing what they considered blasphemy.

She's smart, Quark thought. He understood why she had given voice to a heterodox point of view. By doing so, she had been able to immediately follow it with her own denial, and even if everybody watching hadn't made it to that part, her address would be replayed again and again. Pralon also undercut the shock that the Ohalavaru clearly wanted to create on Bajor; yes, the sacrilegious contention still stunned Bajorans, but hearing it from their own spiritual leader softened it.

Quark wondered if Laren had postponed their dinner that evening because she'd known about the kai's address. He thought it likely, considering that members of her own crew regularly patrolled Endalla, and they had obviously been on the moon at the time of the attack. It actually made Quark feel better to know the reason he hadn't been able to see Laren, but he also worried what impact Pralon's announcement would have on her. He knew that the captain didn't categorize herself as a believer in the Prophets, but many in her crew did, including—

Including Cenn Desca. Laren's first officer rarely visited the bar, but Quark knew that he had a reputation as a pious man. His behavior in the bar two nights previous suddenly came into sharp focus.

I should contact Laren, Quark thought. He really would have preferred to go see her, but he knew that he couldn't do that. In fact, even if he simply tried to reach her, he undoubtedly wouldn't be able to; she would have too much to deal with in the wake of the kai's address.

Maybe I'll go to her quarters later tonight, he thought, *after things have calmed down.* He had done that on a few occasions in the past, offering her support in times of crisis. She had also done the same for him.

Quark secured his companel. He also shut down his many displays, though his data-mining programs would continue to monitor the incoming comnet feeds. He then headed out into the bar, unsure what the next few days would bring.

Ro entered the conference room off the Hub and took a seat at the head of the table. Her command crew—but for the notable exception of Colonel Cenn—had already arrived. Along the side of the table to her left sat her chief of security, Lieutenant Commander Jefferson Blackmer; tactical officer, *Dalin* Zivan Slaine; communications officer, Lieutenant Ren Kalanent Viss; and the second officer, Lieutenant Commander Wheeler Stinson. To her right sat Chief Engineer Miles O'Brien; operations officer and assistant chief engineer, Lieutenant Commander Nog; science officer, Lieutenant Commander John Candlewood; and chief medical officer, Doctor Pascal Boudreaux. They all looked to her expectantly, probably not just because she had called them to a meeting at the beginning of gamma shift, but also because they'd seen, or at least heard about, Kai Pralon's statements to the Bajoran people.

"An hour ago, we received a priority-one transmission from a Federation research facility," Ro said without preamble. She saw several surprised expressions around the table, likely because those present had expected her to address the Ohalavaru situation. "Some time ago," she continued, "the crew of a Starfleet science vessel evidently detected an unusual energy burst inside a star system. They tracked the readings to an asteroid belt. They found a number of subspace anomalies in the vicinity, but they were unable to ascertain the cause of the burst. Their investigation did lead them to an asteroid on which they discovered an unusual substance, which they concluded might be a massive shape-shifter."

Ro saw a number of expressions around the table. O'Brien and Nog exchanged concerned glances. Slaine narrowed her eyes in distrust. Even ten years past, ghosts of the Dominion War haunted the Alpha and Beta Quadrants. Despite the subsequent isolationism of the Founders and their empire, and a decade of peace, suspicions of them still remained.

"The readings of the Starfleet crew led them to believe that the substance probably wasn't a Changeling," Ro went on. "But they couldn't tell with certainty whether the substance was a shape-shifter, or if it was alive, hibernating, or dead. So they collected it from the surface of the asteroid and delivered it to the research facility."

"What research facility?" Boudreaux asked.

"That information is classified," Ro said. The captain saw several looks of disapproval, and she understood why. She had obviously called her command crew together in their off-hours because they would need to deal with a problematic situation. In order to do that most effectively, they would want as much information as they could get, and Starfleet

Command restricting their access to potentially useful data could prevent that.

"Once the substance had been taken to the research facility," Ro said, "the scientists there examined it. Over some significant period of time, all their efforts to conclusively categorize it either as a shape-shifter or as something else failed. At that point, they invited Odo to join them."

The Changeling—and Ro's predecessor as chief of security aboard the original DS9—had visited the old station around the time that Bajor had joined the Federation. He had also been in the Alpha Quadrant for these last two years, essentially cut off from the Gamma Quadrant and the Dominion after the wormhole had collapsed. All of her command crew had met Odo and knew him to some extent, and O'Brien and Nog had served with him.

"Two days ago, Odo attempted to link with the substance," Ro said. "It attacked him and several scientists, then fled the research facility. It evidently is a shape-shifter of some kind, and possibly—perhaps probably—intelligent. It utilized gravitational fields within a planetary system to propel itself out of that system, at which point it accelerated to warp speed. The facility's long-range sensors have been tracking the shape-shifter, and it has maintained a direct course for Bajor."

"For Bajor?" Candlewood asked. "Why would it be headed for Bajor?"

"We don't know," Ro said.

"Maybe it's not headed for the planet," offered Slaine. "Maybe it's headed for the wormhole."

"If it is a Founder, that would make sense," O'Brien said. "Maybe it just wants to go home."

"Or if the scientists are correct and it isn't a Changeling," Nog suggested, "maybe it knows about the Great Link and wants to join them."

"Those are all possibilities," Ro said. "And if this shape-shifter is only interested in traveling through the wormhole, that's acceptable. My concern is that we don't know its aims. It already attacked ten people at the research facility and left at least two of them dead. I don't want to take a chance that it has designs on attacking either Bajor or this starbase." Ro's officers all nodded in agreement. "Wheeler," she said, "I want you to take the *Defiant* out and intercept the shape-shifter. Kalanent, attempt to communicate with it and ascertain its intentions. If you believe that either Bajor or Deep Space Nine is a target for attack, warn it away."

"What if we're unable to determine its purpose?" asked Stinson.

"Until we know for sure what it wants," Ro said, "I don't intend to let it enter Bajoran space. Zivan, employ a tractor beam or other nonlethal force to keep it away. If necessary, and as a last resort, fire on it."

"Understood," said the tactical officer.

"John, I want you to go to provide whatever scientific analysis you can," Ro told Candlewood. "I want you on board as well, Pascal. Jeff, Miles, you will stay on the starbase, just in case the shape-shifter somehow gets past the *Defiant*."

The officers offered assents all around and started to rise, but Ro held up a hand to stop them. She motioned for everybody to take their seats again, and they all did. "There are two more issues," she told them. "First, Odo is apparently in critical condition. His color has changed and he is nonresponsive. The doctors at the research facility aren't even sure if he's still alive, or if he is, if he'll be able to recover from the attack. They've requested assistance with his care."

"The medical doctor most familiar with Odo—or with any Changelings, for that matter—is Julian Bashir," said O'Brien. The captain detected an edge in his voice, betraying his sympathies with the doctor. Ro knew he wasn't alone in thinking that Starfleet Command's decision to capture, imprison, and court-martial him was unjust. The captain knew that Bashir had violated orders—some of them hers—but the results of his disobedience spoke for themselves: the Andorian reproductive crisis had at last been resolved, Andor had rejoined the Federation, and the UFP had a new president whom all the people had rallied behind.

"The research facility has contacted Starfleet Command about procuring Doctor Bashir's help," Ro said, "but it's unclear if that can happen. In the meantime, they've asked Doctor Girani for her help." O'Brien and Nog had served with Girani Semna, but the captain offered a précis of her service record for the rest of her command crew. "She has agreed, so the *Defiant*'s first stop will be at Bajor to bring her aboard. After you deal with the shape-shifter, you will deliver Doctor Girani to the research facility. You'll be given instructions at that time where to go and how to approach."

"Yes, sir," said Stinson.

Ro leaned back in her chair before broaching the final subject she needed to discuss. She knew it would be uncomfortable, not only because of what she had to tell her crew, but also because of the decision she'd made. "You all know that Colonel Cenn took a few days of leave after the incident on Endalla," Ro said. "I visited him earlier to check on him, and I'm pleased to report that he is in much better spirits. Unfortunately, he has made the decision to resign from the Militia, and from his position aboard this starbase." The captain saw surprise on most of the faces in the room, as well as sadness. Most of the officers present had served with Cenn Desca for years.

And was that a fleeting glimpse of anticipation on Wheeler's face? Ro hoped not. Stinson had made no secret of his desire one day to attain the rank of captain and the command of his own ship. A bump up to first officer of Deep Space 9 would grant him an obvious next step on that path. Ro didn't begrudge Stinson his ambition, but she would not appreciate his taking even a small amount of pleasure at Cenn's departure.

"For the time being, Jeff, you will serve as acting first officer," Ro said. The security chief's eyebrows rose, the announcement plainly a surprise to him. She suspected that it also displeased Stinson, but she trusted that he recognized it made no sense to appoint him as acting exec when he would shortly be leaving the starbase aboard *Defiant*. "Once we've dealt with the shape-shifter and I've made my recommendations to Starfleet, I'll determine a permanent chain of command." Ro knew that she would also need to consult with the minister of state regarding a replacement for Cenn in his position as Bajoran liaison, but she had several candidates in mind.

"That's it," the captain said. "Dismissed."

Lieutenant Commander Wheeler Stinson sat in the command chair on the bridge of *Defiant*, trying to concentrate on the task at hand. He felt the pulse of the warp drive translating through the deck, listened to the hum of the ship around him, watched the starscape on the main viewscreen as the ship hurtled through the void. He worked hard to stay in the moment and not think beyond the current mission.

It had been more than two days since *Defiant* had departed Deep Space 9. After diverting to Bajor to bring Doctor Girani aboard, the crew had set course for the last reported coordinates of the alien life-form that had attacked scientists and escaped the Federation research facility. Since then, Girani had been in communication with the scientists at the outpost—via a relay located in the Oort cloud of a remote star system—in an attempt to help them nurse Odo back to health.

As the ship's sensors scoured surrounding space for any sign of the fleeing shape-shifter, Stinson watched the stars on the viewer. He could readily imagine the early treks of humanity away from the blue world it called home. He knew all of the firsts—Yuri Gagarin, Neil Armstrong, Verna Mitrios, Zefram Cochrane—had known about them since he'd been a boy, listening to his mother recite stories from the history of Man's extraterrestrial exploration. As a teen, he had devoured accounts from the first days of the United Earth Space Probe Agency all the way to modern-day Starfleet. He'd read all the classics, including *Small Steps and Giant Leaps*, *First Captain*, *The Stars Within Reach*, and *To Boldly Go*. He loved it all, but he reserved his most intense fascination for the captains—Archer and Hernandez, April and Pike and Kirk, the two Sulus, Robinson and Jang, and so many others.

Stinson fostered no illusions about the origin of his interest in starship commanders. His father had pursued a career in Starfleet, his primary goal to occupy the center seat. When he washed out of the command track, Harvey Stinson refused reclassification to engineering or to security, instead opting to drop out and sign on with a freighter line. On *Betelgeuse* and then *Rings of Meldora*, he worked his way up from deckhand to second mate. He never made it to master, though; he died when a hatch either gave way or hadn't been properly secured, and he was blown out into space. The inquest into the incident never reached an absolute conclusion about the hatch, so Harvey Stinson might have been the cause of his own death.

Just two years old when his father failed to come home from his run aboard *Rings of Meldora* between Andor and

Derenja V, Stinson had few firsthand memories of the man. Most of what he recalled came from holophotos and vids his mother had showed him, as well as from the stories she'd shared with her only child. Marjorie Montero kept her late husband's memory alive for her son, and she never tried to dissuade him from his passion to become a Starfleet captain. To the contrary, she not only supported his dreams, but nurtured them with her own desires to travel the stars. A research librarian, she read voraciously about the most majestic sights and places in the universe—from the perpetual comets in the skies of Remoré VII to the Forge on Vulcan, from the Jeweled Cliffs of Koltaari to the garnet seas on the Canopus Planet—and she hoped one day to visit as many of them as she could.

She'd never gotten the chance. A freak transporter accident claimed the life of Stinson's mother during his final year at the Academy. Coming to see him in San Francisco from her home in Wichita, she never rematerialized.

That had always seemed to Stinson like a particularly impersonal way to die. The loss of his mother had torn him up, especially since she had been traveling specifically to visit him. In the days immediately following her loss, Stinson stopping attending classes and exercises, at first holing up in his quarters, and then walking the campus for hours, and later, spending long, drunken nights in San Francisco.

He had faced expulsion, although the commandant of Starfleet Academy, sympathetic about his situation, had offered the alternative of discipline and counseling. Stinson had no interest in either, let alone both, and so he resolved to just walk away, allowing his superiors to amend and close his record however they saw fit. His father had never made it through the Academy, so what difference would it make if he washed out, too?

Hell, maybe I'll just sign on to a freighter myself, Stinson remembered thinking at the time. And somewhere in the back of his mind, had there also been the idea that maybe, just maybe, he wouldn't remember to seal all of the hatches on whatever hulk he ended up crewing? There seemed a sickly sort of poetry in that.

Stinson had never revealed all of that to anybody—not even to the counselors he'd eventually ended up seeing. One man—a gardener on the Academy grounds—seemed to intuit it. The man never mentioned it outright, but he said enough to finally get Stinson to take a hard look at the choices available to him. He returned to classes and exercises, redoubling his efforts to excel. The time away cost him—he dropped from first in his class to third—but not nearly as much as walking away would have.

"Commander," Slaine said from the tactical console on the port side of the bridge, "we have sensor contact with an object dead ahead."

Stinson blinked, realizing that he had allowed his thoughts to wander far from the current mission. He stood up just to get on his feet, to allow the simple physical act to help him clear his mind. "Is it the shape-shifter?" he asked. "Or is it a vessel?"

"Analyzing the scans now, sir," Slaine said. "It's moving at warp, about the size of a runabout. I'm detecting . . . organic tissue."

"It's the shape-shifter then."

"Possibly," Slaine said. "Commander Candlewood, what do you make of these readings?"

The science officer had clearly been examining the incoming sensor scans, because he responded without delay. "As you indicated, there is organic tissue, but I'm not detecting any biomimetic material," Candlewood said from his position beside Slaine. "At least, nothing that corresponds to a Changeling."

"But would we detect biomimetic material if the shape-shifter has become something else?" Slaine asked.

"No," Candlewood said.

"Sir," said Lieutenant Tenmei from the combined conn and ops panel forward of the command chair. "The object is within visual range."

"Maximum magnification," Stinson ordered.

On the main viewer, the starfield did not change, but in the center of the screen, a shape became visible. It looked bulbous, with a brownish cast. Two spiked appendages protruded forward from its body. It traveled with a gentle up-and-down sort of motion, and Stinson thought he saw wavering movement behind it, almost like that of a fish's fins.

"What is that?" Tenmei asked.

"Commander, I have a match in the species database," Candlewood reported. He worked his station, and a complete overhead view of the entity appeared on the right-hand third of the main screen. As Stinson studied it, the image shifted, showing it from different perspectives. It looked more or less as he'd envisioned it, with two long, sinewy tendrils emerging from the top rear of the entity's main body, and a third trailing out of the bottom rear. "Chief O'Brien reported seeing a creature of this type a decade ago. He and—" Candlewood looked up from his console. "Chief O'Brien and Odo were aboard the *Volga* when they encountered a creature of this type, but it turned out to be a shape-shifter who called himself Laas." The science officer consulted his displays again. "Captain Picard and the *Enterprise* crew also reported seeing this type of creature emerge from the wormhole just before it collapsed two years ago. It was Odo."

Stinson put all of the information together. "We've been told that scientists brought what they thought might be a shape-shifter to their research facility," he said. "They couldn't confirm that, or even if it was or had been a living being, until Odo linked with it. Then it came alive, altered its shape, attacked the scientists, and escaped into space, where it used gravity to leave the system and go to warp." He paused, allowing a moment for everybody to consider the sequence of events. "It's as though that entity out there learned to change its form from Odo, and possibly to that specific form." He pointed toward the main viewscreen.

"Could it be that the entity *acquired* the ability to change its shape from Odo?" Candlewood asked.

"That doesn't sound quite right to me," Stinson said. "But what do I know about Changelings . . . or shape-shifters . . . or whatever we should call that entity?"

"One thing we do know is that Changelings can communicate large amounts of information when linked," Candlewood said.

"Right," Stinson said. He returned to the command chair and sat down. "Commander Candlewood, is there any record of communication with either Laas or Odo when they were in the same form as that entity?"

"Checking," Candlewood said. He worked his station, before adding, "Negative. In both cases, there was no communication with the Changelings while they were in that form."

"All right," Stinson said. "Lieutenant Viss, it sounds as though you've got a difficult job. Open hailing frequencies."

"Hailing frequencies open," said Viss. The communications officer, a member of the aquatic Alonis species, wore a formfitting environmental suit, the helmet of which interpreted the underwater chirps and clicks of her native tongue into Federation Standard.

"This is Commander Wheeler Stinson of the *U.S.S. Defiant*, to the entity moving alone through space," he said. "We wish to speak with you. Please respond." He waited, but he did not expect to receive a reply. After several attempts went unanswered, Stinson said, "I know it's possible that the entity the shape-shifter is emulating is capable of receiving and sending subspace transmissions, or that the shape-shifter could form the necessary components to do that, but how likely is it?"

"There's really no way to tell based on the limited information we have," Candlewood said.

"Right," Stinson said. "So how can we establish communication?"

"I suggest visually," Viss said. "Flash a light in front of the creature in a sequence simple enough to be understood, yet complex enough to be an indication of intelligence and not just a random natural occurrence."

"How can we do that?" Stinson asked.

From the tactical console, Slaine said, "I can tune the shields to emit flashes of light."

"Will that impact our ability to defend ourselves?" Stinson wanted to know.

"No, sir. I can restore the shields to normal operation almost instantaneously," Slaine said.

"Let's try it," Stinson decided.

"I just need to know the sequence," Slaine said.

"I advise either a simple geometric progression—one flash, two flashes, four, eight—and then repeat," Viss said. "Or, alternatively, a Fibonacci sequence, where each number equals the sum of the previous two: one, one, two, three, five, eight, thirteen, and then repeat."

"Let's start with a geometric progression," Stinson said. "Lieutenant Tenmei, bring us out of warp and hold our position in the entity's path. Dalin Slaine, rig shields as needed."

The crew acknowledged their orders and set about their tasks. The bass vibration that accompanied *Defiant*'s faster-than-light drive began to fade. Stinson had never really cared for that sound, that feeling of a starship slowing and stopping. It always felt to him like an interruption in his personal journey; he preferred racing into his future at full speed.

"Thrusters at station-keeping," Tenmei said. "The entity is still traveling toward us at warp."

"Shields are ready, Commander," reported Slaine.

"Viewer to normal," Stinson said, and the screen reverted to showing an empty field of stars. "Initiate geometric sequence."

Slaine echoed the order as she operated her controls. Stinson did not expect to be able to see the results of her handiwork, but light-blue flashes did momentarily blot out the view on the main screen. One, two, four, eight. One, two, four, eight.

After the sequence had repeated a dozen times, Viss said, "Nothing, sir. No response."

"Even if the entity is perceiving our signal," Candlewood said, "and even if it wants to respond, it would have to have the ability to do so, and in a way that we could detect."

"I'm scanning across subspace and radio frequencies," Viss said.

"Sensors are open to all forms of electromagnetic radiation," Slaine added.

"Understood," Stinson said. "Keep trying."

The crew waited, but nothing happened. Eventually, Tenmei said, "The entity will reach our position in five minutes."

"All right, let's try something else," Stinson said. "Lieutenant Tenmei, bring us about. Lay in a course parallel to that of the entity. I want to travel alongside it."

"Aye, sir."

Around Stinson, *Defiant* woke from its slumber. The sonorous beat of the warp drive rose and filled the bridge. Stinson watched as the stars visible on the viewscreen began slipping to port as Tenmei brought the ship around. Once the image stabilized, Stinson said, "Show me the entity."

On the viewer, the spacefaring creature appeared, almost in profile. Stinson watched the graceful wavering of the tendrils, moving like eels through the sea. As it came fully abreast of *Defiant*, Tenmei said, "We are matching course and speed with the entity. It is still headed for Bajor."

"Dalin Slaine, set phasers to one one-hundredth intensity," Stinson said. "Fire across the path of the entity, just as we did with the shield flashes: one shot, two shots, four, eight."

"Yes, sir," Slaine said. She worked the tactical console, then said, "Ready."

"Fire." Feedback tones sounded as Slaine triggered the ship's phasers. On the viewscreen, a beam of amplified, coherent light sliced through space ahead of the entity. After a three-second pause, two of the yellow-red beams followed in quick succession, then after another gap, four shots, and then eight.

"I'm detecting no change in the flight of the entity," Slaine said.

"Communications is not picking up anything," said Viss.

"Sensors remain clear," Candlewood said. "If it's attempting to respond in any way, we're not finding it."

"All right, I guess we're going to have to do this the hard way," Stinson said. "Are the shields up full?"

"Aye, sir," said Slaine.

"Lieutenant Tenmei, bring us to within range of our tractor beam," Stinson said. "Maintain relative course and speed."

"Aye, sir."

"Commander Nog," Stinson said. DS9's chief of operations crewed an engineering panel off to starboard, beside Viss. "Can we use the tractor beam to pull the entity out of warp?"

"Yes, sir," Nog said. "Once we have a lock on the entity, we just need to drop the ship to sublight speed."

"Lieutenant Tenmei?" Stinson said.

"Understood, sir," Tenmei said.

The image of the entity on the viewscreen grew as *Defiant* neared it. Finally, Tenmei announced that the ship had closed the distance. "Commander Nog, engage tractor beam."

"Engaging tractor beam."

On the viewer, a hazy white cone of light swept out across the entity. The creature immediately attempted to veer off. *Defiant* rocked with the effort, but the beam held.

"Slowing to sublight speed," Tenmei said. The sound of the ship changed from the resonant beat of the warp drive to the higher-pitched whine of the impulse engines.

"The entity is trying to get away," Slaine said. It began moving wildly from side to side and up and down inside the white light.

"Sheering forces are increasing," Nog said. "I'm not sure if the tractor beam can hold."

"Increase power to the beam," Stinson said.

"Increasing power," Nog said. On the viewscreen, the brightness of the beam increased, and the entity's movements quieted. "I think we have it. Power consumption—"

Suddenly, the entity moved with lightning speed—not out of the tractor beam, but back along its path. Several of the crew spoke at once. Numerous thoughts rose in Stinson's mind: to order the ship away from the entity, to fire the ship's weapons at it, and to reverse the tractor beam so that it would repel rather than hold. "Cut the beam," he said. "Evasive maneuvers."

Stinson saw the white cone of the tractor beam vanish from the viewscreen, and the pattern of stars beyond the entity begin to shift. Then *Defiant* rocked hard, inertial dampers momentarily failing. Stinson was nearly thrown from the command chair, and he saw Nog and Viss hurled onto the deck. Both scrambled back into their seats, the task a bit more cumbersome for the communications officer because of her environmental suit. The lighting panels in the overhead winked off and then back on.

"Slaine, report," Stinson called out. "Were we fired on?"

"Negative. The entity has rammed the ship," Slaine said.

"Phasers, full power," Stinson said. "Fire." He expected to hear the tones that accompanied the firing of the ship's weapons, but instead, Slaine turned toward him in her chair.

"Commander, we can't," she said. "The entity is no longer in the form we saw it. It has reverted to a liquid or semi-liquid composition and is in the process of enshrouding the *Defiant*. If we fire while it is in contact with the hull, we could damage the ship."

"What is the condition of the shields?" Stinson asked.

"Shields are intact," Slaine said. "The shape-shifter penetrated them as if they weren't even there." Stinson thought to ask how it could do that, but considering that it could change its form, it must have been able to constitute itself in a manner that allowed it through the shields—perhaps it had even made itself essentially into a shield.

"I could reverse the polarity of the tractor beam," Nog suggested. "Try to push it away."

"Do it," Stinson said.

"Reversing tractor beam," Nog said, and a whine accompanied his efforts at his engineering station.

"It's moving one section of the shape-shifter away from the hull—" Slaine began, her words encouraging, but then she stopped herself short. "The shape-shifter has opened a hole in its body around the tractor emitter," she said. "The beam isn't even touching it, just shooting out into space."

"Cut tractor," Stinson said.

"Cutting tractor beam," Nog said.

"Damage report," Stinson said. "What is that thing doing to us?" He glanced over at the main viewer and no longer saw the stars. Rather, the screen had gone blank. *No, not blank,* Stinson realized. *Covered.*

"The shape-shifter has completely coated the exterior of the ship," Slaine said, confirming Stinson's suspicion. "It's encasing the *Defiant* like a second skin."

"Why?" Stinson said. "What is it trying to do?"

"There's no increase in pressure on the hull," Nog said. "I am detecting a subspace variance . . . but nothing that puts the ship at risk."

"It doesn't appear to be doing anything now," Slaine said.

"Lieutenant Tenmei," Stinson said, "full stop." As the flight controller acknowledged the order and worked her console, the ship quieted.

"Thrusters at station-keeping," Tenmei said.

"The shape-shifter has opened holes in itself to allow our thrusters to function," Slaine said.

Stinson stood up and walked toward the tactical console off to port. "What would happen if we opened the doors of the shuttlecraft hangar?" he asked. "Would the containment field be able to keep the shape-shifter out of the ship?"

"Considering how it penetrated the shields, my guess is no," Slaine said. "But why would you do that?"

"Because then we could face it," Stinson said. "Perhaps try to find some way to communicate with it . . . tell it that we mean it no harm, that we only want to ensure that it has no designs on attacking Bajor or Deep Space Nine."

"But what if it does?" Candlewood asked. "What if it is heading for Bajor or Deep Space Nine specifically so that it can attack?"

"Then we try to understand why it wants to do that," Stinson said. "We try to negotiate with it." He turned and looked across the bridge, to the communications console. "Lieutenant Viss, any suggestions on how—"

"Sir," Slaine said, "I'm detecting energy readings within the shape-shifter . . . and inside the ship."

"What kind of energy readings?"

"They read like . . . like scans," Slaine said. "Like sensors. It's doing no damage, but I think we're being probed."

"If we did open the hangar bay doors, and even if it entered the ship that way," Candlewood suggested, "maybe we could launch the shuttlecraft. We know that the tractor beam had some effectiveness against the shape-shifter. Maybe the shuttles could tow it away from the *Defiant*'s hull."

"If the shuttlecraft can even get past the shape-shifter," Nog said. "It could just as easily wrap itself around a smaller vessel as it did around the *Defiant*."

Stinson nodded. "We need other suggestions," he said. "How can we communicate with the shape-shifter, and if we can't, then how do we force it off of the ship?"

"We could try sending an electrical charge through the hull," Nog said. "We could try that as a method of communication, and if that fails, we could increase the power. That might not hurt it, but maybe it would rattle its cognitive processes."

"What if we took the ship to warp?" Candlewood offered. "Would that have any effect on it?"

"I'm not sure if we can even go to warp with the shape-shifter surrounding the ship the way it is," Tenmei said. "It could have an impact on our warp-field generation. Even if we can reach faster-than-light velocities, there's no guarantee that we could maintain a stable course."

"Study the problem," Stinson said. "See if we can go to

warp safely, and if not, determine what we need to do to make that happen."

"Aye, sir."

"To what end, sir?" Candlewood asked.

"It's possible that, if we can go to warp, the shape-shifter might not be able to maintain its position on the hull," Stinson said.

"And if it can," Slaine said, "we could travel to the nearest star."

"Maybe we can boil the shape-shifter from our hull," Stinson said. He moved back to the command chair and sat down again. "Are there any other suggestions?" he asked. "If not, we need to prioritize what we've come up with, based on the chances for success."

"Sir," Slaine said, the single word carrying both excitement and surprise. "The shape-shifter has left the hull."

"What?" Stinson said. He looked at the main screen, and once more saw the stars. In the center of the viewer, the shape-shifter poured through space like a shimmering, free-flowing river. "What's its heading?"

Before Slaine could respond, the shape-shifter altered its form. It spread left and right, up and down, its rounded textures hardening into sharp lines and edges. In just seconds, it twisted itself from an amorphous mass of fluid into a solid shape—a *recognizable* shape.

"What the—?" Stinson said. He saw a compact structure on the main viewscreen, with a snub-nosed bow and warp nacelles hugging tight to the main body of the hull. Out in space, drawn in reflective silver, floated the image of *Defiant*.

"Sensors are reading a Starfleet vessel," Slaine said. "*Defiant*-class."

"Not just *Defiant*-class," Stinson said. "That's a copy of the *Defiant* itself."

"Is it attempting to communicate with us?" Viss asked.

"Sir, that's not just an empty shell," Slaine said. "I'm detecting fully functioning systems: impulse engines, warp drive, shields—"

On the viewscreen, the silver ship began to shimmer. At first, Stinson thought the shape-shifter might be altering its form, but he did not see the faux *Defiant* changing. Rather, the image of it rippled, as though Stinson saw it through moving water.

A moment later, the ship was gone.

"It cloaked," Slaine said. After first contact with the Jem'Hadar, in an effort to prepare for the obvious threat posed by the Dominion, Starfleet had fitted *Defiant*—and later, during the war, its successor—with a Romulan cloaking device. Starfleet had negotiated its continued use after the war, with the prohibition that it not be utilized in either the Alpha or Beta Quadrants.

"Sensors," Stinson said at once, remembering what Captain Sisko had once told him. "Search for subspace variances." Cloaked vessels traveling at warp velocities radiated such variances.

"Scanning," Slaine said.

Stinson waited. He also knew what he would have to do if they could locate the shape-shifter. He hadn't known the capabilities of the entity, but he knew well what *Defiant* could do. And if the shape-shifter had mimicked the ship well enough to cloak, then could it generate phaser beams and possibly even quantum torpedoes? Stinson didn't think that Changelings could do such things, but then he hadn't believed that they could emulate the function of a cloaking device either. Unwilling to risk the lives of the crew to find out, he decided that if they could find the shape-shifter, they would have to fire on it.

But a complete scan of surrounding space turned up nothing. That might mean that the faux *Defiant* had not gone to warp and therefore remained in the area, but they couldn't know for sure. They had lost the shape-shifter.

Jefferson Blackmer peered across the Hub from an unfamiliar perch. If he'd sat down in the first officer's chair, he certainly would've felt out of place. Seated in the captain's position, though, he almost expected members of his own security team to show up and clap him in irons for impersonating a commanding officer.

The security chief had not been surprised when Cenn Desca had resigned his commission in the Militia and had decided to leave not only Deep Space 9, but the Bajoran system. In the more than three years that Blackmer had served under Captain Ro, he had come to know the importance that the colonel placed on his religious beliefs. Down on Endalla, and then almost a week later, outside Quark's, the security chief witnessed firsthand the impact that the Ohalavaru discovery had on Cenn. The exec seemed not just hurt or angry, but shaken.

On the other hand, Captain Ro's decision to appoint Blackmer as the starbase's first officer—even temporarily— *had* surprised him. As Ro's second officer for the last few years, Lieutenant Commander Stinson appeared the logical choice to succeed Cenn. When the captain announced the security chief's ad hoc appointment as exec, she hadn't offered an explanation, nor had she done so once Stinson had departed aboard *Defiant*. Afterward, though, she did suggest that Blackmer could use additional command experience. To that end, she assigned him to take the Hub as the acting CO during gamma shift, and to remain available during delta shift. The two met at the beginning of alpha shift to review critical issues, with respect to the starbase and to his performance.

Back at Starfleet Academy, Blackmer had actually begun his training in the command track. He initially qualified, but during his first year, he did not distinguish himself. He wanted to stick it out, to improve in the areas where he most needed it, but his advisor strongly suggested otherwise. Blackmer didn't know whether he could have or should have fought to stay as a command trainee, but he accepted reclassification to security. Among his fellow gendarmerie, he graduated the Academy near the top of his class.

Blackmer's Starfleet career, two decades long, had proceeded without many twists or turns. He served in perhaps a few more places than most—Deep Space 9 marked his eighth posting—but through all of those transfers, he continued to progress through the ranks—not quickly, but not slowly either. It gratified him when he made chief of security aboard *Perseverance*, and then when Starfleet accepted his request for transfer to assume the same position on DS9, since he preferred duty on a space station rather than aboard a starship.

By the time Ro named him as acting first officer two days prior, Blackmer hadn't thought about command in years. When he first got routed into security at the Academy, he still retained a desire to make the switch back. He initially thought that would happen in his second or third year of studies, and then out in the field once he received his first posting, to Starbase 189, but he didn't think the idea had crossed his mind since.

Across the Hub, doors parted and a crewman stepped out of a turbolift. Blackmer recognized him from the starbase's personnel files, a young Dedderac named Verlon, who had been posted there a few months earlier, when DS9 had first become fully operational. The crewman walked along the perimeter of the Hub, past the communications and dockmaster stations and over to the command chair.

"Sir, I have the mid-gamma operations status report," Verlon said, holding out a padd.

Blackmer took the device and scanned its display, which listed various operational systems throughout the starbase, such as communications, sensors, life support, and power generation. The security chief—and acting first officer—verified the green status of all but one category: under recreation, which had been listed as yellow, one red mark appeared, beside the antigrav envelopes that allowed visitors to soar above Nanietta Bacco Park. "What's going on with the flying zone in the park?" Blackmer asked.

"A power-transfer relay failed for the antigrav that covers the space above one of the landing zones," the Dedderac said. Typical of his species, he had striped, black-and-white skin. "It just happened an hour ago. Lieutenant Thorne thought it wisest to shut the entire system down until the unit could be replaced." Leslie Thorne, Blackmer knew, worked on Chief O'Brien's engineering staff. "She estimates a twenty-six-hour turnaround."

"All right," Blackmer said. He tapped at an upper corner of the padd, along its edge, to release the stylus stored there. He could have affixed his signature to the report using the tip of his finger, but he always felt silly doing that—it always reminded him of a child in kindergarten painting with his hands. After signing the report on the display, he reinserted the stylus and handed the padd back to Verlon.

"Thank you, sir," the young crewman said.

"Carry on, Mister Verlon," Blackmer said. "Dismissed."

As Verlon headed for the nearest turbolift—just behind Blackmer and to his left—Ensign Zhang spoke up from the communications console. "Commander, we're receiving a transmission from the *Defiant*."

"Put it on-screen," Blackmer said. A ring of four curved displays depended from the overhead above the situation table at the center of the Hub. Blackmer watched as the image of Wheeler Stinson appeared. "Go ahead, Commander."

"Commander Blackmer," Stinson said, *"we have located the shape-shifter and had an encounter with it."* The second officer detailed finding an entity traveling at warp through space, attempting first to communicate with it and then to snare it in a tractor beam. He described how the shape-shifter traveled back along the beam and enveloped *Defiant*, then replicated both the ship's form and function, to the point of cloaking. The crew subsequently lost sensor contact with it.

Blackmer considered how Stinson should proceed. It occurred to him that he could, or perhaps even should, contact the captain to allow her to make the call. *But that's not why she put me in command, even if it is gamma shift,* Blackmer thought. To Stinson, he said, "Implement a search grid for the shape-shifter. Treat it as a cloaked vessel unless there's a reason to think it's altered its form again. Scan for an echo of the *Defiant*'s power signature, and also use gravimetric sensors and tachyon beams if necessary." The latter two methods could be utilized to detect cloaked vessels.

"What if it's already somehow slipped past us?" Stinson asked. *"It could already be on its way to Bajor again. Shouldn't the* Defiant *return to defend the system?"*

"If it's already back on course for Bajor, you won't be able to catch up to it," Blackmer said. "Not if the shape-shifter has taken on the form and capabilities of the *Defiant*."

"But that will leave Bajor undefended." Blackmer wondered if Captain Ro's passing Stinson over for first officer, at least in the near term, contributed to Wheeler's arguments—perhaps to demonstrate that he could fulfill the role better than the security chief.

Blackmer tapped at the console in front of the command chair and quickly accessed a chart of Starfleet vessels. He saw two, *New York* and *Sacagawea*, within two days' travel of Bajor. "There are a pair of starships closer than the *Defiant*," he said. "We'll contact them to provide defense."

"How long should we conduct the search?" Stinson asked.

"Until you're sure that the shape-shifter is no longer in the area," Blackmer said. "What about Doctor Girani? Where is she with respect to providing assistance for Odo's medical care?"

"She's been in contact with the scientists at the research facility throughout our journey," Stinson said. *"I haven't spoken with her since our encounter with the shape-shifter."*

"Find out how urgent she thinks it is for her to reach the research facility," Blackmer said. "If she believes it vital, assign a pilot to take her there on one of the *Defiant*'s shuttle-craft."

"Aye, sir," Stinson said.

"Is there anything more?" Blackmer asked.

"No, sir."

"Keep us apprised of your progress," Blackmer said. "Deep Space Nine out." The security chief looked to the communications console. Ensign Zhang ended the transmission. "Open a channel to the *New York*," he told her.

As he waited for Zhang to raise the *Nebula*-class starship, Blackmer realized that he was enjoying the reactiveness of command. Security certainly provided such opportunities, but typically in a less cerebral, more physical vein. As Deep Space 9's security chief, he spent far more time planning ahead and providing visible, but often otherwise unused, support. He didn't know how long he would get to act as the starbase's first officer, but he resolved to make the most of it while he did.

"Commander," Ensign Zhang said, "I have Captain Wright from the *New York* for you."

"Put him on-screen."

When the door opened to reveal Altek Dans standing beyond it, a tremulous sensation wiggled in Ro's belly, even though she had made the choice to visit him in his quarters. It wasn't a bad feeling, but it wasn't a good feeling either. *Well,* Ro thought, *maybe it's a little good.*

"Captain," Altek said. His face quivered through a rapid range of emotions, from shock to confusion, and then on to trepidation, and finally—thankfully—to delight. "I'm surprised to see you, especially so late."

"Not *too* late, I hope," Ro said. "I know that you often read late into the night, so I thought you'd still be awake." More than halfway through gamma shift, she had debated about whether or not to call on Altek—not just because of the hour, but because of what had happened the last time she had come to his quarters. Four nights previously, after attending evening services at the temple with the kai, she had walked with Altek back to his cabin and then gone inside with him to continue talking. Their conversation had ended in a kiss.

Not just one kiss, Ro thought. They'd spent several minutes locked in a clinch on his sofa, and it easily could have gone past that. She could tell that Altek wanted it to go further, and the moment tempted her as well. More than sex enticed her; though that certainly held its appeal, a night of romance promised even greater fulfillment.

But Ro had excused herself before the kiss—the kiss*es*— could progress to something more. Her reason—more duties to perform—did not sound better to her for being true. She heard in her parting words an undercurrent of fear, which she did not completely understand. She wondered if Altek heard it, too.

"No, it's not too late," Altek said. "Please come in." He stepped back to allow her to enter, and the door closed behind her. "What can I do for you, Captain?"

The question struck Ro as an indictment. Not only had she hastily left Altek's quarters after they'd kissed, but she'd then stayed away for four days, only contacting him a couple of times by comm to inform him of the political and religious upheaval instigated by the Ohalavaru discovery, and that she had yet to hear from the kai about his request to return to Bajor. Ro understood that Altek had not intended his simple question as an accusation; her own mind had furnished that interpretation because of the guilt she felt for fleeing from him.

"I suddenly had a taste for something sweet," the captain said, "and I was wondering if you might consider having a late-night dessert with me."

Altek smiled. "I'd like that," he said. "I'm not sure if Bella's Confections is open now, but we could go to the Replimat, or to Quark's."

Quark. Ro's thoughts had turned to the barkeep after her brief dalliance with Altek. For a decade, she and Quark had spent a great deal of time together. Long periods occasionally passed during which they saw little of each other, mostly because one of them—usually Ro—would get busy, but they always seemed to find each other again. Ro liked Quark. More than that, she loved him—but as a friend. A *good* friend. Yes, they sometimes shared more than friends typically did, but despite its longevity, their relationship never progressed. The two of them had much in common, which had brought them together in the first place. They each provided the other with a strong shoulder to lean on and a sympathetic ear to listen. *And if you claim a Ferengi has a sympathetic ear, that's saying something,* Ro thought, and she knew that Quark would see the humor there, too.

"I don't really feel like going out," Ro said. Right or wrong, she did not want to run into Quark while in Altek's company. "If it's all right with you, maybe we could just order something from the replicator."

"Of course," Altek said. He took her elbow for a moment to guide her toward the dining table on the far side of the room, and Ro felt something like an electric charge at his touch. "By the way, you were right about my reading." He pointed to the low table in the sitting area, on which lay a padd, lines of Bajoran text visible on its display. "I'm in the middle of a novel."

"Anything I'd be familiar with?"

"Perhaps," Altek said. "It's called *Meditations on a Crimson Shadow*, by Eleta Preloc." Ro stopped in her tracks. Altek walked past her a few steps before turning back around. "What?" he asked.

"You're reading a *Cardassian* novel?"

Altek's right shoulder rose in a half-shrug. "Yes," he said. "I thought it was considered a masterpiece of modern literature."

"The Cardassians may think so, but . . . isn't it about the Union essentially running roughshod over the Alpha Quadrant . . . obliterating the Klingons, destroying the Federation . . . Bajor, utterly defeated and in servitude?"

"I haven't finished the book," Altek said, "so I can't speak to all of that, but yes, some of the elements you mention are in there. I take it that you haven't read it."

"No," she said. "Why would I? I spent my childhood under the bootheels of the Cardassians. Why would I want to read about the twisted hope that they might someday subjugate the entire quadrant?"

"If that were the point of it, I don't know that you

would," Altek said. "But that's not how I've been reading it. It seems to me a lot less like wish fulfillment and a lot more like a cautionary tale. I get the feeling that the writer was not proposing the dream of Cardassian conquest, but the inevitability of such a dream's failure. Throughout the novel, at least as far as I've read, there is a vein of principled opposition that continues on even as its adherents die." Altek paused, and Ro saw that he no longer looked at her; rather, his eyes focused on the middle distance as he looked inward. "It's actually inspiring to read such a subversive message cloaked in the trappings of bellicose patriotism and the glory of an authoritarian state."

"I have never heard the book described that way," Ro said. "I don't think I've ever heard of *any* piece of Cardassian writing described that way." As she made the assertion, though, some vague memory told her otherwise—that she had years earlier heard not just about subversive elements on Cardassia, working in secret to overthrow the stratocracy, but seditious groups—such as the Oralian Way—speaking out and acting to end the military's rule of the Union. "I don't know. Maybe I have heard that," she admitted. Ro walked the rest of the way to the dining table and sat down. Altek followed, took a seat, and turned it to face her. "Maybe I have heard that, but maybe I just didn't *want* to hear it."

"Why wouldn't you want to hear it?" Altek asked gently.

"I think because I didn't want to have to differentiate among Cardassians," Ro said. "It was easier just to hate them all."

Altek leaned forward and took one of Ro's hands in his own. "I can't imagine what it must have been like living under the Occupation," he said, his voice full of emotion. His touch felt warm—almost hot. "I watched a segment of my society forced into servitude . . . treated not only as inferior, but as something less than people." When Altek had first come aboard, he had been questioned by Lieutenant Commander Blackmer, and he'd eventually spoken about the enslavement of the Bajora by the Aleira.

"You fought that," Ro said. "You fought against your own people."

"How could I do anything but fight against it?" Altek asked. "Nothing really separated the Aleira from the Bajora other than our religious beliefs. Some did claim a genetic difference, a physical purity of the Aleira over the Bajora—which was preposterous; we were all Bajorans—but even if that had been true, so what? The Bajora were still people. There can be no justification for slavery—or for mistreating people at all."

"Of course not," Ro agreed.

"It seems like you're rebuking yourself for jumping to a conclusion about a novel written by a Cardassian," Altek said. "And because you used to generalize about all Cardassians. But you also stopped yourself from doing that."

"Because I no longer paint all Cardassians with one brush," Ro said. She thought in particular about Akellen Macet, a *gul* in the Guard and cousin to the evil Skrain Dukat, but a man who had fought against the Dominion and his own people at the end of the war. When she'd commanded Deep Space 9, Captain Kira had worked on a number of occasions with Macet, and since then, so too had Ro. "I'm sorry," she said. "I didn't come here to talk about the Occupation or slavery or prejudice, and certainly not to question your choice of reading materials."

"It's all right," Altek said. "I don't mind talking about those things. In fact, I like it. Those values—not just tolerance, but acceptance—are just about the most important things to me. They're worth discussing."

"So is chocolate."

"Ah, right," Altek said. He leaned back in his chair, letting go of Ro's hand as he did so. Her body took keen notice of the loss of that physical connection. "So what can I get you? A *jumja* stick? *Tuwaly* pie? Or were you serious about the chocolate? I saw a listing the other day for something called a Ktarian puff that's supposed to have something like fifteen different types of chocolate in it."

Ro thought about what sort of dessert she wanted. She'd been telling Altek the truth when she'd spoken of her desire to have something sweet. "I think . . ." she started, but then she looked into his eyes, which were rich and deep and dark. *Almost the color of chocolate,* she thought, and the idea pleased her. "I think I want something even sweeter than that," she finally said, and she leaned forward, parted her lips, and kissed Altek deeply.

When she pulled back, Ro saw that he had closed his eyes. When he opened them, she said, "Dessert can wait." She stood up, took him by the hand, and led him into the bedroom.

Doctor Girani Semna stood in the isolation ward, outside the sealed chamber containing Odo—or what had once been Odo; she could not tell from his state whether or not he was alive. She had just arrived at Newton Outpost with Ensign Edward Baiers, who had conveyed her there from *Defiant* aboard one of the ship's shuttlecraft, *Sagan*. When they'd departed three days earlier, the crew had been engaged in a laborious search for the mysterious shape-shifter, which had apparently learned how to cloak itself. The uncertainty of how long a search would take, combined with reports of Odo's grave condition, had motivated Girani to accept Lieutenant Commander Stinson's offer to convey her there as quickly as practicable.

"We did everything you suggested to us, Doctor," said

Mennil Farran. A strikingly tall man, the research biochemist had been assigned with half a dozen other scientists to study the massive shape-shifter that the crew of *U.S.S. Nova* had discovered on an asteroid. Since the team's leader, Doctor Norsa, continued to recuperate from the effects of a concussion, Farran filled in for her.

Girani had been in continual contact with the scientists at Newton Outpost ever since they'd reached her on Bajor with the news of Odo's injury and his unresponsive condition. During her time on Deep Space 9, the doctor had gotten along well with the Changeling; they appreciated each other's directness and lack of sentimentality. Regardless of her opinion of Odo, Girani would have agreed to assist in treating him, considering that, other than Doctor Bashir, she had more hands-on medical experience with Changelings than anybody else in the Federation.

Girani gazed through the observation port into the isolation chamber. "That's Odo?" she asked, pointing to the lone bio-bed, atop which sat a large transparent container perhaps two-thirds full. Inside, a leaden material barely moved. It looked more solid than liquid.

"Yes, that's Odo," Farran said. "Since we collected his substance and placed him in the isolation chamber, his density has decreased and his mass has increased. We're not sure whether that's an indicator of his health improving or failing, but we do see more movement on the exposed surface of his biomimetic material."

"What sort of movement?" Girani asked. "Has Odo made any attempt to shape-shift at all?"

"Not that we can tell," Farran said. "But we are continuously scanning him, so it's possible that you can make that determination better than we can."

"Yes, I'd like to take a look at those readings," Girani said. She hoped that she had enough familiarity with Odo and the way he moved, the way he changed his structure and appearance, that she could recognize his will at work, even in failing to successfully shape-shift. "So if you don't believe he's tried to alter his form, then what kind of movement are you talking about?"

"When we initially placed Odo in the isolation chamber," Farran said, "his biomimetic material had an extremely high viscosity. The flow of air across his exposed surface would not even result in ripples. As you can see—" He pointed through the observation port. "—that has changed. We now see undulations in his surface layer."

Girani watched until she saw what Farran had pointed out. She noted that the diagnostic panel above the bio-bed registered almost no activity on any scale, not unusual for a Changeling in his amorphous state. She backed up a step and gazed down at the control panel just below the observation port. "You've adjusted the environmental factors and maintained them as I advised," she said.

"Yes, we have, Doctor," Farran said. "The atmospheric composition in the chamber, the temperature, the pressure, and the humidity have all been set as you prescribed. We've also modified the intensity and color of the light according to your specifications."

Girani nodded slowly. "Odo could alter his form in almost any environment," she said, "but different sets of conditions impacted the ease with which he did so. Obviously, given the trauma he's suffered, we should make it as easy as possible for him to shape-shift, and the way you've configured the isolation chamber will do that. Depending on what has caused Odo to revert to his amorphous state, it may be that he will be able to heal himself if he's able to start changing his form again."

"Do you mean that he will be able to shape-shift away his injuries?" Farran asked, clearly astounded by the concept.

"Possibly," Girani said. "If, for example, only some of his cells have been damaged, he may be able to employ his other cells to re-form them. It will be contingent upon the nature of Odo's wounds." Girani peered again through the port. "I've never seen Odo take on this color in his unvariegated state." She could hear the concern in her voice. "His biomimetic material usually shines with a golden hue, tinged with orange. It also shines reflectively."

"What about when he was infected with the morphogenic virus?" Farran asked.

"I never saw Odo when he had the virus," Girani said, "but I studied the readings and images that Doctor Bashir made of him at the time. Nothing corresponds to what we're seeing here."

"Our theory is that Odo is either suffering from the physical attack he endured, which caused his biomimetic material to spatter," Farran said, "or that when Odo linked with the other shape-shifter, he became infected with some sort of pathogen."

"From the available evidence, nothing else seems to make sense," Girani agreed.

"When the *Nova* crew found the specimen, they could not determine if it was alive, or even if it ever had been," Farran said. "We did no better with our analysis once the specimen was brought here. It is obvious now that the shape-shifter was alive, but does the state it was found in suggest that it was suffering from a disease that it then passed on to Odo?"

"Perhaps," Girani allowed, "but that would mean that the shape-shifter not only infected Odo with the disease, but spontaneously cured itself. I'm not sure that's possible, but . . ." Something else occurred to Girani, an event that took place on the original Deep Space 9, at a time when Odo had been rendered an unchanging "solid" by the

Founders. She described the incident to Farran, telling him about how a dying, unformed Changeling had integrated itself into Odo's morphogenic matrix, thereby restoring his shape-shifting abilities. "Perhaps something like that happened here, but in reverse. If the specimen had some sort of condition—not a disease, but a physical handicap—could it somehow have made itself whole by taking something from Odo?" She didn't expect an answer—even a speculative one—from Farran, and he didn't provide one.

"I'll need to take a look at all of the readings you've taken of Odo since he's been in this condition," Girani said. She recalled how exposure to massive amounts of tetryon radiation had doomed the unformed Changeling that had given Odo back his shape-shifting abilities. Girani and Doctor Bashir had both worked to save the dying Changeling, but they hadn't been able to do so. She wondered if that experience could help her, first in diagnosing Odo, and then in determining a treatment that would return him to health.

"I can get you every reading we've taken," Farran said.

"I also need to know every test you've run on Odo," Girani said. An idea had begun to form in her mind, but if Odo suffered in any way like the unformed Changeling had, she would have to work fast. She hoped that it was not too late.

As Blackmer spoke with Lieutenant Aleco at the tactical station, he noticed Ensign Zhang look up from the communications console and across the diameter of the Hub at him. "Commander," she said, "we have an incoming transmission from the *Sacagawea*."

"Put it on-screen, Ensign."

On the ring of displays above the situation table, the bridge of *Sacagawea* replaced the view of local space. The ship's captain, John Augustine Swaddock, sat in the command chair. *"Commander Blackmer,"* he said.

"Captain Swaddock, it's good to see you." Three days prior, when the shape-shifter that attacked and then imitated *Defiant* had cloaked, Blackmer had contacted the two Starfleet vessels nearest to the Bajoran system. The *Nebula*-class *New York* could not divert from its time-sensitive mission of mercy to the Cassiterides, a mineral-rich Federation colony in the midst of a botanical plague, but the *Niagara*-class *Sacagawea*, on routine patrols in the sector, set course immediately for Bajor. Captain Ro concurred with Blackmer's plan to request another starship to guard the planet until either the shape-shifter could be located or *Defiant* returned. "What can I do for you?"

The lean Swaddock had a long, youthful face, but the gray hair at his temples hinted at more advanced years. *"I was hoping you could provide an ETA for the* Defiant. *Starfleet has a mission for us, but it's predicated on when we can depart Bajor."*

"Let me get that information for you, Captain," Blackmer said. He nodded to Zhang, who muted the transmission. "Ensign Wat, when does Commander Stinson expect the *Defiant* to reach Deep Space Nine?"

"Checking, sir." Denor Wat, a Bolian who served as the operations officer on gamma shift, worked his console. Blackmer knew that the *Defiant* crew had spent more than half a day searching unsuccessfully for the cloaked shape-shifter. Afterward, with Doctor Girani already on her way to the research facility aboard a shuttlecraft, Captain Ro had ordered the ship back to base. "The *Defiant* is expected to arrive just under thirteen hours from now."

"Thank you," Blackmer said, and again he nodded at Zhang, who unmuted the transmission. "Captain, the *Defi-*

ant is due back within thirteen hours. Will you be able to remain in the system until then?"

"*That shouldn't be a problem,*" Swaddock said, "*but I think Starfleet will have us departing shortly after that.*"

"I'll inform Captain Ro."

"*Thank you, Commander.* Sacagawea *out.*" The display reverted to its view of the space surrounding the starbase. Blackmer saw a number of ships arriving as others headed away from DS9.

The security chief and acting first officer continued his conversation with Aleco. They had been discussing the new relay that Captain Ro had proposed for deployment in the Gamma Quadrant, and the lieutenant finished filling him in on the particulars. Unlike previous relays, which allowed only for communications from the Gamma Quadrant back to DS9, the new unit would also contain a long-range sensor array. Two and a half years previously, when the Federation and its Khitomer Accords allies had agreed to allow Typhon Pact vessels to transit the wormhole, Starfleet had seeded sensor buoys along mandated travel routes in the Gamma Quadrant. During the two years that the wormhole had been closed, those buoys had disappeared, either stolen or destroyed. With the Bajoran system accessible from the Gamma Quadrant again, Ro wanted to know as early as possible whenever ships headed toward the wormhole.

When he had concluded his discussion with Aleco, Blackmer returned to the command chair. He tapped at his console to check the current status of various starbase functions. He reviewed the vessels presently docked at Deep Space 9—seventeen freighters, four transports, and two prospectors—as well as the arrival and departure schedules for the rest of gamma shift. He had just begun reading the security report from the Plaza—which typically received most of its entries as the time approached zero hundred—when the red alert klaxon sounded. Blackmer looked up from his console in time to see a three-dimensional holographic image wink into existence above the situation table.

"Commander," Aleco said from the tactical console, "the tachyon grid has detected the passage of a cloaked vessel." Blackmer had previously heard similar alerts called out, but only during drills. During construction of the new DS9, a tachyon grid had been installed around the starbase specifically to prevent cloaked vessels from approaching unobserved. Located at a far enough remove from Deep Space 9, the detectors gave the crew time to react to the arrival of a cloaked starship. "Shields raised automatically," Aleco said. "Phaser banks are online and energized, quantum torpedoes are loading. Thoron shield generators in standby mode."

Blackmer quickly stood up from the command chair, stepped to his left, and descended the stairs down into the Well, the inner deck of the Hub. He studied the holographic display above the sit table. It showed a representation of DS9 at its center, surrounded at a distance by a light-blue, many-sided polygon, the vertices of which marked the positions of tachyon detectors, and the edges, the complex network they defined. A bright-red dot marked the encroaching ship, which flew in the general direction of the starbase. "Bearing: from one-hundred-thirteen degrees, mark forty-one. Projected course: the wormhole. Distance: one-point-seven-five million kilometers. Velocity: one-half impulse."

"Blackmer to Captain Ro," said the acting first officer, knowing that the comm system would pick up his command and route it appropriately. "Please report to the Hub immediately." While the automatic triggering of the red alert should already have caused the computer to notify the captain of the emergency situation, Blackmer believed in taking no chances.

"Hub, I'm on my way," came Ro's immediate reply.

"I need an identification on that ship," Blackmer said.

"The detection grid is working to scan through the cloak," Aleco said. "Picking up characteristics now. Reading dual warp nacelles, configured directly on the main hull. Mass: three hundred fifty thousand metric tons. Length—" Blackmer knew what Aleco would say before he uttered the words. "Commander, it's the *Defiant*."

"No, it's not," Blackmer said. "Ensign Zhang, hailing frequencies."

"Hailing frequencies open."

"Deep Space Nine to approaching shape-shifter," Blackmer said. He didn't know whether or not the entity possessed the capability of receiving transmissions, but he reasoned that if it could emulate such complex functions as cloaking, it could also produce a working copy of *Defiant*'s communications equipment. "Please decloak and reduce your speed. If you wish to travel through the wormhole, we are amenable to that, but we wish to speak with you first." The captain had discussed with the crew the possibility that the shape-shifter might be a Changeling, or even a link of Changelings, and therefore might seek to return to the Dominion. Even some other form of shape-shifter might have learned of the Founders and wanted to visit them. Captain Ro had no issue with allowing passage to the Gamma Quadrant in such circumstances, but she also wanted to ensure as best she could that the entity had no inimical designs either on the wormhole or on the Eav'oq.

"No response," Zhang said.

"No change in velocity," Aleco said, "and it remains cloaked."

"Deep Space Nine to approaching shape-shifter," Blackmer repeated. "We must speak with you before permitting you to continue on your current course." At almost the same instant, two of the four doors leading to turbolifts opened. The captain entered from one, and Chief O'Brien from the other. "Please respond or we will be forced to fire on you."

Ro descended into the Well while O'Brien took over at the main engineering station from Crewwoman Antigua Brown, who moved to a secondary engineering position on the periphery of the Hub. "Anything?" the captain asked Blackmer.

"Not so far," Blackmer said. "The intruder reads as the *Defiant*, cloaked, but the actual ship is still a half-day's travel from the starbase. It is clearly the shape-shifter that attacked the real *Defiant*. It is headed for the wormhole and refuses to respond to hails."

"Captain," Aleco said, "the detection grid is reading shields and charged phaser banks on the entity."

"Damn," Ro said. "If all it wanted to do was travel through the wormhole to the Gamma Quadrant, why is it running with shields up and weapons charged?"

"After the *Defiant* crew attempted to capture it, maybe it just wants to protect itself," Blackmer said. "Do we risk letting it go?"

"No," the captain said decisively. "Not without some indication of its peaceful intentions. We can't risk an attack on the Eav'oq, or an attempt to damage the wormhole." She looked up at Ensign Zhang. "Open hailing frequencies."

"Frequencies open," Zhang said.

"Deep Space Nine to shape-shifting entity. This is Captain Ro Laren. You must stop, decloak, and reply, or we will have no choice but to fire on you." Ro waited. Blackmer didn't expect a response, and he didn't think anybody else in the Hub did either, but then Aleco reported one.

"Captain, the entity has changed course," the tactical

officer said, the tension in his voice presaging what would come next. "It's heading directly for Deep Space Nine."

Ro exchanged a concerned look with Blackmer, then glanced at the holographic display projected above the situation table. In it, a representation of *Defiant* soared toward Deep Space 9, a red arc behind it tracing the alteration to its course. "Raise the thoron shield," Ro ordered.

"Raising the thoron shield," Aleco said. The new type of Starfleet defense provided a seamless energy covering around all of Deep Space 9, along the inner sides of the starbase's three orthogonal rings. A second casing formed around the Hub, which sat at the upper intersection of the *y*- and *z*-rings. The thoron-based defense provided greater protection than normal shields, safeguarding the starbase not only against energy weapons and transporter beams, but also against physical objects. On the downside, it hindered long-range sensors and communications. "Captain, the entity is not reducing speed."

"Fire phasers," Ro ordered, and she peered up at the ring of displays above the sit table. She watched as yellow-red beams streaked out into space, at no discernible target. The phasers abruptly ended, as though they had struck an invisible wall—which they essentially had. The image wavered at that point, and then the shape-shifter faded into view, looking precisely like *Defiant*. Except that the ship-form had none of *Defiant*'s coloring—no grays and whites of the hull plating, no red glow fronting the warp nacelles, no blue radiance emanating from the navigational deflector, no black characters spelling out the name and registry. The simulacrum of the ship showed entirely in reflective silver. It looked to Ro more like a ghost than something real.

"Captain, the phasers have reduced the entity's shields, but it is still not slowing down," Aleco said. Though he spoke urgently, his voice was steady. "It's on a collision course with us."

"Fire phasers and quantum torpedoes," Ro said.

"Phasers and quantum torpedoes, fire!" Aleco said.

On the overhead displays, yellow-red beams cut once more through the void, followed by the blue-tinged white pulses of a quartet of quantum torpedoes. The phasers reached the *Defiant*-shape—and passed through it. A moment later, so too did the torpedoes.

"What—?" Ro started to ask, but she could see what had happened: apertures had opened in the shape-shifter–*cum*–starship, allowing the weapons fire to pass cleanly through it. As the captain watched, the openings sealed themselves.

"Brace for impact!" Aleco called out.

No, Ro thought as she rushed to the sit table and took hold of its edge. Blackmer did the same beside her. She prepared herself for the crash. The regular defensive shields would not hold back the mass of the shape-shifter, but the thoron shield should. Even so, Ro expected the impact to rattle the starbase.

Nothing happened.

"Captain," O'Brien said. "Look!"

Ro backed away from the sit table and lifted her gaze to the display ring. She saw a view of Deep Space 9 from high up near the Hub, looking down toward the main sphere. The golden cast of the thoron shield spread in an ovate shell bounded by DS9's three rings. A nebulous silver blemish tarnished one portion of the shield. As Ro watched, the blotch spread in what looked like a random fashion, like a liquid spilled on top of a ball, but then suddenly it fell inward, toward DS9's main sphere.

"What happened?" Ro asked.

"The shape-shifter has passed through the thoron shield," Aleco said.

"What?!" O'Brien exclaimed. "How is that even possible?"

Ro quickly mounted the steps between the tactical and main engineering stations and turned to her right to study Lieutenant Aleco's displays. As she did, Blackmer moved beside the tactical officer, to the adjoining station, where he took over the security console from Ensign Ernak gov Ansarg. Ro reached in past Aleco to a screen showing a live feed of the shape-shifter, and she dragged the time indicator backward, to the moment when the entity had penetrated the thoron shield. The captain then tapped several times at the point where the shape-shifter had come through the powerful defensive screen. The image magnified again and again, until Ro held a fingertip on it steadily. A series of numbers and descriptors appeared that described the two substances—the shield and the shape-shifter—and their interaction.

"It's possible," Ro said, able to interpret what she saw to find justification for her conclusion, "because the entity altered its form to correspond to that of the thoron shield. It became a part of it . . . became *one* with it . . . and then changed its form again, back into itself, but on the inside of the shield. It's essentially how Commander Stinson described the entity getting past the *Defiant*'s shields."

"The shape-shifter has attached itself to the hull," Aleco said, pointing to another monitor on his console.

"It's dispersing itself, Captain," O'Brien said.

Ro watched the entity as it oozed across the hull in all directions. "This follows the pattern of attack Commander Stinson described on the *Defiant*," she said, more to herself than to her crew.

"What's it doing to the hull?" O'Brien asked. He operated his own console, clearly searching for answers.

"Vel? Denor? Jeff?" Ro said. She had an intuition that the shape-shifter intended no harm to Deep Space 9 and those aboard it—an optimism based on the experiences of *Defiant*'s crew with the entity. Still, she would take nothing for granted.

"I don't see anything, Captain," Aleco said. "There's no evidence of an attempt to break through the hull . . . or to 'become one with it' and breach the starbase that way. There's no increase in temperature or pressure on the hull, nothing that would suggest an energy weapon. There's no radiation . . . check that: I'm reading some subspace radiation, but it appears to be trace amounts spread evenly through the entity. It poses no danger to us."

At the operations console beside O'Brien, Ensign Wat said, "All starbase functions show green, Captain." He sounded as though he didn't quite believe it.

"All security systems read green as well," Blackmer said. "There are reports of issues with moving residents to their cabins and visitors to designated shelter areas, but most of the civilians have responded well to the alert. There are obviously a lot of questions and concerns."

"Captain," Zhang said, "we are receiving communications from the masters and crews of almost all docked ships. They all want to know what's going on. Some of them sound on the verge of panic."

To Crewwoman Grandy, the dockmaster on gamma shift, Ro said, "Arleta, coordinate with all vessels. Have them undock and withdraw to a distance of a hundred kilometers."

"Aye, sir," Grandy said.

"Suyin, try to calm everybody down," Ro told Zhang. "Tell them I'll speak with them as soon as I'm able, but emphasize that neither Deep Space Nine nor any of the ships, whether docked or not, are in any danger."

"Sir?" Zhang asked. Ro thought it was the first time she had ever heard the young communications officer question an order.

Beside the captain, Aleco quietly asked, "How can you be so sure?"

Past him, Blackmer said, "Agreed, Captain. This *feels* like an attack."

Ro nodded, then she began walking along the outer circle of the Hub. As she passed behind the tactical and security stations, she said, "I know it would be easy to view what's happening as a threat to the starbase, but I don't think it is." She moved past one of the sets of steps that led down into the Well and then past the first officer's position. When she reached the command chair, she stood behind it and continued to address the crew. "The shape-shifter is doing exactly what it did when the *Defiant* crew encountered it. Commander Stinson tried to communicate with the entity, and when that didn't work, he tried to warn it to stop. It redirected itself toward the *Defiant* only after an attempt to capture it. That's when the shape-shifter covered the hull of the *Defiant*, but it did not harm the ship or crew."

"But why did it do that?" O'Brien asked. "Just so that it could learn to copy the ship? For what purpose?"

"To communicate, maybe," Aleco ventured.

"No, not for communication," Ro said. "It seemed as though as soon as it could copy the *Defiant*, it did so, and as soon as it took the ship's form, it cloaked and left the area."

"Then why?" Blackmer asked.

"I don't know," Ro said. She looked up at the display ring and saw the shape-shifter continuing to spread itself across the hull of the starbase. She also saw the vessels that had been docked at DS9 moving away.

Ro genuinely believed that the entity did not pose a threat to the starbase, or to any of the docked or nearby ships, but she also recognized that she could not be certain. "Suyin," she said, "contact Captain Swaddock aboard the *Sacagawea*. Explain the situation and tell him that I'm requesting he bring his ship to Deep Space Nine immediately."

"Aye, sir," Zhang said.

To the rest of her crew, Ro said, "If we need to force the shape-shifter away, how can we do that? And what else can we try to communicate with it?"

The ideas that followed echoed many of those that the *Defiant* crew had suggested, and some that they had attempted, all of which Commander Stinson had detailed in his report. New proposals included polarizing the thoron field, but that seemed as likely to keep the shape-shifter inside the field as to force it out. At some point, Ro made the decision to shut down the thoron shield altogether, given that it had been ineffective in preventing the entity from passing through it. Lieutenant Aleco advised launching many, or even all, of DS9's dozen runabouts and having them employ their tractor beams in concert to pull the shape-shifter from the hull. Chief O'Brien talked about using all of the personnel and cargo transporters throughout the starbase to attempt to beam it away.

At intervals, Blackmer announced the proportion of the hull that the entity had covered. *Thirty-five percent. Forty percent. Fifty.* On the display ring, images of the starbase transmitted by various nearby ships showed the shape-shifter's progress. Considering the enormous size of Deep Space 9, nobody initially believed that the entity would be able to disperse itself thinly enough to coat the entire hull, but as time passed, it showed no signs of slowing. When the silver veneer of the shape-shifter had concealed most of the main sphere, it began creeping the length of the crossover bridges toward the horizontal x-ring, and then eventually up the two vertical rings toward the Hub. *Sixty percent. Seventy-five. Ninety.*

None of the schemes to remove the entity from the starbase appeared likely to succeed, nor did any of them appeal to the captain. Ro preferred communication to conflict, but she was not convinced of the efficacy of the proposed methods for conversing with the shape-shifter. In the end, Ro could think of only one reasonable way to proceed.

"We can try the direct approach," she said from where she sat in the command chair.

"The direct approach, Captain?" Blackmer asked from the tactical station.

Ro stood up. "I can go out there and face the entity."

"Begging the captain's pardon," O'Brien said, "but 'go out there' how?"

"In an environmental suit," Ro said. "Through one of the maintenance ports not yet covered."

"I strongly advise against such a course, Captain," Blackmer said. "For one thing, the scientists at the research facility came into contact with the shape-shifter, and it did not provide them with a means of communication. It left two of them dead. For another thing, your place is here, sir. With all due respect, if anybody is to make such an attempt, I must insist that it be a member of the security staff."

"It may not matter," Aleco said. "The entity has now wrapped itself around the entire starbase. All of the maintenance hatches are covered." Ro peered back up at the display ring to see Deep Space 9 shrouded in silver.

"I'm picking up increased energy readings in the entity," Aleco said.

"And there are corresponding readings inside the hull," Blackmer said. "It's not a weapon. It appears that we're being scanned."

Ro moved to the steps and headed down into the Well. A holographic representation of Deep Space 9 hung above the situation table, its exterior smooth and featureless. Ro studied it, then said, "We've already shut down the thoron shield. We can shut down the regular shields as well, and I can beam onto the hull."

"Onto the shape-shifter itself?" O'Brien asked.

"Or in space just beside it," Ro said.

"Captain, as both chief of security and acting first officer, I cannot allow you to endanger yourself like that," Blackmer said, his manner very serious. "I'm not clear why you think that such an attempt to make contact with the entity will work, but if somebody is to try it, it has to be a security officer. I volunteer."

Ro considered the security chief's perspective. She knew that he held himself partially to blame for the assassination of the Federation president, because when Bacco and the other dignitaries at the DS9 dedication ceremony had refused the use of defensive screens during their speeches, he had not insisted. Ro also understood that she had just appointed him as acting first officer, and he plainly took his responsibilities to heart.

"Jeff—" she started to say, but then movement on the holographic image drew her attention. She looked and saw a line of silver streaming away from Deep Space 9. "Vel, what's happening?"

"The entity is beginning to move away from the hull," Aleco said. Even as he did so, Ro saw portions of the starbase becoming visible as the silver extent contracted toward the part of the shape-shifter jetting out into space. "I'm still detecting no damage to the starbase."

"Where is it going?" Ro wanted to know.

"Bearing: two hundred seventy-three degrees, mark thirteen," Aleco said. The tactical officer paused as he operated his controls, then said, "It's stopping in space approximately two thousand meters away."

"Suyin," Ro said, "show us."

"Aye, sir." Zhang worked the communications station, and the starfield on the display ring changed. "Magnifying." The viewscreens blinked, and the flow of silver became visible. It spilled to a point in space, where it collected into a growing sphere.

"What is it doing?" O'Brien asked.

Ro thought she knew. She reached forward and tapped a control on the situation table. The image of starbase disappeared, replaced by the accumulating silver mass. It did not take long for the entity to begin taking on a recognizable shape.

Blackmer said it first: "It's Deep Space Nine."

In the conference room just off the Hub, Miles O'Brien sat across from Lieutenant Commander Blackmer and Lieutenant Aleco, all of them waiting for Captain Ro. The four of them would shortly begin discussing the unlikely occurrence of a massive shape-shifter forming into an exact copy of Deep Space 9 in nearby space. *And,* the chief engineer assumed, *what we should do about it.*

The attendance at the meeting felt light to O'Brien, but of greater import, so did the collective experience of the few assembled. The captain's conferences with her senior staff usually included Wheeler Stinson, Ren Kalanent Viss, John Candlewood, and Pascal Boudreaux, as well as Zivan Slaine in Aleco Vel's stead; until a week prior, they had also included Cenn Desca. O'Brien had been in Starfleet for three and a half decades, and he knew that Blackmer had been in for two. Even Aleco, who'd first come to the original DS9 as a fresh-faced corporal in the Bajoran Militia, had served for ten years. Despite the record of O'Brien and the two other officers, though, it seemed a formidable proposition for them to adequately stand in for the wealth of experience and knowledge missing from the room.

The doors parted and the captain entered the conference room. She sat down at the head of the table. "The shape-shifter is continuing to form into a replica of Deep Space Nine," she said. "The main core is complete, and the crossover bridges, and now it's forming the rings."

"Why?" Aleco asked.

"That's the big question, isn't it?" O'Brien said. "That, and what should we do about it?" Having the starbase enveloped by the shape-shifter had made the chief engineer feel claustrophobic—not an easy thing to accomplish, considering the great size of DS9. He had also found the experience unnerving, almost like being swallowed alive.

"It seems to me that this must be an attempt to communicate," Blackmer said.

"I might agree," O'Brien said, "if the shape-shifter hadn't done the same thing to the *Defiant* and then immediately left the area."

"Do you expect that to happen now?" Ro asked.

"You mean as soon as it finishes molding itself into a silver-plated Deep Space Nine?" O'Brien asked. "I don't know. If it reproduces the starbase's structural integrity field and its thrusters, it would have the capability of moving away in that form. But if it leaves, what does that mean? And if it stays, what does *that* mean?"

Blackmer leaned forward on the table. "The entity took on the form of the *Defiant*, but not as an attempt to communicate," he said. "It immediately set course for the Bajoran system."

"More specifically, for the wormhole," Ro noted. "But the shape-shifter didn't head for Bajor only after its encounter with the *Defiant*. As soon as it left the planetary system housing the research facility, it started in this direction."

"Again, why?" Aleco said. "Is it from the Gamma Quadrant and trying to return home? Is it a Founder? Or did it learn of the Founders when it linked with Odo?"

"It *was* traveling toward the wormhole," O'Brien said, recalling the sequence of events just past. "We tried to contact it—first Commander Blackmer and then you, Captain—and we even threatened to fire if it did not stop, but we didn't actually use our weapons until *after* it turned away from the wormhole and toward Deep Space Nine."

"And we now know that we *can't* stop it," Blackmer said.

"Maybe it didn't know that until after we fired on it," Ro said. "Our first phaser beams struck the entity. It was only with our subsequent weapons fire that it determined a way to avoid our attacks."

"That's right," O'Brien said. "Our weapons are ineffective against this shape-shifter, and it knows that now, too. So why doesn't it just resume its course and go through the wormhole to wherever it's going?"

The four officers regarded one another silently. Nobody had an answer. Blackmer held up his open hands and leaned back in his chair, at an obvious loss. O'Brien agreed: none of it made sense to him.

"Is it possible," he finally ventured, "that we're giving this entity too much credit? Could it be that it's not a shape-shifter in the same way that Odo is, that the Founders are?"

"What do you mean?" the captain asked.

"Maybe this entity is alive, but it's not intelligent," O'Brien said. "Maybe the choices it's making aren't really choices; maybe they're instinctive responses . . . simple reactions to complex stimuli."

"Like a cephalopod changing its color and texture," Blackmer said.

"But this isn't camouflage," Ro said.

"Not all metachromatic animals change color to disguise

themselves," O'Brien said. "But maybe this is a form of camouflage . . . an attempt to assimilate to surroundings. Or maybe it's just a physical consequence . . . mindless."

"But if it is just a reaction," Aleco said, "there still has to be an evolutionary reason for it. In order for such an autonomic response to survive in a species over time, it has to serve a useful purpose."

"Or at least not prove a detriment to survival," Blackmer said.

"That's if the species evolved and wasn't engineered," Ro said. "We know that the Founders essentially created the Jem'Hadar and the Vorta."

"Do you think that's what this shape-shifter is?" O'Brien asked. "A product of the Founders' genetic engineering?"

"No, not really," Ro said. "I suppose it's possible, but I can't imagine them attempting to manipulate their own kind." The captain looked weary to O'Brien, and he completely understood. He had been close to getting into bed himself when the red alert had sounded.

"We may not know why the shape-shifter is doing what it's doing, and we may not be able to puzzle it out," the chief engineer said, "but we are going to have to figure how to deal with it."

"Even if we could determine a way to successfully attack it," Blackmer said, "I don't really see a reason to do that. I know it killed at least two people when it escaped the research facility, but it didn't harm anybody aboard the *Defiant*, and it hasn't harmed anybody here."

"So I guess we're back to finding a means of communicating with it," O'Brien said.

"Or we could just ignore it," Aleco said, and he shrugged. "I know it's not Starfleet's usual way of addressing a problem, but what else can we do?"

"I see your point," Ro said, "but I don't think that either

Starfleet Command or the Bajoran government will accept that as a solution."

"And it would probably discourage a lot of traffic from coming to the starbase," O'Brien said.

Ro sighed heavily. In addition to being fatigued, she seemed more than a little frustrated. O'Brien couldn't blame her on that score either. He thought she would say something more, but then the tones of the comm system interrupted.

"Hub to Captain Ro," came the voice of Ensign Elvo Minnar, who had taken over for Aleco at tactical. *"The shapeshifter has finished forming into a copy of Deep Space Nine, and something's happened."*

Ro didn't bother to respond verbally. She pushed up out of her chair and strode toward the door that led into the Hub. O'Brien immediately stood up, as did Blackmer and Aleco, and the three men followed the captain out of the conference room.

Blackmer stood with O'Brien and Aleco beside the captain at the sit table, studying the holographic image of the shapeshifter there. It looked like DS9, if the starbase had been crafted entirely in silver. To Blackmer, it looked dreamlike.

"This is a depiction of the entity at the moment it completed forming this shape," Ensign Zhang said from the communications console. "Not long after, this is what happened."

Blackmer watched the hologram closely, but he almost missed the lone bit of movement. It took place on the top, flat side of the *x*-ring, in a rounded, rectangular depression. A hatch slid open. On the real Deep Space 9, it led to one of the runabout hangars.

Blackmer waited to see if anything would emerge from

the space, but nothing did. He pondered the reason for it, but he discovered that the captain had developed her own interpretation. He immediately wished she hadn't.

"It's an invitation," Ro said.

But not an invitation we're going to accept, Blackmer thought, but refrained from saying. He understood his responsibilities both as the starbase's chief of security and as its acting first officer, but he also knew that he should allow the captain her say before opposing her. Perhaps she would not choose to put herself in harm's way.

"Elvo, how closely does the entity match Deep Space Nine's dimensions?" Ro asked.

The Betazoid ensign peered down from the tactical station into the Well, his dark eyes intense. "It is essentially an exact replica, Captain, and not just in dimension," he said. "I'm reading fusion reactors, shield generators, phaser banks, even the equipment to produce a thoron shield."

"Is all of it functioning?" Ro asked.

"Much of it is," Minnar said, "but even though there appears to be an infrastructure for life-support, I'm not detecting internal gravity, atmosphere, or lighting."

Ro nodded, and Blackmer could see that she had already reached her decision. Before she could articulate it, he tried to outflank her. "I volunteer to take a runabout over there and investigate," he said.

The captain gazed at him appraisingly, and for just a moment, he thought she would permit him to lead the mission he knew she wanted to undertake herself. "I think we do need to investigate," Ro said, "but the circumstances are too uncertain for me to allow a member of my crew to do it." She paused, then said, "I'll go."

"Captain, I can't let you do that," Blackmer said. "The situation *is* too uncertain, and therefore too dangerous.

"Jeff, we need answers," Ro said. "We can't just sit here

and wait to see what will happen. For all we know, the shape-shifter out there could be marking this area for an invasion."

Blackmer shook his head. "You don't believe that, Captain."

"No, I don't," Ro said, "but what I believe is immaterial. We have more than enough theories; what we need are facts. And that means sending somebody over there to get them."

"I don't object to that," Blackmer said. "I object—strongly—to *you* going over there."

"With all due respect, Captain," O'Brien said, "I have to agree with Commander Blackmer. This crew needs its commanding officer." The chief engineer didn't add that it had not been even four months since the assassination, which had so profoundly impacted every person aboard Deep Space 9, and that they did not need to lose their captain on top of that. Still, Blackmer could see in O'Brien's eyes that the chief thought it.

Ro took a deep breath and let it out slowly. She walked away from the sit table and up the steps closest to her command chair, but she stopped once she reached the upper level of the Hub. When she turned around, she regarded Blackmer. "I appreciate your perspective, Commander," she said, "and yours, too, Chief." Blackmer took note of the captain's use of his rank, since she typically practiced informality with her crew, referring to her subordinates by their given names. "I'm also sorry for the position I've put you in, Commander Blackmer. I made you acting first officer, and less than a week later, I'm undercutting your authority."

"Captain—" Blackmer began, but Ro held up a hand to stop him.

"I urge you to make your objections to my decision in your first officer's log, and in your security report," the captain said. "I truly believe that the shape-shifter intended the opening of the runabout hatch—" She pointed toward the holographic image above the sit table. "—as an invitation. But I've also realized something else. Commander Stinson attempted to communicate over subspace with the entity, and it didn't respond, other than to re-create the *Defiant* and leave the area. You also tried to communicate with it over subspace, Jeff, and it didn't respond. But when *I* sent it a message, it turned toward Deep Space Nine." Ro walked back down the steps and over to Blackmer. "The shape-shifter didn't just offer an invitation. It offered it to *me*."

Although Blackmer could not dispute the captain's account of events, it seemed more reasonable to him to attribute the timing of the entity's course change to coincidence, rather than to the conclusion Ro had drawn. "Captain . . ." He didn't finish, because he knew there was nothing more he could say to change Ro's mind.

Ro piloted *Senha* away from Deep Space 9 and toward its duplicate—a duplicate clad in silver and alive. She wore an environmental suit, although she had set her helmet on the chair beside her at the runabout's main console. She maintained an active comlink with Blackmer and the rest of the command crew in the Hub, but beyond providing an occasional status, she had said nothing since departing the starbase.

Ro had left Blackmer in command. She had always found him a capable officer—at least after her initial, erroneous misgivings at the time of his transfer to DS9—and she believed that he had turned a corner in the crisis of confidence he'd suffered in the aftermath of the assassination. Starfleet Command had questioned his competence, and she had done so as well. Her review of his service record under her command acted not only to exonerate him of having made any mistakes, but also to demonstrate the keenness of his abilities and his dedication to duty.

And do I recognize something of myself in him? Ro wondered. She had been much younger when a choice she'd made had resulted in the deaths of eight crewmates, and it had taken her a long time to recover from the completely justifiable actions that she nevertheless wished she could reverse. Like Blackmer, she came under the scrutiny of Starfleet Command, though she ended up paying a steeper price for that incident than Blackmer did for the assassination. In part, that was because Blackmer was not responsible for President Bacco's death, but it was also partially the result of Ro standing by him. *And that's ultimately how I recovered: by somebody standing by me.* Captain Picard supported Ro not once, but twice. Without him, she never would have been able to return to Starfleet, much less be permitted to advance from security chief to exec, and from exec to commanding officer. Even almost seven years after the fact, Ro sometimes found it difficult to believe that she had ever been promoted to the top post on Deep Space 9.

The captain in no way regretted assigning Blackmer as the starbase's interim first officer, but she did feel sorry that circumstances had unfolded to put him in such a difficult position. He had been right to speak out against his commanding officer conducting such an uncertain and potentially dangerous mission, but Ro also felt justified in refusing to risk the lives of her crew on what amounted to a hunch. Although she believed that the shape-shifter had specifically invited her to visit, she could not be sure.

Up ahead, through the forward viewport of the runabout, the doppelgänger of Deep Space 9 grew closer. Ro scanned the structure. With impressive exactitude, the readings mimicked those of the original. Ro registered a lack of life-support functions, just as Ensign Minnar had reported, and no life-forms. It put the captain in mind of the construction of DS9. At some point, the exterior of the starbase had been completed, while efforts continued inside it to render it habitable.

Ro narrated her findings—though not her personal thoughts—as she made them. The open channel on her environmental suit picked up her words and transmitted them back to the Hub, where Blackmer and the others monitored her progress. Other than Zhang, they said little; the communications officer periodically reaffirmed the continuing function of the comlink.

Eventually, Ro said, "I am approaching the open runabout hangar." The reproduction of Deep Space 9 looked completely familiar and recognizable, but its monochromatic sheen made it feel both unknown and alien. The idea that Ro would land the runabout on—and *in*—a living being unnerved her.

As *Senha* neared the open hatch, the readings on the sensor panel changed. "I'm suddenly showing artificial gravity inside the hangar," Ro said. "I'm also detecting increases in the levels of heat and light." She paused, then said, "It seems as though it knows I'm coming."

"Captain," said Blackmer, *"I recommend that you don the helmet of your environmental suit before you land the runabout."* Ro could hear the concern behind her acting first officer's words, even as he kept his voice level. Once Blackmer had come to understand that he could not prevent her from visiting the shape-shifter in its DS9 guise, he had suggested that she beam over, since the two structures were close enough to each other to accommodate transport. Ro considered the idea, but finally rejected it for two reasons. First, they could not be sure that the shape-shifter would not raise shields to prevent transport once she boarded. Second, the entity had proffered its invitation in a very specific manner—by way

of the open runabout hangar—and the captain believed she would have the greatest chance for success in communicating with the shape-shifter if she met it on those terms. Blackmer had insisted on maintaining a transporter lock on Ro for as long as she remained off the starbase, and she had quickly acquiesced. Not only would it reassure Blackmer and the rest of her crew, but it would provide her a swift means of escape, should she need to beat a hasty retreat. Ro would willingly enter dangerous situations when the need arose, but she had no wish to die.

"I'm putting my helmet on now," the captain told Blackmer, and she quickly did so. She would maintain the function of her environmental suit for as long as she was aboard the imitation starbase.

"Understood," Blackmer said. *"Thank you, Captain."*

Another reading appeared on Ro's sensors. "A navigational beacon just activated," she said. "I'm going to follow it into the hangar."

"Acknowledged," Blackmer said.

"One hundred meters," Ro said, and she began counting down the distance by tens. At thirty meters, she stood up and peered through the forward viewport to her destination. "I can see part of the hangar," she said. "It's difficult to make out detail because the lighting level is low, but also because of the uniformity of color. Are you able to see?" A monitor in her helmet transmitted real-time images of what she saw back to DS9.

"Affirmative, Captain," Blackmer said. *"We have it on-screen."*

Senha continued to descend toward the starbase-emulating shape-shifter. "Twenty meters," she said, and then, "Ten meters," and finally, "The runabout is passing through the open hatch."

Ro switched from impulse propulsion to antigravs to

effect her landing. *Senha* alit gently. Ro placed the runabout on standby but did not power it down.

"*Captain*," Blackmer said anxiously, "*the hatch is closing, and shields have activated.*" That quickly, both of Ro's avenues of escape—the runabout and the transporter—had been blocked.

"I'm all right," Ro said. "That's standard operating procedure for Deep Space Nine, so perhaps the shape-shifter is imitating that as well." Ro didn't actually believe that—she thought that the entity wanted to ensure that she would not leave before it wished her to—but she didn't want her crew to worry any more than necessary.

Through the forward viewport, diffuse lighting from above revealed what looked like a standard hangar for auxiliary craft, despite its steely finish. It surprised Ro to see a runabout, as well as a work pod and a cargo management unit—also rendered all in silver. She squinted and could just distinguish the outline of the runabout's registry on its bow: NCC-77548. Ro knew that the number—one greater than that of *Senha*—belonged to *Taaj*.

"I'm going to exit the runabout," Ro said.

"*Acknowledged,*" Blackmer said.

Ro strode to the airlock amidships and operated a control panel. The inner hatch glided open with a hum, and she stepped inside. When it had closed behind her, she depressurized the airlock and opened the outer hatch. She waited a moment, then checked the readouts that displayed on the inside of her helmet. "Except for the obvious differences, the hangar matches the configuration of those aboard Deep Space Nine," Ro said. "I am exiting the runabout."

Ro tentatively stepped one foot onto the deck of the hangar. She realized that she expected it to be malleable, perhaps even soft, a supposition that no doubt came from her observation of the shape-shifter readily sculpting itself into various forms. Instead, the footing was solid.

The captain stepped completely onto the deck. Ro paced away from *Senha* and then turned in place. The light from her helmet reflected off every surface at which she looked. But for the lack of color, the setting precisely resembled its counterparts on Deep Space 9.

Suddenly, directly in front of Ro, something on the deck stirred. The captain bent to take a closer look, but then realized that the deck itself moved. A patch began to rise in front of her, like a column draped in a silver cloth. As it climbed higher, it started to shimmer and twist, fashioning itself into another shape—a *humanoid* shape.

The form had reached a height taller than Ro, and a width broader, when it stopped rising. Its features sharpened from head to toe, like a view at a distance coming into focus. Although its flesh matched the silver hue of everything in sight, Ro nevertheless recognized the likeness.

The shape was in the form of Taran'atar.

As little as Ro had fathomed the entity's replicating the form of *Defiant*, and then of Deep Space 9, she understood the Taran'atar-shape in front of her even less. It seemed to indicate that the shape-shifter must have come from the Gamma Quadrant, from the Dominion, and that it must have knowledge not only of Taran'atar, but of Ro's association with him. *For that matter, the entity must know who I am.* That lent credence to her belief that the shape-shifter had changed course toward DS9 when she had identified herself.

"Captain, is that a Jem'Hadar?" Blackmer asked.

"I need to concentrate," Ro said quietly. She slowly reached up to her helmet and muted the transmissions from the starbase, though the crew would still be able to monitor her open channel. Zhang would see on her communications console what the captain had done, and she would report the action to Blackmer.

Before Ro could identify herself or ask a question of the figure standing before her, it spoke. "Ro Laren," it said, the words reaching her not through the external sensors on her helmet, but through her environmental suit and its connection to the deck.

"I am Captain Ro Laren," she said, assuming that the sound of her voice would likewise translate through the deck to the entity. "I am the commanding officer of Deep Space Nine, the starbase that you have copied."

"This is not the Deep Space Nine familiar to me," the Taran'atar-shape said. "But the records we scanned indicate that the former Cardassian ore-processing facility was destroyed some time ago."

"'We'?" Ro said.

"There are many of us here," the Taran'atar-shape said.

"How many?"

"Thousands." He paused, then added, "Some of those here are no more, but their remains are still present."

"Who are you?"

"You know me. I am Taran'atar."

"No, you're not," Ro said. Though she knew the claim for a falsehood, it still angered her. "Taran'atar died in this star system."

"You thought that I died," the Taran'atar-shape said. "Aboard a ship called the *Even Odds*."

It seemed to Ro that the entity intended its statement as proof of its identity, but that didn't follow. "You already told me that you scanned Deep Space Nine's memory banks," Ro said. "The information about how Taran'atar died is stored there."

"It is," the Taran'atar-shape agreed. "I had hoped initially to speak with Captain Kira Nerys, but I saw in the records aboard the *Defiant* that she left Deep Space Nine, and that she was eventually lost."

"Yes," Ro agreed. "She died in the collapse of the wormhole more than two years ago."

"That is unfortunate," the Taran'atar-shape said. "Although . . . it is perhaps intriguing as well."

"I don't know what you mean by that," Ro said. "You are in the form of Taran'atar, but I would like to know your true identity . . . who you are, who your people are. Why have you come here? I would like to open a dialogue with you. My people are curious about all life-forms, and we seek peaceful coexistence with them."

The shape stepped toward Ro, its legs attached by waves of silvery material to the deck. It gazed down at her and closed its eyes, as if in concentration. Ro did not feel threatened, but neither did she know what the entity intended to do.

The light flickered. *No, not the light.* Everything around Ro blinked, changed for a fraction of a second from a wholly metallic version of a hangar bay to a more genuine one. A light blinked on and then off, and then the one-colored compartment returned.

It lasted only an instant. Color reappeared—not bright, vibrant colors, but the muted tones of an actual hangar bay. It faded quickly, but then snapped back to a realistic echo of the same space aboard the real Deep Space 9.

Though branches of silver still connected him to the deck, the Taran'atar-shape looked genuine, too. It had a coarse gray-green hide. Bony, teeth-like protrusions lined its jaw and climbed up the back sides of its head. It had dark, deep-set eyes.

"I am Taran'atar," it repeated.

"I know that you're not," Ro said again. "Please stop saying that. Taran'atar was my friend."

"I know," the entity said. "It was eight of your years ago, though I could not have told you that before gaining access to your records. Since then, time had lost meaning to us. Or perhaps we had been lost to time."

Ro shook her head. "I do not know what you are talking about," she said. "You sound as though you are intentionally speaking in ways meant to confuse, rather than enlighten."

The Taran'atar-shape glanced away, not at some point in the hangar bay, but as though looking inward. "Yes," it said. "It has been that long—eight of your years—since I used words in this way. But I will seek to be clear: I am Taran'atar."

Ro chose not to contradict the entity that time. *I may as well let it have its say.* She might not learn its identity or what it truly wanted, but she might at least learn how and why it wanted to represent its identity and its needs.

"I left Deep Space Nine almost nine of your years ago," the Taran'atar-shape said. "Captain Kira and Commander Vaughn led the effort to recover me from an alternate universe, and from the control of Iliana Ghemor. The captain gave me the choice of remaining on the station, or leaving on an old Bajoran scoutship. I left, not to claim the freedom Kira Nerys offered to me, but to seek the judgment of the Founders for my failures.

"I took the scoutship and traveled through the Anomaly," the Taran'atar-shape continued. "On my way to the Dominion, I intercepted a distress call from the crew of the *Even Odds*. Seeing a means of fulfilling my role as a soldier, I responded. Afterward, once I had saved the *Even Odds* crew, I set myself a new purpose, and I stayed aboard to provide them security."

Ro knew the beginning of the story—the capture and

control of Taran'atar by Iliana Ghemor, and the DS9 crew's attempt to rescue him—but she knew nothing about the Jem'Hadar's life between his decision to depart the station and his arrival back in the system almost a year later, aboard *Even Odds*. What the Taran'atar-shape told her could all be fantasy, a tale designed to produce some response in her, but she wanted to hear the rest of it.

"Eventually, the *Even Odds* traveled to Idran Four," the Taran'atar-shape went on. "There, we discovered a fleet of Ascendant vessels massed near the entrance to the Anomaly. I learned that they were being led by Iliana Ghemor, and that she had a subspace weapon with which she intended to destroy Bajor."

Again, the Taran'atar-shape listed details that had become a matter of record. Ro knew that the best way to lie was to tell as much truth as possible. Still, she discovered that she wanted to believe all of what she heard.

"I protected the city on Idran Four from an attack by a small force of Ascendants," the Taran'atar-shape said. "When they moved to rejoin their fleet, I stranded the *Even Odds* crew on the planet and went in pursuit of Ghemor. On my way to Bajor, I spoke with Captain Kira. I explained the situation to her, and when I saw the Ascendant ships massing to attack, I tore open a subspace irregularity."

"A what?" Ro asked. She remembered well the explosion that had consumed *Even Odds* and sent subspace waves rippling through the Ascendant fleet.

"An irregularity . . . an incongruence in subspace," the Taran'atar-shape said. "I cannot describe the abnormality more completely or more accurately than that. I studied it enough to conclude that it was a threshold between points in space-time. That threshold might have linked the normal continuum with subspace, or it might itself have been a part of subspace. I didn't know, and I still don't. But I had determined that if I increased its level of energy, it would give way."

"You fired an energy weapon," Ro said, recalling Kira's account of her last contact with Taran'atar.

"Yes. And the threshold failed, releasing a barrage of subspace waves, as I'd anticipated."

"Waves that triggered Ghemor's subspace weapon," Ro said.

"But, as I have come to learn, it was not *just* a subspace weapon."

"It was an isolytic subspace weapon," Ro said.

"It was not *just* an isolytic subspace weapon. It had been augmented by one of the Ascendants with a transformative fuel."

"What . . . what does that mean?" Ro asked.

He told her.

Interlude

Nova

On the Quest

In a distant patch of space, Aniq piloted her bladelike vessel toward the rapidly fading star. She skirted a vast expanse of dust and ionized gases that colored the void mostly in shades of violet and blue. The shape-shifters who called themselves the Founders—who had, in fact, *founded* the Dominion—had until recently called a planet in the nebula home. Aniq had hoped to be a part of the force that eradicated them from the universe, but before that could happen, the Changelings had abandoned their world for another, in an as yet unknown location.

Teniq waited too long, Aniq thought. She had never uttered that statement aloud, for fear of risking the label of impudence, and the penance that would come along with it. A young knight who had not lived even a full century could not speak out against the Archquester to whom she reported without provoking consequences.

And yet it remained the case that a more timely attack on the Founders could have vanquished their particular breed of sinner. Unlike those who dared to falsely worship the True, or those who deified beings other than the actual gods, the Founders had constructed an empire in which they inculcated in their subjects—and sometimes *bred* into them—the belief in the divinity of the shape-shifters themselves. Such arrogant sacrilege seemed almost unimaginable to Aniq, and it could be met with only one response: extermination.

Aniq eyed the nebula as she passed it to port. She hoped that she would eventually get the opportunity to rid the universe of the Founders and the filth they propagated. She believed that she would, because such an accomplishment would be worthy of the End Time, and recently, she had heard tell of other knights reporting foretokens of the Path to the Final Ascension.

Aniq had never doubted that she would one day enter the Fortress of the True, that she would stand before the Unnameable and burn beneath their gaze, that she would be found worthy and allowed to join with her gods. She knew that some who had endured the Quest for centuries considered her self-centered belief the egotism of youth. All knights knew that their people would one day reach the Fortress and achieve the Final Ascension, but many accepted as likely that it would not occur within their own lifetime, but during some future generation. Aniq believed otherwise, and she took every opportunity to make her beliefs reality.

To that end, the young Quester had pursued a great, changeable being—not one of the Founders, as best she could tell, but a shape-shifter of considerable size and age. She first encountered the vast creature cycles earlier, in a confrontation that destroyed Aniq's ship and left her stranded on a primitive world. Two older Ascendants in her Order rescued her and provided her with a new vessel. They also counseled her to allow the experience to teach her a modicum of humility and caution when it came to the performance of her duties.

Aniq had accepted the proffered guidance meekly, but with no intention of necessarily heeding it. When she later seized a trophy from a civilization of heretics that she destroyed, a plan began to form in her mind. She viewed the subspace weapon she had taken as her personal tribute to the True, as well as a tool to aid her—and her fellow Ascendants—in burning before them. And in the enormous shape-shifter, she suddenly perceived a means of facilitating her—and the Ascendants—joining with their gods.

Aniq had searched out the massive, variable being. When she found it, she tracked it. Over time, she learned its patterns of behavior, which included occasionally going to ground by settling into a star system, emulating a piece of planetary flotsam, and hibernating.

During one such period of dormancy, when the shape-shifter had dropped into orbit about a white dwarf—one star of two in a binary system—Aniq had recognized her opportunity. Utilizing a technology appropriated from another race of blasphemers the Ascendants had long before annihilated, she accelerated the accretion of hydrogen by the white dwarf from its companion star. A runaway fusion reaction ensued. The white dwarf went nova.

Aniq had withdrawn to a safe distance as the star began to brighten. It ejected material from its surface and emitted massive amounts of radiation. From her observations of the great shape-shifter, Aniq calculated that it would not have enough time to awaken from its slumber before the effects of the nova reached it.

Since then, Aniq had resumed her life on the Quest: searching for the Fortress of the True, seeking out heretics and making them pay for their profanation, looking for omens that the End Time approached. But while other Ascendants contented themselves with merely being receptive to auguries of what they had for so long sought, Aniq would work to make them come to pass.

Aniq had kept a dedicated scan locked on the nova she had hastened. When its effects receded enough for her to inspect what she had wrought, she set course for the white dwarf. It pleased her to think that she had neutralized a creature that had acted against the Ascendants—that had almost killed her—but it inspired her to imagine collecting its resources for her own ends.

Past the nebula that had previously sheltered the Founders, the white dwarf still blazed more brightly than when Aniq had first visited the system, but far from the peak radiance of the nova. Long-range sensors confirmed that the current conditions would allow safe entry into the system. Aniq continued on her course at superluminal velocity, waiting for the immense shape-shifter to appear on her scans.

At last, it did. It read as a static, dome-shaped object orbiting the white dwarf. Aniq saw no movement, and no signs of life.

At the edge of the system, Aniq dropped her vessel to its maximum sublight speed and set course for the remains of the shape-shifter. She rendered the canopy of her ship transparent so that she could see it as she neared. More than once, she glanced aft, at the missile she towed behind her vessel.

As her ship drew closer, Aniq took care to ensure that the shape-shifter had been rendered lifeless. Once she had, she charted an orbit around it. She sampled radiation measurements from its surface, eventually locating the least irradiated area just where she expected it: in the center of its dark side. Choosing that as her destination, Aniq took her vessel down into the shadows. Her ship landed softly, the pull of gravity real but weak on the sizable mass.

After activating her ship's external lighting, Aniq donned an environmental suit. She then sealed the cabin off from the rest of her ship and purged it of atmosphere. Reaching her gloved hand into the hatch release, she took hold of the handle, pulled it toward her, and twisted it. The canopy of her vessel rotated upward.

Aniq hauled herself out of the cockpit and used two lines of indentations in the hull to climb down the side of her ship. The external lighting banished the darkness for several times the length of her vessel, in all directions. When she stepped onto the shape-shifter, wisps of fine, dry material puffed up all around her boots. She watched as the tiny clouds settled slowly back down. After they had, she kicked at the surface. An arid spray of the shape-shifter's remains arced upward. It took a long time to drift back down.

The moment felt like victory to Aniq. It also seemed inevitable. She had always known that she would reach the Fortress of the True, and now she knew why. When the Ascendants burned, she would provide the means by which they joined with the Unnameable.

Aniq strode along the flank of her vessel and then past it, to the missile towed there. Fitted with antigravs, it floated above the surface, double the length of Aniq's ship. She beheld its long, narrow form and the bold whiteness of its casing, as well as her modifications to the weapon. A tubular black ring encircled the projectile near its nose cone, while a second girded it at its midpoint. A trio of long conduits, also black, connected the two rings.

Aniq moved to a control panel on the missile and tapped in a series of commands. Along the forward half of its length, panels rotated out of position, revealing empty compartments. Once, they had held components that Aniq had deemed unnecessary for her purposes, or that she had condensed into other sections: she had eliminated a redundant guidance system, a sublight engine, and a shield generator, and she'd reconfigured its thrusters and an overly complex triggering mechanism. She had then isolated those empty compartments and fitted them with a means of evenly distributing their contents at the moment of the weapon's detonation.

With a specific movement of her head, Aniq activated the external sensors in her environmental suit. She studied the readouts that streamed across the inside of her helmet and saw exactly what she wanted to see: biomimetic material, relatively free of radiation. Although lifeless, the material still possessed the essence of its physical nature. Buried deep in its structure hid the potential of change—of change, and of the ability to *link*.

Aniq bent and scooped up two gloves full of the shape-shifter's ashes, then stood up and deposited them inside an empty compartment in the missile. She could have used a tool to do so, but she wanted to do it with her hands. Somehow, it made the experience more real, more vital.

When the time came, when she and her fellow Ascendants stood in the Fortress of the True and faced the Unnameable, Aniq would see to it that the fire in which they burned also transformed their existence. She and her people would literally join with their gods. That would be the Final Ascension.

III

Ascent

December 2385

"Are you *truly* Taran'atar?" Ro asked. She thought she understood the implications of his story. Standing before a perfect reproduction of the Jem'Hadar soldier, in a perfect reproduction of a DS9 hangar bay, it seemed eminently believable.

"I am Taran'atar," the entity said.

Ro wanted to believe him, but she didn't know if she could. The entity had linked with Odo, and it had scanned the memory banks of both *Defiant* and Deep Space 9. It therefore effectively knew everything that the captain knew.

No, not everything, Ro realized. *Not my thoughts and experiences—at least not those that there's no record of.* "Did you ever write me a note?" she asked. Ro had never told anybody about the brief missive Taran'atar had left for her just before he'd departed the original DS9 for good.

"Once," the entity said. "I left it beside the door to your quarters. I wrote it in Bajoran. It said, 'I'm sorry.' I signed it with my initial."

The description, perfect in its detail, satisfied Ro. More than that, it thrilled and amazed her. She felt pressure mount behind her eyes, and she forced back her tears. "You *are* Taran'atar."

"I am Taran'atar, and more. I was fused in the fire of the isolytic subspace explosion to the shape-shifting substance Aniq had loaded into the weapon. In that form, my consciousness survived the blast and was thrown through subspace. How far, I cannot say, but a considerable distance. Light-years, at least, I have no doubt, but I eventually emerged back into normal space."

Ro remembered the great fissures that the isolytic subspace weapon had opened above Bajor. Those long, jagged rifts had been explained to her as places where the boundaries between the normal space-time continuum and its underlying foundation had been torn asunder. Could Taran'atar—could *anything*—enter subspace through such a fracture and surface back into normal space somewhere else—perhaps through an unsealed cleft? Ro didn't know, but it didn't seem unreasonable to her—and she did believe that Taran'atar, or some part of him, communicated with her at that moment.

"We floated freely for a while," he said. "Time passed, whether slowly or quickly, we could not say. Eventually, through sheer chance, we came into physical contact with a mass of rock. We attempted to reach out to it, to take hold, but we did not know how. We struggled mightily, our continuous but fruitless efforts painful and frustrating."

The captain took note of Taran'atar's shift from an individual to a collective pronoun. She also heard emotion in his words. The act of remembering did not seem easy for him.

"Though we could not explain how we did it," Taran'atar continued, "we at last managed to . . . melt. We seeped onto the surface of what we would later learn was an asteroid. We clutched at a portion of its surface and returned to our solid state.

"We remained there for a period of time we could not begin to define," Taran'atar went on. "We had nothing but ourselves, but many of us railed against the commingling of our thoughts . . . of our life-forces. It was a new existence. For some, it represented rescue, an escape from the nothingness that death would have brought. For others, it came as salvation, a reprieve from lives lost during their existence to what suddenly appeared to be a lie. For still others . . . for *me* . . . it was torture: my existence laid bare, my failures no longer serial but comprehensive, my weaknesses not a difficult internal struggle but a beacon of flaws broadcast to an entire *link* of unknown beings."

"A link," Ro said. She had not intended to speak—she wanted to hear the tale that Taran'atar wanted to tell—but one too many questions had risen in her mind.

"I was not the only consciousness transformed by the detonation," Taran'atar said. "So too were many of the Ascendants. Many also perished, overcome by the explosion, by the destruction of matter, before the transformative wave could sweep them up and fuse them into it."

Taran'atar raised an arm to the side and pointed. Ro looked and saw another figure rising from the deck, painted all in silver and attached by numerous tendrils of shape-shifting material to the surface from which it grew. Unlike Taran'atar, it was not standing; it lay on its side in the fetal position. Ro could not see the face from her position, but she recognized enough details of the figure that when Taran'atar identified it, it did not surprise her.

"Iliana Ghemor," he said. "She did not survive the blast of the metaweapon. Like many of those nearest the point of detonation, she died in its initial fire." Around the silver-clad figure of Ghemor, other forms began to appear, all of them Ascendants. But for the shoots of shape-shifting material that bound them to the deck, and the large eyes that did not show as gold but as silver, they looked very much like Raiq, the lone Ascendant Ro had ever met.

A thought occurred to the captain, and she immediately voiced it. "What about the Bajorans on Endalla? Are any of them with you?"

"There are no Bajorans within our link," Taran'atar said.

"A subspace fracture was drawn by the power sources on the moon," Ro explained. "It obliterated the ecosphere on Endalla, ripped away the atmosphere, destroyed the scientific facilities there. Everybody there—thousands of men and women—were killed."

"Their violent ends must have come before they could be

encompassed by the biomimetic material," Taran'atar said. "Or maybe that material never reached them. Maybe it had all been fused to others. I don't know what happened. I only know that they are not here."

The information saddened Ro anew. The people of Bajor had mourned the loss of those lives eight years earlier, but in some ways, the enormity of it never completely left them. It also reminded Ro that two scientists had been killed on a Federation research facility, and Odo had been badly, perhaps mortally, wounded.

"You killed two scientists yourself," Ro said. "And you attacked Odo."

"I know of what you speak," Taran'atar said, "but what you say is not accurate. We know from Odo that we were found on the asteroid by a Starfleet vessel. Its crew had been drawn to our location by readings of an energy burst, which I assume was generated when we reentered normal space. Once in the system, the crew tracked some anomalous subspace scans to our location. They removed us from the asteroid and brought us to a place Odo knew as Newton Outpost."

Ro had never heard of Newton Outpost, but the Federation research facility from which the shape-shifter had fled had never been identified to her. Taran'atar also provided additional information of which she had been unaware, including the name of the ship whose crew had found the specimen. Other details, such as how the *Nova* crew had discovered the shape-shifter on the asteroid, tracked with what little Ro had been told.

"We did not know where we were," Taran'atar said. "We did not know anything but our internal life and our link."

"Could you perceive your surroundings?" Ro asked.

"Mostly no, and not at all in the way you mean," Taran'atar said. "And then Odo linked with us, and everything changed. In an instant, all of his knowledge became ours. The experience completely overwhelmed us, but of all the information we learned, one piece of knowledge superseded all others: we suddenly knew how to change our form. The second-most important thing we knew was that we were being held prisoner, and that we must escape.

"We foolishly viewed Odo as a threat in those first moments, and we did strike him," Taran'atar said. "But we did not attack the scientists. If they were injured or killed, it must have been an inadvertent consequence of our hurried attempt to flee."

Ro believed Taran'atar. "I understand wanting to escape captivity, but what are you doing now?" she asked. "What do you want?"

"I wanted to speak with you," Taran'atar said. "I would have wanted to speak to Kira Nerys as well, and to Elias Vaughn, but I know from your records that they are dead." He paused before continuing. "But that is what *I* want. It is not what *we* want. What we want is to return to the Fortress of the True. That is what the Ascendants call the Anomaly, what the Bajorans call the Celestial Temple. Once we escaped from Newton Outpost, we knew that was where we had to go."

"So you were heading for the wormhole all along," Ro said. "Not for Bajor, nor for Deep Space Nine."

"We were heading for the wormhole," Taran'atar confirmed. "When you attempted to make contact with us, I heard you identify yourself, I wanted to speak with you, to see you. I convinced the others to allow me to do so."

"Why?" Ro asked.

"Because you are the last available connection to my life as I once knew it," Taran'atar said. "As alien to me as my assignment was to observe life in the Alpha Quadrant, it now seems like a natural part of my existence as a . . . as a *solid.* I believe—*we* believe—that once we enter the Fortress of the True, we will never leave it. I accept that, but it also made me want to make one final connection to my old life."

"But why would you want to enter the wormhole?" Ro asked, and then she revised her question. "Why would you want to enter the Fortress of the True?"

"It has been the generations-long desire of the Ascendants, and the lifelong goal of those with whom I am linked," Taran'atar said. "Even if I did not wish to go, I could do little to prevent it from happening. I cannot separate myself from the link."

"Can't you?" Ro asked. "Odo could. Other Founders could."

"I do not know how," Taran'atar said, "but even if I did, that would not change the situation. I am part of this link . . . this community . . . and I do not wish to leave it. I am also eager to enter the Fortress of the True and see it as something more than the Anomaly that I knew. My life . . . my *former* life . . . was beset by doubt—doubt in myself, and doubt in my gods. I look forward to reestablishing my faith, this time in the truly divine."

"Are you talking about the Prophets?" Ro asked.

"I do not know," Taran'atar said. "*We* do not know. But yes, we think that *Prophets* is just another name for the True."

"What do you expect to happen when you enter the wormhole?" Ro had no doubt that the first minister and the kai and probably just about everybody else on Bajor would not want to allow a link of shape-shifters—comprising a Jem'Hadar soldier and some number of Ascendant zealots—to enter the Celestial Temple. The captain didn't know whether she wanted to permit that either. Based on all that had taken place, though, she had no idea how she and her crew—or anybody else, for that matter—could realistically prevent that from happening.

Perhaps the scientists on DS9 could eventually figure out a solution, but she doubted that the Ascendants would wait.

"We do not know what will happen," Taran'atar said. "Once, the Ascendants believed that they would burn beneath the gaze of their gods, and then join with them, but they see that the events alluded to in their holy texts have already taken place. At Bajor, they burned—*we* burned—and none would disagree that the event fell within the perception of the True. The surviving Ascendants then joined, not with their gods, but with each other. There has been debate, but it seems settled that what has transpired is a valid interpretation of scripture. The only action that remains is for the Ascendants to reside in the Fortress of the True. There, we expect to live as we were ultimately meant to: within the gaze of the Unnameable, joined to them in a spiritual way, and joined to each other physically."

Ro nodded, not to agree, but as a simple response to an overpowering narrative. She saw one of the inert bodies—or body-shapes—on the deck behind Taran'atar, and she looked around at all of them, including the one approximating Iliana Ghemor. "What about the dead?" she asked, pointing to the form of the Cardassian madwoman.

"These are not the true corpses of the dead," Taran'atar said. "They were reduced to ashes. Some of that material does reside within our link, but without consciousness, without life." Around them, the body-shapes began to dissolve back into the deck. In short order, none of them remained.

"I'm glad that I'm getting to speak with you," Ro said. "I'm glad that I can tell you that your note meant a great deal to me . . . that your friendship meant so much to me. I'm glad that I can show you that I'm all right, that I've recovered. But mostly, I'm glad that you're alive."

For a long while, Taran'atar did not move, and he said nothing. At last, he closed his eyes and nodded once, slowly.

When he looked at her again, the moment had passed, and he said, "The Ascendants have a request."

"Yes?" Ro asked, immediately on her guard.

"We know from Odo that Raiq is still alive," Taran'atar said.

"Yes," Ro said. "As far as anybody knew, she was the lone surviving Ascendant."

"She is living on Bajor," Taran'atar said. "At the Vanad-wan Monastery."

"Yes," Ro confirmed, understanding that there was no point in denying it.

"According to Odo, she has taken a vow of silence until either an Ascendant returns, or Kira Nerys does."

"I've heard that," Ro said.

"Raiq should know that the Ascendants have returned," Taran'atar said, "and that we would welcome her to join us."

Ro did not know how to respond to that statement, so she chose to agree. "I can speak to Raiq," she said. "I can inform her of everything that's happened. The choice would have to be hers."

"Of course," Taran'atar said. "On behalf of the Ascendants, thank you. And for myself, I also thank you . . . for everything."

Ro again felt pressure behind her eyes. She fought it, and she fought the impulse to embrace Taran'atar. He seemed to perceive the emotion within her, as well as the fact that their conversation seemed to have reached a natural end. Without saying anything, the shape of Taran'atar began to lose its form, almost like an ice sculpture thawing. The hangar bay flickered, once, twice, thrice, the color draining out of it each time, until only silver remained.

The captain took a long look around, and then she boarded her runabout. She unmuted her comlink to Deep Space 9 and was immediately faced with questions. Ro shut her crew down, telling them that she was all right, and that she would soon be back on DS9.

Once Ro boarded the runabout, the shields surrounding the phantom starbase dropped, and the exterior hatch opened. The captain piloted *Senha* upward, taking it back out into space. Then she pointed the bow of the runabout toward the real Deep Space 9.

Raiq sat beside Captain Ro at the forward console of the runabout. The Starfleet officer had contacted her the night before and requested that she travel to Deep Space 9. Ro had been circumspect about the reason for the journey, but she'd hinted that she possessed information that the Ascendant would want—likely about Kira Nerys, Raiq had thought.

The conversation had not been an actual conversation, since Raiq had not spoken since the disappearance of Vedek Kira more than two years earlier, when the wormhole had collapsed. Ro did all of the talking, although she didn't say much either beyond presenting the invitation to the starbase. In the end, Raiq agreed with a nod.

The captain had said that she would send a ship for the Ascendant, but Raiq hadn't expected Ro to be piloting it herself. The reason soon became obvious. The captain told a story to Raiq about the fate of the Ascendants, and since Ro had been the only person to hear the account firsthand, she had wanted to relate it herself.

The tale had been fantastic, and yet much of it made sense to Raiq. She remembered hearing Aniq tell the Fire and Grand Archquester Votiq that she had modified her powerful weapon with "transformative" fuel. The correspondence between the fact of the Ascendant fleet being caught in the detonation of the subspace weapon in the general vicinity of the wormhole, and the belief of the knights that they would burn beneath the gaze of the True, appeared too close to be coincidental. Likewise, the linking of the Ascendants via biomimetic material seemed similar to the notion of them joining with the Unnameable.

And I felt that there were still Ascendants out there somewhere, Raiq thought. That might have been hope masquerading as intuition, but it had turned out to be true after all.

Raiq believed what the captain had told her. She felt ecstatic to learn of the survival of many of her people, even though their physical nature had changed. That they had come back for her before reentering the Fortress of the True touched her deeply. While she did not wish to relent on the vigil she held for Vedek Kira, Raiq could not possibly turn down the opportunity to rejoin her people.

Up ahead, through the forward viewport of the runabout, Deep Space 9 came into view, as did its silver twin. Ro had described the events that had brought about the recreation of the starbase, so the image did not surprise Raiq. Still, the Ascendant found the scene surreal.

"I have to ask you again," Ro said as the runabout veered toward the replicated DS9. "Are you certain that you want to do this?"

Raiq regarded the captain. She considered making an analogy about all of the Bajorans lost during the Occupation, and that Ro, after running away from Bajor, had eventually returned to her people, but she chose not to do so. Instead, she said, "I thought I was the last of my kind. Now that it turns out that I am not, how can I not do this?"

Ro accepted that, and other than contacting her crew aboard Deep Space 9 and providing them a status, she said nothing more for the remainder of the voyage. The captain navigated the runabout through a hatch on the silver starbase's horizontal ring, and she set the vessel down in a large compartment.

"I assume that, for your transformation, the Ascendant link will need to touch you," Ro said. "That means that you can't wear an environmental suit, but since there's no atmosphere in the hangar bay, I'm going to pump air into it from the storage holds of the *Lorus*." The captain pointed a thumb toward the aft section of the runabout. "It won't take long."

Raiq didn't know the length of time the process actually did take, but it felt like one of the longest waits of her life. Eventually, Ro told her that she could safely exit the vessel. The captain walked with her to the rear of the cockpit, to an external hatch, and opened it with a set of taps to a control panel.

Outside the ship, the silver compartment seemed empty, but as Raiq started through the hatch, a shape began to rise from the deck. As it grew, it took on the general contours of a body. When it reached its full height, its appearance suddenly clarified.

Although she expected it, or something like it, Raiq still could not believe what she saw. Gratitude welled within her that Captain Ro had told her the truth, that her people had survived, and that they had come back for her. Raiq strode forward in the compartment. "Seltiq," she said. Behind her, the hatch of the runabout closed.

"Raiq," the Grand Archquester said. "It is good to see you."

"I . . ." Raiq began, but words failed her. She had never felt more joy in her life than at that moment.

"It has been explained to you what has happened?" Seltiq asked.

"It has," Raiq said, finding her voice. "Aniq's 'transformative' fuel for the subspace weapon actually worked."

"It did," Seltiq said. "Perhaps not in the way she envisioned, but yes, it worked."

The Grand Archquester's use of the word *perhaps* caught Raiq's attention. "You do not know what Aniq envisioned?" she asked.

"I do not," Seltiq said. "I never spoke with her about it, as I only became Grand Archquester shortly before the weapon detonated."

"Then that means Aniq is not with you."

"She is not," Seltiq said. "Aniq died in the subspace explosion."

The news pained Raiq. "How . . . how many of us are there?"

"We have not counted," Seltiq said. "We know that some of us are missing, but there are enough of us to go on. We are legion."

The Grand Archquester's declaration elated Raiq. "I want to join you."

"And we want you to join us." Without another word, Seltiq dissolved, her single-colored visage pouring back onto the deck—*into* the deck.

And then a wave surged upward from where she had stood. Raiq closed her eyes as it rushed forward and crashed upon her like surf upon sand. She expected heat in the embrace, but wrapped in the swirling, shape-shifting slurry, she felt a chill run through her body.

Raiq heard movement all about her—*on* her. The link of Seltiq and the other Ascendants twisted around her body, covering every point of her exoskeletal sheath. When she breathed in, their essence mixed with the air and entered her lungs, filling her up.

Anticipation filled her as well. Raiq wanted so much to be with her people again. The Bajorans had been remarkably accepting of having an Ascendant in their midst, and Vedek Kira had been kind and compassionate, but Raiq wanted to be among those with whom she shared a heritage.

She waited for the moment of *joining*, that instant when she would become one with her people. After all that she had endured, that moment shined just ahead of her like the ultimate fulfillment of her Quest.

But nothing happened.

By degrees, Raiq grew aware that nothing any longer touched her body, nothing moved around her. She opened her eyes to see Seltiq once more standing before her. Raiq knew what she would tell her before the words left her mouth.

"I'm sorry," the Grand Archquester said. "We hoped that we could do this."

"You . . . hoped?" Raiq said. "You didn't know."

"We didn't know," Seltiq said. "Our contact with another shape-shifter suggested that it would not be possible for us to join with a solid, but he was different than we are, and so we hoped. Forgive us, but we wanted to try."

"Yes," Raiq said. "I'm pleased that you did." Her voice, her words seemed to belong to somebody else. She felt cheated, and angry, and sad.

"Your Quest is at an end," Seltiq said. "Let that be your solace."

Raiq nodded. A moment passed silently, and then another. She did not know what to say any more than she knew how she would go on.

You will, she told herself—although the voice in her head sounded like that of Vedek Kira. *You will get on with your own life, even though you have no idea what that means.* She accepted that her Quest had definitively come to an end, but she also realized that she could, if she so chose, begin another.

Before her, Seltiq bowed her head. Raiq returned the gesture and then watched as the Grand Archquester melted back into the deck. When she turned back toward the runabout, the hatch slid open. She strode back inside, still feeling cheated and angry and sad.

But she no longer felt alone.

For the third time in the span of twenty-six hours, Ro guided a runabout toward the silver copy of Deep Space 9. She'd barely slept in half again as long, though she had managed to nap on the trip to Bajor to collect Raiq. The captain had taken the lone remaining "solid" Ascendant to the real DS9 after the shape-shifting link's failed attempt to join with her. Ro expected that Raiq would later return to Bajor.

Except that might be an open question, Ro realized. Raiq might not want to go back to Bajor, although Ro had no idea where else she might want to go. *But that's not my decision either to make or to approve, so I don't need to think about that right now.*

After the Ascendants had failed to assimilate Raiq into their link, Ro had gone back into the hangar bay on the ersatz Deep Space 9. Taran'atar reappeared, and the two spoke again. The captain reconfirmed his intention, and that of the link, to travel into the wormhole. They truly believed that they would achieve the Final Ascension by doing so, but Ro wanted to know what they intended to do if nothing happened. Taran'atar told her that few of the Ascendants considered such a possibility, but of those who did, they reached a consensus that they would depart the Fortress into the Gamma Quadrant and seek to find an uninhabited world where they could explore their new reality in peace. The captain then asked if she could accompany the link into the wormhole, simply as a witness to whatever took place, if anything did.

That idea had been Ro's. She developed it after a series of long meetings with people who mostly wanted her to do the impossible. Virtually everybody with whom she spoke believed that the shape-shifting collection of one Jem'Hadar and many Ascendants represented an existential threat, and they tasked Ro with ending that threat. The captain understood their perspective.

Starfleet Command viewed the wormhole as a Federation asset—for exploration, trade, and defense—and they did not want to risk its collapse, either temporarily or permanently. Neither did they want a link of hostile shape-shifters to head into the Gamma Quadrant to form an alliance with the Founders and stir up old hatreds. Admiral Akaar ultimately ordered Ro to resolve the issue in some way that did not prove deleterious to Bajor or the Federation. Though a vague directive, the captain preferred it to something more definite; it allowed her a great deal of latitude. It also demonstrated that the commander in chief had finally come to trust her, something he had first shown signs of doing as Ro had handled events in the wake of President Bacco's assassination.

Captain Swaddock had also offered his opinion about the Ascendant link when *Sacagawea* had arrived at Deep Space 9. He supported a military solution. Fortunately, Ro outranked Swaddock based on their respective tenures as Starfleet captains, and her firsthand experience in dealing with the Ascendant link gave her view more weight. When Lieutenant Commander Stinson finally returned to DS9 with *Defiant*, Swaddock had departed so that *Sacagawea* could begin its next mission.

The Federation president, Kellessar zh'Tarash, had also voiced her concern with allowing the link into the wormhole. First Minister Asarem had grave misgivings as well, especially given the current uproar on Bajor over the Ohalavaru discovery on Endalla. Kai Pralon and the Vedek Assembly echoed those fears.

Ro had reviewed the facts with all of them, and had presented her argument about what she thought should happen. The linked Ascendants had enveloped both *Defiant* and Deep Space 9, and though it seemed likely that they could have meted out considerable damage to both, and maybe even destroyed them, they had not done so. Ro also pointed out that, even if the decision was made to prevent the link from entering the wormhole, nobody knew how, realistically, to stop them. Moreover, the captain believed Taran'atar when he told her that he and the Ascendants intended only to enter the wormhole, and that if nothing happened, they would be content to locate an uninhabited planet somewhere in the Gamma Quadrant to call home.

Ro opened a channel. "*Rio Grande* to Deep Space Nine," she said, and she had to smile. The crew utilized the starbase's runabouts on a rotation, contingent on maintenance and repair schedules, with an eye toward balancing out flight hours for each. The captain had first taken *Senha* to the duplicate DS9, and then *Lorus*, and for her current journey, she piloted *Rio Grande*. The runabout had been among the first delivered to the original DS9, long before Ro had ever served there. While the other runabouts initially assigned to the station, and numerous others after that, had been lost, *Rio Grande* had survived. Some of the crew—including Chief O'Brien—regarded the use of the venerable runabout as a talisman for success. Ro did not count herself as superstitious, but she had to admit that it pleased her whenever she boarded *Rio Grande*.

"*Deep Space Nine here. This is Stinson.*" Upon *Defiant*'s return to the starbase, the ambitious second officer had taken no time in getting back into the duty rotation. Ro knew that she would soon have to name a permanent replacement for Colonel Cenn—both in his position as exec and as Bajoran liaison—and she would have to take care with Stinson. He would expect to be elevated to first officer, and if she made another choice, he might well request a transfer.

"Wheeler, I'm approaching the link now," the captain said. "I will—" Ro stopped as she detected motion through the forward viewport. She watched as the imitation DS9 began to collapse in on itself, its surface glittering as it did so. "Are you seeing this, Wheeler?"

"Yes, sir."

The vertical rings gave way first, their smooth lines buckling, but all of the pieces remained attached to one another. The horizontal ring moved next, the thick section crumpling as though made of paper. All of it fell inward to the main sphere, the surface of which puckered and condensed. In just seconds, the shape-shifting link emulating Deep Space 9 went from the form of the massive starbase to a gleaming silver globe not much bigger than a runabout.

"I'm going in," Ro told Stinson.

"Acknowledged, Captain."

"Rio Grande out." Ro closed the channel, then adjusted her course to take it past the new shape of the Ascendant link, just as she'd worked out with Taran'atar. The captain didn't know if he and those with him in the link knew that she wanted to watch them enter the wormhole in order to ensure that they truly had no hostile aims, but she understood that it likely wouldn't have mattered if they did know that, or even if they did plan to commit some heinous act. As she had pointed out to Admiral Akaar and everyone else, there would be little she could do to stop them.

As *Rio Grande* came alongside the globe, she activated the runabout's tractor beam and took it in tow. She then set course for the wormhole. It blossomed open before her in spinning blues and whites, and she took *Rio Grande* toward its brilliant heart.

Scans showed high proton counts, neutrino disturbances, variably changing wave intensities. Ro compensated as she had numerous times before to establish a smooth transit. *Rio Grande* responded accordingly, and then the captain directed the runabout into the wormhole.

Inside the great subspace bridge, everything appeared as it normally did. Ro checked the tractor beam and saw that it still operated, but when she attempted to verify the load on it, she saw that *Rio Grande* towed nothing. She quickly worked her controls to activate the runabout's rear monitor. She saw the iridescent white cone of the tractor beam, but no globe—no shape of any kind—within it.

Ro attacked the flight controls, intending to double back, a maneuver she had never attempted within the confines of the wormhole. Before she could even plot a course, *Rio Grande* began to slow. Ro searched for the cause, but she could find none.

"Warning," the computer announced. *"Impulse system overload. Auto shutdown in twelve seconds."*

Ro swore under her breath. She had no choice but to disengage the engines. *Rio Grande*'s velocity continued to fall, telling her that she had little chance of reaching the Gamma Quadrant. She would be caught within the wormhole until somebody from DS9 came to find her and tow her out. When the captain didn't return to the starbase, Blackmer would not wait long to mount a reconnaissance and rescue.

Suddenly, the runabout thudded. Ro recognized the cause at once, though it made absolutely no sense to her. *Rio Grande* had landed.

"Landed?" she said aloud in the empty cabin. "Landed on *what*?" Ro had some vague memory that Captain Sisko had once reported setting down inside the wormhole, but he hadn't been sure whether the experience had been real or had occurred solely in his mind.

The wormhole no longer remained visible through any

of the viewports. Bright white light had replaced the kinetic blend of colors that adorned its length. The captain checked the hull sensors and, to her surprise, read an atmosphere surrounding *Rio Grande*—a *breathable* atmosphere.

"I guess this is where I get off," Ro said. She stood up and headed to the runabout's hatch. She reconfirmed the external atmosphere, then thought about retrieving an environmental suit from equipment storage and putting it on, but she reasoned that anything that could fool the sensors doubtless had many ways of killing her beside asphyxiation.

Ro opened the hatch. Outside, a dark and forbidding landscape stretched away as far as she could see. Lightning flared above sheer cliffs and black plains, and chasms cut wide gashes in the terrain. Gray clouds filled the sky, and thunder rumbled in the distance.

Ro headed to an equipment locker and retrieved a tricorder. She then moved back to the hatch, took a deep breath, and stepped outside. Oddly, she felt no wind, and the air temperature seemed no different than that inside *Rio Grande*.

"What is this place?" she asked. She activated the tricorder and started to try to scan her surroundings, but then the entire scene blinked. For an instant, Ro saw bright, natural colors, but then they immediately disappeared, replaced by the stormy skies and bleak terrain she had first seen. She turned in place to view everything around her, and as she did, the vista flickered again. She suddenly stood in a glade, with green grass underfoot and tall trees all around. Flowers of vibrant hues dotted the landscape. Sunlight cascaded down from a cloudless, azure sky.

"Thank you."

Ro whirled to see Taran'atar standing there, not in silver, but restored to his normal appearance. No silver tendrils connected him to the grass. He wore the same black coverall he had back in the days when he had stood motionless in Ops, on the old station, treating Odo's orders to observe life in the Alpha Quadrant as literally as he could.

"What is happening?" Ro asked.

"The Ascendants have achieved their Final Ascension," Taran'atar said.

"And they've left you?"

"No," Taran'atar said. "We are still one." He closed his eyes as though in concentration, and the color washed from his body, leaving him painted in the silver of the Ascendants. In the next instant, the entire tableau paled, every hue leeched away.

And then everything returned to its previous appearance, including Taran'atar. "We are all here," he said. "Existence is different in this place, we have discovered."

"How could you have discovered anything?" Ro asked. "You just arrived here."

"No," Taran'atar said. "We have been here for some time, it turns out, and we will be here yet longer."

"I don't understand," Ro admitted.

"Nor do we," Taran'atar said. "But we will exist here."

"On a planet inside the wormhole?"

"No," Taran'atar said. "This—" He spread his arms wide, a gesture clearly meant to encompass everything around them. "—is who we are. We are a living, breathing world, and we will be so for as long as we endure."

Ro had seen many remarkable things in her travels, including some that she had never come to understand, but the sense of confusion that filled her at that moment carried with it a trace of comprehension. She could not articulate it, but she wanted to—if for nobody else than for herself. "How is this possible?"

"We know only some of what you ask," Taran'atar said. "The isolytic subspace weapon, the biomimetic yield placed inside it, learning of our new nature and how to alter our form from Odo. The rest is the will of the True."

"The True?" Ro still had difficulty believing that Taran'atar wanted to replace the Founders with another set of gods.

"The True," Taran'atar said. "The Prophets. The Siblings."

It surprised Ro to hear the Jem'Hadar use the Eav'oq name for the inhabitants of the wormhole. He could have learned that during his time on the original Deep Space 9, or he could have gotten it from the scans of *Defiant* and DS9's memory banks. *And the Ascendants probably knew,* Ro realized.

"Have you spoken with the . . . the Prophets?" Ro asked, opting for her people's own name for the denizens of the wormhole.

"No," Taran'atar said. "But we feel their presence, and their will is clear to us. Or, at least, as clear as is possible."

"And this is what you want?" Ro asked, genuinely concerned for her friend, no matter his form.

"Yes," Taran'atar said. "And it is what the Ascendants want."

"Very well," Ro said. "Will I see you again? Will anybody?"

"You speak of the future," Taran'atar said. "That is no longer a distinct concept to us, at least not in the way you mean. The future is the present, the present is the past, the past is yet to be, and all of it has always been."

"That makes no sense to me," Ro said. "I don't know what you mean."

"Nor need you," Taran'atar said. "We are here. We have

been here. We will be here. And if the True . . . if the Prophets . . . will it, then others may come here, too. But . . ."

"But?" Ro asked when the Jem'Hadar did not finish his statement.

"I do not know," Taran'atar said. "I believe that we are here for a purpose, but I do not expect that we will see many others."

Ro nodded, though she had trouble parsing Taran'atar's meaning. It definitely put her in mind of the way in which Captain Sisko—the Emissary—portrayed the Prophets, as beings who existed nonlinearly in time. As implausible as it all seemed, it nevertheless sounded *right* to Ro. More and more, she felt compelled to reconsider her long-held beliefs that the Prophets were members of an advanced alien species, but not gods. *What more proof of divinity do I need?*

The captain asked Taran'atar, "Will I be able to leave here?" Until that moment, the possibility that she would be trapped there had not occurred to her.

"Yes," Taran'atar said. "But it is likely that you will be unable to return."

Ro sighed. She did not wish to say good-bye to Taran'atar again, but at least she would not have to mourn him. "I wish you a fulfilling existence," she told him.

"I have a new purpose," Taran'atar said. "I am fulfilled."

Ro didn't know how much the Jem'Hadar's "new" purpose differed from his old: to serve his gods. *But my opinion doesn't matter,* she told herself. *As long as he's happy—or as close to happy as a Jem'Hadar can get.*

"I wish you your own fulfillment, Ro Laren."

"Thank you," the captain said. "I have my purpose, and it does fulfill me." Some days when she thought about the satisfaction that command brought her, she could not believe how far she had come from a childhood best left in the past. "Good-bye."

Taran'atar bowed his head. Ro turned and walked back to the runabout. Once aboard, she turned to the open hatch as she reached for its controls. The beautiful setting still lay before her, but Taran'atar had gone. "Good-bye," she said again. Then she closed the hatch and lifted off, on her way back to Deep Space 9.

Epilogue

Return

January 2386

Doctor Girani Semna walked into the isolation ward as she studied Odo's latest readings on a padd. She had been at Newton Outpost for five weeks. While she found the work rewarding, she also missed Aroya back on Bajor. Girani hadn't been permitted to contact her directly from the facility, but only to send her brief messages channeled through Deep Space 9. The two had been seeing each other for nearly a year, and their relationship had grown serious. Girani hated to be away for so long.

Even so, she believed that her efforts had been worth it, and she felt sure that Aroya would have thought so, too. Girani had worked nonstop since arriving, regularly putting in twelve- to sixteen-hour days. The last few weeks had not been quite as hectic as the first few, since Doctor Norsa, the facility's chief of staff, had returned to her duties after recovering from concussion-related symptoms. Though not as well-versed in Changeling physiology as Girani, Norsa offered significant contributions to Odo's care.

Girani's notion that the shape-shifter that had injured Odo might have taken something from him had initially not panned out. A careful reexamination of all his biological readings revealed nothing that the Newton Outpost staff had overlooked. Scans for tetryon and other forms of radiation likewise turned up negative.

The day after Girani had arrived at the facility, she'd received a message from the chief medical officer on Deep Space 9. Doctor Boudreaux informed her that the biomimetic substance of a shape-shifter had been caught in the isolytic subspace detonation that had taken place over Bajor eight years prior. According to Boudreaux, that explosion resulted in a Jem'Hadar soldier and a number of Ascendants assimilating the morphogenic matrix of that shape-shifter and forming an unprecedented link. It had been that newly amalgamated life-form that had been brought to Newton Outpost, and with which Odo had joined.

Girani had spent considerable time after that searching for some trace of biological material corresponding to the Jem'Hadar or the Ascendants. Starfleet had a good deal of information about the former, but very little about the latter. Just a single Ascendant had ever undergone medical examination, and only rudimentary data had been collected. When the Jem'Hadar line of inquiry failed to produce any results, Girani contemplated contacting her colleagues on Bajor and having them request that Raiq consent to in-depth testing.

Before she had done that, though, she'd thought about something else. So far as she knew, nobody had ever survived within the immediate vicinity of an isolytic subspace detonation. She wondered what impact that could have on a living being, and so Girani enlisted the aid of some of the scientists at Newton Outpost to examine Odo from that perspective. They detected nothing biologically wrong with him—their tests had not been designed to do so—but they did identify a subspace variance within many of his cells. Though nobody could know for sure, it seemed reasonable to assume that Odo's contact with the Jem'Hadar-Ascendant link had effected those changes in him.

Over the next few weeks, Girani had worked with the scientists to realign the subspace signature of Odo's impacted cells. It was a painstaking, round-the-clock process. Before undergoing the treatment, Odo had begun physically deteriorating further, his biomimetic material growing darker and less flexible by the hour. Once the subspace therapy began, his condition plateaued.

Girani had hoped that once the treatment had been completed, Odo would start to convalesce. That hadn't happened. He didn't get worse, but neither did he get better.

Girani had then reviewed all the records of Odo's care during the time he'd served on DS9, which she had ordered from Starfleet Medical before she'd left Bajor. She performed a statistical analysis on all of the treatments he'd received, however minor, and determined several adjustments she could make to his environment in the isolation ward. She switched out the cylindrical glass container in which he had been placed for one she designed and replicated herself. The new vessel had a cubic shape and a softer interior coating, with intricate patterns etched into its base and sides. She adjusted the lighting and temperature centered upon Odo's compromised state.

Nothing had worked. Desperate, Girani requested Norsa's permission to enter Odo's isolation chamber. The chief of staff initially denied the request, citing Odo's own determination to link with the specimen that had ultimately put him in critical condition. Girani argued her case, showing Norsa the records of an incident where a "solid" had, through personal attention and hands-on care, helped improve the medical condition of a shape-shifter. Girani hadn't bothered to mention that the "solid" had been Odo himself, at a time when the Founders had stripped him of his ability to alter his form, and that the unformed Changeling had eventually perished from tetryon poisoning. With no other prospects for Odo's recovery, Norsa had relented.

Using Odo's own notes from his care for the unformed Changeling, as well as Doctor Mora Pol's more comprehensive records from his observations at the time, Girani had begun to care for Odo directly, inside his isolation chamber. Since Odo's cells had been repaired of their subspace variance, she believed that he should be able to change his form, but he showed no indications of even attempting to do so. Girani reasoned that if the Founders could physically divest a shape-shifter of its transformative ability, perhaps severe trauma could result in a comparative mental or psychological condition. She just hoped that his memory and cognitive function had not been impacted.

Girani had used antigravs to manipulate the container holding Odo. She moved him around, in a way that she viewed as similar to helping exercise a humanoid patient's impaired motor control and atrophied muscles. Girani also spoke to Odo as she proceeded.

Eventually, Odo had shown the first signs of moving on his own. He did little more than shift the top of his mass, causing a motion that looked like a wave in a fish tank. A day after that, Odo copied the designs incised in his container. Each day brought improvement, not only in his shape-shifting abilities, but also in his appearance. The gray shading suffusing his substance faded, replaced by his natural orange-gold tones.

Girani looked up from her padd and through the observation port in the isolation ward. Odo's container was empty. Girani dropped the padd and pressed her face against the port, peering around in search of her patient. She saw a patch of color near the inner corner of the chamber, but she could not make out any detail.

Fighting the urge to storm inside, Girani worked the bio-sensors on the panel below the port. They registered Odo's biomimetic substance as alive and showing vital signs that registered on the low end of healthy for a Changeling, but better than they had since he'd been attacked.

Girani strode to the chamber door and worked the control panel there to open it. She stepped inside, then took the time to close the door behind her. Once she had, she looked down to the inner corner where she had seen a patch of color.

Odo lay there—not in his amorphous, unformed state, and not even as some geometric figure or pattern. He had resumed the roughly Bajoran shape in which Girani had seen him on DS9. The simulated clothing appeared different to her, but then, Odo had not served in the Militia for a long time. He lay on the deck in the corner, his back propped up against the bulkhead, his eyes closed.

"Odo." She spoke softly, striving not to startle him.

"Doctor Girani," he said without opening his eyes. Perhaps he had recognized her voice, or even her footsteps, but she thought it more likely that Odo had been perceiving her for days or weeks, even without taking on his humanoid form. "I'm . . . surprised to see you."

Girani approached him and squatted down beside him. "I've been here for a while," she said.

"I know," Odo told her. "I meant that I didn't expect you here, at Newton Outpost."

It delighted Girani to hear that Odo knew her, and that he knew where he was. It suggested that his memory had survived his ordeal. "After you were hurt, the acting chief of staff contacted me directly to request my assistance with your care. I came immediately."

Odo nodded. His movements seemed sluggish. Girani hoped she could attribute that to fatigue. "Thank you," Odo said.

"How are you feeling?"

"As though a massive shape-shifter shocked my system and splattered me against a bulkhead," Odo said.

"You remember what happened," Girani said, more statement than question.

"Yes," Odo said. "I lost consciousness sometime soon after that. The next thing I remember is being maneuvered around in a container and you talking to me." He looked into her eyes with a steady gaze. "What you did helped," he said. "Thank you."

"You're welcome, Odo," Girani said. "How are you feeling? Have you completely regained your biomimetic abilities? Do you have any injuries?"

"I'm fatigued," Odo said. "It took a lot of energy to take on my humanoid form. I'll need to revert to my amorphous state soon to regenerate. Other than that, I feel . . . normal."

"I'm so glad," Girani said. "If it's all right with you, I'd like to take some readings, make sure that everything looks good."

"There's nothing I enjoy more than being poked and prodded by humanoid physicians," Odo said, but his words carried no bite. Still, it pleased Girani that Odo's personality—curmudgeonly though it might be—appeared intact.

"Can I help you up?"

"Thank you," Odo said again as he started to stand. A little shaky on his feet, he allowed Girani to take his arm as he moved over to the bio-bed. "Tell me, Doctor, what happened to the shape-shifter? I don't know how, but it contained within it a Jem'Hadar and a large number of Ascendants." He lifted himself onto the bio-bed, where he sat beside the container there. He paused, as though trying to recall some other detail, and then he said, "Not just any Jem'Hadar—Taran'atar."

"As I understand it, that's correct," Girani said. "I'm not completely clear on what happened. Deep Space Nine's chief medical officer gave me the information he thought I would need to aid in your treatment. I understand that once the shape-shifter fled Newton Outpost, it traveled to Bajor."

"Not to attack?" he said, concern evident in his voice.

"No," Girani said. "I'm told that there has been a peaceful resolution. I suggest you contact Captain Ro for details."

"I will, Doctor," Odo said. "I think I need to regenerate now."

"Of course," Girani said. "Is this container sufficient for your needs?"

Odo regarded the open cube. "For now, it is," he said, "but I would prefer an opaque version."

"I'll have one replicated for you," Girani said. "In the meantime, I'll black out the observation port to give you privacy. There's a comlink active in here, so once you've rested, please contact me."

"Yes, Doctor." Somehow, Odo managed to fit a paragraph's worth of annoyance into just the two words. For what it said about the state of Odo's personality, Girani loved it.

She headed for the door and worked the controls to open it. Girani would have to speak with Doctor Norsa, and probably with Lieutenant Commander Selten as well, about moving Odo out of the isolation ward and into the main infirmary. They would both want to make sure that he sustained no continuing effects of his joining with the Jem'Hadar-Ascendant link, but she didn't think that would be a problem.

Before leaving, Girani looked back at Odo. "It's so good to see you," she said. Odo nodded his head once, sharply, in a gesture she had seen him make uncounted times back on the original DS9. On her way out of the isolation ward, thinking of that nod made her smile.

Odo waited until the observation port had darkened, and then he gazed inward. As he always did, he visualized circular motion, wheels within wheels—

The effort exhausted him. He kept at it, struggling to maintain his concentration. Eventually, he envisioned the change he would make, and then he became that change. His body morphed from its humanoid shape into a rush of biomimetic potential. With his last measure of energy, he drew himself up against gravity, over the lip of the container, and down into the comfort and tranquility of its enclosed form.

As Odo drifted down into his regenerative state, he felt a burst of gratitude for Doctor Girani. Under other circumstances, he would have expected Doctor Bashir to make the journey to Newton Outpost. At the time Odo had traveled there, though, Bashir had been confined by Starfleet and made to stand court-martial. The doctor's crimes had been reported, but so too had his reasons for committing them, including solving the Andorians' reproductive crisis, which in turn spurred them to rejoin the Federation. It never ceased to amaze Odo what counted for justice in the minds of most beings—including Changelings.

Changelings. It had been a long time since Odo had been back among his own kind. Even though his joining with the hybrid shape-shifter had injured him, he still experienced a moment at the start of that encounter that reminded him of the joy of linking.

Maybe it's time, Odo thought. *Maybe it's time for me to go back to the Dominion.* He guessed that Laas would still be there, as well as the few Changelings who had come back after the mass exodus that had sent the Founders scattering all over the galaxy. He hoped to find that more of them had returned since he'd been gone.

And what about Weyoun and Rotan'talag? he asked himself. From the moment Odo had arrived in the Dominion and taken his place in the Great Link, he had worked to lift up the Vorta and the Jem'Hadar. He sought to demonstrate to them that they could live their own lives, free of the worship of the Founders that had been bred into them. Odo had seen some progress, but he had also watched them regress. He had no notion of what he would find when he went back, but he bore responsibility for whatever had transpired, even in his absence.

Why did I stay away so long? It was a foolish question because he knew the answer—an answer just as foolish: *Nerys.* He still loved her, and he missed her, but he must give up his ludicrous hope that she had not been killed in the collapse of the wormhole, and that she would one day return. When the wormhole reopened two years after she had been lost, Odo still thought that she might suddenly reappear. But that never happened.

It's time, he thought more decisively. *It's time for me to go home.*

The door glided open, and he started into the holosuite.

"Nog?"

Although the word had been whispered, Nog recognized the voice instantly: Ulu Lani. Nog set the simulation tester down, stepped back out into the corridor, and saw the woman of his dreams peeking at him from around the corner. She motioned him to her, and he hurried over. "Hi, Lani," he said. "It's good to see you." Nog didn't lie; it was *always* good to see Lani. One of his uncle's servers—and not a *dabo* girl, as he'd initially assumed—she had long red hair that framed her beautiful Bajoran features. Taller than Nog in an alluring way, she filled out a dress in a manner that proved beyond doubt that the Ferengi tradition of keeping females unclothed could not have been more idiotic. That night, she wore a black-and-white print that hugged her body from her shoulders to her thighs in way that Nog wished he could.

"It's good to see you, too," Lani said. She carried a circular tray with several empty glasses on it, and Nog guessed that she had sneaked away for a moment, which she immediately confirmed. "I only have a second. I have to get back to work. I just wanted to see how you were coming with the program."

Lani had first learned about Vic Fontaine from Quark, but since then, in the few stolen moments when she visited him outside a holosuite, Nog had regaled her with wonderful stories about the lounge singer. She had listened with great interest, laughing at all the right parts. She continued to say that she wanted Nog to take her to Vic's casino, and that she couldn't wait for him to succeed in restoring the program from the simulation tester—an artifice he continued to maintain. Nog worried that if Quark found out about the changes that had taken place in the program, he would make the choice to shut it down and restart it, thus wiping out the Vic Fontaine that Nog considered a close friend.

If he's even really still himself, Nog thought dejectedly. It had been six weeks since Nog had successfully loaded the program to the holosuite and he'd gotten to see and speak to Vic. But the meeting had been short-lived, with Vic running out after telling Nog to meet him there the next night. Nog had shown up as instructed, but his friend had not. *And I did that every night I could until my "adventure" with Chief O'Brien.* Nog had begun to worry not just about the integrity of Vic's matrix, but about the holographic singer's safety within the program.

"It's going all right," Nog told Lani. He considered telling her the truth—just as he did whenever she asked about Vic—but he decided not to. At first, he had worried that his uncle had sent Lani to spy on him, but he no longer believed that. If Nog shared his progress with her, though, then he would be burdening her with having to keep a secret from her boss—never a good policy when you worked for a Ferengi.

"Just 'all right'?" Lani asked with a disappointed tone. "I was really hoping that we could visit the casino together soon."

"I know, I know, so do I," Nog said, and then he thought of the same thing he thought of whenever Lani talked about going to Vic's. That night, he finally found the confidence to say it: "Maybe we could pick another holosuite destination."

"Maybe," Lani said, though she sounded less than enthusiastic. "It's just that . . . for our first date, I want to do something special."

"First" date? Nog thought. The Ferengi in him knew all about ordinal numbers, and the notion of a *first* date implied the promise of a *second*. "I'm doing my best," he said. "I'm sure I'll get it soon."

"I'm looking forward to it," Lani said. She glanced quickly over her shoulder for an instant, then looked back at him and held out her empty hand. At least, Nog *thought* the hand not carrying the tray was empty. Instead, he saw that she had a small, covered metal dish.

"What's this?" he asked, reaching for it.

"Take it and find out," she said.

As Nog took the dish, his fingers brushed against Lani's. His lobes immediately began to tingle, and he feared that they had flushed as well. To cover his embarrassment, he removed the cover of the dish with a grand gesture. His eyes widened at what he saw: "Toasted tubeworms!"

"Shhh," Lani warned him. "You'll get me fired."

"Never," Nog said with a smile. "I have some pull with the owner."

"Mmm," Lani purred. "I love a man who's not afraid to throw around his influence."

Nog heard the turbolift doors open two corridors away, and at the same time, Lani peered back over her shoulder as though she'd heard the noise herself. *Wow,* Nog thought. *They may not look like much, but those are some great lobes.*

"I should go," Lani said.

"Okay," Nog said. He held up the dish she'd given him. "Thanks."

"It was my pleasure."

Just Lani's use of the word *pleasure* made Nog's lobes tingle again. He watched her disappear around the corner, and then he leaned heavily against the bulkhead. He popped a couple of tubeworms into his mouth—so succulent and tasty—and thought about how much he wanted to go on that first date.

The sound of approaching footsteps woke Nog from his reverie. He quickly headed back to the holosuite and closed the door behind him. He ate a few more tubeworms, and then a few more, and finally he set the dish down on the deck beside the simulation tester. "Computer," he said, "run program Bashir Sixty-two."

Once more, as had been the case every time he had executed Vic's code since reloading it, a run-down hallway materialized around Nog. As was the case most nights, all of the doors were closed. Nog walked over to the one labeled with the number *23*, reached up, and tapped one finger against its surface. He expected no response, but the door swung open at once. Vic stared at him. "Nog—"

Heavy footsteps suddenly thundered up the staircase. Nog saw Vic's eyes go wide. "Don't get involved!" the singer whispered urgently. "The fat lady's about to sing!" Vic threw the door closed.

Nog turned toward the top of the stairs just as a large, well-muscled man appeared. He had a square jaw and square shoulders, and he wore a rumpled suit that still outclassed the hotel around them. When he saw Nog, he stopped. Two equally large men climbed out of the stairway behind him. Nog saw the glint of gunmetal in one of the men's hands.

"Who're you?" Square Jaw demanded.

"Nobody," Nog said, taking a step back down the hallway.

"Is he one-a Conterelli's guys?" asked the man with the gun.

Square Jaw stepped toward Nog, appraising him. "Mebbe," he said, and he looked over his shoulder at the others. "All dem guys is funny lookin.'" Then he turned back to Nog and lurched toward him. "And dey're always tryin to take what isn't theirs." He reached the door and slapped his meaty palm against it. "Fontaine's ours," he said. "You let Mistuh Conterelli know dat."

Nog said nothing, and the man paid him no more attention. Instead, Square Jaw stepped back, lifted his massive, booted foot up, and kicked the door hard. It flew open in a hail of splintered wood, its lower hinge tearing loose from the jamb.

"Where d'ya think yer going?" Square Jaw asked, looking through the doorway. Nog could only imagine that Vic was attempting to flee through the window. Square Jaw pointed into the room, and the two other men rushed inside.

The obvious danger to Vic snapped Nog out of his shock. "Hey," he told Square Jaw. "What are you doing?" Nog strode forward, the safety protocols of the holosuite making him brave. He'd had enough difficulties loading his friend's matrix to a Deep Space 9 holosuite, and even more trying to locate him within the program. He had no intention of putting up with . . . whatever this was. "Mister Fontaine is a friend of mine," Nog said, stepping directly up to Square Jaw. From that vantage, the man looked more like a mountain. "You better leave him alone."

Square Jaw moved so quickly that Nog didn't even see

his hand coming toward him. He struck Nog in the center of the chest and sent him flying backward. He landed in the middle of the hallway. The safety protocols ensured that Nog's ribs had not been broken and that he landed relatively softly on the floor.

Vic suddenly called out, but the sound came out garbled, as though his mouth had been covered. Nog rushed to get back up, but as he started down the hallway, the two thugs emerged from room 23, hauling Vic between them. A gag had been tied tightly around his mouth, and one eye was swollen shut. Blood spilled down the side of his head from a nasty gash.

"Vic!" Nog cried out, and he raced forward.

Square Jaw held up both his hands, one to his colleagues, and one to Nog. Then he reached into his suit coat and pulled out his own gun. He held its barrel up to Vic's forehead. "If this guy's really yer friend," Square Jaw said, "I'd advise ya take a step back and don't follow."

Nog stopped. The safety protocols would not protect Vic; if he died in the program, he died. There was no bringing him back. "Okay," Nog said. "Okay."

"That's bettuh." Square Jaw pointed with his gun toward the end of the hallway, and the two thugs dragged Vic along in that direction.

Nog watched as the entire group disappeared down the stairs. He waited until he heard them reach the first floor, and then he raced into room 23 and over to the window. He threw the dingy curtains open with such force that the rod they hung from tore from its mounts and clattered to the floor.

Outside, the three men hustled Vic into a long, dark automobile, then followed him inside. Nog studied it even as it peeled away, its tires leaving skid marks on the street. He wanted to remember every detail so that he had somewhere to start in trying to find his friend.

Find him, and rescue him.

"This won't take long," Ro said, aware that the end of alpha shift rapidly approached. She had gathered her senior staff in the conference room off the Hub: Jefferson Blackmer, Wheeler Stinson, Zivan Slaine, Miles O'Brien, Nog, Ren Kalanent Viss, John Candlewood, Pascal Boudreaux, and Dockmaster Vendora deGrom. She had also invited Aleco Vel. "I want to address the vacancies left by Colonel Cenn."

"Have you heard from him at all, Captain?" O'Brien asked.

"No, I haven't," Ro said. Nearly six weeks had passed since Cenn Desca had left Deep Space 9. *He didn't just leave the starbase,* the captain thought. *He left the system.* Ro had verified the safe arrival of the ship on which he'd departed—the Alonis freighter had been on its way to its home port—but she'd lost track of him after that. She thought that he might contact her at some point. They had been crewmates for almost a decade, and she considered him a friend, even if they hadn't been especially close. *But we did work closely together,* Ro thought. *We relied on each other, trusted each other.* The fact that she hadn't heard from her former first officer hurt Ro's feelings, but mostly, it signaled to her the depth of Cenn's despair. "I haven't heard from him, and I don't know of anybody who has."

"He was in bad shape after what happened on Endalla," Blackmer said. "I'd never seen him as upset as he was that night in Quark's." He didn't need to specify the incident any more than that; virtually everybody on the starbase, civilian and Starfleet alike, knew about the broadside he'd leveled at the kai.

"I spoke to him the morning he left," O'Brien said. "He seemed better. Accepting of everything, I think."

"If he had truly been accepting," Slaine offered, "he would have stayed on Deep Space Nine." She did not sound angry, but Ro thought that the matter-of-fact tone of her statement demonstrated a decided lack of empathy.

"If Cenn wasn't truly accepting, he wasn't alone," Ro said. "Right now, there are a lot of people on Bajor, and on this starbase, who are having trouble accepting the Ohalavaru actions on Endalla and their claims about the meaning of their discovery." Since the kai's initial public address about the events on Endalla, Bajor had erupted on several occasions. First Minister Asarem had sought to reassure the people, as had the Chamber of Ministers, but the comnets and the public squares had regularly exploded in strident rhetoric. Demonstrations had been staged across the planet, with some of the faithful demanding that no further examination or analysis be permitted on the so-called Endalla falsework. There had been demands for the kai to step down, and a split in the Vedek Assembly had weakened both sides of the argument. There had so far been several incidents of violence on Bajor, but fortunately none that had resulted in casualties.

If one good thing had come from the clamor, it had arrived that morning. With seemingly everybody on Bajor concentrating on the Ohalavaru, Kai Pralon had finally convinced the First Minister to have her government issue identity and travel documents to Altek Dans. Ro looked forward to sharing the good news with him—which she planned to do right after the briefing.

"Speaking of people having trouble these days," Ro said, "I want to commend Commander Blackmer and his staff for the exceptional job they've done since all of this happened. We've had some peaceful demonstrations on the Plaza, but that's it."

"Thank you, Captain," Blackmer said with a grin. "There's also been an occasional screaming match, but overall, security has excelled at allowing people their freedom, but still maintaining the order. I'll pass along your commendation."

"Good," Ro said. "Regarding the vacancies left by Colonel Cenn, we needed to fill his position as the Bajoran liaison. I came up with a very short list of people who I wanted to see in that role, but because it's one traditionally held by a member of the Militia, I also reached out to the minister of defense to find out if he had any exceptional candidates on his end. It turns out that he did, but there was one name that appeared on both our lists. So Minister Ranz consulted with Minister of State Gandal, and I checked with Starfleet Command. With their approval, I offered the position to Lieutenant Aleco Vel. He accepted this morning."

All eyes in the room turned toward Aleco, and then O'Brien began thumping the table with his palm. Everybody present followed his example, including Ro. Aleco did his best to suppress a smile, but he didn't completely succeed.

When the applause died down, Aleco said, "Thank you, Captain. I appreciate this opportunity. I'll do my best to live up to the high standard Colonel Cenn set."

"Don't worry about what anybody else has done in that post, Vel," the captain said. "Just perform your duties to the best of *your* ability."

Aleco nodded. "Yes, sir," he said. "Thank you, sir."

As quickly as everybody's attention had turned to Aleco, it turned back to Ro. They all knew what would come next—the promotion of a permanent first officer—but not whom the captain had chosen. Ro had not even spoken with the two obvious candidates. She had consulted only with Starfleet Command about her choice.

"Obviously, in addition to replacing Colonel Cenn as the Bajoran liaison," Ro said, "we need to fill his position as first officer on a permanent basis. As you all know, Commander Blackmer has been acting in that capacity since the colonel's departure. He has done an outstanding job."

Blackmer nodded, but said nothing. That pleased Ro, who just wanted to get through the meeting. "At the same time, Commander Stinson has served as my second officer for more than four years now. He too has done an outstanding job, not only as the second officer on Deep Space Nine, but as the first officer, and even more frequently these days, as the commanding officer of the *Defiant*."

Stinson had the good sense to remain quiet and let Ro continue. "I have nothing but respect for both of you, and choosing between you has been difficult." She looked across the table at Blackmer. "Jeff," she said, "congratulations." Blackmer's eyebrows rose, and Ro saw him make a conscious effort to lower them. The captain waited for a new round of applause to stop, and then she said, "Starfleet Command has approved my request, and your promotion to first officer of Deep Space Nine begins with alpha shift tomorrow."

"Thank you, Captain," Blackmer said.

"You've earned it," Ro said, and then she gazed over at Stinson. To his credit, he did not allow his disappointment to show. "Commander Stinson, as I said, I have tremendous respect for your abilities, and even for your ambition. I think I speak for everybody present when I say that we all know that you're going to occupy a center seat somewhere in Starfleet, and probably sooner rather than later. It might even be mine one day, if that's what interests you, though I suspect you'll want a command that takes you around the quadrant, and beyond." Stinson looked abashed for a moment. Ro knew that she could have spoken to him in private, and maybe she should have, but she wanted her senior staff to hear what she had to say about the young officer, and she wanted him to hear her tell them.

"I trust you, Commander," Ro went on, "and I believe that you have a long and successful career ahead of you. I hope that you will not take my promotion of Commander Blackmer over you as a repudiation of your capabilities as much as an acknowledgment of his. I know that you must be disappointed, but I value you as an important member of this crew. I hope that you'll consider staying with us." Ro understood that Stinson would be within his rights to request a transfer to another posting, but she hoped he saw the value in continuing on at DS9.

"Thank you, everybody," Ro said, and she stood up from her chair at the head of the table. "Jeff, meeting in my office tomorrow at oh-seven-hundred," she said. "Don't be late." She offered her new first officer a wink, and he smiled.

"Aye, Captain."

"Wheeler, I want to see you at thirteen-thirty," Ro said. "Don't you be late either." She then exited the conference room into the Hub, crossed behind the tactical station, and entered a turbolift. She ordered it to take her to the residential deck—not to her own quarters, but to those of Altek Dans. The night before, they had agreed to meet for a late lunch.

If our recent time together is any indication, Ro thought as the turbolift whirred into motion, *we'll never make it to a meal.* Alone in the lift, she smiled. Since their first night together five and a half weeks earlier, they had been spending more and more time with each other, mostly in his cabin. Ro had yet to break the news to Quark of her new relationship, but she knew that she would have to do so soon—not just because it was the right thing to do, and not just because

Quark shouldn't find out from anybody other than her, but also because of the depth of her feelings for Dans. It had been a long time since she'd experienced such emotions.

Who am I trying to fool? Ro upbraided herself. *It might be the first time I've ever felt like this.*

The turbolift continued on its journey from the Hub to the residential deck. As it descended, Ro's thoughts drifted back to her experience in the wormhole—not an uncommon reflection in the days since she had accompanied the shape-shifting mass of Taran'atar and the Ascendants to their new home. *Or maybe not so new,* the captain corrected herself, recalling what the Jem'Hadar had told her about the world upon which she'd landed inside the Celestial Temple: "We have been here for some time . . . and we will be here yet longer."

Once Ro had returned to Deep Space 9, she had researched the planet—or, at least, she'd attempted to do so. She could find only one direct reference to it, in reports filed by Benjamin Sisko and Jadzia Dax when they had first discovered the Celestial Temple—an event that had taken place seventeen years prior. The timeline didn't add up: How could Taran'atar and the Ascendants have become the world within the wormhole *after* it already existed? Yet Captain Sisko's description perfectly matched what Ro had witnessed for herself. Perhaps two distinct worlds populated the wormhole, but Ro truly believed that they were one and the same, further corroboration of Captain Sisko's claim that the Prophets existed nonlinearly in time.

And if the Prophets can see the past and the future as easily as They see the present, what does that say about Their nature? Ro wondered. How much more evidence did she need of Their divinity?

As the turbolift slowed and changed direction, the comm system suddenly chirped. *"Hub to Captain Ro,"* came the voice of Ensign Allasar, who worked as the duty officer on beta shift.

"This is Ro. Go ahead, Allasar."

"Captain, a small vessel of unknown configuration has just emerged from the wormhole," Allasar said. *"It stopped almost at once and broadcast a transmission directly to you."*

"Directly to me?" Ro said. "Not to Deep Space Nine?"

"No, sir," Allasar said. *"Directly to you."*

"Very well," Ro said. "Computer, hold." The turbolift eased to a halt. "Pipe it down here, Allasar."

"Yes, sir."

Ro waited, and a moment later, she heard the transmission: *"Kira Nerys to Ro Laren."*

Acknowledgments

Thanks, as always, to my editors, Margaret Clark and Ed Schlesinger. My *Star Trek* literary work always begins and ends with Margaret and Ed, who set me on my way into the wilderness and remain by my side until I emerge back into the light of civilization. They are able partners on the journey from blank page to published novel, and I am grateful for their considerable assistance.

Away from my keyboard, I am supported by a long list of individuals whose very presence in my life allows me to slip the bounds of the here and now so that I can venture into the bright, shining future. Matt Harris and Adam Rogers are two of those people. Both are exceptional human beings: smart, loving, dedicated, and involved. Together with their beautiful boys, Javier and Marcel, they provide hope for a better tomorrow.

Steve Pilchik is another person who bolsters me. Though he and I go back a long way, we have always shared a common vision for the future. Steve has always been there for me, and I value his friendship beyond measure.

Thanks also to Colleen Ragan, a kind, compassionate, and raucously funny woman who has become another sister to me. I have known few people as brave or as adventurous as she is. Her presence in my life is a gift.

I also want to express my gratitude to Walter Ragan. A Navy man—a submariner—he is a genuine patriot, a man who has willingly served his country by putting himself in harm's way. I thank him not only for his continuous love and support, but also for the example he sets.

Thank you as well to Anita Smith, another woman who has become my sister. She is kind and caring, fun and funny, and simply one of the best people I know. And if that isn't enough, she's also pretty good out on the links.

I am also grateful to Jennifer George, my sister by birth and my friend by choice. Jen is an amazing woman, whose many accomplishments are too numerous to mention. Although I am the older sibling, Jen has still taught me much in this life, and I cannot thank her enough for all she has done for me and all she means to me.

I also want to thank Patricia Walenista for . . . well, literally for everything in my life. She is the wellspring not only for my existence, but for much of what populates my world. I would not be here at all if not for her, nor would I be as happy without her loving influences.

Finally, thank you to Karen Ragan-George. She and I fly together in this life, and there is nobody I would rather have by my side. Karen provides the riotous laugh at the end of a tough day, the loving smile in a moment of sadness, the tender kiss that banishes any inkling of isolation. More than that, she simply makes life worth living. Every day with her is a joy, every second a treat. I love her more than words can say.

About the Author

David R. George III has frequently explored the *Star Trek* universe. *Ascendance* marks his sixteenth such novel. He has most often added to the *Deep Space Nine* milieu, with the novels *The 34th Rule, Twilight, Olympus Descending* (in *Worlds of Deep Space Nine, Volume Three*), *Rough Beasts of Empire, Plagues of Night, Raise the Dawn, Revelation and Dust,* and *Sacraments of Fire.* He also wrote the *Crucible* trilogy—*Provenance of Shadows, The Fire and the Rose,* and *The Star to Every Wandering*—which was set during the original series and helped celebrate the fortieth anniversary of the television show. Another of his novels, *Allegiance in Exile,* takes place during the final part of *Enterprise*'s five-year mission. David also penned a pair of *Lost Era* books featuring John Harriman and Demora Sulu, *Serpents Among the Ruins* and *One Constant Star,* as well as an *LE* novella, *Iron and Sacrifice,* which appeared in the *Tales from the Captain's Table* anthology. He also provided an alternate-universe *Next Generation* novel, *The Embrace of Cold Architects,* for *the Myriad Universes: Shattered Light* collection.

David first contributed to the *Trek* universe on television, with a first-season *Voyager* episode titled "Prime Factors." He has also written nearly twenty magazine articles about the shows and books. Of his non–*Star Trek* work, his novelette "Moon Over Luna" is available on Amazon.com. A second novelette, "The Instruments of Vice," appears in *Native Lands*, the third volume in the *ReDeus* universe, which tells stories set after the return of the gods to Earth. A third novelette, "The Dark Arts Come to Hebron," is included in a genre anthology called *Apollo's Daughters*. David's work has appeared on both the *New York Times* and *USA Today* bestseller lists, and it has been nominated for a Scribe Award by the International Association of Media Tie-in Writers. His television episode was nominated for a *SciFi Universe* award.

David is an ardent—though often unfulfilled—New York Mets fan. He enjoys playing baseball and racquetball. He and his lovely wife, Karen, enjoy traveling, theater, concerts, and museums, count themselves as cinephiles, and have spent many a fun evening tearing up the dance floor. David and Karen currently reside in Los Angeles, California.

You can contact David at facebook.com/DRGIII, and you can follow him on Twitter @DavidRGeorgeIII.